CITIES OF SMOKE & STARLIGHT

CITIES OF SMOKE & STARLIGHT

GATE CHRONICLES BOOK 1

ALLI EARNEST

Dragon Page Entertainment

For Jason & Joey

Contents

the
WORLD
of
Yalvara

Tevi Sea

Tev Rubika

Sunken City !

Kavost Peaks

Jaydle

Narden Pass

Fort Achilles

Cerulene

Leqara Canyon

Rune Bay

Narden Range

Kyvena

Forest of Gilan

Sol Adrid.

Silver Coast

Bay of Storms

Josei Ocean

Vatn Wood

Jasara

Sali Bog

Haddon's Pass

Myrra

Vadri Wastes

Dragonar Lands

Varáni Mountains

PART I: MISSION

CHAPTER 1

THE BEST STARS-BLASTED PILOT

Kase

RAIN BEAT A STEADY RHYTHM on Kase Shackley's leather jacket. After three years spent earning it, he wore it with his chest puffed out and shoulders high as the moons.

Beowulf, Odysseus, and King Arthur, all heroes from ancient First Earth stories, had nothing on Kase's piloting skills. If they'd had hover technology, he knew he'd outstrip them by miles. With a small smile playing at his lips, Kase pulled the collar higher.

Leading his hoverbike into the alleyway behind the

hangar, he shook more water droplets from his dark brown curls and tugged down his pilot goggles. The buildings of stone and metal loomed over Kase like specters in the early evening. Dark clouds blotted out any chance of a decent sunset, though the gray light peeking through cast a pale glow on Kase's skin. Perfect weather for the usual induction ritual—no one other than the pilots would be out in it, of course, and as usual, Kase had already paid off the guards.

The soft tut-tut-tut of the yalvar fuel engine overpowered the rain. Kase swung one leg over the seat and pressed the button to lift the craft a foot off the mossy cobblestones below. Without a thought, he tightened his stomach and kept the bike upright.

Easy.

The technology keeping hover vehicles afloat wasn't new, but it was only in the last twenty years that the nation of Jayde's Engineer Corp had untangled the secrets nearly lost to time.

The rain's damp, earthy scent mixed with the smell of burning fuel as Kase sucked in another breath. Yes, this was the perfect night to show the new pilots who ran the airfields. A low rumble sounded from around the corner, and a grin tugged at the corner of his mouth. The fresh meat, Kase's first opponent, had arrived.

It was the greenie pilot's *stars-rotten* luck to be going up against Kase his first day on the job, but that wasn't Kase's fault. All the *dulkop* had to do was swerve before the bike rammed him—not difficult, even for the greenie. After his pompous words today, he was asking for a beating.

"The handbook states the speed of a hover should be considered when making a turn. If one wishes to do so, slow the speed of the hover and ease into the turn."

He'd peed his pants when Kase made the next *perfect* turn at full-speed three seconds later. How did Kase get stuck with such an uptight greenie to train?

Bike fighting usually ended with at least one busted-up engine from the less experienced pilots scraping them against the hangar walls, but the machines were only a cheap practice tool anyway. New pilots crashed them all the time trying to get a handle on the controls. Starting on the bikes made it easier to fly the larger airships, which were like the sleek spaceships the ancient peoples of First Earth used to soar among the stars before getting stranded on Yalvara without their fancy tech.

Kase thumbed his nose and eyed his opponent.

The greenie was fresh out of school, and one look at his thick gray trainee jacket had Kase rolling his eyes. He landed his bike, holding up a hand.

"Judging by how you've buttoned that jacket up to your ears, you have no blasted idea what you're doing, do you?" The drizzle didn't dampen the echo of his voice on the hangar walls. "We went over this earlier."

The man was only three years Kase's junior, but at eighteen, the bloke's large brown eyes peeking out through the goggles made him appear much younger— though it didn't stop his tongue. "Pilots must look professional, and leaving buttons undone makes us appear disheveled. Lead Jay said that..."

Ugh. Had Kase been that whiny and priggish when he was that age? "Yeah, yeah, yeah. But Jay isn't here, is he? This is a contest of men, and you don't even remember how to turn on the hover components."

"According to the handbook, when preparing the bike or hover for use, one should first make certain all safety features are engaged. If one is unsure about one or all of the safety indicators..."

Kase shook his head and strolled over to the greenie's bike. His boots splashed in small puddles growing from cracks in the cobblestone. "You don't need to explain it to me. Just press that button there—"

"What're you doing, Kase?" came a gruff voice from the end of the alley. "Hurry up!"

Kase's ears caught the familiar clipped Kyvena accent, and he rolled his eyes at the other senior pilot hovering on his own bike a few feet away. The rest of the pilots had arrived only moments before, bikes rumbling. "Just because your greenie beat you in that training exercise yesterday doesn't mean you can rush me. I'm helping my greenie here with his bike." He winked at his opponent. "You'll be fine."

"But according to Lead Jay, we shouldn't even be here—"

Kase reached over and pressed the hover button in the center of the handlebars. The new pilot nearly slid off the seat.

"Whoa, there. Tighten your abs and hold on." Kase caught his arm before he smashed his face into the ground. "And it's tradition. Legend says Jay started this little induction ritual of ours."

The boy—because that's what he was, even if Jaydian law considered him a legal adult—paled as he clenched the handles with a rock-crushing grip. He nodded, the goggles slipping down his face with rain and probably a good bit of sweat. "But what if I can't swerve in time?"

"Pull up. No shame in losing to the best." When Kase was sure he wasn't about to slide off again, he stepped back.

"But what about the Hover Colonel? And what

happens if I don't pull up or swerve?" He looked down the alley where more catcalls came from the assembled pilots. "All the training manual states is that—"

"Good luck, greenie!" Kase jogged back to his bike, ignoring jeers coming from both sides of the alleyway. It was time for Kase to put on a show. Too bad the greenie had to suffer for it.

Pinpricks needled his chest and fingers as Kase lifted his bike into the air and revved the engine. The craft responded, vibrating under his fingertips. "Let's duel!"

With a battle cry ripping from his throat, Kase darted forward, his bike's engine whining against the sudden speed. Rain and wind nipped at his uncovered hands as he roared down the alleyway toward the— *toward the stationary greenie.*

The fool hadn't moved forward. Was he giving up?

"Pull up! Pull up!" Kase's voice wasn't the only one screaming the words as he sped down the alley. "Pull up, you *stars-idiot!*"

"And what happens if—" the greenie's nasally voice was just audible over the wind rushing in Kase's ears. "What happens if we get caught?"

At the last second, the greenie yanked the handles toward his chest, whipping the bike straight into the air. The hover components screeched with the sudden force, shattering Kase's concentration on his own bike. Greenie and machine roared over his head, the wind of their passing chilling Kase's wet face.

The bike climbed higher and higher, the greenie still pulling on the control, until the bike flipped in midair, his feet flying over his head. With a deafening crunch, the greenie landed on the neighboring hangar roof. The bike crashed at the end of the alley, judging by the other shouts and splintering shriek of metal on stone.

Kase slammed his brake. The force threw him from his seat, and he rolled and skidded across the uneven cobblestone, the knee of his trousers ripping, but he didn't care. He was up and running toward the limp figure sliding off the edge of the roof.

Not again. Heavens and stars, not again.

As the body plummeted, Kase dove underneath it, catching the boy before his head slammed against the stone.

"YOU RECKLESS PIECE OF—HOW many blasted times must I—"

Kase knew by the lack of complete sentences that his father teetered at the edge of the abyss of his fury. Lord Kapitan Harlan Shackley smoothed his steel-gray mustache and paced the private study of Shackley Manor, his polished black boots clacking with each step and squeaking with each turn. Kase tugged at his rain-soaked collar and winced. Though it would've made a good shield right about then, he'd left his jacket at the door.

Focus on the shelves. Focus on the books. Focus on anything else.

But nothing about the weathered spines organized by height on the shelves flanking the large brick hearth comforted him. Instead, all he saw was the broken, bleeding body in his arms. He'd shouted for the others to fetch a medic while Kase administered what first aid he could, but that was his brother Zeke's specialty. No, Kase was vastly more talented at screwing things up. Just like the night his sister died in the fire.

The gas lantern sitting like a king on his father's desk was the only illumination in the room. The Lord Kapitan refused to have electricity in his own home, even if the lower classes also had the new technology. With each crackle, a flicker of light flitted over Kase's clenched fingers. After the crash, he'd told the rest of the pilots he'd take the blame for the night's events. He knew the Hover Lead wouldn't do anything to punish him.

Kase never thought they'd bring his father, the supreme commander of the military, into it.

Dealing with him on a good day was less than ideal, but late at night after a man was on the brink of death? Kase rubbed his shoulder and refused to look up. "It isn't my fault the greenie didn't pay attention in training."

Harlan spun and kicked the leg of Kase's chair. It screeched across the floor an inch, and Kase gripped the arms as his father bent down. Exhaustion and exasperation warred in his sharp hazel eyes. "The boy nearly *died* because you didn't use your blasted head." He stood, running a hand down his aging face. "After everything I've done..."

Kase gritted his teeth. "How was I supposed to know he'd yank the bike hard enough to send him to the stars? How'd he even test into the Crews in the first place?"

Harlan's eyes flashed. "Trainee Laurence Hixon had the highest scores on the written examination. They put him with you for a reason, even if you just earned your jacket. You were to be...but of course, you..." His father marched toward his desk and snatched a piece of parchment. He held it up. "You know what this was?"

Kase squinted at it, but the writing was too small

and the lighting too dim to tell what it said. Harlan grasped it in both hands and ripped it, the pieces fluttering onto the desk and immaculate green carpeting. "Jove recommended you for a mission. Your brother and your Hover Lead think you're the best blasted pilot we have, yet you can't make the simplest decisions when your head isn't up in a hover."

Jove had a mission for him? If Jove was heading it, the Watch was involved…"Where were you sending me?"

"Doesn't matter. You aren't mature enough to decide your next steps."

Kase stood, his chair scraping back. "I didn't do anything!"

"You're facing charges that could lock you up for stars know how long, destruction of government property and trespassing being the least of your worries. I thought you would've learned responsibility after these three years, but you're a sorry—"

Kase slammed his fist on the desk, the lantern light quivering and casting strange shadows on his father's face. "I *am* the best *stars-blasted* pilot you have, and I did that without your *shocking* help."

The resounding slap reverberated through Kase's skull as his body listed sideways from the momentum of his father's hand. He caught himself on the edge of the desk and blinked away tears.

Harlan's voice dropped to a temperature colder than the snow falling in the Narden Range. "You're dismissed from the Crews on my orders as Lord Kapitan. I'm through with you disgracing the Shackley name. Now get out of my sight."

Kase's eyes still stung, but he gritted his teeth. His blood heated, his rage simmering near the surface, scorching, *burning*—

A small voice in the back of his head told him to stop, flames igniting at the edge of his memory, their orange glow hovering in the night sky.

That would happen again if he retaliated. And that wasn't something he could return from.

Instead, he spit on the floor and stalked from the room, out of the Manor, and into the empty streets of Kyvena.

CHAPTER 2

YOU NEED ME

Hallie

HALLIE WALKER CRACKED HER KNUCKLES through protective gloves. The image of her aging yet eccentric professor traversing the wilds of neighboring Cerulene just to get his hands on the document before her made her smile.

She allowed herself a silent chuckle.

Definitely not Professor Christie's style, but it would've made for an interesting epic. If he had, the University might have commissioned a marble bust of him to display like the others lining the ends of the library's towering shelves. It would've certainly earned him a spot next to General McKenzie, the man who'd led the Life Ships from First Earth to Yalvara.

That is, if the document had anything worthy

scrawled upon it; Hallie's gloved hands and golden eyes would decide that. The first half of the document hadn't been anything ground-breaking—only a bit about Yalven cultural history before the Landing. Hallie already knew about those bits.

While it was too early in the year to need a proper fire, the one in the University library's hearth added a lovely crackling that echoed off too-tall ceilings and wooden beams. Sunlight through stained-glass depicting the heroics of the First Settlers painted pictures across the sparsely populated tables tucked between bookshelves so tall, one needed a ladder to reach the top shelf.

Hallie thought it poetic that the first victory against the ruthless Cerls danced across the parchment in front of her. They were the ones who had chased off the Yalvs two decades before.

She squinted a little and tried to translate the next few words. *Stars.* The discoloration and faded symbols were one of the many ways Hallie could tell the parchment was ancient. Really, it was remarkable her professor had acquired such an important historical artifact as this.

Grabbing a cheap and slightly stubby charcoal pencil, she scratched out a rough translation in her open notebook. Both only cost her a half bronzer total at the market. Some vendor wanted to get rid of the notebook in particular, and Hallie gladly took it off his hands...even if the binding didn't want to hold all the pages.

She just hoped it lasted until the end of the semester.

Hallie blew her auburn hair out of her eyes. Blasted pins didn't keep her too-slick locks in place long enough. Of course, her mother would've chastised her, saying she hadn't done her hair up properly, that a lady's bun was free of stray hairs, tighter than a miner's grip, and decorated with fine braids and twists.

But her mother wasn't here, was she? Bless the stars for that.

As the wisps weren't cowed by the force of wind, she dug her fingers into her hair, keeping the offenders at bay, and kept writing.

They came with sparking...

The next word wasn't as clear. She peeked around at the other students near her. Each bore down on their documents like bees to mountain lilies. With a sigh, she looked at the faded word once more. "Could it be science? Maybe? It might also mean something unnatural with nature. Good stars, could Professor Christie have not found this earlier?"

While her mumblings were too loud for the library room, not even one of her fellow university scholars moved. Except she was sure she noticed an eyeroll from the glossy-haired girl next to her.

That would've been her friend Petra, who Hallie swiftly kicked underneath the table. Only the jingle of Petra's jeweled bracelet told Hallie she'd gotten her point across. It wouldn't do well to get kicked out of the library again this week. Hallie grinned.

With a tapping of her pencil, she inspected the Yalven document once more. Professor Christie had assigned each of her classmates a piece of the artifact, hoping they'd get some good practice in. While Hallie loved the man like a grandfather, she was certain he simply didn't want to translate it himself. Not that he was lazy, but with each passing year, Hallie feared his eyesight grew worse.

Then again, Hallie didn't mind being tasked with this. That meant she would know the secrets of the ancient natives before just about anyone else in Jayde. She didn't know why Professor Christie hadn't handed the entire document to her. She *was* top of his Yalven Language Level 3 class. Translating Yalven into Common came to her almost naturally.

Leaving a small blank for the word she couldn't quite make out and copying the nearly illegible symbols below that, she moved on.

...*We welcomed them to our destruction. Yalvara is not meant for man.*

"Interesting." Hallie finished scrawling the last word and tapped her pencil on Petra's parchment.

The young woman looked up, her thin, obsidian eyes hard. "What is it you want? Are you trying to get us kicked out again?"

Hallie swiveled her head to where the librarian dealt with some sort of issue at the desk. "We're fine. Madame Terry is busy with a first-year student who seems to have lost a book."

"Your point?"

Hallie shoved her notes across the table and pointed to the blank and the symbols beneath. "I can't seem to figure out this word here. It's too faded. Will you take a look?"

Petra raised a slim brow but nodded. "Don't know why you're asking me. You're loads better at this than I am."

"Except my superior brains can't decipher something not there," Hallie said with a grin, and passed over her portion of the ancient text as well.

Petra took it in her own gloved hands, squinting and chewing on her lip as she inspected it. She smoothed non-existent stray hairs back into her immaculate coal-colored lady's bun.

A dark stain had smeared across the fingertips of Hallie's left glove. *Blast.* Probably from her pencil. Hopefully the old hag of a librarian she borrowed them from wouldn't mind terribly. The woman already hated Hallie after the *incident* earlier this week.

Eyeing Petra's fountain pen, Hallie shoved down her resentment. If only she hadn't had to work her way through school after that first year at the University, maybe she could afford to be so luxurious in her choice of writing utensils. Not that she blamed Petra herself, of course. That was just the way things were—though it didn't make the bitterness any sweeter.

Regardless, Hallie would rather be poor in Kyvena than wealthy back home in Stoneset.

Petra's eyes narrowed further as she chewed the end of her pen. Must be nice to have the privilege of chewing up the end of one's writing utensils, as daddy could buy another when the teethmarks became visible.

Hallie cracked her neck and stroked the pocket watch hanging around her neck. She sucked in a few long breaths, an attempt to calm the pins and needles pricking her chest.

The pocket watch had never worked properly, even when it had belonged to her twin brother Jack, or their father before him, or even their grandfather if family legend was to be believed. Jack had tried to fix the heirloom many times, but even as skilled with his hands as her twin was, he hadn't been able to make it work. Hallie didn't exactly mind. Besides, the engravings on the cover intrigued her the most. Worn down with time, they were somewhat difficult to make out, but in the right light, she could just see the picture they painted.

The wide face detailed a city Hallie had never seen before. Granted, she'd only ever been to Jayde's capital, Kyvena, but the city didn't match any depicted in old First Earth storybooks either. A castle-esque structure sat tucked into the side of a mountain with other buildings dripping like rain all the way to the valley, each with oddly slanted roofs building to thin points.

She rubbed her thumb once more across the memorized scene. *Breathe in, breathe out.* This was her last year of school, and after graduating, she'd open a school in Lower Kyvena and would never have to think of home again.

Petra blew air out of her lips in a very unladylike fashion, which interrupted Hallie's thoughts. She looked over at her friend. "Tsk, tsk, what would your mother say if she heard you make that noise?"

"She wouldn't, because I'd conveniently blame it on you," Petra said, her words laced with subtle mirth. "She thinks you're a bad influence."

Hallie shrugged and leaned her elbows onto the table, another rub of the pocket watch taking the unintended sting out of Petra's words. "I try ridiculously hard to be. Now, I assume you can't figure it out either?"

Her friend shook her head. "My guess is as good as yours. If Ellis were here, he might be able to figure it out with those eagle eyes of his, but for now, we're stuck."

Hallie took back her sketchpad and the document. Ellis completed their trio, but his mother had needed him for a function of some sort that afternoon. Probably one involving too-expensive tea, coattails, and dignified handshakes. All were pretentious in Hallie's opinion.

Before either of them could say anything else, the clock tower struck the hour.

The University had built the stone monolith keeping the capital on schedule nearly three centuries prior. University legend said the Yalvs had aided its construction, and the High Council, which was comprised of the two Head Guardsmen, three elected Stradats, and Lord Kapitan, had kept one of the Yalvs captive, forcing him or her to work the bells ever since.

Yet Hallie had met the bell ringer in her first year. Or she should say bell *ringers*. The University employed street urchins from the lower city to ring the bells at the appropriate times.

Hallie counted each peal unconsciously as she stared at the impossible word. *One, two, three, four...*

Then silence.

Four o'clock. Didn't realize it was so late. Wasn't there something...

"Mother of ash!" she squealed, leaping up, her chair toppling over behind her. The librarian and every student turned toward her, the former giving her the nastiest look with eyes narrowed to slits and nostrils flared.

Crashing stars.

"For all the moons in heaven, what—" Petra started.

Hallie shoved her sketchpad and pencil into the satchel and righted the chair. "I was supposed to be at work at three! Oh stars, Jess will be so...ugh!" She flung the satchel over her shoulder. The contents slapped her leather-clad back. "Will you take the document and tell Professor Christie I'll give him my report tomorrow?"

Petra took the artifact before Hallie upended the table. "I'll pick you up at a quarter after seven to eat before the play?"

Hallie nodded and took off toward the front of the room, ripping off her gloves and flinging them at the librarian's desk and ignoring the woman's low growl.

Hallie didn't care. She'd already been late twice that week. Trying to ignore the thought of the bookshop owner's quiet, disappointing words as he berated her once more, she fled through the streets of the capital, praying Jess didn't fire her this time.

THE BELL ATOP THE BOOKSHOP door clanged and nearly fell off its perch as Hallie blew into Beckham Books on Callan Street twenty minutes later. The lacy shirt underneath her jacket clung to her back awkwardly, and auburn strands stuck to her face during her mad dash to work. She'd sprinted through alleyways and side streets all the way to the lower city, as she knew without a doubt the marketplace and main thoroughfare would be full to the brim that time of day.

Stars, I still need to pay for next semester and if I lose this job...oh stars...

"I know I'm late and I *know* I swore I wouldn't be, but I didn't hear the blasted bells until four and I was translating something in the library..." Her words came out jumbled as she wove her way through the too-close shelves and to the back where Jess, her employer, waited.

But the look in his brown eyes said it all. Hallie stopped short, her breath coming in sharp bursts. "I'm so, so, so, so sorry." Unable to stay upright any longer and face the disappointment lacing Jess' features, she bent over, hands on her knees and satchel falling off her shoulder onto the floor. "I came as fast as I could! I only got to wave at Edward as I passed him, but I did stop and give Gemma a copper. She hadn't sold any daisies I don't think, and I—"

"Who's Edward?" Jess' voice was tired and slow like each word trudged through the mountain snows.

Hallie glanced up, a bead of sweat perched on the lip of her brow. "You know...he's the beggar with that really long red beard? Sits on the corner of Brooks and Flincher? And I'm pretty sure he combs that beard of his, because it's not tangled and matted like some..."

Jess rubbed his cheek, then the smooth skin on top of his head. "Hallie, this is the third time this week you've been late and the seventh time this month alone."

Hallie straightened, the fingers on her right hand finding her pocket watch. A tingling started in her chest, mixed with heat that felt like the fire in the library hearth. "But you know how hard this semester is. I've told you that the workload is much heavier, like Tuesday with my Professor holding me back and then today with the translations and...and..."

She took several deep breaths. It wasn't Jess' fault, even if he didn't quite understand. In the silence, Jess spoke, his voice hard—though not in the way her mother's got whenever she chastised Hallie for ruining yet another skirt playing out in the spring rains. "I do realize this, yet Evie and I have a business to run, Hallie. If this was a one-off thing every so often, I wouldn't mind, but you're late at least once a month if not more—even in your summer months—and mainly because you get distracted on your way over. After our conversation Tuesday, I thought I'd made myself clear."

The tingling in Hallie's chest turned to hot, flaming knives. "I know I said I wouldn't be late again...and I didn't...I'm so sorry. I just...and what you said about the probationary period..." Tears hotter than the blasted sun clouded her vision, but she blinked them back. "I'll not be late again. I swear...I swear on Tovo's name!"

Jess rubbed his cheek once more, and the light from the chipped electric lanterns hanging from the ceiling reflected off his bald head. His cheeks pinked even more under his copper skin as he looked at her again. "You shouldn't swear by Tovo unless you want the gods after you." He swallowed as his eyes scanned the shelves. His next words were quiet. Hallie had to lean in to hear each one. "We agreed that if you were on time for every shift the rest of the month, Evie and I would rethink your probation." He stopped inspecting the haphazard book piles and looked her square in the eye. "But I have to go through with what I said."

Hallie's fingers ached from gripping the pocket watch too tightly, and at least one tear liberated itself from her hold. "You can't fire me. You can't do that. Not now! I promise you by the stars and moons in the sky, I'll be on time tomorrow and through the rest of the month. You can count on me. I'm the only one who knows where the Shakespeare books are! Conor can't do this all by himself, and neither can you. You *need* me." Heart pounding in her ears, she took more deep breaths. "And you and I both know Conor can't take on more hours."

Jess came around the counter at last and put both hands on her shoulders. He gave them a light squeeze. "I'm truly sorry this had to happen this way, but like I said earlier, I have a business to run, and sometimes I have to make difficult decisions." His smile was sad and droopy as if melting in the summer heat—yet the air was starting to turn crisp. "Finish out today, and I'll bring your last pay sum down when we close at six. I'm certain you'll be able to find something before the end of the month. Maybe even talk to Owen?"

As if Hallie would tell Professor Christie she'd gone and lost the job he'd helped her get a year ago. She swallowed the pain and tightened her fists. "Fine."

Jess gave her one last squeeze before turning away and limping toward the stairs. His knee, an old injury from the War two decades earlier, seemed to bother him more and more lately, but at that moment Hallie couldn't find the strength to care.

Once the upstairs apartment door opened with a creak and closed with a thud, Hallie finally made her way around the counter. She dropped her satchel underneath. Working her lips to try and keep the breakdown contained, she fell onto the stool and collapsed into her arms.

It's all right. It's okay. Maybe someone at the University needs an assistant. The librarian?

Another few tears leaked from her eyes, dripping down the bump on her nose from where she'd broken it nearly three years prior and plopping silently onto the rough wood of the shop counter.

I still get to go to the theater tonight, and Ellis said he's taking us to that tavern he's been raving about the last month or so. I'll worry about finding a job tomorrow.

She grabbed a stack of books needing to be put away. Part of her wanted to fling them against the wall, but she settled for slamming them on the shelf in random places. Each thud drowned out the conversation replaying in her head.

Bless the soul and stars of whoever walked into the shop during her shift.

CHAPTER 3

CLEAREST SAPPHIRE

Kase

KASE SPENT THE NEXT DAY flitting around Kyvena, avoiding the Manor at all costs. Whether it was a good or bad sign that the Lord Kapitan hadn't sent soldiers after him yet, he didn't know. His gut told him Harlan hadn't wanted to draw attention to the fact that his youngest son was a problem. A *disgrace*.

But Kase no longer cared. His father could go blast himself to the moons.

After failing to finish a mug of ale at one of the lower city's seedier taverns, he inspected Kyvena's busiest market square, various wares flashing between patrons like dusty electric bulbs in the early evening light. Running his fingers through his mess of curls, he leaned against a tall building—an apothecary, judging by the sharp scent of lavender and some chemical wafting out every time the door opened. Kase dug in the back pocket of his trousers and tugged out a piece of crumpled parchment. Smoothing it with his thumb, he squinted and tried to decipher the messy cursive blurred by his own sweat.

Callan Street, Apartment 303, Lower Kyvena

He scanned the colorful market, attempting to figure out which direction Callan was, but apparently the lower class didn't believe in street signs. *Ridiculous.* It didn't help his foul mood.

He pushed off the wall with a soft scraping noise and fought through the mass of shoppers. The capital had grown over the millennium since the Landing, but the city's population had erupted in the last decade. He'd read more than one scholar attributing that growth to the Eighth Industrial Revolution, which wouldn't be the first time they'd compared something here to distant First Earth. But that place of legends no longer existed. All Jayde had left were stories and crumbling artifacts—and all these blasted people jostling him. If only he could get out of the city and live somewhere in the mountains. That'd be nice. He'd take all his favorite books and read them under the uninterrupted blue sky.

One day.

As he stuffed the slip of parchment away and wove past hagglers of all shapes and sizes and the rich, pungent scent of cooking spices, his eyes caught on a blade seller's wares. He paused and grabbed a scabbard with a decadent flame pattern. It reminded him of something Beowulf might have carried as he went to slay Grendel.

"Fifteen gold tenners for that!" the vendor said as

Kase unsheathed the knife. He inspected the strange bronze-colored metal. "That Zuprium comes all the way from Sol Adrid itself!"

All the way from the Cerulene capital? Right. Did people believe that rubbish? It barely took a moment for him to spot the telltale freckles of a well-done fake. Life must be difficult for blade sellers, seeing as electropistols were the weapon of choice. Still didn't excuse lying to people.

Kase sheathed the knife and bent down to the man's height. "You and I both know this is a Rubikan imitation not worth three bronzers. I suggest you be honest with patrons, or you might find yourself explaining to the Watch how you got all the way to Cerulene and back with your head intact."

An empty threat, seeing as he couldn't go tell the Watch on the man without turning himself in to his father. Minor details.

The man gulped. "Yes, yes...no need! I'm trying— my family—we're starving. Please don't tell the Watch! I won't do it again. Swear on Tovo's name!"

Fishing a couple bronzers from his quickly depleting money pouch, Kase straightened. He'd need to sneak back to the Manor soon and steal more. Pushing the coins across the table, Kase leaned in. "If I ever hear of you lying to a customer again, I *will* tell the Watch. Got it?"

The man snatched the coins as Kase stood, flicking invisible dust off his shoulder. "Now, which way is Callan Street?"

The man pointed a trembling hand to the west side of the square, and the afternoon sunlight burned Kase's eyes as he looked that direction. Trudging half-blind through the crowds, he put up a hand to block it as he moved away from the blade seller's stand. If the man kept his word about lying, all the better, but he wasn't the only one conning people. Jayde was on the verge of collapse, even if no one knew the extent of it. The influx of even more refugees from Tev Rubika didn't help the city's already bulging population.

Kase moved past a peach-colored awning and nodded to the daisy seller wearing a tattered headscarf. Turning the corner, he froze.

Many buildings in Kyvena were constructed of white-washed stone with hints of Zuprium mined in the Nardens, but here on Callan, faded black marks crawled up the walls like macabre floral creepers, marring the bricks and sending a shudder down his spine.

How many reminders of the past would he face this week? First the fight with Harlan, now this? *Shocks.*

The fires that had ravaged much of the city three years ago were burned into his memory. Some parts were worse off than others. The upper district only had a few manors catch flame, but several sectors of the lower city had been an inferno with their cheap wooden housing.

Just breathe.

Bending over, Kase put a hand on the corner shop's rough stone wall and calmed his racing heart. When his brother had given him the address before the greenie's accident, he hadn't thought twice about where it'd be located. He didn't know the lower city well enough to realize, and Zeke couldn't have known how much the marks would affect him. He squeezed his eyes shut and took another deep breath.

Stop being a stars-idiot. You're making a fool of yourself.

Eyes opening once more, he passed the black stains.

It was a quiet lane and sparsely populated—the perfect place for his brother to live. Smaller shops dotted the street with their signs jutting out above the doors. *Soran's General Supply, Tailor for Hire,* and *Beckham Books.*

A bookstore? Kase smiled.

He'd been searching for Homer's *Iliad,* specifically Marisee's translation. It might've been useless now as he had no plans to return to Shackley Manor, but buying a book—any book, Marisee or not—would make him feel better. And it would help clear his head so he could better coerce Zeke into lending him proper clothes for the theater that evening.

The hanging sign creaked in the brisk breeze like the loose hatch underneath his old hovership. He flinched a little at that thought. If Harlan got his way, there'd be no hovership—old or new.

No. He wouldn't let the blasted Lord Kapitan stop him.

The Crews were an autonomous branch of the Jaydian military, so Kase had more freedom than others, but that was all about to change. Kase needed a way to absolve his guilt or prove himself to his father.

He shook his head, laid a hand on the shrinking money pouch at his waist, and pushed open the bookshop door.

A bell pealed above him as he shut the door, and he breathed in the musty scent of decaying parchment. The smell calmed his nerves enough that he could almost forget the scorch marks outside.

But that small amount of peace didn't last long. Of course, it never did.

A soft curse broke his reverie—a flustered feminine voice. "*Stars,* I mean...welcome. Have a look around but make it quick. We close in ten minutes."

Furrowing his brow, Kase checked his pocket watch, the parchment from earlier fluttering to the ground. It was just past six. He scooped up the parchment and shoved it into the opposite pocket.

In a moment, the owner of the voice appeared from the back. The first thing he noticed was her outfit—trousers tucked into calf-high boots instead of long skirts. It was a recent trend, and one his mother frowned upon. Kase didn't care either way, though his sister, Ana, would have liked the new fashions. She'd always hated lacy dresses tangling around her ankles.

Kase swallowed hard. Those thoughts were best left forgotten beneath the ash.

The second observation was the girl's eyes, which reminded him of golden honey on toast. *Should've eaten dinner beforehand instead of trying to drink that ale.* Ignoring his stomach grumbling, he stuffed his timepiece away.

Her gaze narrowed at his clothing. "And I *mean* ten minutes."

Shocks and stars. What'd he do to earn such a glare? Kase glanced down at his pilot's jacket. His clothes were stiff from the rain, the same he'd worn during the bike fight. At least his jacket hid the blood.

Kase ran a hand through his curls and frowned. "Is that how you treat paying customers?"

"Depends on if you actually pay or not, doesn't it?" She swiped bits of dark auburn hair out of her eyes. Little pieces had escaped the messy bun. "Please let me know if you require any help."

"Thank you so kindly. The service here is just so blasted lovely!"

The girl's face clouded before she spun on her heel and disappeared behind one of the shelves. "Eight and a half minutes!"

With a huff, he entered the labyrinth of tomes and crackling parchment. Really, it was abhorrent to have so little time to explore a place such as this, but at least he had money. No one would refuse a paying customer.

Many of the books looked like an inebriated patron had stacked each shelf. *Shameful.* He passed by two, finding nothing of note. Maybe he wasn't meant to find a copy of Marisee. He certainly wasn't traveling all the way to Tev Rubika. Their civil war...no, he'd keep looking. Maybe he could ask the *kindly* attendant if she knew where he might find one.

Cautious of speeding up his time, he peeked around the end of the first row. The girl organized some books and muttered under her breath just low enough that he couldn't hear.

Kase narrowed his eyes. He loved a good sparring match if it sharpened his wit and tongue, but her attitude was borderline rude. For once, he hadn't done anything to deserve such treatment. She wasn't terrible to look at, though. Her long nose had been broken at least once, but that only enhanced her soaring cheekbones.

When she turned back to the desk, Kase darted back into the maze and searched the next shelf. He sent up a quick prayer to find his quarry sooner rather than later. He'd come in to find solace, yet the time crunch only made him feel worse. Maybe he should leave and continue to his brother's apartment? He worked his jaw for a moment and pulled out his watch once more.

He still had plenty of time before he needed to head to the theater, and the more time he wasted here meant less time for Zeke to interrogate him about the previous night's events.

As he brushed his fingers over the spines on the next shelf, his eyes caught on a flash of gold. Squeezed between two monstrous volumes, the shining, embossed letters of *Iliad* glinted at him. With a soft grunt, he tugged on the book, keeping the others from tumbling onto his head with his other hand, and flipped it open, glossy pages sliding through his fingers.

He scowled. This was a more recent edition written in the queen's Rubikan. While most living among the nations of Yalvara spoke Common, a sect in Tev Rubika still spoke Rubikan—they'd been the ones who'd instigated the war to begin with. Blasted rebels. The war led desperate citizens to try anything to bring in a few coppers. Kase didn't blame them, but the quality of products was terrible. This specific version of *Iliad* lacked several elements from the original epic.

He rifled through the rest of the shelf to no avail and moved on. How did anyone find anything in there? Was there not a section dedicated to ancient classics?

He inspected each shelf for any sign of what it might hold. A few Rubikan copies of other novels littered the shelves. Great shocks, why would any bookshop carry those?

A red leatherbound book sat upon a large volume about plant life in Cerulene and others whose titles had rubbed away. Kase pulled it out and smoothed a hand over it, wiping the grime onto his trousers. They were already filthy anyway.

"Is this an authentic Sond?" he whispered to himself. He didn't recognize the cover itself with its embossed title written in some language Kase wasn't sure of, and an imprint of a large archway. He opened the book, coughing as a cloud of dust took flight from the pages. *This place is a health hazard.*

What it was, he didn't know, but it was rare, maybe even an original Sond—a man from the Landing who'd written dozens of books about their journey from First Earth to Yalvara. Good stars, his mother would love this, whatever it was. It might even have something to do with the Yalvs. Most copies of anything to do with Yalven culture had been lost once they'd disappeared. Some said they'd died off. Either way, only the University of Jayde had any copies of Yalven texts.

By his brother Jove's standard, their mother had far too many books, yet not enough for Kase's. He ran a hand over the cover and mysterious title once more. In fact, the gift might propel him past Zeke as her favorite son. With another cough, he tucked it under his arm.

But he was never going back to the Manor. Blast. Maybe Zeke could give it to her? Double blast. His brother would get the credit.

He wandered a little more and found the young woman reading an enormous book at the counter. Was reading it worth the back ache from carrying it around? Odds were it was. She looked up at his polite cough. "Do you need assistance?"

Kase ground his teeth at her tone. Maybe he should have just gone to Zeke's. "Your shelves would benefit from more organization, I'd say."

She set down her book, pages rustling. She arranged her face into a smile, though to Kase, it was more a pained grimace—as if she knew she should be a friendly shopkeeper, but she'd much rather dice him to bits. Even her voice sounded fake. "Again, I would be *happy* to help you locate any texts you desire in the next five minutes. Because we close. And I won't be selling any books to you after that." She gave him the once over again. "No matter how much *money* you might have."

"Oh, no, I'm fine. Just enjoying my time here at this establishment. Good thing I don't have asthma." He coughed and swatted imaginary dust out of the air. "Though I wouldn't complain if you shelved all the books by topic."

"Thank you for your insight. I don't own the shop, but your time limit is now down to..." She brushed her fingers across a locket hanging from her neck and looked to the dust-clouded clock on the wall. The second hand needed oil, judging by its subtle creaking. "...Three minutes. I'd give you that entire time, but I'm not in a forgiving mood. You have two-and-a-half instead."

Kase held up the rare book and placed it on the counter. Hopefully, he would be able to buy it with the small sum in his pouch. Blasted girl probably didn't know what it might've been worth anyway. "Most other shops close around seven at the earliest. What makes this one so special?"

"We've always closed this early." She pressed her fingers into the countertop. "Now, is that all you're looking for?"

Kase cleared his throat as he drew a finger through the dust on the nearest shelf. Because he couldn't ever help himself. "I'm in the market for a copy of Marisee's *Iliad* translation, but the monstrous volume you've got there intrigues me."

Her nostrils flared, the only sign that his silent insult about the dust landed. He would have to try harder.

Her words came out stilted. "We don't have any *Iliad* translations other than a Rubikan copy."

"I saw. Shame they leave out Achilles dragging Hector's body around, that's one of the best parts."

"I know, it's rather—" She caught herself and scowled. "Is that all? Just that one?"

"How about your book?" Kase tried to move closer, but she picked up the text and tucked it clumsily to her chest. He grinned. "I'll give you a silver fiver for it."

"*Gracious day*, my textbook isn't for sale."

A female student at the University? Rare indeed. Impressive, and if she hadn't hounded him about leaving, he might have told her so.

"Shame you have to work. Paying your way through school, I assume?" Kase caught a peek at the author on the spine. His stomach flipped unpleasantly, and he frowned, twisting the ring around his finger. "Huh, Owen Christie's a bit of an old fart, to put it kindly. I'd set that aside. You'll thank me later."

The girl's ears reddened as she slammed the book on the counter. The action sent a charcoal pencil to the floor. She tried to catch it before it fell but failed. She scooped it up and clutched it in her fist. "I see you must be one of those elitists who believe us poor peasants worship the privy you defecate in. Well, *Lord Pilot*, if you'd deigned to read the sign outside, you would've known we closed at exactly six, and ten minutes was generous since I accidentally left the door unlocked."

She waved the pencil around like a knight brandishing a sword.

Sign? What sign?

Heat flooded the back of his neck. Who was this girl to make such ridiculous assumptions about him? Most people at least waited a half hour before deciding he was a cocky *dulkop*.

Don't lose your temper. You'll regret it. Remember what happened last time...

"So you're rude *and incompetent*? What a wonderful

employee you are! In that case, I'll leave you to your rotting ramshackle dump. Don't expect me back."

He stuffed the red leather book on a nearby shelf. *Stupid, blasted—*

He whisked through the shelves, coughing as the hem of his jacket upset layers of dust, but before he made it to the door, she shouted, "I bite my thumb at you, sir!"

He stopped. Of all the things she could have said, she'd chosen to insult him with Shakespeare? If he hadn't been so frustrated, he might've laughed. Instead, he slammed the door and headed off toward Zeke's.

Blasted girl.

FINDING HIMSELF AT HIS BROTHER'S apartment a short walk from the bookshop, Kase threw his stiffened, bloodstained clothing onto the spotless floor and ignored how terribly it stuck out. Zeke kept a ridiculously clean house—must've been the soldier in him.

After a quick wash and a dash of woodsy fragrance, he shrugged into a borrowed broad-shouldered shirt and used a leather belt to keep the trousers from falling to his ankles. Not the best, but it would work. He was thankful Zeke had even let him in the door. Otherwise, he'd have to go in his old clothes, and the steward might not have allowed him in the theater for the smell.

He eyed his blood-soaked trousers and gave them a swift kick for good measure. As for his pilot's jacket, it lay across the bed and out of harm's way.

Kase was about to grab the tie from the nearby chair when voices sounded down the hall and shattered the small peace he'd found in the last half hour. Glancing into the mirror set on the wash basin, Kase ruffled a few curls as his eldest brother, Jove, flew in like a maelstrom, eyes wild.

Zeke caught the door before it could bang into the wall and shut it quietly. Had Zeke snitched and told Jove where Kase was hiding? *Traitor.*

His older brothers were both strong-jawed and broad-shouldered, but sparse patches of black stubble spotted Jove's cheeks. Apparently, he was trying to start a beard. Almost twenty-five and not able to grow proper whiskers. Just terrible. While Kase was sure he could produce enough facial hair to reach his ankles at his mature age of twenty-one, he preferred to keep his face clean-shaven. Food might get caught in his mustache if not. Ridiculously embarrassing.

Zeke, on the other hand, wore his face clean and his hair shaved on the sides, the longer locks on top smoothed back toward his crown.

"Hiding, are we?" Kase knew Jove was one step from losing his cool by the way his nostrils flared. Jove didn't wait for an answer before launching into another question. "*Where have you been?*"

"Nowhere important." Kase jerked the blue silk tie around the back of his neck and did up the knot. Ana's dainty ring on his pinky finger glinted in the light filtering through the open window.

"Just wandering around the city then?" Jove's ears flushed from the color of parchment to ruby-red in seconds. "Or perhaps chasing Lavinia Richter's skirts?"

Kase finished up his tie, biting back another sharp retort. He hadn't spoken to Lavinia since she'd gotten engaged to that *stars-idiot* from Tev Rubika, but Jove was too busy with his new High Guardsman duties to pay attention to Kase's life. As an ultra-important member of the Watch, he believed he had the authority to boss everyone around.

Zeke cleared his throat and put a hand on Jove's shoulder. His sturdy face was as calm as a cloudless day. "Let's be calm about this..."

"I *am* calm," Jove growled. Kase snorted, and Jove shook off Zeke's hand. "Kase, after what you did last night—"

"I didn't do anything."

Jove threw his hands in the air as Zeke rubbed his eyes. The latter spoke first, his voice soft, almost placating. "There's a pilot fighting for his life in the city infirmary. The Guild medics don't know if he'll ever walk again."

Kase glared. "You think I meant for it to happen? *Shocks*, Zeke, it wasn't my fault, whether you believe me or not. And on top of that, they brought the blasted Lord Kapitan into this, and now I'm off the Crews. So I don't shocking care what either of you have to say about it."

"Listen." Jove scratched at his budding beard, the irritation leaving his face. "I didn't come to yell at you. I swear. Though your attitude needs a major adjustment, as usual."

"What did you come here for if not to berate me for *besmirching* the family name?" Kase crossed his arms and went to the window. "And my attitude is fine, *thank you very much.*"

Jove merely sighed. "The Watch would like you to join a mission."

Kase laughed, still not facing the other two. "Your orders are probably still on the esteemed Lord Kapitan's study floor."

"Kase." Zeke's voice was steady, annoyingly so. "Listen to him. It might be the only way out of the mess you've made."

Kase gritted his teeth and breathed sharply out his nose. "I didn't do anything wrong! I only took the blame because I thought I was the only one who *could* without getting disciplined."

Zeke's jaw shifted a little, as did his feet, but he didn't say anything. Jove spoke instead: "Will you just listen? I'm trying to *help* you."

"*Fine.* Talk."

Jove took a deep breath, fingers twitching like he was imagining strangling something—probably Kase's neck.

"Let's go to the parlor and sit, shall we?" Zeke asked, opening the door once more.

Both Kase and Jove followed, each refusing to acknowledge one another. The parlor wasn't nearly as grand as the one at Shackley Manor. The apartments were rented to those of higher station in the military, but it was cozy enough with its plush armchairs and soft electric lighting. Kase knew Zeke was proud of it with his recent promotion—and pay upgrade—to Lieutenant Colonel. He was only overshadowed by Jove, who'd been given the title of High Guardsman by the Watch, the top rank in the intelligence and police service. A prestigious honor—especially for someone as young as Jove. Both brothers' accomplishments made Kase's promotion to full pilot pale in comparison. He slumped into a chair, the material of his too-large shirt bunching up at the shoulders. Jove leaned forward, elbows on his knees and fingers pressed together.

"I know Father's taken you off the mission, and he's still contemplating the charges."

"I didn't—"

Jove held up a hand, cutting Kase off. "For moons-sake, I didn't say I agree with him. But the mission is vital to Jayde's survival, and I wouldn't trust it in any other pilot's hands. Your Hover Lead agrees with me."

"But you'll still have to deal with Father."

"And I will." Irritation laced Jove's voice. "If the mission's successful, we can drop the charges. You'd have proven yourself to him."

Kase sat forward and ran both hands through his hair, mussing it further. They would drop the charges? Was Jove implying if he didn't go, he'd be facing them? "And where would I have to go?"

Jove picked at his fingers. "I can't say right now. You'd not only be working with Zeke, but you'd also have Agent Ben Reiss as your co-pilot."

Kase's head shot up. "Skibs said yes?"

"*Agent Ben Reiss* will be head of the mission, and Zeke will be along to represent the military's interests and be the on-crew medic, but you'll be the lead pilot."

If Skibs was going, it couldn't be too bad. He and Kase had been friends since they joined the Hover Crews together three years ago. A year after joining, Skibs decided he'd rather go into the Watch after a near-death experience with the highly corrosive yalvar fuel. Kase didn't blame him. Having to strip naked on the airfield after getting the liquid on your clothes was embarrassing.

Only one question left. "Would this give me back my place in the Crews?"

The words sounded forced, almost choked, but Kase couldn't help it. After everything he'd gone through in the last twenty-four hours, that was the weightiest thing bothering him. He just wanted to be free. And freedom meant a hover and the wide-open sky.

Jove nodded. "I'll make it happen. I need you, Kase. *We* need you. You're the only one I trust to do this."

Kase finally met Jove's gaze. Blue as the clearest sapphire, like his own. No matter how stern he seemed, Jove believed in him, trusted him to do the right thing, for some reason. He had always stepped in to protect him. Kase should feel more grateful.

His brother knew all along Kase couldn't say no. Because for all of Jove's faults, they were still brothers, and they trusted one another. After Ana's death, he, Zeke, and Jove were all the other had. Kase twisted the ring on his finger.

This could be his *only* chance to escape.

"All right." Kase didn't take his eyes off his brother's.

Zeke's shoulders relaxed as Jove smiled, his eyes crinkling slightly at the edges. "You'll report to Professor Owen Christie's office on the University campus at three tomorrow for a briefing."

Instantly, calm resignation burst into blazing rage. Bookshop girl hadn't known about his past, so her reading a book hadn't bothered him nearly as much, but Jove *knew*. "Owen Christie? Are you crazy?"

"He's one of the most respected professors at the University," Jove barked.

"I don't blasting care what he's done. He can go—"

Zeke's voice rang out over the other two, his deep baritone stopping Kase mid-sentence. "You're not the only one who lost a sister, Kase."

Kase snapped his mouth shut and gritted his teeth. "Why do you think this has anything to do with Ana?"

Zeke rose from his chair and placed a hand on Kase's shoulder. "I know everything's been different since then. But you can't blame Professor Christie, or anyone—"

Kase shrugged off Zeke's hand and turned away. His heart thudded at the burning memory of that day. He worked his jaw, pleading for the screams to go silent. Neither of his brothers stopped him as he grabbed a bowler hat from the hook by the door and stifled his curls with it. He put a hand on the doorknob, not turning, trying to breathe through the memory. "Don't...don't bring her into this." He opened the door and paused. "I'll be back late tonight, Zeke, if that's okay. And I'll show up to your meeting, Jove. Just make sure *he* isn't there."

With that, he walked out, closing the door with a sharp snap. After the past twenty-four hours, Kase didn't want to think about the memories hiding in the darkest corners of his mind. He hired a cab and hopped in. He would enjoy the night at the theater, then he could figure out his next steps.

CHAPTER 4

SPEAK, O MEMORY

Hallie

AROUND THE CORNER FROM BECKHAM Books and tucked into an even quieter side street, Hallie fumbled with the key to her apartment. Blasted thing wouldn't go into the hole properly. It wasn't because her hands were shaking. Nope. Not at all.

It didn't matter she'd been fired and carried her last pay sum in her satchel, nor did it matter that some egotistical jerk had insulted her, making the night even worse.

It was fine. Everything was *fine*. She would get a job at the University, maybe—even though most of the assistant positions in her department had been filled weeks earlier when term started. She would figure it out. Hallie wouldn't have to move back home to

Stoneset, the place where she'd slowly forget all the wonderful things about Kyvena and her dream life studying the ancient Yalvs. No, she would find a way to stay.

She swallowed as she finally got the key into the lock properly and turned it. Stuffing all of her worries behind the wall in her mind, she breathed slowly through her nose. As she did, the smaller clock tower down the lane built in remembrance to those who'd died on the long journey from Earth to Yalvara rang out the time.

Seven.

"Oh crashing stars and moons!" Hallie wrenched open her door and flew in. Petra would be there to pick her up for the theater in fifteen minutes, and Hallie was still wearing trousers.

The piles of books on the shelves in her tiny parlor might look messy and disorganized to some, but she had a system. She'd organized each pile by genre, author, and even color. Yet, they were all reminders of the job she'd lost, so she ignored their judgmental eyes as she flew past them into her bed chamber.

After throwing on a proper skirt and not bothering to change her blouse, she tied on her red maiden belt and attacked her hair. Hallie didn't have her mother's clever fingers, so after some deliberation and painful twisting in the mirror, she left it in its too-messy bun but pinned back the wayward hairs that always seemed to come loose. She wouldn't miss a second of Odysseus' trials because of her hair.

Beep, beep!

Blast. Petra's motorcoach.

Stuffing her money pouch into her satchel, Hallie hurried out the door and back into the living area. She grabbed her jacket from where she'd thrown it over the second-hand couch with the threads fraying at the seams and flung open her door.

"Hurry! We're going to be late!" Petra called over the rumble of the engine, her ebony hair shining in the fading sunlight.

Hallie's gray skirt tangled around her ankles as she rushed to the coach and slid in beside her friend, shutting out the putrid scent of yalvar fuel. The use of the caustic fluid was better than the steam engines, but she hated its scent. It reminded her of toasted flesh. Repulsive. "Sorry, Petra. I lost track of the time."

"To West Jayde Street," Petra told the driver instead of answering.

Hallie ran her hand over her pocket watch and breathed deeply. "What time is it?"

"Quarter after seven."

"What?" Hallie groaned. "I was on time? Why'd you shout at me?"

The coach jerked into motion as her friend straightened her shoulders. "If I hadn't, you wouldn't have hurried."

"I *might* have."

Petra's thin, dark eyes landed on the bag in Hallie's lap, and she laughed. "Please tell me you didn't bring your sketchbook?"

Hallie clutched her satchel. "Does it matter if I did?"

"Well, no." Petra sat back, her crimson dress rustling, and folded dainty hands in her lap. "But we're going to the theater. You won't need to draw anything there."

"I always sketch when we go. There's always a little bit of light if we sit near the stage."

"But I thought this was your favorite."

Though she fisted her hands, Hallie kept her tone light. "Good stars, will you relax? Let me be my weird self and sketch during the play."

"Fine, fine. My teachings are lost on you."

Hallie rolled her eyes as their driver waved people out of the way through his open window. The streets hadn't been built to accommodate both motorcoaches and people when the city was first established. According to the writings, everyone believed all the advanced technology was lost to another time now that they were on Yalvara. Some writings even blamed the Yalvs for its demise, but Hallie wasn't sure she believed them. "Did you tell Professor Christie about why I couldn't stay?"

Petra instructed the driver to honk because a group of about twenty Rubikan refugees refused to move out of the road. She smiled at Hallie. "Of course, and he said he'd meet you in the library tomorrow at nine."

Good thing I no longer have to be at the bookshop at nine.

Petra tapped her manicured nails on her silk-covered knees. "You're the only one who translated nearly a paragraph. No surprises there. Rosalie Gunnar thinks you're making us all look bad, you know?"

Hallie snorted. "Except she's only there because *daddy* gives thousands of gold hunders to the University each year."

"Too right you are. I told her to stuff it anyway." Petra checked her reflection in the window. "Now, how do I look?"

"Ellis will think you're beautiful." Hallie gave her a wicked grin.

Petra whipped around, a few stray hairs coming loose from her twist, and narrowed her eyes. "That's not what I meant."

"That's *exactly* what you meant. You've been eyeing him for months. And with us graduating soon, it's only natural..."

"Not so loud!" Petra glanced at the driver and pushed back the offending hair. "If Papa finds out, he'll have my head! He doesn't think Ellis has the status and...well, you know."

Hallie bit her lip. "Any wedding updates?"

"Anderson and I have an official date. The Sunday after we graduate." Petra's shoulders fell. "What was the point of sending me to school if all he wanted was for me to marry someone wealthy?"

This wasn't the first time Hallie questioned society's rules. The elitists in particular had such antiquated practices. People had fallen back onto those when they'd landed on this strange planet and were thrust back into the dark ages. Something about religion and not wanting to mix bloodlines with the other peoples already established on Yalvara. That still didn't mean Hallie agreed with any of it.

"At least Anderson is handsome. Do you remember that guy Zetta married? I mistook him for a pig the first time I saw him." Hallie put a hand on her friend's shoulder. "She wasn't too pretty either, but..."

"Oh, Hallie, that isn't a kind thing to say," Petra giggled.

"Would you rather me lie?"

"You're hopeless!" Petra's face fell. "What am I going to do without you?"

"Well, you won't be teasing me about my sketchbook," Hallie said as the motorcoach rumbled through the back streets to avoid the marketplace, which was surely overflowing this time of night. Jess' bookshop hours made little sense, which she'd no longer have to worry about. She held back a grimace. "Getting married doesn't mean moving all the way to Tev Rubika."

"I'll be the wife of the City Governor's son. Lots of stupid engagements where my husband will force me to interact with other uppities."

"You're still one of those."

Petra glared. "Not anymore."

"A work-in-progress, but I'll corrupt you yet!"

Petra rolled her eyes, and both girls continued to gossip as the driver took them through the city streets and into the upper district with the buildings towering over them, reminding Hallie of the mountains she'd left far behind. She missed the view, if nothing else...not that she ever wanted to go back. But worrying about the future was futile. *The Odyssey* awaited her, and she wouldn't let anything ruin her night. She could worry tomorrow.

Finally, the motorcoach came to a halt, and Petra fidgeted with her own maiden belt. "Don't mention Anderson at dinner, please? I'd rather enjoy my night."

"As you wish." Hallie gathered her skirts. "But Ellis making eyes at you might compel me to pull it out."

"Oh, quit that."

"Well, I'd prefer you still have your head at the end of the day."

AFTER EATING *STARS-FANTASTIC* ROSEMARY potatoes and lamb at a new restaurant with Petra and Ellis, the trio headed out into the early evening. Petra dismissed the motorcoach in favor of a stroll after Hallie's insistence, and Grieg's Theater was only a block away. Early autumn was always more pleasant in the city. The slight crisp felt like someone had laced the air with coffee cake crumbles.

"I'm still mad at you, El." Hallie pulled her jacket tighter around her shoulders as she looked over at her friend, his blond hair reflecting the soft street lantern light. "That restaurant was expensive!"

Ellis held out both arms for Hallie and Petra to take. "I didn't know either. I went with my parents last time and didn't pay attention to the prices. I'm sorry, but now you're simply in my debt. I'll come up with something good."

Hallie rolled her eyes and tempered the heat rising in her cheeks. Of course, Ellis wouldn't realize how much something had cost. His parents supplied his every need and whim, but that wasn't Ellis' fault. "It's a good thing you weren't lying about those potatoes being delicious. Otherwise, you'd be in trouble."

That was the only positive.

"Close call." His green eyes glittered as he poked her shoulder.

"You must pay more attention." Petra shook her head. "However, I'd say you've redeemed yourself from that last atrocity."

"Yes." Hallie's laughter chased away her worries. "At least now I know how much I despise pig tongue."

Petra blanched. "Oh, that was horrid!"

"You both *chose* to order it!" Ellis laughed.

"Sure, but you told us it was the best meal you'd ever eaten." Hallie shivered, thinking about the rough texture—ugh. Repulsive.

"Good stars, neither of you have the required refined palate."

Hallie punched him lightly in the shoulder as they

reached Grieg's Theater. The building was taller than if she'd stacked the bookshop and her father's inn back in Stoneset on top of each other. Pillars carved with images from some forgotten tale Hallie had yet to read supported the structure.

The entire front facade past the pillars was a masterpiece of floor to ceiling windows glowing from within. Dozens of other theatergoers climbed the stairs to the three entrances where stewards awaited. Hallie bounced on the tips of her toes.

"Of course, as he's on the board, father got us decent seats." Ellis gestured for the ladies to enter ahead of him. "One box didn't fill."

"Oh." Hallie swallowed. "How high up will we be?"

Fingering her gossamer cloak, Petra groaned. "*Hallie.* You won't fall out of the box."

"But what if...I read an article about someone leaning too far and something startled them, then...oh stars. Are you sure?"

Ellis gave their tickets to the waiting man, who counted them. "Didn't you want to see this play more than anything?"

Petra tapped Hallie's shoulder. "I distinctly remember you saying you'd haunt Ellis for the rest of his life if he didn't beg his father for tickets."

Hallie narrowed her eyes. "Because I'd *die* if I couldn't see the show."

"Then don't worry about falling out of the box!"

"But if I *should* start falling—"

Ellis shook his head. "We'll grab you before you fall to your death. Deal?"

Hallie didn't answer, because as soon as she laid eyes on the opulent foyer, her fear vanished. It was her second favorite at Grieg's, the stage itself being the first, if one considered that a room. She imagined the Cerulene palace's foyer in Sol Adrid might look something like it. Their king ruled at the lavish castle-esque home, squirreling away all that realm's money. That was what the Rubikan merchants had said when they'd stayed at her father's inn, at least. Stoneset was on the border of both, which meant they got more traffic than most. Hallie didn't know if their word could be trusted, but nothing else she'd learned upon arriving at the capital had refuted their claims.

After Hallie handed her jacket to a mousy attendant with a murmur of thanks, Ellis held out both arms again so he could lead the women up the left stairway.

Ruby-red carpeted stairs stood to the right and left, taking attendees to upper floors and expensive boxes, and each banister reflected the gentle glow of the chandelier dangling above. Hallie was certain she could see her reflection in the polished metal.

Once they reached the carpeted landing, Ellis took them to the last box. The light from more delicate lanterns drew shadows on the floor as they passed.

The box only seated four, but it had a magnificent view of the stage. Decorated like the hall outside with red carpet and gold trimmings, it was fairly cozy, and Hallie could almost ignore the drop on the other side of the railing. Once she spotted the stage itself, she couldn't contain the squeal that escaped her lips. The soft chatter of the waiting audience below only heightened her excitement.

"This is lovely, El! Your father deserves a promotion!"

Ellis laughed and took a seat next to Petra. "You're only saying that because it's *The Odyssey*. You wouldn't care so much if it was one of those new Rubikan shows.

Every single one has the same plot twist where everyone dies. Absurd."

He wasn't wrong; they *were* awful, though that didn't mean Hallie would say no to a free ticket. Besides studying at the library, going to the theater was her favorite thing to do in Kyvena.

"Look at this program!" Hallie took hers from Ellis and smoothed a finger over the embossed title. "It's so fancy!"

"Are you sure you'll make it through this?" Petra asked with a laugh.

"I promise to shut up as soon as the curtain rises." Hallie straightened her skirt with her free hand.

Ellis chuckled. "I don't believe that for a minute."

She swatted him on the knee with her program. "Hush. The only reason I talked through that last one was because it was…gracious day, I can't even find the word to describe it. The actors were stiff, and—"

"Yes, yes, we know, you could do a much better job." Petra fanned her face with her own program.

Hallie huffed and pulled her satchel off her shoulder, digging for her drawing supplies. She grabbed her sketchbook and set it in her lap. "You're not wrong." The other two ignored her; she selected a hard pencil for light sketching and peeked at the program. "Sterling Goslan as Odysseus? Wasn't he in—"

The flickering of electric lights down below and the hush falling over the expansive room interrupted her.

"Quiet!" Petra poked her and pointed to the stage as the thick velvet curtain parted.

"How about you not give me a bruise—oh!" Hallie swallowed her words and stuffed the program down beside her satchel. She leaned forward as far as she dared, a grin pulling at her lips as nine actors—must have been the Muses—waited, lights reflecting off their pale, masked faces. Their voices echoed as they recited.

"Speak, O Memory…"

Hallie put her chin in her hands, her sketching supplies forgotten as they fell off her lap, pencil rolling across the floor. And for once, she didn't even care.

Kase

FOR A SMALL TRAVELING TROUPE, Kase thought the performers had done a decent job with the play. They couldn't fit every little detail into the two-hour performance, but the actor playing Odysseus—Sterling something or other—was wonderful. The director accomplished quite a feat with the ending scene. The surprised looks on the suitors' faces as the beggar transformed into Odysseus were fantastic. However, to Kase, the man's reunion with his wife was the most touching scene.

If only love was actually like that. His mother and father certainly didn't have it. Jove and his wife seemed happy enough, but he wasn't sure she'd wait twenty years for his brother to return from war.

Kase wouldn't stick around that long for Jove, that's for sure. His older brother's more corrosive words from that afternoon still stung. But then again, he'd be leaving the city soon, so did it matter?

Stepping into the corridor with the plush red carpet, thoughts of the mission clouded his mind. What was it? *Where* was it? Maybe it was a covert mission into neighboring Cerulene? The furthest he'd ever gone was to ferry a local Governor to the Crystalfell region on this side of the Narden Range. Once. He and Skibs had been in one of the larger, fancier hovers and had also flown through a storm. Not ideal. The other missions had been within an hour's flight.

The relationship between Jayde and Cerulene had never been pleasant, but it'd been at least two decades since the last major conflict. That had started because of clashes over the use of the Narden mines, which held Zuprium, an ingenious native metal that didn't rust. It also seemed to have other superior, almost magical qualities, as Kase's uncle found nearly twenty years before. His discoveries led to the construction of hovers. Something about fusing the metal with electricity made the devices fly.

Either way, the war ended with Jayde the victor after five long years and left Cerulene in the dark and hungry for revenge.

In the last few years, there'd been whispers of unrest, something about border raids and people disappearing into the wilds, but Kase didn't follow politics. All he knew was that some said Cerulene was the reason the Yalvs had disappeared some years ago.

As he followed the trail of people leaving the boxes, the faint memory of he and Ana sliding down the banisters crept into the peripheral of his mind and interrupted his thoughts. At the bottom of the staircase, he turned away from the spot where he'd fallen off said banister and cracked his radius clean through on the edge of the stone stair. That was before the theater had added the carpet that reminded him of blood. He remembered his mother's tear-choked voice and his father's hard, unblinking stare promising retribution for their childish actions, although Kase had been only seven, Ana six.

Blasted memories.

He rubbed at the spot on his wrist where the bone had cracked. Even fourteen years later, the phantom pain resurfaced when he thought too long on the occasion. Shaking his head clear, he pulled out his timepiece as he walked on. If it wasn't too late, he might be able to swing by a tavern on his way back to Zeke's for a drink or two. He could afford a morning with a pounding headache, the only perk of not being allowed within ten feet of his hover.

Hopefully that would change soon, so long as Jove kept his word.

Either way, he failed to see the tall woman in his way. He nearly knocked her over and into the mouse-like coat room attendant, who squeaked.

"Stand in the middle of the foyer, why don't you?" Kase growled as he let go of the woman's arm. Thankfully, he'd kept them both from falling. He coughed a little as a sweet fragrance reminiscent of mountain air pervaded his senses.

"Oh good stars, of course it's *you*," a light feminine voice said, the words sliding from her tongue like silk.

Kase stopped dusting off his too-large frock coat.

She looked different than she had earlier that day, her stray hair pulled back and her clothes much finer, but he remembered that golden-brown glare.

Blast.

Throwing his shoulders back, Kase scoffed. "Bookshop girl! Well, isn't this such a *pleasant* surprise? Here I was hoping I'd never see you again."

The girl's hand curled into a fist. "The feeling was mutual."

Kase gritted his teeth and gestured for the attendant. "My hat, please."

The girl quirked a dark eyebrow as the man

scurried off. "You think you're something, don't you? I'm surprised you even said *please*."

With a short bow that made the electric lighting shine off his bald spot, the attendant returned a moment later and offered Kase his bowler hat. He snatched it from the man's fingers. "Can't come up with a better insult? How tragic."

"Would thou wert clean enough to spit upon."

"A plague upon thee! Thou art too bad to curse." Kase gave her a satisfied grin as her eyes narrowed. "I'm surprised you've heard of Shakespeare. From your accent, I'd say you're from the mountains, and everyone knows the further up the peaks, the more teeth you lose." The girl's nostrils flared, but Kase didn't stop there. "Maybe you came here to better yourself? To see if you could pass for someone important?"

"Of course someone as *high and mighty* such as you would think so little of us 'lessers.'" Her words were stilted and stiff, like stones falling from her lips. A few theater patrons paused to look, but continued after a quick glare from the girl. "At least I don't barge into bookshops after hours and demand to be served."

"I didn't *demand* anything."

But she wasn't to be deterred. Her voice dropped low. "The world doesn't revolve around you, you know, but your head is so far up your—"

Kase gripped the hat brim so hard he nearly ripped it, a roar of agitation drowning out her words. Who in the moons was this girl? Why did she insist on antagonizing him so? Why couldn't he leave through the front doors? Others milled about them, grabbing their personal effects and bleeding into the moonlit night, laughing and chattering, perfectly pleasant, yet red creeped in at the edges of his vision.

"—so excuse me if I don't bow to your every blasted whim!" she finished, her breaths coming in huffs.

Kase mashed the hat onto his head. "At least I'm not a two-blistered wench begging for scraps at the University's table."

The words were out before he could stop them. A momentary silence fell over those nearest as bookshop girl's hand flew through the air. Kase's head listed sideways, his cheek smarting from the blow.

Several passersby gasped. Kase caught a few scandalized whispers, but no one stepped in to help. Selfish creatures.

Bringing a hand to his face, he blinked once, twice. His father's words came back to him in that moment.

I'm through with you disgracing the Shackley name.

Maybe Harlan was right.

Glassy tears pooled at the corners of the girl's eyes. Kase ignored the clawing sensation in his chest. There was no taking the words back now; they hung in the air like the night's gathering frost. He hadn't meant them, but her unfounded prejudice drove him to the edge of his sanity. Especially after his past couple of days.

"Hals! The coach is here!" a new voice interrupted. "Is Petra with you?"

Bookshop girl blinked and hurried away, but not before she made sure to shove past Kase, her shoulder digging into his upper arm as she did.

"Hey! How dare—" His words died on his tongue as he exited the theater and watched her stomp toward a young man at the bottom of the stairs, a motorcoach with gleaming hubcaps stalling nearby. Kase's stomach dropped when he made eye contact with the gangly young man sporting golden blond hair.

"*Kase?*" His voice was light and airy, opposite to

what Kase felt in that moment. "Is that you?"

The bookshop girl spun, eyes still glistening and scowled up at him. "Ellis? Who are you—"

Blast, blast, blast.

Kase attempted to force his way back into Grieg's, but a woman dressed in rustling scarlet blocked his way. She gave him an appraising look before slipping past.

"Kase!" Ellis called again.

Kase didn't acknowledge him, but footsteps slapped the stone stairs before a slender hand grabbed his shoulder. Kase fixed his face into what he hoped was a pleasant expression before turning around. "Ellis! I didn't recognize you."

Ellis gave him a short bow before waving to the bookshop girl and the woman in scarlet who'd prevented Kase's escape. He nearly groaned aloud. Of all the rotten luck...

"How long has it been? Three years? Four?" Ellis asked as his companions joined him. The girls whispered as they approached, the scarlet-dressed one tugging bookshop girl along as they climbed. The latter faced away from them a few steps down, her shoulders taut.

"Around the time I joined the Crews." Heat crept up the back of Kase's neck as he watched her from the corner of his eye, probably only making the handprint he was sure graced his cheek even worse. He hadn't meant to let his temper get the better of him, yet here he was again. Fingering the ring on his little finger, he cleared his throat and avoided looking at the young woman.

Ellis probably could've guessed the actual reason he'd dropped out of school, but it wasn't a topic for polite conversation. Nor did Kase want his entire life story spilled into the open air. That required too many pints of ale in the darkest booth in the dirtiest tavern Kyvena had to offer.

"Right." Ellis' voice was as warm as the sun and oblivious to the subtext of Kase's clipped words. "And you've been good?"

"Fine."

The gangly man turned to his companions. "This is Petra Lieber of Kyvena. Her father owns most of Stawson Street."

The young woman in scarlet silk held out her hand. Kase took it and offered it a swift kiss though his stomach was still in knots.

"And—"

"*We've met*," the bookshop girl interrupted, looking over her shoulder.

Kase caught the Lieber woman's whispered: "Hallie!"

Ellis coughed. "This is Kase Shackley. We went to school together before I enrolled at the University."

Kase shoved his hands into his jacket pockets. "I apologize for my rudeness, El, but I need to go. It was good to see you. My driver..."

Hallie snorted and spun around. Her eyes no longer glistened with unshed tears.

Kase clenched his hand. "I'm sorry, did you want to say something?"

"Not at all." She waved a hand. "Run along. Your chauffeur must be in fits waiting for you."

"Indeed, he had a few of those on the way here. Poor chap. I'll let him know you're concerned—Hallie, was it? Again, it has been a *pleasure*," he spat through gritted teeth.

He bowed to the others and turned away. Hallie's

stare burned a hole in the back of his head until he disappeared down the stairs and slid into the hired motorcoach.

Hallie

WATCHING THE VEXING KASE SHACKLEY'S motorcoach drive away, Hallie ground her teeth. Why did he have so much power over her? Why didn't she simply shrug off his insults? In fact, she might have even forgiven him if it hadn't been for him calling her...calling her *that*. Tears of frustration budded once more. And of all days for someone to bring up just how much she'd had to do to stay at the University. He'd deserved the slap ten times over.

His name sounded familiar, but she couldn't place it. Her friends looked at her with varying degrees of irritation.

"Really, Hallie?" Petra shook her head, stray hairs busting loose from her elegant twist. "You embarrassed us!"

Hallie shrugged and tried to push down the heat rising in her cheeks. Ellis spoke up next, fingers pinching the bridge of his nose. "Do you know who that was?"

Hallie fingered the strap of her satchel as she shook her head.

Ellis groaned. "He's the son of Harlan Shackley!"

Again, familiar. "Harlan Shackley...wait...isn't that..."

Petra stepped next to her and whispered, "Yes, *Lord Kapitan* Harlan Shackley. The man who runs the military. Part of the High Council."

This time Hallie couldn't stop the blush. "Oh, yes,

that Harlan Shackley."

"And you just insulted his son," Petra added. "I hope they don't send you to the dungeons. You'd never survive."

"Dungeons?"

Ellis scoffed. "She's kidding, but Hallie, what were you thinking? You don't go insulting those of higher station than you!"

"Those of *higher station* need to learn manners." Hallie crossed her arms tightly over her chest. "He came into the bookshop today, and he was rude and inconsiderate and he called me a—"

Ellis threw his hands in the air. "We need to go before you get us *all* thrown in the dungeons."

"But you said—"

"Let's go," Ellis interrupted, opening the coach door.

Hallie clamped her jaw shut, but it was painful.

Ellis helped Petra inside.

Hallie shook her head, and Ellis rolled his eyes. "You're being ridiculous."

"I'd much rather walk."

Ellis paused halfway into the coach. "And if you get mugged on your way back?"

"Better than riding with you lot."

"*Hallie.*" Ellis' voice thinned. "You know how society is. People like you have to play by the rules same as the rest of us."

"People like me?"

"I didn't mean it like that."

"Then how *did* you mean it?"

He blinked and shook his head. "My point is, it'll be less stress on you in the long run."

She simply crossed her arms until Ellis cursed

under his breath. "Suit yourself. I was just being honest."

And with that, he climbed into the vehicle.

As Petra's motorcoach putted down the lane, leaving its foul stench behind with Hallie, she pulled her jacket tighter around her lean frame. She tried not to think of the warm interior of the coach. But she didn't want to be lectured any further for treating the illustrious Kase *blasting* Shackley like the scum he was. Just because someone had wealth didn't mean that person was better than anyone else.

Besides, the walk would also give her time to calm the emotions raging in her chest so she didn't feel the need to slam her apartment door and wake her landlord. She couldn't handle another soft-spoken speech riddled with disappointment about how the landlord's wife had been unable to get back to sleep after Hallie woke them up in the wee hours of the morning because she'd forgotten her key. That had happened ten times too often.

The last time hadn't been *that* late. Only near midnight. But to hear her landlord describe it, Hallie had banged like a madwoman on the door at two in the morning. Crashing stars, she'd thought she was going to have to hole up in an alley somewhere and hope no one preyed upon her while she slept. The Watch kept most crime under control, but they couldn't be everywhere. While her apartment wasn't in the slums, petty thieves still roamed the market for pockets to pick.

Hallie shook her head and started down the lane. Point was, after arguments with both her friends and Kase Shackley, she'd need all the time she could get to calm down.

Her boots tapped lightly against the cobblestone

street as she made her way to the main market square. Thankfully it wasn't nearly as crowded at night, but because the city was so populated, several people were still out and about this late. Hallie made sure to avoid the ones weaving from one tavern to the next. Those kinds of establishments littered the main road running from the market to McKenzie Square up in front of the glittering Jayde Center atop the hill.

Hallie nodded to a few Watch patrolmen standing on the corner near one of the rowdier taverns. They looked bored, but one had a steaming cup of coffee. The man raised his drink in her direction and continued to chat with his partner.

Must be a quiet night if they could take a break. What else did the Watch do besides walking the streets looking for troublemakers? She'd heard there was a specialized unit that undertook covert or undesirable missions. However, she might only think that because she and Jack had once read a book about undercover agents working to thwart the lord of a crime syndicate on a far-flung world at the edge of space.

That distraction still wasn't enough to make her forget Kase's harsh words. They stung like a red mountain hornet and burned in her ears. He'd gone too far—not that she'd helped. As always, her mind and mouth didn't always communicate before spewing forth whatever words formed first.

Her mother always said Hallie's tongue was a deadly weapon that needed dulling, and Hallie would be hearing those words all too soon if she didn't find a new job before the month was out.

As she walked, music leaked out into the street from a few taverns. The notes of a popular drinking song pierced the air, and she tried to focus on the words.

"I once was high on Mount Loma, all pretty in the south..."

Hallie blushed even as her lips mimed the words. Her brother used to sing it at the top of his lungs whenever Ma made him clean the inn's dining tables.

The song grew rowdier as more voices joined in, the peppy melody and words echoing off the stone walls. Another late-night wanderer picked up the tune and nearly bumped into Hallie. His voice was gruff, and the sickly stench of alcohol on his breath was enough to turn her stomach.

He threw open the door to the tavern, and the song ticked up a notch in volume followed by the stomping of feet and clanking of mugs. She hurried past.

A few minutes later, she entered the near-empty market square. Another pair of Watchmen patrolled the perimeter and nodded to Hallie. She bowed back and hurried past the empty booths and fluttering tent-like roofs. Her boots trod on discarded daisies already beginning to brown and wither. A pinprick of pain bloomed in her chest. Gemma, the sweet little daisy seller, must not have made her quota for the day after all. It didn't surprise Hallie, but that didn't mean it made her any less empathetic toward the girl. If Hallie hadn't had Professor Christie or the University, she might've found herself in the same situation.

If she saw the girl in the morning, she would give her an extra copper.

When she reached the other side of the square, another song caught her ears. This one had even more meaning behind it, but she couldn't bring herself to sing the words.

"Carry my soul in yours
All the days through.

Over dales and misty moors
Shall I go with you..."

The woman's soprano rang out the song for destined sweethearts. Once, she'd hummed the tune to herself for hours and danced with an invisible partner on her warped bedchamber floor. Her heart clenched painfully, and she squeezed her eyes shut even as she walked, praying the image of a blond boy with laughing brown eyes would simply disappear. Stars. What a terrible night. First Kase Shackley. Then memories of her brother. Now Niels.

Seeing *The Odyssey* was supposed to make this the best day she'd ever had. But reality was the real two-blistered wench. Not Hallie.

At least the memories better left in the dusty, forgotten corners of her mind finally drove out the ones of anger and embarrassment from the day. She blinked away tears and left the market square and its music behind.

CHAPTER 5

FIFTY GOLD HUNDERS

Hallie

SKIRTS SWISHING AROUND HER BOOTS, Hallie blocked the morning sun with one hand and with the other, waved to a few of her professors as she passed by the Yalven Studies building. The stone bricks on that one had ivy crawling up the sides and pushing its way into each crevice, but at the corners, there were no invasive plants. Those were outlined with Zuprium, the miracle metal that had saved Jayde from the dark ages. She appreciated the fact she no longer had to use a candle or gas lamp to read by at night, but she hated the metal. Zuprium made electricity possible here on this strange planet, but it still reminded Hallie of home.

As she entered the shadow of the great columns of the University library, her mind took her back to another time when bits of Zuprium flakes dusted familiar blond hair. Niels.

Blast it.

Hallie really didn't need to cry—it wouldn't help her with the librarian, who was the only reason she wore skirts that morning. Believing the trend to be rather ostentatious, the ancient keeper of the books didn't appreciate the new fashions like women in trousers, and Hallie needed all the help she could get if she wanted a job.

Maybe she was stupid in thinking the old hag would say yes, but Hallie had to try.

The great arched oak door scraped against the library's stone floor as she pushed it in with both hands. Her satchel slid off her shoulder while doing so, but she quickly righted herself and dusted the bag off. It was one of the few new things she'd bought for herself upon arriving in the capital two years prior.

Once the door had closed behind her, the flickering, dusty electric bulbs in the chandelier above did nothing to calm her nerves. Pushing back a few escaped locks of hair, Hallie took a deep breath.

It was time.

She had purposefully arrived a half hour before she was supposed to meet Professor Christie for this reason—an amazing feat, and one she wished Jess could see. Either way, she needed all that time to convince the deranged bat lady to give her a job.

I should probably start by not calling her the deranged bat lady...or old hag. It's not her fault she's crazy.

Hallie smirked and strode forward, her chest out and head high. She'd thought about roping either Petra or Ellis into her scheme by having them need help and Hallie offering guidance, but she was still angry with them for the previous evening.

Therefore, her back-up plan won out—impress and beg if needed.

As she exited the grand foyer with its marble columns and tapestry-filled walls, Hallie spotted the *kind and gracious librarian* ahead at her large oval desk, books stacked high on one side. At Hallie's footsteps, the woman looked up from a yellow-paged ledger, her faithful sword against those horrible students who kept books past their return date. Hallie had never failed to return a book on time. That should give her a leg up, right?

The crevices in the woman's face deepened when she recognized who it was, but Hallie took a deep breath and gave the hag, *ahem, the lovely librarian*, her biggest smile. "Good morning, Madame Terry. Isn't today perfect for cozying up to a good book? Have you read the latest Gardier mystery yet? His characters leap off the page!"

Madame Terry patted the braided knot on top of her head and grunted. Hallie bit her lip to keep from saying something nasty. Instead, she smiled again. "It's really good, I swear. I think you'd particularly enjoy the fact the mystery is set in this haunted library back in the Dawn era, so the Cerls would be the heroes of the story...which might turn people off, but I found it quite refreshing to read, even if it was rather gruesome at times. There was this one part where the killer murdered the main character's love interest with only a..."

The librarian went back to her ledgers, and Hallie trailed off, holding back all the Shakespearean insults that flooded into her mind, *froward and unable worm* being the most prominent. "You see, Madame Terry,

I'm actually here to—"

"No, you may not use the Ancient Manuscripts room. You've lost your privileges."

"I was starving, and I didn't get any crumbs on anything!" Hallie's heart sped, but she tried to slow it down. "I'm still filing an appeal with Dean Himmel, and he—"

Hallie cut herself off before she lost her temper and completely blew her chances...though they may have already been at the bottom of the ocean with the countless ships lost trying to find the Tasava continent. She cleared her throat. "What I meant to say was that I don't need to use that room today. I only wanted to ask—"

"And I'll need to check your bag for any contraband." The woman's voice was as gravelly as ever. She held out a withered hand and smiled with her perfect teeth. Though the latter wasn't comforting.

I was a fool for thinking she'd say yes.

"It was just a muffin," Hallie whined as she opened her bag and held it out for the woman to inspect. "I hadn't gotten to eat breakfast that morning, and I needed to examine that Yalven document before Professor Christie's class. You and I both know I'd never do anything to damage a book or manuscript."

Madame Terry said nothing, only used the tip of her fountain pen to push Hallie's notebook out of the way. She poked Hallie's books as if expecting a pastry to pop out.

I should've worn trousers. Now I'll have to ask Professor Christie for a job...

When the librarian finally gave her the okay, Hallie trudged over to a table nearest the fireplace. The small flames in the hearth didn't do much to warm her. She'd hoped to avoid asking Christie, because then she'd have to explain why she'd lost the last one he'd helped her get.

Blast all the stars.

With a burning in the corner of her eyes, Hallie got out her Yalven Language book as well as yesterday's unfinished translation. Working on it would keep her mind busy until the Professor arrived, and hopefully she'd figure out a plan to talk to him about an assistant's position.

GOOD STARS, HALLIE HAD NEVER been so stuck on a translation. It wasn't technically her fault, granted. With half the word faded out, trying to figure out what it said was nearly impossible. Underneath the offending blank, she had a running list of possibilities, but each were more nonsensical than the last—the most recent being 'netherbee,' a type of disgusting insect who lived under the ground and whose sting induced mild to severe hallucinations. Hallie doubted the Yalvs meant that because 'they came with sparking netherbees' nearly made her laugh out loud.

It was a good thing she didn't do so, as the old hag of a librarian kept a wary eye on her, probably hoping Hallie would mess up. That way Madame Terry could officially ban her from the hallowed library halls.

Hateful froward worm.

Yes, that insult fit nicely. It also helped dry the remnant of tears from Hallie's eyes.

After sticking her pencil in her hair, she tapped her fingers on the parchment. "But what could it be?"

Two words near the top of her list were contenders,

but they didn't quite fit with what she knew about the Yalvs. Maybe she should ask Professor Christie whenever he finally arrived? The nine o'clock bells had rung nearly ten minutes prior, yet the elderly teacher was nowhere in sight. Should Hallie go to his office? She didn't think he had students at this time, but she wouldn't see him until her own class that afternoon. Why he wanted to meet with her beforehand was a little confusing, but Hallie didn't mind. She didn't have a job anymore.

Traitorous tears burned again at the corners of her eyes. "Blast it."

"Miss Walker, I'm glad you're here!" a crinkled voice said.

Hallie's head shot up, her hands flying to her eyes and brushing away any leaked moisture. Striding toward her was Professor Christie himself, bushy white mustache and all, his spectacles pushed into his fading hair. He must be nearing seventy, but bits of hair tucked behind his ears were still a soft red, much brighter than her own auburn.

With a smile, she stood and tripped over her tangled skirts. She caught herself on the edge of the table before she could make a complete fool of herself. Not that the boy sitting three tables away hadn't seen her tears earlier.

"Professor! I was getting worried you'd forgotten all about me." Hallie rearranged her skirts to avoid another catastrophe.

Stars-blasted fancy clothing.

Professor Owen Christie grinned, showing off his mismatched teeth, and straightened his gentleman's morning coat. "I apologize, my dear. I was busy studying part of the document I set you lot to translating yesterday, and time just ran away from me." He chuckled while patting his portly middle. "And a few pastries might've been involved. I found the most delightful bakery en route to the University. Elaine isn't too happy with me skipping breakfast with her, but bless her soul and stars, her cooking just can't compete with those cinnamon buns."

"It's quite all right, Professor. I've had more time to stare at my list of impossible translations, which in turn led me to ruminate on leaving University and exploring the wilds of Cerulene."

"That bad, huh?"

Hallie took her seat again, and Christie followed suit. She handed over her notebook. "I have several possibilities, but as you can tell, parts of the word or phrase were too faded to translate accurately. However, based on my knowledge and the little research I've done, the two words near the top seem to be the most feasible."

She pointed to those, and Christie leaned in closer, pulling his spectacles down. Hallie continued, "If I have to go with my gut, the word is 'magic,' but 'abstract sciences' might also fit. Both kind of mean the same thing, but I'm leaning toward the former seeing as most of the older texts, Rayvon Chorzle's *Cultural Practices and Beliefs of the Yalvs* included, point to the Yalvs having some sort of power the scholars couldn't quite understand. They were alluding to the Essences, of course. Therefore, the use of magic here would work, even though it confuses me."

Her professor nodded. "Why would that confuse you, dear? I know you've already taken Yalven Arcane Theory."

Hallie took back her notebook and ran her hand

over the words. "Except all the records we have show the Landing and subsequent settling here on Yalvara were peaceful, barring the fact that many panicked when all of the technology went dark."

Out of the corner of her eye, a man entered the library and stopped at the front desk. He removed his fisherman's hat to reveal short, dark hair where the longer ends seemed to want to go their own way. He tugged at his jade green Watch uniform sleeves as he argued with Madame Terry. Hallie blinked and focused on Christie's next words.

"I knew it!" His smile had grown, all his very crooked teeth glinting in the light from the lanterns and windows. "You did excellent, my girl! You'll do nicely."

"What?"

She never got her answer. The professor turned toward where the Watchman and the librarian were still at odds based on the red staining the man's cheeks. Hallie felt sorry for him.

Christie waved. "High Guardsman, you may join us."

Hallie's stomach flipped. *High Guardsman.* That man was a member of the High Council and head of the Watch—not simply a patrolman like she'd assumed. Oh gracious stars. What was he doing here? And with Professor Christie?

Her heart hammered as the man left the librarian and headed toward them. He wove through the tables with a sure stride even though the blush still proved his frustration with the ever-vexatious Madame Terry.

He bowed to Hallie as she got up and curtsied. What else was she supposed to do when meeting someone who had a hand in ruling all Jayde? Her right knee popped. She winced and stood, heat coloring her own cheeks. The man gave her another short bow before turning to Professor Christie.

"Are you sure she's the one?" He asked in a curt accent that bespoke of the wealthy class.

Christie hadn't stopped smiling. "Absolutely."

Hallie chewed her lip and stared at the men. "What do you mean?"

The High Guardsman turned toward her. "It would be best if we discussed this in a more private setting." He eyed the boy sitting a few tables away before focusing back on Hallie. "It's a matter of the Watch."

Hallie swallowed as her body flashed hot then cold. What did this mean? She looked to her professor, who gave her a reassuring nod.

After packing everything into her satchel, she followed the two men toward the front of the library and to the left, to the door to the Ancient Manuscripts room. Hallie paused and looked back at Madame Terry. The woman's eyes narrowed, and a few teeth escaped her scowl, almost like a wolf's grin. "I'm not supposed to be in there. A mishap earlier this week made her kind of hate me."

"It's quite all right," the High Guardsman said. "I've cleared it with the librarian."

But the woman in question did not look happy. At all. Hallie spun back around. "Are you certain? Madame Terry holds quite a tight grudge if she's perceived you've wronged her in any way, and she hates my guts."

Professor Christie chuckled while the High Guardsman shrugged. "She knows her place. Not that it didn't take a little arm twisting, but I've had good practice at that."

His face was dead serious, so Hallie didn't know if he was trying to crack a joke, but Jack had always said that the Watch had unsavory ways of accomplishing their goals when needed. "Um, okay then. If you're sure..."

With that, the High Guardsman led the other two into the room. The ceiling chandelier was much less opulent than the one in the foyer, but it gave off just as much light. Each of the four thick wooden tables inside also had an electric lantern in the center, just in case. Studying Ancient Manuscripts required more light than most, which was one reason Hallie didn't understand why there wasn't a single window, only tables and several rows of bookshelves laden with scrolls and other large tomes.

The High Guardsman gestured to one of the seats, and Hallie sat, her satchel making a soft thump against the side. She let it slide off before setting it on the table just as Professor Christie took the seat in front of her. The High Guardsman didn't sit. He paced.

"I'm sorry I didn't introduce myself earlier, but my name is Jove Shackley, High Guardsman of the Watch. It's a pleasure to meet you, Miss Walker, is it?" He held out a hand.

Shackley? Like Kase Shackley? Oh blasted, burning, *crashing* stars and suns.

Hallie half rose from her seat and gave him her hand, on which he placed the customary chaste kiss. She tugged it out of his grip as politely as she could manage. "Yes, Hallie Walker. It's a...it's a pleasure to make your acquaintance as well...I hope."

Jove Shackley raised a brow. "You hope?"

Heat blazed upon Hallie's cheeks again. "I didn't mean...it's just that I don't understand why someone so important in the Watch would want something with me. I swear I haven't done anything illegal!"

The last part came out a little squeaky, but both the High Guardsman and Professor Christie laughed. The latter reached over and patted the table before her. "No worries, dear. I told High Guardsman Shackley here that you'd probably pass my little test, especially as none of the other students would. You're correct on your translation. The faded word is indeed magic."

Hallie gasped. "I was the only one, really? I mean, it was difficult, but I would assume someone else would have also..."

She trailed off when the older man shook his head, a few wisps of thinning hair falling into his eyes. He pushed them back. "I didn't doubt it'd be you. As you correctly stated, the Yalvs did have a sort of power which some might refer to as magic, and of course coming from First Earth, it was a bit of a shock, but...I digress. I'll let the High Guardsman continue."

"Yes." Jove Shackley folded his arms and looked her straight in the eye. "While I cannot say much here, you, Miss Walker, have been selected to join a mission for the Watch. With your expertise and Owen Christie's high recommendation, I believe you are the correct person for the job."

Mission for the Watch? What in the blazing stars?

Hallie waited a moment, but at his silence, she said, "I'm not sure what—"

"It's complicated, and I'm not allowed to say much." The High Guardsman rubbed a hand over days-old stubble. "I've been put in a tight bind, but this mission is quite serious and of the utmost secrecy. We don't know how long you'll be gone, but what you accomplish will save *many* lives. I can't say more than that. I'll understand if you decline, of course."

"You expect me to say yes based on such scant

information?" Hallie's nerves tingled. No return date? Would this also mean she wouldn't have to return home? "What about my studies? I have to graduate next spring."

Professor Christie held up a hand. "I'll be your required mentor for a sabbatical. I've already talked with the Dean of Students as well as the head of the University."

Hallie's mouth popped open. "But that isn't available to undergraduate students!"

"I've taken care of it, Miss Walker, I assure you," her professor said, leaning thick elbows onto the table. "You are the best choice out of all the students, and a far better one than a paunchy old man past his prime."

New tears blurred Hallie's vision. After the day she had yesterday, it was a miracle she wasn't babbling at that response. "I—I don't know what to say."

The High Guardsman leaned his hands onto the table, his long fingers splaying out on the deep-stained wood. "This mission is in service to Jayde, and you would be paid fifty gold hunders upon your return."

"*What?*" Hallie sat back as far as her chair would allow. *Fifty gold hunders?* That would pay for another three years of tuition and then some.

The High Guardsman looked back toward the door before making eye contact with her again. "As I said, this mission is important. It doesn't come without risks, but—"

"I'll do it." Staring that money in the face and rejecting it would be ludicrous.

The High Guardsman's bushy eyebrows rose so high they nearly disappeared. "You don't need any time to think?"

Hallie shook her head; any reserve vanished. That

morning, she'd believed moving home was her only option, but with fifty gold hunders...shocks and bolts and stars twinkling in the sky. "If Professor Christie believes I'm qualified, and you pay me that sum when I return, I'll fly to the *blasted* sun and back if you ask me to." She clapped a hand over her mouth. "Sorry."

Both men looked at her for a moment and then burst out laughing—the relieved kind, not out of derision. It was the High Guardsman who spoke. "Stars, Owen said you'd be willing to help." Professor Christie nodded, a smile fixed in place. Jove Shackley continued, "But I didn't expect—well, I appreciate your cooperation, Miss Walker. We'll meet this afternoon at three in the Professor's office to discuss further."

With a bow to both her and Christie, he left through the door, his hat back on his head. Hallie turned to her professor. "I don't know—thank you—I—" She played with her pocket watch, trying to find her words. "After yesterday, I didn't think I'd be able to...just thank you, Professor."

He squinted. "Of course, dear. You've done me proud. Now, say, what is that you're playing with? May I see?"

Hallie's fingers closed around the family heirloom for a moment. "You mean this pocket watch?"

He nodded. "I've never noticed the carvings on the cover before, though I know you wear it religiously."

"All right." She lifted the chain over her head and passed it to him. "It was my brother's, but he passed it onto me before I came to Kyvena."

Not the whole truth but not a complete lie. Even though she and the professor were close, she didn't think he could stomach the details of how it had passed to her. When she'd told Ellis and Petra the story of how her brother had been crushed in a mine collapse, they'd refused to treat her the same for a week. Hallie couldn't stand for anyone to walk on eggshells around her, and if the professor knew just how unstable she was inside—especially with the loss of her job—he might not let her go on this mission, whatever it was.

He took the watch with wrinkled fingers and inspected it. "Curious. Do you know what city it is?"

"All I know is that it's been in my family for ages, so who knows."

"I understand why you keep it so close to you, then." Christie furrowed his brows, but eventually held the watch back out to her. Hallie took it, and he stood, using the table to aid him. "Anyway, you've done me proud, Miss Walker. Now enjoy the journey of a lifetime…just make sure to document it so I can live vicariously through you."

And with a small pat on her head, he left the room.

Hallie slipped the chain over her head, and the slight weight of the watch thumped lightly against her chest. *Fifty gold hunders.* Her heart pounded as tears of joy sprang to her eyes. Holy stars, her dream had just become a reality.

HALLIE PUSHED THROUGH THE DOOR and welcomed the lazy breeze from the open window. It danced with the wisps of hair framing her face and rustled the numerous maps and pieces of parchment tacked to the walls of Professor Christie's office.

Usually, she could find a new map when she came for a visit, but this time, he'd added people instead. Not by his own invitation—that had been High Guardsman

Jove Shackley and the promise of fifty gold hunders. She couldn't stop those words from replaying in her head ever since the conversation in the library that morning.

The University bells tolled three o'clock just as she shut the door.

See? I can be on time.

In front of the fireplace, two other people waited, and not one of them was the High Guardsman or Christie—though she didn't think the latter would join them, as she was supposed to be in his class at that very moment.

Careful not to trip over the skirts she'd yet to change, she walked up to the others gathered around the empty hearth. "Hello! I'm Hallie Walker from Stoneset."

Hallie winced at her own too-loud words. *Just act normal.*

The tiny young woman in a faded floral armchair with fraying edges stopped jiggling her leg and looked up, black curls bouncing as she did so. She gave a short wave with a small, russet-brown hand. "Ebba Fleming. Kyvena."

"Nice to meet you." Hallie turned to the next occupant. The man towered over her, his immaculate green military uniform making him seem even taller. His dusty brown hair was shaven on the sides but longer at the top in the usual soldier style. The insignia on his shoulders told her he was high up in the military's pecking order...impressive, for someone only a few years older than she. He uncrossed his arms and held out a calloused hand. *Stars, he's handsome.* "My name is Zeke."

Hallie gave her hand for him to kiss and raised an

eyebrow. "No surname? Just a random soldier crawling in from somewhere?"

Zeke's mouth quirked. "I'm from Kyvena, same as Miss Fleming here."

"It's Ebba. And technically, I moved here from some town you've probably never heard of," Ebba said.

"Still counts."

The girl shrugged. "So, Hallie, you said? Why're you here?"

Hallie walked over to a matching floral armchair and took a seat. She slid off her satchel, placing it on the low table in front of her, and leaned forward. "High Guardsman Shackley asked me." *And offered more money than I've seen in my whole life.* "And you?"

Ebba raised an eyebrow. "I can fix anything."

"Anything?"

The girl sat up straighter in her chair. "I completed the University's mechanics course at fifteen. Youngest ever."

Zeke laughed. "Your confidence could rival Kase's."

Ebba whipped her head around and groaned. "That *dulkop* rejected my request to join his ground crew."

"Kase?" Hallie's stomach clenched. Surely, they weren't talking about the same one.

"My brother."

"Oh." Hallie swallowed. Still might be a different one...

"Don't hold it against me." The soldier grinned, a sparkle in his hazel eyes. "Not all Shackley men are—"

Three Shackleys? Burning stars. There were three of them? She should have run screaming in the other direction.

The door opened, interrupting Zeke. Hallie recognized the High Guardsman, but the man right behind him was new. He had hair the color of the sun, and his pointed features were reminiscent of the fox living in her parents' back garden. He was much shorter than Jove Shackley, only coming up to his shoulder. A third person shut the door.

A soft growl escaped her lips. Hopefully no one heard.

It was him again. *Kase Shackley.*

What had she done to deserve such a cruel and unusual punishment?

When his eyes fell on Hallie, he smirked as he went to stand beside his brother Zeke. She glared back. Kase finally broke eye contact as the High Guardsman spoke from in front of the hearth; Hallie took the small victory with a smug smile.

"Thank you for coming," the High Guardsman began, scratching his stubble. "The Watch is grateful to each of you, even when you didn't know what the mission was. I assure you, your service will be invaluable to the realm and its survival."

He looked at each of them. Hallie peeked at Kase as he gave a slight roll of his eyes. How did he get invited to this? He must have thought he was so important with his pilot goggles around his neck like a wealthy woman's jewels. Ugh.

"Before we begin, a few introductions are in order. Most of you know each other, but Miss Walker does not."

The blond cleared his throat and stepped up. "I'm Agent Ben Reiss. Used to be a pilot in the Crews before joining the Watch."

Ebba sat tall in her chair, hands folded on her knees. The action drew Hallie's attention to the girl's trousers—not skirts. A small part of her warmed at the sight.

"Ebba Fleming." She blew a rogue curl out of her face.

"Miss Walker and I just met." Zeke stepped forward to shake Ben's hand. "Good to see you again, Agent Reiss."

Agent Reiss smiled, but it didn't reach his eyes. The soldier nodded and stepped back. Now that all three Shackleys were together, the resemblance was as plain as light on the water. Kase was a blending of the two, but she couldn't figure out where that hair came from.

All heads turned toward the pilot, but he looked directly at Hallie. "*We've met.*"

Blasted stars-idiot.

In his clipped Kyvena accent, the echo of her words at the theater was even worse.

Out of the corner of her eye, High Guardsman Shackley clenched his hands. Maybe she wasn't the only one irked by Kase's behavior.

No matter. It was fine. Kase Shackley could think what he wanted. She arranged her face into one of calm.

"My name is Hallie Walker, and I hail from the illustrious town of Stoneset on the other side of the Nardens. I'm the scholar on this mysterious mission." She offered a blinding grin to Jove.

The High Guardsman looked taken back by her introduction. "Thank you, Miss Walker." He paused and took in the group once more. "I've assembled the finest team possible, and I expect each of you to show the *utmost respect* for one another."

His gaze lingered on Kase, who inspected a dusty terrarium on the shelf near him. Hallie narrowed her eyes. Sure, the petrified toads inside were dressed in ruffled tunics and tights, and they'd been staged like one had stabbed the other in a duel of swords, but if the High Guardsman had been glaring a hole through *her* head, she wouldn't have been quite so unconcerned.

The High Guardsman tucked his hands behind his back. "With a mission this dangerous, I'll give you one more opportunity to back out." He paused. "If you stay, know this is for the good of the realm and its future. This is your last chance to say no. No one will penalize you for that decision."

Fifty gold hunders. Fifty gold hunders. The words beat in time with Hallie's heart.

When the silence threatened to crush her, he continued, "Your reputations are not unfounded. Thank you. Now, let's talk. Pilot Shackley, secure the room."

The messy-haired brother's nostrils flared, but he obeyed, shutting the window and locking the door.

"Secured, *High Guardsman* Shackley." He rejoined the group.

The High Guardsman stared at him for a second before moving on. "As you know, relations between Jayde and Cerulene have never been amiable." *What an understatement.* "However, over recent years, our cache of Zuprium has dwindled dramatically, while Cerulene's has done the exact opposite."

He waited for a reaction, but everyone wore the same expression—confusion. Hallie spoke without waiting for him to call on her. "The mines in the Nardens are still in operation, aren't they?" Many in her village were miners, including Niels. He'd been more interested in that than helping Jack prepare for University, but that was *before*.

"Yeah." Ebba scratched her head. "How'd the *sterning* government run out of it? I've only ever seen it on hovers and electropistols." She thought for a moment. "Or in knife blades worth more than this whole blasted city."

The High Guardsman shifted his weight from one foot to the other. "We believe our mines have been compromised. And those that haven't aren't producing nearly enough."

Hallie's words spilled out of her mouth. "Cerulene's stealing our Zuprium?"

"Get to the point, Jove," Kase said. Zeke elbowed him. Stars, why *was* he invited?

"We're handling that issue," Jove Shackley continued, his tone flinty, "but we need an alternative solution, which I shall explain momentarily. Your main objective is twofold. The first is to secure a source of Zuprium."

Ebba raised her hand. "Aren't the miners the best ones for this job? I'm a *mechanic*."

A muscle quirked in the Guardsman's jaw. Hallie bit back a laugh. This was *not* going as the man had planned. "No, Miss Fleming. Allow me to finish, and I will take any questions you have."

He waited a second. No one spoke, so he continued. "You'll search for Zuprium beyond our borders."

Hallie bristled. "Like in Cerulene? But that would mean we'd..." Someone snorted, and she caught Kase molding his expression back into one of abject boredom.

"Let me finish, and you'll understand. I promise," the High Guardsman answered.

So what was Hallie's purpose on this mission? Her expertise lay in other areas. Why make a big deal about her going if all she was going to do was search for some resource so Jayde could build new airships?

The High Guardsman pulled out a folded parchment from inside his jacket. "The second half of your objective is a bit more complicated."

He unfolded the parchment and placed it on the low table in front of Hallie. She quickly moved her satchel to her lap as the others leaned in close. Yellowed and crinkled, the parchment was weathered with age. A bit of one corner had been burned off, by mistake or on purpose, it was hard to tell. To the south of Jayde, the Silver Coast, a small kingdom that had broken off nearly a century ago, wasn't even on the map. Gracious day, this map was old.

The High Guardsman pointed to the continent to the south of the one they were currently on. "The most important part of your mission is to contact the Yalvs, ally with them, and in turn, secure Zuprium trade. They have more efficient ways of mining it than we do."

"But," Hallie interrupted, "no one's seen them in at least two decades, and only in Cerulene even then. The Jaydian clan disappeared hundreds of years ago. Many sources suggest they died."

"Which is the lie the Watch and Jaydian government spread." A slight pink tinted his cheeks. Hallie's eyes widened as the man continued, "As far as we know, the Yalvs are still on Tasava."

"*Tasava?*" Hallie hardly believed the words coming out of his mouth. All expeditions of engineers sent to explore it had returned with tales of terrifying beasts and other horrors. And those were the few who'd survived the return journey.

Kase crossed his arms. "You're cracked, Jove."

"And you're toeing the line, Pilot Shackley."

Zeke stepped up between his brothers. "Let him finish, and then we can discuss. You're only making fools of yourselves."

The three brothers glared at each other, but the High Guardsman broke away first. Hallie wondered if their poor parents had any hair left. "Here," he said, pointing to a point on the map. It was deep in the wilds of Tasava, though with a map this outdated, who knew what was there now? "This is where we think the Yalvs' main city is, Myrrai."

"That means starlight," Hallie whispered, but quickly shut her mouth at the stern look she got in return. She just caught Kase's raised eyebrow in response.

"At least, this was its last known location as of twenty years ago when we lost contact with them. We simply assumed they didn't want to be bothered after suffering so much during the Great War." The High Guardsman then pointed to a portion of the map labeled *Bay of Storms.* "While you'll have trouble enough in the wilds of Tasava, this is the best place for you to land on the continent...as dangerous as that is. From others' accounts and our own intelligence, the only way to land on Tasava is to fly over the massive storm here. There's something with the temperature of the water and the hot air or something colliding, making an almost everlasting storm this time of year. Our own scientists haven't been able to explain much more than that. If you can't fly over, aim for the eye of the storm. All evidence points to the fact the eye is partly over a good portion of the coast."

"That's nearly impossible, Jove." Kase snapped. "Are you sure that's our only landing point?"

The High Guardsman nodded. "Everywhere else is too far to reach without refueling, and there aren't islands to do so. You *must* find a way through the Bay of

Storms, and quite frankly, that's why you're on this mission."

"If you say so."

"Yes, now," the High Guardsman coughed. "That's not all, either. I'll let Agent Reiss explain the rest."

The blond man stood straighter, and everyone else leaned back from the map. He folded his hands in front of him. "We've intercepted recent Cerl communications saying they intend to find the Yalvs and take control of a certain weapon. With this and other indicators, we think Cerulene is preparing for possible war. We don't know much about the weapon itself, only that the Yalvs were in possession of it, but we've...uh..."

He scratched his cheek and looked to the High Guardsman. "We also think they may have discovered something not quite natural in Cerulene...something to do with the Yalvs themselves. We don't know specific details, but it seems the Cerls have captured what some believe to be a Yalven Essence."

"How in the blazes did they do that?" Hallie burst out. "That religious practice died out centuries ago!" The stories of great power being passed down through generations of Yalvs flooded her thoughts. "It was dangerous, and the Yalven-Jaydian Treaty of 3664 made sure no one could take part in it again. The Yalvs agreed for the power to die with the last Essences. I can pull up their death records at the University library if you wish."

Essences were difficult to find in the ancient literature, because those who possessed a facet of power from the Yalven god could do unspeakable things, and no one wanted to dwell on a problem that no longer existed. Many Yalvs also died in the process of taking on an Essence, which was the main reason the natives of Yalvara had agreed to the treaty. Hallie wished she knew more. Her mind also went back to her translation. *They came with sparking magic...*

If the Yalvs had that sort of power, why were they scared of whatever man had brought with them to Yalvara?

Agent Reiss' blue eyes darted again toward the High Guardsman. "That was what we intercepted. It'll be our job to confirm the Yalvs haven't broken the treaty, and bring them into an alliance before Cerulene does."

She cocked her head. "But all the sources say they were never friendly. I've read about their customs and—"

Jove Shackley tapped the table. "And that's why you're here, Miss Walker. Your knowledge of the language, Yalvs, and history is vital to persuading them to join our fight. We're at a distinct disadvantage if war breaks out. That is, if Cerulene obtains whatever the weapon is...and is indeed in possession of an Essence."

An icy cold sensation spread through her stomach, like she'd swallowed a handful of snow.

The High Guardsman looked them all in the eyes before speaking again. "We can't risk sending more than your small group with the tensions being what they are. Find the Yalvs before the Cerls do, bring them into an alliance, and if possible, secure more Zuprium."

He straightened and folded the map back up. "The reality is, we're running out of resources. Quickly. If we can attain more Zuprium and re-establish an alliance with the Yalvs, we can prevent this war and save millions of lives. It's up to you, the crew members of the *Eudora Jayde,* to find a miracle."

Ebba cleared her throat. "But what about our

families?"

The young woman looked so small sitting there, swallowed by the armchair. How old was she? Seventeen? Eighteen? What had she said earlier about completing the University mechanics course at fifteen? Hallie bit her lip. They would send a girl barely old enough to be out on her own into the unknown?

"We'll protect them here in Kyvena. That's the most we can do for you. I'm sorry it's not more," the High Guardsman answered.

"What about mine?" Hallie interjected. "They're all the way in Stoneset. Pa runs the inn, and Ma won't want to leave her garden."

"They'll have the option of moving to Kyvena."

"But—"

Agent Reiss interrupted her. "Unless you prefer they stay there in the direct path of an invading Cerl army?"

Hallie clamped her mouth shut. *Holy moons.* It was that serious. Her small lunch of chicken and greens bubbled in her stomach.

Another moment of silence. Zeke shifted his weight. "When do we leave?"

"At dawn in five days." The High Guardsman paused and waited for anyone else to speak up. "If you have questions later, please contact me through the Professor. Otherwise, you're dismissed." He looked each of them straight in the eye before any of them could move and spoke once more, "I'll also remind you any word outside this room about the specifics or objectives of the mission will be construed as treason. Thank you."

No wonder they were offering a fortune upon their return. The Watch believed it was nearly impossible.

As the new members of her crew filed out, they all avoided eye contact. They must've been thinking the same thing Hallie was.

Failure wasn't an option.

Because it meant something much worse than her returning home.

CHAPTER 6

YOU'LL BE BACK

Kase

ONLY FOUR PEOPLE WERE AWAKE at that stars-forsaken hour. Some antiquated folk tales and legends called the time before dawn the witching hours, but Kase never put much stock in those stories. Shackley Manor's numerous busts of dead old men and the occasional griffin knocker would certainly frighten away unfriendly spirits...and anyone who didn't share the Shackleys' prestigious, mostly pretentious, family history.

Kase didn't feel comfortable there either.

He didn't care to say goodbye to his father, who'd strode down the great marble stairs without acknowledging his youngest son in the corridor seconds before. Harlan Shackley's pristine uniform and too-sharp eyes were too good for Kase's rumpled shirt beneath his pilot's jacket. Of course. Instead, the Lord Kapitan left without thanking the butler for opening the door.

Kase couldn't complain. The ice-cold shoulder was better than anything else he expected from his father. His mother, on the other hand, was different.

With each clack of his boot heels on the polished stone, Kase counted the seconds until he reached his mother's library. Portraits of forgotten family members judged him with brush-stroked eyes as he passed. The candlelit sconces lining the corridor were dark. At least they reflected his mood.

Golden light blazed out and stretched upon the floor as Kase approached the room he sought. It wasn't even dawn, but of course, his mother was up with a cup of black tea and her nose in a book. While Kase loved reading, he would never wake before the sun to do it.

Hiking his pack higher, he stepped over the threshold. "I do admire your dedication, Mother."

Lady Celeste Shackley, called Les by those who knew her best, looked up. She didn't put her book down on the carved side table, merely held her golden-brown finger in her page and set it in her lap.

In her growing years, laughter lines had decorated her face. She hadn't gotten those because of his father. No, those had been lovingly placed there by her children. However, she wasn't smiling now.

A rock of guilt dropped into Kase's stomach. Zeke had stopped by the night before, he knew, but Jove must not have told her Kase was going too. Blast him. Kase always drew the proverbial short straw.

He shifted his weight. "I'm going with Zeke."

A bead of sweat formed on Kase's brow. After a

minute too long, his mother took a small strip of cloth from her lap, put it in her book, and closed the volume. It looked to be *King Arthur*—one of her favorites. She set it on the side table with peacock feathers carved onto the surface and legs.

"You're leaving as well?" Her blue eyes took in his pack.

He rubbed a hand through his hair once more.

"Don't do that," she scolded lightly, "you're making your hair messier than it already is."

Unlike Kase, who didn't care which mind his curls took, she'd tamed hers into her usual fashionable bun at the nape of her neck.

He put his hand down. "You must have heard about...about the other night. I don't have a choice. If I don't go..."

Shocks, he couldn't say it. His lips couldn't even form the words. His throat closed around each syllable, but Kase didn't fight it. He only looked down at the floor. While much of the manor boasted fine marble from the Narden Range, his mother covered it with rugs in her library. Some were soft, some showcased scenes from the Landing, and other nondescript ones were for merely covering the gaudy floor beneath.

"Where are you going?" her voice was too soft.

Kase peeked up through the hair falling into his eyes. "I can't say where we're going."

His mother bit her lip. "How long will you be gone?"

Kase shrugged. "Might be a while."

"Then, why?"

Kase didn't answer. He could only swallow. This was his chance to get out of the city at last. If he was successful, he could prove himself to his father. Jove also promised any charges brought against him would be dropped. He needed to do this. It wouldn't help the greenie in the city infirmary walk again, but it might heal Kase.

Blasted stars, he was a terrible person.

His mother rose and came to stand in front of him. It'd been a while since he'd been shorter than her. Now, she had to look up at him just to see his face. He grimaced. "I'm sorry."

She shook her head and grabbed his arms. "You'll be back."

"But..."

"No, I refuse to believe otherwise. *You'll be back.*"

He couldn't say anything, only pulled her into a tight hug. Her subtle scent encompassed him, and he almost broke the promise to his brother.

Hallie

WITH EACH DAY BRINGING HER closer to departure, Hallie occupied herself by scouring the University library for any information she could find on Tasava. Unfortunately, even those who'd survived to write about their experiences hadn't given many helpful details.

Sure, they described beasts never seen on this side of the world, and Hallie was especially interested in one description alluding to what she would call a dragon, though she didn't see any records of it shooting fire like the old legends from First Earth. A part of her wished she'd run into one—a sadistic side of her, that is.

Another account detailed other odd occurrences, like hearing voices or seeing specters, but not one account mentioned the Yalvs.

Not a single one.

They *must* have encountered them. The Yalvs wouldn't just allow people to wander their lands unchecked, not after Cerulene nearly wiped them out. They would've defended their villages until their last breath. So how could there be *nothing*?

Five days of near-fruitless research later, the day of departure arrived, and sweat beaded on Hallie's brow in the cool predawn air as she sprinted through lower city streets to reach the airfields. It was all her fault she was running late, of course. She knew she shouldn't have stayed up rereading parts of *The Odyssey*, but she thought Odysseus' courage might make her feel better about her own journey.

Though she hoped this mission wouldn't last twenty years.

Back aching from her pack and heart still racing, Hallie whipped around the side of a small building—a cheesemaker's shop, judging by the smell. At the end of the lane stood her goal, the top of the outer city wall crested with the tell-tale golden gleam of early dawn. The gate to the Kyvena Airfields itself was only a simple door manned by two guards, one of whom slumped against the wall in sleep.

I'm with you. I don't want to be up now, either.

She waved as she came up to them, the sleeper perking up at her footsteps. Both wore matching dark green uniforms, the Jaydian symbol of a tree inside the outline of a sun emblazoned near the right shoulder. The other soldier pulled off his military cap to reveal hair dark as the night sky and tipped it toward Hallie. His face looked like it'd been carved from the Nardens. That fact made his intended smile more into a grimace. "It's rather early, Miss, but good morning. May we help you?"

The sleeper soldier nodded, but his hand went to the sword at his side. From Hallie's understanding, the thing was ceremonial and used as a last resort, but the move made her heart thump a little too loudly. She didn't know which was worse, the soldier spearing her through the chest or shooting her with the electropistol holstered on his other hip. Rock-Face put a hand on his partner's shoulder. "Rest easy, Buck. It's just a pretty lady out for a stroll...at dawn."

Hallie fiddled with the strap of the pack on her back. "The High Guardsman said to meet at the airfields about five minutes ago, but I overslept, and I'm running late. Will you please let me in?"

Both soldiers raised brows, but before they could say anything else, hobbled footsteps came up behind her. This time, Rock-Face also went for his weapon, but he chose the electropistol. He relaxed, though, when a hand landed on Hallie's shoulder.

"Miss Walker, good morning. Glad I caught you." The man's voice reminded her of the sea crashing into the rocks along the Silver Coast. She'd only visited once—with Ellis. With that voice, though, all the anxiety building up like cement in her chest disappeared.

Hallie half-turned and caught sight of the man's bushy white mustache in the bit of sunlight peeking up over the outer wall. "Professor Christie!"

He nodded to the guards. "Miss Walker is here on the High Guardsman's orders, so do let us pass."

"Not without papers," Rock-Face answered.

Professor Christie dug in his jacket's inner pocket for his identification papers. Hallie hadn't thought to bring anything other than what she'd need to survive or entertain herself on a mission she didn't know how long she'd be on. Granted, only top government officials and other important people were given identification papers such as that. Like anyone else would ever need to use the airfields or enter important government buildings.

The last time she'd ridden in a hover had been with Ellis, but his father had booked the trip through his connections, and the hover picked them up right outside the Carrington estate in the upper city.

Professor Christie gave the man his papers, and after a minute of inspection, the soldier nodded. "And the girl?"

I'm twenty-one, you stars-idiot.

Christie's hand grasped Hallie's shoulder, which prevented her from saying something she'd probably regret. "Miss Hallie Walker has express permission from me and the High Guardsman to enter the airfields. Therefore, if someone objects to you allowing her in, send them to me. Thank you."

The sleeper soldier finally took his hand off his sword, and Rock-Face sighed. "Fine, but I'll be taking this up with the Crews Commander."

"Be my guest," Christie retorted and pushed Hallie forward, leading her through the door.

The Kyvena Airfields covered the remnants of the old city just outside the eastern wall of the modern-day capital. Hallie and Professor Christie passed relics of times near forgotten littering the sides of the cobblestone lane—a rusted lamp post here, a crumbling stone foundation there. The High Council really needed to clean the place up, but Hallie made a mental note to sketch the rusted lamppost when she had time. She couldn't let such history pass her by.

"Miss Walker?" Professor Christie whispered as they passed a guard contingent patrolling the grounds.

Hallie looked up. "Yes, Professor?"

He paused outside the first large metal hangar and gestured over to the alley between it and the next. Curious, Hallie followed.

As the older gentleman inspected the space, Hallie spoke, "I need to find hangar number three, Professor, and I'm already late."

The alleyway wasn't large, only wide enough for roughly three people to walk abreast. She scuffed her boot on cracked and mossy cobblestones below, the golden light streaming over the hangar roofs making each stone glow with morning dew.

Her professor dug in his jacket and pulled out a slim, rectangular wrapped package. He held it out. "Take this."

The packaging was yesterday's newspaper. The headline on top read: "Stradat Millicent Sarson Leads Charge to Raise Wages amid Rubikan Refugee Surge." A black-and-white picture of the scar-faced woman watched Hallie as she untucked the corner of the wrapping, but Professor Christie stopped her with the clearing of his throat. "Wait until you're alone on the hover. This...this is...well, no one outside of me and you will know about it. Read it and find out what you can when you arrive in Myrrai."

Hallie's fingers froze as she looked up. "What do you mean?"

Christie looked around, behind him down the deserted alleyway and toward the main road. "I trust the High Guardsman, but I feel like something's amiss about it all. There's a reason no one's been able to contact the Yalvs in two decades, and there's a reason why that book in the package has been banned everywhere. It's a wonder Jess still had this copy, though the blasted man had it out for sale. Thank the stars I got it before anyone else. And lucky for me, I guess."

Hallie looked down at the package once more, the scarred Stradat glaring up at her. "You're frightening me, Professor. What do you mean something's amiss? I really need that money the High Guardsman promised..."

"No, just study the book whenever you're alone, and tell the Lord Elder that Jasper will be in touch." He stepped past her but paused right before the entrance to the alley and turned. "I need to go if I'm to make it in time for fresh cinnamon buns."

A tingling sensation started in Hallie's chest. "Who's Jasper? What's going on, Professor?"

He faced the sun once more, and Hallie barely heard his next words. "Be safe, my girl. I've never told you this, but you do remind me so much of my...of my grandson, the one we lost in that horrid fire three years ago." He sniffed and still didn't turn toward her. "My lovely Elaine agrees with me, so take care of yourself, all right?"

Hallie blinked away the moisture flooding her gaze and nodded. "Thank you, Professor."

And then he was gone, disappearing into the glow of early morning.

OUTSIDE THE HANGAR MARKED WITH the number three, Hallie cleared away the dirt from a window embedded in the door. A shiny brown airship filled her vision. Having only flown in a little hover cruiser, this one was vastly different; it reminded her of the merchant ships in port near the sea with its long body, but instead of sails on top, this monstrosity had wings jutting out from the sides. Underneath those, great propellers hovered on the lip of each engine barrel.

"Nice, isn't she?"

Hallie jumped and found the small woman from the meeting behind her. She put a hand on her satchel, hoping the edges of the newspaper-wrapped book didn't peek out. "Ebba, right?"

The young woman nodded, adjusting the strap of her pack higher on her shoulder. "Impressive. I can remember thousands of hovership parts, but names of people? Forget it."

"Hallie." She held out a hand. Ebba took it.

"Was gonna guess Holly. Not too bad for me. So, are we gonna go inside?"

"I assume this is what we're flying to Tasava and back?"

Ebba nodded. "She's the nicest ship I'll have ever worked on."

Hallie opened the door. Without the haze from the smudged glass, she saw the airship with even more clarity, and she halted. "You weren't kidding."

Ducking under the engine, Ebba walked toward it, and Hallie tried not to think of the razor-sharp propeller blade chopping off anything important. The wings themselves didn't look like they'd hold anything up, but that was where the hover components came in.

"This beauty's much bigger than the ones I usually work on," Ebba said, "but I can fix anything, so we shouldn't have a problem if we have...problems."

Hallie chuckled. "I didn't know hovers of this size existed. I'll have to sketch it later."

"You're an artist?"

Hallie patted her worn satchel. "It's more of a hobby."

"My pa's a painter." Ebba placed a foot at the edge of the ship's stairs. In profile, her pack was nearly as large as she was. "Thought moving to Kyvena would help, but it doesn't bring in much." She glanced around and whispered, "The money from this mission should make everything much easier, I'd say."

Hallie snorted. "You've got that right."

Professor Christie's words echoed in her mind. With the book tucked in her satchel, those words weighed heavier than they should have. Her professor was hiding something from the High Guardsman, and then there was the absurd sum of money Hallie'd receive when they returned. She shook her head to clear her thoughts.

It was still better than moving home, and if she was honest with herself, the idea that she was in on some sort of secret made her heart thrum with excitement. Professor Christie wouldn't have sent her on anything too dangerous. She hoped.

She followed Ebba up the folding staircase. Before going through the door, Hallie ran a hand across the letters engraved along the side. *Eudora Jayde.* The smooth metal around the words contrasted with the rough etchings. "So does the *Eudora Jayde* run on yalvar fuel like the others?" Yalvar fuel was foul-smelling, but it had been found to increase efficiency and speed over the old steam engines.

Ebba nodded, absently, but Hallie wasn't sure she'd heard the question. "I just love the name. Wasn't Eudora the name of that one guy's wench?"

Hallie flinched. "I'm sorry?"

"You know, the guy who led the Life Ships here?"

"Oh!" Hallie's heart fluttered. "You mean General McKenzie?"

"Sure?"

"Yes, Eudora was his wife. She also founded the Engineer Corp when technology went dark."

"Yeah, yeah. That's right." Ebba grinned so wide a few crooked teeth on the bottom row showed. She stepped into the ship's corridor. "But to answer your question, *Eudora*'s a hybrid. She uses more electricity than the others. First of her kind. I'm surprised the High Council's letting us use her."

"They don't know you're using it," a voice said behind them. The High Guardsman.

Hallie furrowed her brow and stopped on the stairs. "What do you mean?"

Was this what Professor Christie meant?

"Political reasons," was the only answer he gave. Vagueness must've been a job requirement in his field. He gestured for them to go inside. "We're missing Pilot Shackley and Agent Reiss. Of course, my brother is late, but I'm slightly worried about Reiss."

Hallie bit her lip to keep from saying anything, though it was nice to know someone was later than her.

But just as she stepped into the ship, a voice called from behind.

"Sorry I'm late, High Guardsman." Hallie turned to see Ben Reiss hurrying into the hangar, his pack high on his back. "I got caught talking to Christie. He says he's going to take some time off in the country to throw off the Stradats..."

The High Guardsman turned. "Did you see Kase?"

99

"No, but you know him." Agent Reiss gave the oldest Shackley brother a small grin and sped past the others on the stairs. Hallie and Ebba moved out of the way quickly so as not to get hit by his swinging pack.

The High Guardsman ran a hand down his face. "When will he learn..." He led the women onto the ship.

The inside wasn't as impressive as the outside, and it was cramped, like they'd needed to conserve space but had forgotten real-sized people would still use it. Jove Shackley had to duck slightly to walk.

Hallie noticed everything—even the walls and the flooring—was made from the same brown, shiny metal as the outside.

"So much Zuprium." She ran a hand along the side of it, her fingers sliding effortlessly across the surface. To outfit an entire hovership would've taken weeks, if not months, of mining in the Nardens. The smooth touch reminded her of home, yet for some reason, a feeling of safety accompanied it. Hallie shook her head. Stoneset was far from safe. Stars, she should've gotten more sleep.

The High Guardsman winced as he knocked his head on some pipe. "The *Eudora* is the first to be made solely out of it."

"So, if we find Zuprium, they'll use it for more—"

"You'll both share that room there. There's a privy with a small tub for bathing in the middle, and the men's chamber is on the other side." He pointed to a door on the left. "Put your packs in the trunk provided and meet us in the cockpit up the corridor."

"Yes, High Guardsman," Ebba said with a salute.

Hallie frowned. Why had he interrupted her?

The High Guardsman saluted in return and went back down the stairs, presumably to find his missing brother. Hallie bit her lip. "Was I supposed to salute, too?"

Ebba shrugged. "I think you're fine. You're a regular citizen."

"Oh." Hallie opened the door the man had pointed out. "I guess that's a good thing."

They stepped into the room. It was small, with two beds jutting out of one metal wall and a little wooden table and chair on the other. If needed, they could bolt the furniture to the floor, including the steamer trunk at the foot of each bed. Hallie unpacked a few essentials like her extra trousers and lacy blouses, some toiletries, and a new bag of her favorite caramels. They could make even the worst situation a little less terrible.

When everything had a place, she slung her satchel over her shoulder and started off in what she hoped was the direction of the cockpit.

"I'll be along in a minute," Ebba said, heading toward the privy.

The cockpit was larger than the bedchamber, and its ceiling was taller than the one in the hallway, with enough room for a row of seats behind the pilot chairs. The walls on the right and the dash were covered with an assortment of buttons, knobs, and switches, all in a variety of colors. It reminded her of a flaky pastry her mother used to make. Hallie had always asked for extra sprinkles on top.

Her fingers itched to try a few. She'd get kicked off the mission for sure if she did something crazy, so she didn't dare, but maybe the pilot would let her try a few later. Wait. No. Kase was the pilot. *Blast.*

"I wouldn't touch those if I were you," said a smooth voice as the door opened. It was the other Shackley brother, Zeke. He smiled. "I won't either if it makes you feel any better. I'm not sure even Kase knows what all the buttons do."

Hallie's shoulders relaxed, and she grinned. "How can he? All that hair must take up half his brain space."

She shut her mouth as heat flooded her cheeks. Ellis would really have to free her from the dungeons now she'd insulted Kase to his brother's face...his very strong, soldier-y brother. Who was the stars-idiot now?

Instead, Zeke chuckled, his hazel eyes sparkling. "I'm afraid Jove's already used that insult more than once. You'll have to be cleverer than that to outmaneuver Kase. All that's left after the hair is wit." Hallie laughed despite herself, and his small smile grew into a grin. "Good to see you again, Miss Walker."

Hallie nodded, placing her hand into his when he offered it, and he gave it a small peck.

"Ah, here you are, dear brother."

That familiar mess of hair came into view before Kase's face, and she groaned.

Zeke let go of her hand. "I was just inspecting your cockpit. Lots of buttons. Lots of knobs. However, you'll have a pleasant view."

Kase sidled up beside his older brother, frowning at his surroundings. He was a few inches taller, but that might have been because he wore his pilot goggles pushed into his hair, which made it stand up even more. "Seems I will."

Hallie pointed to the window with her thumb. "You won't need goggles on this trip, you know." The front glass was angled to help with air resistance. She'd read about hovers before she'd boarded one last spring. Knowing more about them helped with her fear of heights. Slightly.

"You never know. The glass might break, and at that

point I'll be thankful for these, Hallie Gwen Walker." He tapped the side of his goggles.

"You expect me to be impressed you learned my full name?"

He put an elbow on Zeke's shoulder. The soldier rolled his eyes but didn't move. Kase answered, "It pays to have friends in high places. Something you understand, I'm sure."

"For your information, I'm the top Yalven scholar at the University of Jayde." Hallie tapped her chin thoughtfully. "But what are you, again? The High Guardsman's brother? Sounds like a pity invite to me."

Kase's arm slipped as he lunged forward, but Zeke grabbed his shoulder.

"I'm the best stars-blasted pilot in the *realm,* for your information!" Kase tugged against the other man.

"Stop." Zeke's voice was low and authoritative. "Both of you."

The soldier held Hallie with his firm gaze, and she tried in vain to hold back the heat flooding her cheeks. She gritted her teeth and left, shouldering Kase out of the way.

"Listen, you—"

"Kase, don't—" Zeke's voice was tight with frustration.

Hallie ignored both and kept walking until someone grasped her arm. She yanked it, but the grip was firm. She growled as she spun. Messy hair, blue eyes, bronzed skin, and permanent scowl. Kase.

"Unhand me." Her tone could have cut glass.

His blue eyes narrowed, but he didn't let go. She pulled her arm again. "I said, unhand me, or I'll use whatever means necessary to make you. I know *exactly* where to kick."

"Very ladylike," Kase scoffed, but he let go of her arm. She stuck her tongue out at him before storming off, her boots clacking on the metal floor. She tried to force the blush from her cheeks as she went. Had she honestly stuck her tongue out at him? Gracious day, how old was she?

Once she reached her room, she plopped onto the bed and slung her bag to the mattress beside her. She shuffled through it until she found her sketchbook and pencils. Just what she needed to calm herself down. Ebba had disappeared, too.

Her pencil was an anchor in her hand, the strokes across the page holding her together as the conversation with Kase replayed in her head. His smirk, his tousled hair, his too-straight nose—

Ugh. Stop thinking about him!

"Miss Walker?"

She looked up, ready to fling her sketchbook in Kase's face, but thank the moons, it was only Zeke, his light brown hair smoothed back from his forehead. She sighed, slowly lowering her weapon. "You can call me Hallie. No sense in being all formal if we're seeing each other every day."

Zeke cleared his throat. "Of course. Then please, call me Zeke." Hand rubbing the back of his neck, he stepped over the threshold. "I'm sorry about my brother. He promises to be on his best behavior."

Hallie quirked her eyebrow.

"Well, he'll at least try." He tapped his fingers on the doorframe. "I thought you wouldn't want to miss take-off."

She put her materials back in her bag. "I've never been in a ship like this before. It seems to run on that magic they say the Yalvs had."

"I don't know if I believe all those stories." Zeke moved out of the doorway and allowed her to pass, then caught up with her once she'd strode into the hall. "I know the High Council releases new tech to the public once they approve it, but this ship is unlike anything I've seen before."

Hallie glanced sideways at him. "Why are they keeping so much from us?"

Zeke shrugged. "I'm sure they have their reasons. Ben would be the one to ask."

"Well, then, I'll start putting together a list of questions. What else will I have to do on this mission to nowhere?"

IGNORING THE FACT THEY HURTLED miles above the ground, Hallie worked up the courage to peek out the window of the cockpit—an admirable feat, if she did say so herself. She could just make out the tops of trees, fields, and ant-sized people before she fell back into her seat, blood draining from her face.

In the name of adventure, she *would* conquer this fear.

To distract herself, she filled her sketchbook with the glimpses of what she saw on her daring attempts. Off to the side, Kase and Agent Reiss quietly chatted with each other. Hallie tried to listen in on their conversation, but their words were mere murmurs, too soft to hear over the hum of the hover engines. Zeke and Ebba had left to go rest, so it was just the three of them.

Hallie hummed to herself as she sketched what she thought was a decent rendition of one village she'd spotted, and what it might look like from the ground. But as the landscape came into focus with each stroke, the trees and housing style melded into one reminiscent of Stoneset. Trying to find the best angle to draw, she adjusted her body in the chair as the bitter smell of heated metal seared her nose. Her elbow brushed against the side panel, and—

A loud beeping sound broke the silence in the cabin, jolting her like an electric shock. Hallie sprang back.

Kase whipped around. "What'd you do?"

"I was trying to get comfortable!" Hallie shook her head frantically.

He growled, pushed a button on the steering device, and got up from his seat. Agent Reiss pressed a few buttons on his end and continued to fly without so much as a glance around. Kase stomped over to the console near Hallie.

"Didn't your mother teach you not to touch random buttons?" He fidgeted with a few knobs. The beeping cut off. "You nearly destroyed a village with an electrobomb."

Horror and doubt in equal measure slid through her stomach. Had she really almost done that? "I'm sorry, I didn't...I was just...is it normal for a hovership to have its weapon button all the way over here? What if you needed to fire it quickly?"

"Do something else besides bother us, please."

Fury burned away the last of her horror. "I didn't mean to touch it."

Kase plopped back into his chair, pushed a button, and stared forward. "Doesn't matter what you meant to do. You're in a real airship. Why don't you go look out a different window? Maybe one that's far away from me?"

"No," Hallie said. "I like this one. By the way, would it hurt for you to slow down? I can't draw anything substantial at this speed."

"Oh for moons-sake—"

Agent Reiss cut him off. "Sorry about that. We have to get outta Jayde before anyone figures out what's going on."

Was that because they took the ship without the High Council's permission?

Kase glanced back for a quick second, trying to glimpse her sketches. "Besides, it's only random villages. Not sure why you'd bother drawing them."

Hallie clutched the book to her chest. "Keep your eyes on the sky! And I'm drawing them because they're fascinating. Each one has different people and everything!"

"You're how old, and you just figured this out?" Kase snorted.

"I'm rolling my eyes at you, just so you know," Hallie shot back. Agent Reiss chuckled.

Kase glared at his co-pilot. "Don't encourage her." He turned to Hallie. "Seriously, go bother someone else. Skibs and I are trying to concentrate."

"On what? You're not doing much."

The blond chuckled again. "The wonders of technology. Kase's uncle was the one who discovered how to combine electricity with the Zuprium—our own brand of magic."

Kase's shoulders tensed. "Skibs..."

"Really?" Hallie leaned forward in her seat. "Oh! I think I've heard of him. His name was—"

"Ezekiel. And I'd rather not talk about him," Kase said.

"Why?" Hallie rested her elbow on the seat arm.

Kase and Agent Reiss shared a look before the latter answered, his voice soft. "He's dead."

Hallie's stomach dropped. "Oh...sorry, I didn't realize—I didn't mean—"

The following silence settled upon the cabin like a thick mountain fog. From the way Agent Reiss had said the words, Hallie assumed the death wasn't natural. The whisper was hoarse and a little strained.

She looked anywhere but the back of Kase's head. Her sketch of the village had smudged a little when she'd tucked it to her chest earlier, one of the evergreens.

After several minutes, Hallie couldn't take it any longer. She needed to fix her mistake, so she asked the first thing that came to mind that had nothing to do with dead uncles...at least, she hoped. "So where does the name Skibs come from?"

Agent Reiss groaned. "This *dulkop* thinks he's hilarious."

"Private pilot training information. Confidential," Kase growled at the same time.

"Now *I'm* rolling my eyes at you, Kase." Agent Reiss pushed a button on his side. The engine hummed in response. "You can tell her the story. Maybe she'll take pity on me."

Kase thumbed his nose. "Skibs messed up during a training exercise. He was naked. End of story." He pushed a button on his steering wheel and got up. "Nature calls. Can you handle it for a moment?"

"Don't take too long." Agent Reiss cracked his neck. "Ah, that's better. I'm going to take a break soon, too."

Kase left Agent Reiss and Hallie alone. She put her drawing materials into her satchel. "He must need to remove that stick up his—"

"He's a good friend, even if he's acting like a stars-idiot. Not to excuse his behavior or anything, but he's been going through stuff. Hence the foul mood."

"Like what?" Hallie was grateful he couldn't see her blush. "Is it to do with...with his uncle? Now that I think about it, wasn't he the one who..."

"Yeah, he sold the Cerls our hover secrets, which was part of the reason for that stars-blasted war." He shook his head. "But that's not why he's acting like he is now. I know it has something to do with the Crews and his father. There was also another family thing a while back, but that was before me. Regardless, his position in society comes with its own challenges."

"What happened?"

Ben scratched his chin where a bit of amber stubble peeked through. "Not my story to tell, sorry."

She bit her lip. Different tactic. "Being the Lord Kapitan's son can't be too difficult. He can do anything he wants."

Ben gave a humorless laugh. "If that's what you wanna believe."

Slinging her satchel over her shoulder, Hallie got up from her seat. The contents clunked together as the bag hit her hip. "As a matter of fact, I do."

She walked toward the door. As she reached for the handle, it swung open and collided with her, pain exploding in her head and knocking her backward. She caught herself before she could fall completely flat, but the contents of her bag crashed to the floor.

"Ouch," she moaned, climbing to her knees. That *hurt*. Thank the stars she wasn't wearing skirts.

"Don't you know better than to stand in a doorway?" Kase bent down to help her, and she braced herself for a glare—but instead, those blue eyes met hers with a look that could've almost been concern. They were so close...

She shook herself out of her daze. "I'm *fine*." She grabbed her notepad, and Kase handed her a stray pencil. She snatched it and gathered up the rest before standing. Kase did, too.

After a moment too long, Hallie nodded. "As you were."

She ran off, but there was no denying those eyes burning holes into the back of her head as she closed the door behind her.

CHAPTER 7

BELLIGERENT BOWL OF BOIL-BRAINED BEEF

Hallie

THE FACT THE *EUDORA JAYDE* had crossed such a large distance in only three days was incredible. They were nearly to the Narden Pass. The trip would've taken at least a week and a half in a carriage pulled by the fastest horses.

Did all ships fly that fast? The one she'd ridden with Ellis to the coast had gone just above the speed of a motorcoach, but at this speed and this height...stars, there was a possibility that space travel could be achieved in her lifetime. What had it been like for her ancestors to travel the stars? To flee from the only home they'd ever known? Exhilarating as the idea was, imagining the height made her slightly queasy.

As had been their ritual for the past few days, Kase set the ship down far away from any town, forcing them to cook their food on a fire and sleep on the ship. It wasn't terrible...so long as their supplies didn't run out any time soon. Though judging by the cupboards in the storage room, dried beef and vegetables would be on the menu for the foreseeable future.

Hallie busied herself stirring a stew she'd made with the limited supplies in the pot hanging over their fire. Towering pines were interspersed between the reds and golds of oaks surrounding their campsite, and the atmosphere only made the meal taste even better. It warmed her inside and out with the chill beginning to creep in each evening.

It reminded her of nights spent sitting in front of the hearth back home with her brother and playing a game of *Stars and Blasts*. Jack had been terrible at the card game, always losing the cards he needed to gain a system. Hallie hadn't minded beating him one bit. With each decisive victory, her bragging rights had grown.

She swallowed hard as loud voices reached her ears. Kase and Ben trudged closer, wood for the fire piled in their arms. The machete they'd used to cut it hung from a loop on Kase's belt. Probably dangerous, but Kase didn't seem to care one bit.

Ebba didn't look up from where she fiddled with some sort of metal mind-game she'd brought along. "What're you two fighting about? I'm trying to concentrate here."

Kase threw down his pile, the wood clattering against a large rock jutting from the ground. Hallie focused on the woodsy aroma mixing with the fire's smoky scent, because if she didn't, she might say something to Lord Pilot that she'd regret. Again.

Kase brushed his hands against his trousers. "Then tell Skibs here I'm an expert tree climber."

Hallie snorted and dropped the spoon into the stew. She cursed, trying to grab it without burning her fingers.

Ben's voice cut through Ebba's laughter. "And pray tell, what trees have you climbed, city boy?"

Kase unhooked the machete and stuck it into the ground beside his haul. Instead of sticking, it fell over with a soft clack against the stone. "The Manor's courtyard is full of them."

"And that's supposed to prove you can climb that one there?" Ben pointed at a towering oak with lower branches as thick as Hallie's torso.

A smart clacking on the stairs announced the arrival of the final crew member. Zeke's laughter joined the fray. "I could beat you both easily."

Kase whipped his head around. "Is that a challenge?"

Stars, even his voice oozes with conceit. Like pus. Yech.

Zeke crossed his arms. "And if it is?"

Hallie caught sight of Kase's rakish grin. "I'd say we—"

But before he finished, Ben was off and running toward the oak at full speed. Kase let out something akin to a growl and sprinted after him. Filling the bowls, Hallie handed one to Ebba and another to a laughing Zeke before making one for herself.

"I'll put a bronzer on Kase falling first." Ebba took the bowl and grabbed a spoon. She ate three big bites before smacking her lips. "*Sterne*, I'm starved."

Zeke chuckled. "Don't count him out. If there's one thing he has going for him, it's sheer determination."

Shouting and laughter flittered on the breeze as Kase slid to the ground, his hands clawing at one of the lower branches. Hallie snorted, but quickly covered it up with a cough.

"I stand corrected." Zeke shook his head.

Ebba finished her meal and set the bowl aside. She sauntered over, her voice crackling with mischief as Kase pulled himself up over another branch. "I guess the least I could do is heckle from below."

Hallie couldn't see Ben, but the branches shook a third of the way up the giant.

She ate a spoonful of her stew and sat on the large stone set up near the fire, brushing a few of Kase's wood scraps away with the toes of her worn boots. Little outcroppings such as this were common this close to the Nardens. The sight and feel of it brought up memories of Stoneset, of her mother's garden with the mazelberry patch in the back corner. Of those she'd left behind. Her heart clenched at the thought. All the warm feelings of stew and autumn weather dissipated.

I was the one who left. I don't have any reason to feel sorry for myself.

The stew soured in her mouth, and she set the bowl next to the forgotten machete.

"Thanks for making dinner." Zeke blew off a spoonful. "I'm terrible at cooking, so be glad I didn't volunteer."

Hallie gave him a small smile. "I'd say this is my best attempt yet."

Zeke ate another bite, and Hallie reached over and poured out the rest of hers. Zeke turned, a glob of meat falling off his spoon and splattering a little broth over the side of the bowl. "Everything all right?"

No. "Not as hungry as I thought." Hallie knew her

smile didn't reach her eyes, but Zeke didn't comment.

They sat in a few minutes of silence, save for the exclamations of the others. Stars, they must've been terrible at climbing if neither of them had claimed victory by now.

Zeke set his empty bowl aside and stood, stretching his torso. "Would you like to see an expert tree climber in action? Those fools over there are amateurs."

Hallie laughed softly, grateful for the reprieve. Grateful he hadn't pried...because her lie was thinner than the broth. "Think you can beat them even with their head start?"

Zeke's teeth flashed in the dying light of the sun. "Just watch."

He strode over to the tree, still stretching his core and arms, waving them around to loosen up the muscles. Hallie stepped up beside Ebba.

The smaller woman turned as they approached. "Ben's nearly to the top, but Kase's having trouble with one branch—because he's a blasted cheater. *Gets what he deserves!*"

The last part was followed by choice words from Kase, which made Ebba roar with laughter. Hallie's memories faded a little in the joy radiating off Ebba's features.

"Ready to lose, boys?" Zeke called up as he grabbed the lower branch and swung himself up like a circus performer. Hallie had only been to the circus once. After watching the tightrope performers, she'd vowed never to go again, her stomach left in knots.

Both Ben and Kase answered Zeke's taunt with jeers, but the soldier didn't pay any mind, only grabbed the next branch and swung himself up.

Ebba cupped her hands around her mouth. "You

both owe me a copper fiver if Zeke beats you."

"On your stars." Laughter and exhaustion laced Ben's voice. "He won't beat me!"

Hallie looked into the tree as scraping sounds came from the branches. The leaves had started to turn and fall, so she could just make out little bits of the men. In a few moments, a "Huzzah!" echoed down.

"Told you I'd win," Zeke shouted from the top.

Hallie grinned at Ebba's face as she cheered for her two copper fivers won.

Kase

FLYING THROUGH CERULENE TERRITORY WAS bad enough, but to do it on the anniversary of Ana's death? That was just *wonderful*.

As advanced as the *Eudora Jayde* was, it didn't have the capability of traversing the night sky safely. Only stupid greenies with overinflated egos attempted it—though Kase wished he could. Flying always helped clear his mind.

For better or for worse, he wasn't that reckless. He set the hover down on a bare stretch of land near the edge of a rocky cliff. It was safest, hidden from the nearest village by a thick forest to their left and a cascading waterfall about a mile south. A landing like that would've been tricky for anyone other than an accomplished pilot, and it was better than finding a clearing somewhere in the dense forest below. Like it or not, dusk had fallen like the silence after a storm.

According to the map, they'd find the coast in a few days, which would be a nice reprieve from seeing endless trees and skirting around settlements.

After pumping yalvar fuel out of the ground for the ship, Kase tried to ignore the crackling campfire even as he sat beside it. Instead, he faced the cliff's edge and the lush valley beyond. Every time he looked over at the fire, scorchmarks and a careless cigarette danced through his mind, mocking him. And each time he did, he'd spin his head back around and focus on the sea of gold, red, and orange below them, though that too brought back the blasted memories of *that* day.

Ebba and Skibs were still on the ship while Hallie made dinner, and Zeke, ever the soldier, wandered at the edge of the trees. He'd already inspected the waterfall and northern cliff edge. His brother took his job too seriously; circling the campsite six times was overkill. But being a soldier was the one thing Zeke had going for him. He'd struggled in school, which made it more of a surprise when he applied for the medical unit after joining the Regulars.

The stench of beef stew wafted on the breeze as Hallie set the pot over the fire, the spitting sound of sparks hitting Kase's ears, and he swallowed a groan. Only a week had passed, and he was already sick of the food. He hated beef stew, always had, and Hallie's cooking somehow made it *worse*. The beef tasted like old bark.

Not that he'd ever tasted that before.

"Stars, why won't you stay on the stand, you belligerent bowl of boil-brained beef...BLAST!" Hallie exclaimed. Kase looked back over his shoulder just as Hallie jumped back. The entire pot slipped off its holder and crashed into the fire, spraying stew and sparks. And of course, Kase just so happened to be within range.

He leapt away, narrowly avoiding the contents and

stopping short of diving headfirst off the cliff. "Great! Now I have to wait another hour to eat a meal I hate? Why do you insist on trying to make beef stew?"

"Crunchy, dried beef is unnatural and absolutely disgusting!" Hallie spun toward him, brown eyes flashing in the light of the sunset—almost golden. "So, sorry for trying to keep us all from starving."

"And soggy dried beef is better?" Kase inspected himself for stew splotches. None.

Zeke ambled over and grimaced. "I don't think I can stomach eating that with a handful of dirt. A little grimy. Sorry. Not sure why Kase is complaining, though. He's eaten plenty of dirt before."

Kase's nostrils flared. "I thought you were the nice brother."

"I *was* being nice." Zeke bent down to help Hallie clean the mess.

"Such a gentleman. I'm swooning." Kase crossed his arms. "I'll make something with what we have in the food storage. I *won't* be making beef stew."

Hallie glanced up. "You'll come down off your throne to cook for us peasants? How benevolent of you."

With the sunlight fading behind her, her hair was an attractive ruby-red color. He blinked. "Right. You'll be groveling at my feet soon, I'm sure."

"Stop." Zeke put a hand on Kase's shoulder. "I know this day is difficult...if you don't feel like it, I'm sure Hallie doesn't mind."

Tension banded his shoulders, and he shrugged Zeke off. "No, I'll do it."

Hallie set the dirty pot on her hip. "Don't come crying to me when you make something inedible."

Kase rolled his eyes and boarded the airship. He

would show her. And keep his mind busy.

Hallie

HALLIE SLURPED HER VEGETABLE STEW from a small bowl. True to his word, Kase hadn't made beef stew, though she didn't see how this was any better if his complaint was he didn't want his food soggy. *Stupid prat.* She spooned another bite into her mouth and caught a bit of dried celery and minced garlic.

Even though the great waterfall that the Fern River poured into was nearly a mile away, Hallie thought she could just feel the mist moistening the back of her neck as she sat a little away from the others—closest to the trees and not the cliff, of course. She wasn't crazy. She still listened to Ebba's story about her first day at the University from the other side of the fire.

"I raised my hand when he called roll, but he couldn't see me from behind the 453 Engine we were gonna take apart," Ebba laughed. She put a hand to her heart and took a deep breath before continuing. "I knew I was short, but he was more embarrassed than I was!"

"How long did it take him to figure out you were there?" Zeke blew on a spoonful before putting it to his mouth.

"He didn't. I had to go up to his station to let him know I was there."

"And?" Ben asked.

"And after, I had to sit on a tall stool whenever he took roll." Ebba wiped a tear from her eye. "He wasn't the brightest. Taught myself more than anything."

Hallie tried to pay attention to the story, but she didn't find it too engaging. She'd hated her mandatory class on engines. As much as she loved learning, she'd rather talk to people or read than take something apart and put it back together again.

She scooped up the last bit of stew into her mouth and set the bowl on the ground beside her. It hadn't been half bad. The garlic and a hint of some spice she couldn't name were welcome additions. Apparently, Kase was a decent cook, which was...surprising. Practically being king of the world probably meant he had chefs making whatever meal he could ever want, so where did he learn to cook?

Kase, on the other hand, hid outside the firelight nearest the ship's tail. Hallie almost felt sorry for him. It must be hard to go about life so full of oneself.

Thinking about spending who knew how long on this mission fighting with him threatened to give her a headache. But awkward silence would be even worse.

Hallie pushed herself to her feet. It was time she swallowed her pride and made amends. Still being at odds a week into this mission was long enough. She reminded herself he was only a product of his upbringing—no matter that Zeke was the perfect gentleman.

She smiled at the others and made her way over to the ship. Hallie lowered herself to the ground on a decent-sized stone outcropping a few feet away from Kase. No need to get *too* close. He ignored her—well, he didn't scoff at her, at least. She'd take what she could get.

"So," Hallie said, clearing her throat. "I believe we got off on the wrong foot."

Kase didn't even turn.

"I'm so glad you agree with me," she continued, "and I'm sure you'd also agree that it's time we stop this mad game we have going."

He stabbed a piece of carrot with his spoon with a sharp *clank*. "What if I don't care?"

Hallie bit her tongue to keep from lashing out. She remembered what Ben had said about him the day they'd taken off. "I'm sorry to hear that. Ben told me you've been having a rough time, and I—"

Kase stiffened, and now he looked at her, eyes flashing. "What'd he tell you?"

"Only that you've been in a mood lately. Look, I know family can be overbearing sometimes."

"I've been in a *mood?*" Kase huffed and set his bowl aside. "You don't know anything about me."

Hallie's blood warmed beneath her skin, and she took a few deep breaths. Losing her temper again wouldn't help, even if he was doing his best to be a pernicious canker-blossom.

"You're right," Hallie said as evenly as she could, which was about as easy as moving a mountain, "but I'm trying to help."

"Oh, *blast off*. You don't care about me."

Their conversation attracted the looks of the others. Hallie's face burned from the heat of the argument.

"Some gentleman you are." She stood.

"I'm definitely not that," Kase growled, standing as well. "You should be thankful I held my tongue. I could have said you were a—were a—" He cut himself off and took a deep breath. "I don't care about you or your blasted olive branch. *Just leave me the stars alone, will you?*"

And with that, he stomped over to the waste hole they'd dug earlier. After he poured the remains of his meal out, he boarded the ship.

Not once did he look back at Hallie. Though that

was a good thing, because that way he didn't see the frustrated tears budding in her eyes.

Ungrateful, stupid stars-idiot.

THOUGH MOST BELIEVED CERULENE WAS vastly more dangerous than Jayde by any means, Hallie was glad the trees bled from the mountain pines to the golden maples of the valley. But maybe she was a sadist for thinking she'd much rather face a Cerl than Niels and her family tucked away in Stoneset.

Either way, she was currently hiding in her room, because even thoughts of home and Cerulene couldn't melt the glare Kase gave her whenever they made eye contact. Which wasn't often, because Hallie now avoided sitting in the cockpit while they flew and made Ebba give Kase his food at mealtimes.

Ebba joined her a few minutes after they'd taken off once more, sitting cross-legged and organizing a small handful of rocks. Hallie watched out of the corner of her eye, catching a flash of green. "Is that jade?"

Ebba shrugged and picked up the one in question, holding it in her slender fingers. "Don't think so. Found it back before the big freeze out between you and Kase."

Hallie's cheeks burned, and she sat up. "He's the one who started it!"

"Sure, sure." Ebba handed the small stone to her. "You handled it better than I would've. I'd have slapped his stupid face, but I barely reach the middle of his torso."

Hallie snorted, but thinking of the theater that night, her face still heated. Not her proudest moment. "So...um...this isn't jade?"

Ebba shook her head. "From what my brother said, jade is a lighter color and doesn't have so much roughness 'round the outside. And it can only be found in the Narden mines. That little guy was just sitting by the fire pit all by its lonesome."

Hallie's fingernails traced the chalky, webbed crevices spread across the small stone. "You collect rocks?"

"In a sense." She handed it back to Ebba, who took it with a nod and added it carefully to her row. "Everywhere I go, even if it's just to the market or the airfields, I try to pick up a good one. My brother..." She grabbed another one of her stones, this one brown like sand and slightly larger than the green one. "One of my brothers has this...um..."

"It's okay, you don't have to tell me. I wasn't trying to pry."

Ebba shook her head, her dark hair pulled into a tight knot on top of her head with a few elegant strands curling at the nape of her neck. "It's fine. Collecting rocks is the only thing I can think of to make him feel better. He's rather sick." She rubbed her chest as if it pained her and took a deep breath. "And he's not able to get out often. The fever did a number on his sight and overall health. So I bring him rocks. He has about fifty or so lined up along the wall in our—"

She cut herself off and handed the rock in her hand over to Hallie. "Either way, he'll like this one best."

Hallie chewed the inside of her lip as she took it. The stone was rough and craggy and about the size of the divot in her palm. "Why will he like this one best?"

Ebba grinned. "You don't see it?"

She held it closer and squinted. On the back, she caught a gleam along one small fissure. "This looks like—"

"Pyrite. I might even tell Eren it's a bit of gold. Just to see if he can figure out the difference."

Hallie laughed and handed it back. "It's nice of you to do that for him."

Ebba placed it back in line. "Another reason to make sure we accomplish all those objectives the High Guardsman gave us, right?"

Hallie looked out the window. "The money will be nice, too."

Ebba snorted. "You got that right."

She and Ebba spent the rest of the afternoon napping and chatting about nonsensical things such as what they would do with the money when they returned. Ebba wanted to buy her parents a bigger cottage in the nicer part of Lower Kyvena, and she thought it was nice Hallie wanted to start a school for underprivileged kids, though she didn't like the idea of dealing with the kids themselves. They laughed and told stories the rest of the night about their school days and everything under the stars.

Talking about the sunny days of her past made her forget the stormy ones. For that, Hallie was grateful. It was nice to have at least one friend on this ship.

CHAPTER 8

FOOTSTEPS

Kase

THE BEAUTY OF THE CERULENE woods was strange to Kase. Having never been out of Jayde, much less beyond the Narden Range, he'd always imagined the kingdom was a sordid wasteland, fit for the despot that ruled over it.

But these trees stood proud, some so wide he couldn't wrap his arms around their trunks, and their leaves blazed like red fire. The ones in the vast courtyard of Shackley Manor had never turned such a vivid red. Birds chirped high above his head, greeting one another in a song Kase wished he knew the words to. The serenity of it all lulled him into a sense of peace as he and Skibs patrolled near the ship.

Cerulene had caused all sorts of trouble for his

family after Uncle Ezekiel sold the Cerls hover technology secrets, but Jove's hints about the Cerls messing with the mines—well, that was new. It made sense to an extent, but surely the Nardens weren't the only place on Yalvara with Zuprium buried beneath the surface. Kase almost laughed at his own stupidity. Wasn't searching for the metal on Tasava one of their objectives? Maybe that was why the Cerls wanted to find the Yalvs—for their power and Zuprium?

Kase had only read a little about the Yalvs' powers. He hadn't been able to find much on the subject, but he'd also chalked it up to legend, so it wasn't worth his time. He'd much rather read *King Arthur* or any other number of stories.

Ben's voice was too loud in the damp autumn air. "The ice between you and Hallie could rival even your father's stare."

And there went any chance of a good mood.

Kase rolled his shoulders and kept walking. She hadn't known what that day meant to him, but that didn't excuse her prying. *Blasted girl.*

"I don't pretend to understand what's going on in that head of yours, but maybe if you thought a little before you simply went off on someone...it's a wonder she didn't slap you right then."

Kase spun, his movement disturbing a nearby nest of crows who cawed and took flight, frightening their delicate-tuned neighbors into silence. He flinched. Hopefully anyone who saw the birds wouldn't assume it was anything suspicious. Not for the first time, the stories of travelers disappearing into the wilds of Cerulene flashed through his mind. He shook off his unease. "Can we not discuss her, please?"

After a moment under Kase's frosty gaze, Skibs

relented. "Fine, fine. I just thought someone like her might be good for you."

"You're cracked if you think—wait. Stop laughing!"

Skibs clutched his stomach as his laughs came out in barks, tears of mirth gleaming in his eyes. "It's just— oh stars..."

"You're absolutely hilarious." Kase rolled his eyes. "For moons-sake, you sound like a dying dog."

Skibs wiped his eyes and took a few deep breaths. "The look on your face was priceless."

Kase fiddled with the electropistol strapped to his leg. "Whatever. Let's keep walking. I don't want to be out here long, even with Hallie waiting at camp."

With his breathing under control, Skibs took the lead. They trudged in silence for a few minutes, and Kase tried to calm his nerves. Skibs was only trying to make him feel better. That was all. Not that he was doing a good job.

"Finding someone isn't the worst thing that could happen to you." Skibs surveyed the trees for any threats. "I'm not saying you should court Hallie, necessarily. It would be nice to have someone who won't let you walk over them, and you know...understands you."

Kase groaned. They were still on this? "Have you been talking with my mother?"

Skibs snorted. "I don't mean finding someone just for the sake of doing so. Find the right one."

"And you know this because Lucy is the right one for you? You haven't courted long."

"Doesn't matter. I'm planning on marrying her when we get back."

He wants to marry *her? Shocks.* "Three months isn't long enough to know anyone. And Lucy...she's nice enough, but...is that a wise idea?" He gripped his friend's shoulder.

Kase didn't think any less of Skibs because he wasn't wealthy, but he knew Lucy's family would. In fact, he didn't even know if they knew about Skibs. That wasn't why the match made Kase feel uneasy, though—not the biggest reason, at least. Skibs was a bit of a prankster whenever Kase could make him one, but Lucy didn't appreciate getting her skirts ruffled. And she'd never liked Ana, which was the strongest point against her.

"Oh, what would I do without your opinions?" Skibs shrugged Kase's hand off his shoulder.

"I never said—"

His friend shook his head and stormed off. Kase followed at a distance, cursing himself silently. Why did it even matter? Getting back home from this mission would be difficult at best. Why even plan that far?

A good mile later, Skibs still hadn't spoken, but Kase didn't want to be the one who broke the silence. He had been honest, but he hadn't expected his words to upset his friend so much. Over the years since leaving the Crews, Skibs had become a calm and collected man. That wasn't a bad thing, but he *was* different. Skibs' drunken fighting at taverns had stopped, sure, but the light had also left his eyes. Kase suspected Lucy was the cause. It was the only thing that made sense.

Leaves swirled around Kase as the wind picked up, the only sound being the soft scuffle as each hit the ground to join its fallen brethren. If he hadn't been so preoccupied with Skibs' words, he would've appreciated the serenity. But alas, his blood was still hot, and each sound made him flinch. With the last one, something flickered out of the corner of his eye. He whipped his head to the side.

The treetops swayed in the autumn wind, ruby-red leaves fluttering down. A squirrel jumped from a branch and landed on a neighboring tree.

Just the wind. Just a leaf. Just a squirrel. *Get a hold of yourself.*

"What is it?" Skibs' voice was low, his hand going to the electropistol at his side.

Kase shook his head. "Nothing."

Silence fell once more. The trees closed in on them, tightening their hold, their shadows lengthening and drowning out the afternoon sunlight. Kase kept his head on a swivel, but nothing else flickered in his vision. The forest was quiet once more, aside from the soft sloshing of leaves as they waded through.

That was when Kase heard it: a third set of footsteps. Heart pounding like a drum, he put a hand on his electropistol and spun.

Nothing.

Just the trees and brush below them.

"Kase?" Skibs' voice was hollow in his ears.

Kase cocked his pistol. "Did you hear that?"

"Hear what?"

"Footsteps."

Skibs tilted his head in confusion, but he pulled out his own weapon. "Let's hike a little further, and then we'll turn around. Sound good?"

Kase nodded, but something about his words, as innocent as they were, made the hair on the back of his neck stand straight as a board. He didn't like it. *We really should head back to the ship.*

When they had walked even further, the sun gilding the forest with the dying light of day, an unmistakable scuffle and crunching met Kase's ears. He spun once more, his finger pulling the trigger even as his body turned.

The glowing ball of electricity zinged out of Kase's weapon and blasted through the air. A shout and a muffled thump followed as Kase caught the tail end of a cloak flashing behind one of the thick, towering trees.

"I got someone!" Kase yelled as he stumbled toward the tree.

A litany of curses sounded from where Kase had seen the cloak. He rounded the tree, Skibs a breath behind him.

The man's body jerked with each spark leaping up his legs, the muscles reacting to the electricity thundering through his veins. When he twitched, the man's scraggly brown hair shifted and revealed a cluster of three inked diamonds on his neck. Each diamond tip intertwined with one another, and each shone a metallic blue. It was a tattoo meant to identify those in the Cerl army. *Holy moons.*

The man growled, speaking in heavily accented Common, but Kase could only make out every other curse. He held his pistol at the ready, the end still spitting sparks and Skibs' breathing heavy in his ear. Kase hoped the man's cursing hid the tremor in his own voice. "You're following us. Why?"

With another spasm of his legs, the man's spittle missed his mark, landing harmlessly next to Kase's boot. Skibs stepped forward, pushing away Kase's pistol. He bent down with his own weapon out in front of him. The man's eyes widened even as they twitched. Skibs' voice was low. "You're not in a position to anger us, Cerl. Save your spit for your *helviter* of a king. Now, why were you following us?"

"You know why," the Cerl hissed, his silky accent bleeding into each word.

Kase's heart thudded in his ears. Had someone in Kyvena leaked where they were going? Or had someone simply spotted them flying above the clouds? They couldn't have, he'd been so careful—

Blast it.

Skibs let out a wry laugh, a low whine biting the air. "No. I don't."

The man's spit hit home this time, landing on the blond's stubbled cheek. Skibs backhanded him across the face with his pistol for his trouble. Blood spurted from the man's nose as it cracked. Skibs trained the barrel on the Cerl's forehead. "Get Zeke and the med kit. I'm certain we have something to loosen this scum's tongue."

"But what happens if you need help?"

Skibs cocked his weapon. "I can handle him. Go!"

Kase uncocked his pistol and chewed his lip. "*Fine.*"

Fifteen minutes later, with Zeke and the med bag thumping against his brother's back, Kase led him through the trees, hoping he'd remembered the right path.

"He was twitching a bit after I hit him with the bolt. Then Skibs backhanded him, probably broke his nose—"

An unholy shout tore through the air and stopped Kase mid-sentence.

Oh, moons and stars.

"*Ben!*" Kase launched into a sprint.

Zeke's heavy breathing mirrored his own as they ran through the trees. Kase's foot caught on a root, but his brother grabbed his shoulder and kept him steady.

Another shout. A grunt of pain.

"Ben! Where are you?" The boot peeking out from behind a tree made Kase stumble once more. "*Ben!*"

He and Zeke rushed forward and found Skibs sprawled on the ground, limbs tossed in a heap, a gash across his forehead. Both the electropistol and the Cerl were gone.

Kase fell to his knees beside him, feeling for a pulse below his friend's chin.

A breath. Two.

The soft *thump-thump* flittered under Kase's fingertips, and the corners of his eyes burned. "He's alive."

His words rasped against his throat as he thanked whoever might've been listening that Skibs wasn't dead. Kase didn't think he could handle it if he was, if the last real words they'd exchanged had been in anger. He carefully prodded at the gash on his friend's head. For a moment, the greenie pilot's broken body flashed before his eyes.

Kase swallowed hard. That pilot wasn't dead, either—not yet. Finish the mission, and he could make it up to the kid.

"We have to get back." Zeke bent down, examining Skibs' head himself. He unrolled a bandage and blotted at the gash. "We don't know if—"

But another scream, feminine and far away this time, cut him off.

Was that Ebba or...*Hallie.*

Needles of fear spread through Kase's body as he leapt up. "Carry him. I'll go back!"

His words were lost in the wind whipping through his hair as he tore off through the trees, electropistol out. Sparks blurred past as he sprinted. How stupid of them to leave the rest of the crew unprotected. He'd gotten lucky with Skibs, but if something happened to—

He broke through the last of the underbrush, his side feeling as if someone had pierced it with a wicked-sharp stiletto blade. "Get away from them or I'll blast you to the stars!"

He froze when he found Hallie and Ebba cleaning up the overturned pot. Ebba caught Kase's eye, snorting with laughter. "Hal here saw a spider."

Kase holstered the electropistol and took a few deep breaths, holding the stitch in his side. It didn't help his nerves.

"It's not my fault!" Hallie shot back, her lacy shirt speckled with bits of brown stew. "I didn't realize the pot was so close!"

Kase kicked dirt on the fire and grabbed the dirty pot, shoving it into Hallie's hands. "We're leaving."

"What? I just started dinner! And it wasn't beef stew this time!" Hallie grimaced at the dying embers. "We can't waste all that food!"

Ebba raised an eyebrow. "Well, you already wasted it by dumping it..."

Kase ignored them and rushed up the stairs and into the cockpit. While Zeke herded the others into the ship a few minutes later, Kase strapped in and made the pre-flight preparations. He ignored Hallie's panicked shouts—she must have seen Skibs.

Calm. Steady.

"Go, Kase!" Zeke shouted up the corridor as the metal door shut with an echoing thud. Kase nodded and started the ship's engines. "They can't be far behind us!"

Hallie buckled herself in a seat behind him. "What's going on?"

He shook his head. "We need to get out of here."

"But I thought we couldn't fly at night."

"See that?" He flung his hand toward the front

windshield, the dying light of day reflecting off the nose of the ship. "That's what we call sunlight." He hadn't intended to snap at her, but she was the one asking too many stupid questions.

She muttered something, but Kase ignored her because some blasted thing started beeping. The hover capacitor control light. He hadn't engaged the lever before starting the engines. He did so with a soft curse.

Ebba joined them, her voice bubbling with frustration. Her down-country accent deepened with each successive word. "Will someone tell me what's going on? Why's Ben covered in blood? And there's barely enough sunlight to go anywhere fast!"

Kase pushed the button and pedal to get the ship moving. Within seconds, they were airborne, relying on the hover capabilities to lift them. He twisted a knob and responded, "I need to concentrate."

"Oh, good *sterne*," Ebba growled. "It wouldn't kill you to answer my questions."

Zeke entered, his voice echoing off the metal of the ship's walls. "Ben will be fine. Minor head wound."

"But what happened?" Ebba asked.

"Strap in." Kase shifted a gear and flipped another switch. "Found a Cerl. They're following us."

Hallie gasped. "Are you certain?"

"One attacked Ben and escaped." Zeke buckled himself into a seat with a sharp click. "But he'll be fine. Looks worse than it is."

Kase pushed a button to set the oxygen level. "Except for the fact that he's unconscious."

"Just get us out of here."

Kase gritted his teeth at his brother's tone, but he pressed the foot pedal and tapped a few buttons on the steering control, the engines responding in kind as the ship climbed higher. He made the mistake of looking back toward their campsite and spotted a figure coming out of the woods. The broad-shouldered man had a golden braid down his back. A thick, long barreled weapon sat on his shoulder and sparked as he swung it toward the ship. Nausea crept up Kase's throat.

"Blast!" A glowing blue energy ball shot out of the end. On instinct, Kase jerked the steering control. Someone screamed.

Another bolt rocketed toward the ship. He gave the engines more gas, twisted the hover knob, and whipped the steering control the opposite way.

Both shots missed.

Cerulene doesn't have a hover capable of catching up with the Eudora. *I hope.*

But Jove's words came back to him. *We have reason to believe our mines have been compromised.* And the Cerls had the knowledge...

Zeke finally got his attention with a hand on his shoulder. "What in the blazes are you doing?"

Sweat beaded at his hairline and snaked down his forehead. He blinked. "Did you not see...did you not see...the Cerl? He shot—"

"It's okay. Just don't drop us out of the sky."

"I know."

His brother squeezed his shoulder—almost painfully—before returning to his seat. Kase ignored the chatter from the others.

Only when they were soaring high above Yalvara without sign of chase did his rapid heart rate slow to a normal rhythm. As he steered the ship away from the light cluster to their right, he concentrated on why he loved flying: for the freedom the skies gave him. It was the only thing keeping the bile from rising.

Skibs will be fine. The Cerls are far behind us. We can get out of this.

After an hour, Kase set the ship down in an abandoned meadow before the sky opened, rain falling in sheets. Everyone went to bed after picking at their dinners, but though Kase took the first watch, he knew he wouldn't be the only one who had trouble sleeping.

CHAPTER 9

FIVE MINUTES ABOVE THE STORM

Kase

KASE FINGERED THE GRIP ON the steering control. The leather was smooth, and it helped calm his nerves as he guided the craft over the Josei Ocean. Anticipating the moment when the enemy would slaughter them all, every night since the Cerl's attack had been a tense waiting game.

Hallie hadn't been able to shut up about it, and it'd taken everything in Kase's power not to say something nasty. When it got to be too much, he simply hid in the cockpit. But that was only when they had landed for the day. She infuriated him whenever they tried to have a conversation, and they hadn't had a real one since that night by the waterfall.

Not that he was keeping track.

The ocean had been a welcome sight. Somewhere over those sparkling blue waves lay Tasava, and once they reached it, the real mission would begin. They only needed to survive the Bay of Storms first. Easy, right?

Referencing the map Jove had given them, Skibs decided to follow what he believed to be the best path that would also keep them out of range of any Cerl sea scouts and lead them to the Bay. Though both he and Hallie were skeptical about the map's accuracy.

None of the explorers' accounts had been too believable, from the little Kase had read in the days leading up to their departure. Granted, it was difficult to take the word of men who also raved about dragons, visions, and magic.

Regardless, Skibs said if they reached a point where they were at half a tank of yalvar fuel without finding the Bay, they'd turn around and camp on the Cerl coast. Then they'd try again the next day but follow a different route he'd mapped out.

Ridiculous plan. Especially because it was the second day of doing so. But Skibs was the lead.

The image of the spasming Cerl flashed in his mind as Kase checked the oxygen level in the cabin.

"And *that's* a system," Hallie said behind him. Kase clutched the steering control a little harder. The others had been at the insipid card game for the last hour, sprawled out on the floor behind him like children.

They should've been thankful he had to concentrate on flying. Otherwise, he would've said something ugly. Zeke surprised him by playing *Stars and Blasts* with them. His brother must have been extraordinarily bored.

"Blast!" Ebba yelled out, laughing.

That's it.

"For stars sake, can you keep it down?" Kase growled. The Cerls might have been following them, and he still hadn't spotted any sign of land, yet they still thought it okay to shout out like that? Great shocks.

Zeke got up from the floor and stepped up beside him. "We're only having a little fun."

"Too loud." Kase eyed the horizon where the clouds appeared darker than normal. "Skibs and I are trying to concentrate."

Zeke patted the back of the seat. "Kase, it's fine. Try to cool it, will you?"

"I'm trying to keep us all alive, thank you," Kase interrupted.

"Try to *cool it*," Zeke repeated over him, "and we'll keep it down. Deal?"

"Fine," Kase mumbled.

Zeke rejoined his game. With the renewed shuffling of playing cards, Kase focused on the horizon once more. Charcoal clouds spread across it, growing larger the closer they flew. He rubbed his chin. Day old stubble pricked his palm.

"That has to be it." Skibs fingered the bandage still wrapped around his head.

The card shuffling stopped, and someone pressed on his seat. Zeke's hands gripped the top of his chair. Hallie and Ebba were beside him.

"The Bay of Storms. That's it, right?" Hallie leaned over the dash.

"Move," Kase growled. "I can't see."

Hallie sniffed but did as he asked for once. "Sorry."

Skibs pushed a button, one that would give them a quick reading on the winds ahead. "Gale force winds on the outset. The ship can't take that. We need to increase altitude."

Kase gripped the steering control harder. "I have a feeling that isn't going to cut it."

"Then we try for the eye. We don't have a choice."

Kase grumbled under his breath, but he didn't turn the ship around. If he was careful, they'd be fine. He *was* a stars-fantastic pilot, after all.

"Kase!"

He barely registered Hallie's scream as a blistering bolt of electricity screeched down from the clouds and struck the waters. From where they were on the hovership, the lightning bolt was as thick as one of the Scarlet Oak trees near the Narden Pass, and those trees were at least a thousand years old. Kase swallowed hard. Small fissures from the bolt fanned out over the waters below in a jagged ring, then disappeared.

"That was *beautiful*," Hallie whispered. She stepped away and rummaged through her bag, looking for her sketchbook, no doubt. The sound of pencil strokes for hours on end now haunted Kase's dreams.

"Everyone, sit," Kase said, his voice as even as he could make it. "No matter what we do, it's best if everyone has their safety buckles on."

Zeke's grip left his chair as the soldier followed orders. Ebba stayed for a minute until Kase gave her a look, and she scampered to a chair behind him. The satisfying metallic clicks of safety belts being fastened met his ears. At least they listened this time. He'd have to threaten them with a storm more often.

"You sure this is it?" Kase flicked his gaze toward Skibs.

"Yes," Skibs replied. "That's not a natural storm. See those clouds? They're only rotating, not moving any other way."

"Are we really going to do this based on a *possibility* of land being there?"

"This is our only way onto the continent." Skibs tapped his fingers on the steering control.

Kase itched to run a hand through his hair, but he didn't want to let go of the steering control. Not this close. The wind picked up, and he had to work harder to keep the airship steady.

Maybe this wasn't the best idea. But if anyone could handle it, he could.

"We've flown through a storm before," Skibs reminded him. "This should be easy."

That storm had been a small rain shower in comparison, and they'd entered it by accident. But something told him if they went back now, they wouldn't make it home alive. And even if they did, without a successful mission, he'd be ripped from the Crews and possibly face charges.

"Five minutes above the storm," Kase conceded. "After that, if we don't find anything, we'll turn around. Deal?"

"*Fine*, Master Kase."

"Don't call me that," Kase spat.

"Whatever. Ready?"

"I guess."

Hallie interjected, "You don't sound too optimistic."

"You want to fly?" Kase asked.

"No, but I'd appreciate more confident pilots."

Skibs squirmed in his seat a little. "Trust us. Kase could fly this thing blindfolded."

"I'd rather he not." Hallie's pencil scratchings began again. Did she draw whenever she got nervous?

Kase pushed the craft forward. The *Eudora Jayde* closed in on the ominous clouds below. The cloud-to-cloud lightning strikes were visible this far up.

"It's miles long in all directions, I don't see—" Skibs started.

The ship lurched, cutting him short. Everyone screamed, and Kase barely saved himself from banging his face on the steering control. Skibs wasn't so lucky. He slumped in the seat, nose bloody.

"Ben!" he yelled.

No answer.

"Is he okay?" Hallie's voice was shrill.

"What happened?" Ebba asked.

"Zeke, get Ben out of his chair. I'm turning around." He slapped the *Single Pilot* button on his dashboard and strained to hold the ship in position. He forced it with his might and will to stay on course. Kase gave the ship a little boost with his left foot pedal.

"Turn," he growled.

In the corner of his eye, Zeke lifted Skibs from his seat and moved him somewhere behind.

"Help me strap him in, Ebba," Zeke grunted. "Hallie, get the medical kit."

Hallie's pencil clattered to the floor.

"Wait!" Sweat beaded on Kase's brow. The ship headed into the storm like a bug drawn to light. He pulled with everything he had. "Don't. He'll be… fine. Strap in, *now*. Don't know… what's happening. Blasted *ship!*"

Zeke plopped down into Skibs' seat and buckled himself in, inspecting the dash before turning. "What do I need to do?"

"Not the time," Kase growled. "Don't touch anything."

"But you need—"

"Don't distract me! I'll tell you if—"

Another jolt rocked the ship, and Kase cursed. A *thunk* sounded, like someone hitting the wall.

"Ebba!" Hallie screamed.

"Leave her!" Kase yelled, trying to keep his wits about him as they fell sideways into the storm. "The right engine's out! Zeke, hit the green button to your right!"

The soldier pounded it as Kase struggled to straighten the craft. Ebba's body slid along the floor with a sickening sound as the craft tilted dangerously, and Kase yanked the steering control. He wasn't supposed to do that, but he needed to do something. *Sorry, Ebba.*

The glass in front of them darkened as they plunged into the storm. Kase righted the ship. Zeke had diverted power from the back-left engine, and thank the heavens, it worked for the most part. The ship was still a little lopsided.

"Ebba's not moving." Hallie's voice shook as she unbuckled her safety belt.

"Hallie, don't!" He wiped a bit of sweat off his face with the shoulder of his shirt. The following belt click was almost lost in the resounding thunder.

"But Ebba—"

"Stars!" Kase barely held on and avoided a rollover as a great wind rocked the ship. He needed to get them to the ground. Immediately. A grouping of what looked like trees appeared out of the rain.

"Land!"

Zeke leaned forward, straining his safety belt. "You mean the black stuff ahead?"

"Yes!"

"Is that the eye of the storm?" Hallie asked as Kase steered the ship toward it.

"Don't care!"

Another jolt hit from behind, and Kase reacted to it faster than he thought possible. He didn't know if that was the eye ahead, but it might be their only chance if they could hold—

A brilliant flash of light and resounding boom both blinded and deafened him. *Crashing, burning, and falling stars.*

The nose of the airship dropped. Kase couldn't see, but he knew the too-close strike had taken out both engines. He blinked, trying to clear his eyes without releasing the steering control. The craft jerked with his movements, and he was grateful he at least still had some control. After a few seconds, he could see enough, but the bright spots floating in his field of vision made it difficult. The pressure in his head built to a crescendo. He couldn't hear anything.

Stay awake. Don't pass out. Focus.

Blinking back the pain, he squinted with what remained of his eyesight and focused on the stretch of beach he could land on if he could only get there. The winds increased the further he went, but at least they weren't in a straight nosedive. The strike had taken out the power, but with a pounded fist to the dash, little lights sputtered. The engines worked at their weakest strength, running only on yalvar fuel. The *Eudora* was gliding on the whims of the insane wind.

I can do this.

He only had to hold on for a few more minutes.

Darkness encroached on the edges of his vision. He was taking on too many G's. Maybe. Or perhaps the lightning strike had done more than blind him. Something dripped down his neck. Had Hallie and Zeke fared better in the strike? He prayed they were still alive.

Zoning in on the large stretch of sand, Kase punched the button for the ship's landing gear and hoped it worked. He'd never landed on sand before. He engaged the emergency landing parachute, praying it would slow them down enough.

Ten seconds until impact.

The rain dumped onto the window, the wind battered the airship, but Kase held on. And then as suddenly as it began, the rain stopped. Graying sunlight reflected off the ship's nose.

The eye.

But the ship still wasn't responding. The strip of land grew as they fell out of the sky. Kase couldn't hear his own scream as the *Eudora Jayde* hit the beach.

CHAPTER 10

POINT FOR ME

Kase

THE LIGHT WARMING KASE'S EYELIDS contrasted with the icy cold on the right side of his face. Someone rubbed at his cheek with a wet cloth. He should have been able to hear it scratching the stubble he hadn't shaved that morning, but he heard nothing, and his ear hurt like a demon. He tried not to whimper. In his left ear, the roar of waves crashed in a lopsided lullaby. The sound nearly pulled him back into sleep.

Instead, he blinked into the light of his shared bedchamber and squinted. It was only a lantern, but after being asleep for who knew how long, the light burned as if he'd looked into the sun.

Kase reached up to block the brightness, but his arm weighed a thousand pounds. He winced as he turned his neck.

"Are you hurting?"

He blinked again, his eyes slowly focusing. A face swam into view above him, honey-colored eyes sharp as ever. The cold rag left his face.

"What're you doing?" he asked, a painful cough jerking his chest.

Hallie folded the rag over and sat back. "Cleaning blood off your face."

"Why?"

"You looked rather dead. I didn't want that to ruin your reputation."

"Thanks." He closed his eyes again. "Could you fix my ear while you're at it? The right one doesn't work."

"Only if you ask nicely."

Kase tried to sit up, but his muscles wouldn't cooperate, and his neck felt like someone had taken a hammer to it. Hallie helped him to a sitting position, her small hand careful on his back. She winced.

"What?" he asked.

"Probably wasn't the best idea," she said through gritted teeth. Was she in pain?

"Yeah, it didn't feel so great." He grimaced and tried to turn his body. Daggers raked down his spine. *Shocks and bolts.* He peeked over and saw her arm was wrapped and tied in linen around her neck. "Is that a sling?"

She looked down. "Zeke said I dislocated my shoulder."

"Where is he?"

"Cockpit with Ebba. He thinks she'll be okay."

Silence.

Kase cleared his throat. "May I have the rag? Can't have anyone else seeing me like this."

"I'll fetch a mirror for you." She held the wet cloth

out to him. He gingerly put it to his face and tried to move nothing else but his arm. Gritting his teeth, he wiped what he could, hoping it was clean. He patted his neck and checked the rag to see if it came away bloody. Just a few dried flakes.

Busted eardrum, he guessed. Hopefully, it healed quickly.

Hallie appeared in the doorway and handed him a small mirror. It was simple and unadorned, likely something she'd bought for cheap in the lower market. He took it anyway.

Once he'd finished, Kase set the rag on his outstretched leg. He didn't know what else to say. *Sorry* wouldn't fit, as he had saved all their lives, but Ebba could've been dying because he hadn't been able to keep them out of the storm. *Shocks.*

He was glad Zeke was okay enough to help someone else. He didn't even want to think of what he'd have to tell Jove or his mother if something happened to him. Not after what happened to Ana.

"Thank you," Hallie said softly. Her fingers tangled themselves in knots on her lap. "You really are a stars-fantastic pilot. Our injuries should be much worse."

He blinked. "Except I got us caught in that storm."

Hallie didn't say anything, which made Kase feel even worse. Because it was *always* his fault. No matter how hard he tried.

"I guess I'm thankful we lost the Cerls in that." He couldn't take his eyes off her delicate fingers.

"You think they were following us?"

"Yeah." Kase glanced toward the ceiling. He wished he could say something else, but the silence stretched on, beginning to wax awkward.

"I'm sorry for slapping you at the theater and for

arguing with you back by that cliff. You clearly weren't in a good mood, but I butted in." Her words flew at lightning speed, each vying for his attention.

Kase grunted. That was one way to break the silence. But she was going to apologize now? The girl had *impeccable* timing. "Least of our worries right now."

"But I shouldn't have—"

"I deserved the slap in particular."

"But that doesn't mean—"

"Hallie, stop while you're ahead. You're lucky I don't feel like my normal perky self."

Silence.

Hallie sucked in a breath and unsteadily clambered to her feet. "I'll see if Zeke needs help."

Kase started to nod but stopped when he felt the knives again.

Once she was out of sight, he gritted his teeth and worked to get out of bed. He kept his neck as still as possible, and after a multitude of hissed curses, he finally succeeded in standing. Stars, it could have been so much worse. He should be thankful the rest of his body was just sore.

Neck and ear throbbing, he trudged along the corridor and down the steps. The storm circled around them, the sea waves angry until they reached what looked like a sandbar about a mile out from shore. Behind the ship lay a forest whose trees swayed in the remnant of wind in the eye itself. He wondered just how large the center of the storm was. How did it affect the land? He wished he'd read a book on weather. Too late now.

Once he was halfway down the stairs, he regretted his decision to get up. He could barely look down at his feet without pain.

Could he fly without moving his neck? Probably not.

His boots stuck in the wet sand as he trekked to the front of the ship. Stained, thick white canvas covered the windshield. A soft breeze ruffled the edges still attached by cords to the middle of the hover's roof. Stars, what was the emergency parachute doing over the front? Shouldn't it be tangled up behind? He didn't remember that happening, but he had blacked out. Regardless, that'd probably saved them from the worst of it—even in the storm.

Where was Skibs? Hallie hadn't mentioned him, and he wasn't outside. A pang of unease ate away at his insides. After nearly tripping on the stairs back up to the ship, he headed toward the cockpit to check.

He froze after he pushed open the door. Hallie and Zeke knelt in the corner behind his pilot's chair, speckles of blood littering the floor along with something else. In the dim light from the ship's electric bulbs and what sunlight managed to come through the parachute strewn over the windshield, a thousand little bits of glass winked at him. They covered the floor, his chair, the dash.

The front windshield.

It was gone.

He stumbled forward, ignoring Hallie and Zeke's remarks. The front control panel was also soaked, little sparks jumping up every so often from the buttons and switches. Shocks and bolts. That was why the parachute was there.

The windshield being blown out was bad. Even if they were able to get the *Eudora* in the air again, they would have to stay low and go at the pace of blasted motorcoaches on a busy Kyvena street. All that might strain the hover capacities. *Stars*, Jove would be furious when he found out. His father would be worse. Would he execute Kase like he did his own brother-in-law?

He needed to think of something else. He would figure it out—just not right then.

Kase squinted at the front window. With most of the glass missing, the wind would whip in and freeze his face. Possibly dry out his eyes. Neither were desirable. Thank the stars he had brought his goggles with him. He smirked, remembering Hallie taunting him for wearing them that first day.

Point for me.

"How's Ebba?" He moved to one of the passenger seats and eased himself into it. Zeke wasn't injured half as badly as Kase would have thought, only a cut along his browline, as evidenced by little splatters of blood seeping through the bandage wrapped around his head.

"She's alive," Zeke muttered, then went back to his splinting of Ebba's arm. The lump on the girl's head was nearly as big as a gold hunder, but she wasn't as bloody as the metal floor beneath her. Perhaps Hallie had already cleaned her up. He ran silent fingers near his aching ear.

Zeke tied off the bandage holding a thick rod to Ebba's blue and purple arm. It was swollen to twice the size of her other one—definitely broken. Digging through the medical kit, Zeke pulled out vials of liquid and a few syringes.

Kase shifted in his seat. "You'll have to re-splint it once the swelling goes down."

Zeke didn't turn around. After using a bit of cloth and rubbing alcohol to clean the needle tip, he stuck it into one of the vials. "Glad your unneeded opinions didn't leak out your ear."

"Fine, fine. I know you're a very smart medical specialist, but I didn't—" He cut himself off at his brother's glare. Kase ran a hand through his curls but froze when the pain spiked. He tried to focus on something else. "Where's Skibs?"

Kase didn't miss the glance Zeke and Hallie gave each other before turning to Kase. Hallie wouldn't look at him at all, but Zeke looked him right in the eye. "He's gone. Disappeared."

Hallie

THE NEXT MORNING, HALLIE TRIED to focus on Ebba's words instead of the swirling storm clouds around them. The storm hadn't blown itself out nor moved from its location. It wasn't too bad standing outside the ship, but Hallie was ready to bolt inside if the wind picked up. She wasn't sure how much good it would do, but it was better than hiding in the trees.

"I don't know what to do about the windshield, but that isn't what I was hired to do. If it was mostly intact, I could figure out something, but at the moment, it's a lost cause." Ebba wiped her face with her good arm. "Can't fix something not there."

Hallie nodded along with Zeke and hid her shaking hands. They were going to fly without a front window? Shocks and stars. She gritted her teeth. If she ever wanted to get back home, she'd have to deal with her fear. But maybe she could sleep in her room while they flew? Or read? That might work. Plus, it'd only been a day since the crash. Maybe Ebba could come up with something before they left again. If they managed to fix the ship at all.

Kase crossed his arms. "So how long will it be until we're up in the air? I want to scout for Skibs."

"Kase..." Zeke started.

"I *will* find him."

Ever since Zeke had told him Ben was missing, Kase had been obsessed with stalking off into the forest. Hallie agreed they needed to find Ben, but no one was in the best state to go hiking through a forest on this forsaken continent. And who knew just how far inland the eye of the storm went.

She itched to draw something, but with her shoulder only a day into healing, the most she could do was scribble incoherently with her left hand. Trudging up the beach a little way, Hallie found a large rock to lean against. She eased herself down and adjusted her satchel and shoulder comfortably.

The sun shining into their little circle of calm wasn't too hot. The trees looked normal enough, but they weren't the palms they'd seen on the Cerulene coast. Instead, they were some sort of species she'd never seen before, though they distantly reminded her of the firs near Stoneset. Except these had a more wild look about them, draped in vines and moss, and some sported purple star-shaped flowers growing up their sides.

The brush still shone with water droplets, which puzzled Hallie. Wouldn't most of it be dry? Or perhaps it always looked that way? She wished she'd read more about the Rubikan colonies in the far east past the Tevi Sea. She'd heard they were mostly covered in what the First Earth texts described as rainforests, though many modern scholars called the Rubikan versions simply swamplands. Not the same, but who was Hallie to judge? She'd never visited herself. Tev Rubika had been a hot spot for violence and war ever since she'd been born.

While the rainforest before her might hold secrets, monsters, and who knew what else, Hallie still found it serene next to the impossibly blue ocean with its glittering white sand. That is, if you ignored the angrier waves further out to sea that were caught in the massive storm. What a strange phenomenon.

Again, the desire to draw burned within her. To take her mind off the fact she could barely move her shoulder without it smarting, she dug around in her bag for *The Odyssey*. Her fingers glossed over its leather binding and stopped on the one beside it, *The Gate of Time*, which had no author named on the cover.

She'd only been able to peek at that text once on their journey thus far. She'd been too scared the Cerls would attack if she'd tried reading while she was on watch. All she'd managed to do was unwrap the thing and peek at the front cover about a week ago.

Its red leather was fading, as was the golden embossed title, written in Yalven. Whoever published the book had also added a few extra decorations to the cover, including the imprint of a large archway that seemed to glow, though Hallie was certain that was the bright sunlight above her. It was also slim and was barely taller than her hand.

She looked up. All three of her remaining crew members were deep in conversation. Kase in particular waved his hands around in the air like a madman. Ebba pointed her wrench at him and said something Hallie couldn't understand from her position down the beach.

Well, she had time now to read the Yalven text with a rock to her back and everyone else rather occupied. She pulled it out as well as *The Odyssey*. The latter could hide the Yalven text just in case someone looked her way. She opened *The Odyssey* first and ran a finger over the inked inscription just inside the cover:

To Hallie—

Now you won't feel the need to 'lose' my copy just so you can read it once more. Best of luck to you on your next adventure.

Mistress Jules

Hallie's smile wobbled a tad. Jack would've been incredibly jealous if he'd known Mistress Jules had given this to her. It'd been his favorite.

Turning to where she'd bookmarked her page with a scrap bit of parchment, she opened *Gate of Time,* tucking it inside the larger *Odyssey.*

The pages crackled as she inspected them. Most were yellowed with age, and a few had suffered water damage. Stars, why couldn't people take care of their books? Seeing as it was old and damaged, Hallie figured that's how Jess was somehow able to get a hand on this copy. Why it was banned according to Professor Christie was still a mystery to Hallie—especially knowing that Jayde had allied with the Yalvs during the war.

She flipped back to the opening page. It, too, was written in Yalven, though thank the moons, it was a relatively modern dialect—maybe one from only about two hundred years prior.

With a quick look to make sure she was still left to herself, she began to read. The words were slightly faded with age but still legible.

The words here recorded are from my own account, that of Jasper Morgan, one of the few to be given the privilege of being invited to the great Yalven city of Myrrai, known by many as the realm of starlight. All the notes and information inside this book tell the story of the Yalven people. Their ways and history are sacred, and as humans, interfering with their purpose here on Yalvara will lead to our own destruction. I only pray that my account will prevent any such horrors from unfolding.

Jasper? That was the name Professor Christie had mentioned—the one he wanted her to tell the Lord Elder, the leader of the Yalvs, would be in contact soon. And if this Jasper wasn't Yalven, why did he write in their language if he wanted the world to stop interfering with whatever their purpose was on Yalvara? It didn't make any sense.

A shadow grew across the page, and Hallie slammed both books shut. She winced. Probably not the best idea for the books. Looking up, she found Kase, one dark eyebrow disappearing into his mess of curls. "Reading some explicit romance, Miss Walker?"

"No!" Hallie answered too quickly. He smirked. Great. Now he probably *did* think she read *those* novels Petra liked. She cleared her throat and held up her book so Kase could see the spine. "I mean, no. Homer does include a little bit of...spice...but I wouldn't consider it *explicit*."

"You're not wrong, but the ancient Greeks would still make the high society ladies faint." Kase put hands in his trouser pockets and dug the toe of his boot in the sand. "Zeke said we need you over there so we can talk."

"But I just opened my book!"

"The world doesn't revolve around you. Ebba has an update for us."

"In the ten minutes I've been away?" Praying Kase didn't notice the large gap in the pages, Hallie stuffed both books back in her satchel and stood.

"She's one of the best." Kase squinted. "Was that *The Odyssey*? May I see?"

Hallie fiddled with her satchel strap. "Um, sure. I

guess that's fine."

She turned away from him and lifted her book out, making sure *Gate of Time* fell from its pages. Of course, her bookmark also fluttered into the dark confines of her bag. When she faced Kase again, she caught his smirk once more.

"You sure you don't have *Affairs of a Lady and Commander* tucked inside there?"

"I said, no!" She said, holding out *The Odyssey*. "Do you want to look at this or not?" He took it from her and inspected the cover. Hallie adjusted her sling. "And how would you know about *Affairs of a Lady and Commander*?"

"My sister used to read those sorts when she knew my parents wouldn't catch her." He opened to the front few pages of the tome. "Is this a modern translation or one from the Landing?"

Her eyebrows rose. What did he know about ancient literature? "It's one of the first retellings they made when the Life Ships landed, but this isn't nearly a thousand years old. Just a reprint."

He handed it back to her. "I've got a copy in a display case at the Manor of one of the ancient First Earth versions, but Mother wouldn't dare let me take one of her precious books. I brought Marisee's modern translation."

"You have a Marisee with you?" Hallie's heart raced. Robert Marisee was a renowned Rubikan scholar. The original planet from which those of Tev Rubika had descended hadn't had *The Odyssey*, but much of the ancient cultures of it, Cerulene, and Jayde had crept into each other's modern ones. "I love his findings on Yalven culture. The Rubikans were the first of the human off-worlders to settle here and—" She stopped at Kase's stare. "Sorry," she said, "I can get a little carried away."

He shook his head. "I just didn't know you knew so much about fine literature or history, but I should've figured that when I ran into you at the theater."

Hallie blushed.

"Kase! Hallie! Get over here!" Zeke yelled from the ship.

Kase held out her book. She stuffed it back into her bag with one arm and trotted to catch up with him. What other works had he read? If he knew Marisee, he must have heard of Chorzle and Kaylor and Rogers at the very least. And that wasn't even touching on all the ancient literature the first settlers brought with them, and...she was getting carried away again. This was Kase, after all. He'd be back to his normal crotchety self soon.

Regardless, she walked with a little hop to her step. Maybe this journey was beginning to look brighter. Just a tiny bit.

CHAPTER 11

LIKE A HEADACHE

Kase

AFTER EVERYONE HAD GONE TO bed, Kase grabbed an electropistol from the storage closet and strapped it to his leg. He wasn't sure what he'd need to traverse the forest at night, but an electropistol was a good start. A lantern would be helpful, too. Sure, he was supposed to be on watch, but this might be his only chance to go look for Skibs.

As he stepped into the hallway, soft footsteps came down the stooped corridor toward him.

Frozen, he tried in vain to think up a plan. A flimsy excuse bubbled on his lips to give his older brother, but it wasn't needed.

Hallie appeared around the corner, satchel over her shoulder, one hand fumbling to tie her maiden sash around her waist. She held one side in place with the elbow of her sling. She looked up and jumped, the sash sliding to the Zuprium floor.

"Oh, I thought I heard..." She bent and picked up the cloth, tucking it to her chest.

"*Keep your voice down.*" Kase crossed his arms. "You thought you heard something?"

What a lie. He knew he'd been silent, and the women's chamber was too far away for her to have heard him anyway.

"Yes! I was checking to see what it was," Hallie finished in a firm whisper, still clutching the red material.

"With your satchel and sash on?"

She frowned. "It *is* proper. The maiden belt, that is. I don't want to be known as someone who flouts all propriety."

"Ah, I forgot, you mountain people call it a belt, not a sash." Kase shook his head.

After another moment of indecision and a glare, Hallie stuffed her sash away. "Fine. I was going to have a look around at the edge of the forest. See if I could find anything that might tell us where Ben went."

If he'd had any suspicions of her being crazy before, she'd just confirmed every single one.

"Armed with your drawing pad?"

"I wasn't going *into* the forest, you dolt," she huffed. "But if you must know, I *was* about to search the same closet for an electropistol. Just in case. The satchel was for carrying it, of course."

"It's not very useful like that."

She eyed his pistol. "And where are *you* going? Your neck was killing you earlier, and you can't hear out of one ear, much less walk in a straight line."

"I'm not dizzy anymore."

"I saw you swipe some pain medicine earlier. You can't go anywhere in your state."

"Says the girl whose arm is in a sling."

She pursed her lips. Kase puffed out his chest in victory, but she continued, "I'm twenty-one, so I'm not a *girl*."

"Ah, irksome lizard then?"

She rolled her eyes. Kase bit his tongue to keep from saying something about it, and instead, he tried to push past her toward the food storage. He still needed a lantern. He wasn't foolish enough to go off without one in hand.

"You're going after Ben, aren't you?" She didn't move out of the way.

"Yes, and I don't need anyone tagging along. Go back to sleep. You'll only trip over your skirts."

"Well, seeing as I'm wearing trousers..."

He glared at her, and she finally moved out of his path. Once at the food closet near the cockpit, he shuffled a few things around, searching for the lantern.

"Looking for this?"

He spun. Hallie picked up the unlit lantern from a small niche along the hallway outside. "I'd taken the liberty of using it while I read tonight. Problem?"

Instead of putting Hallie in her place, he strode past her and out the door of the ship. Her footsteps clattered behind him as he descended the stairs. Could she *be* any louder?

"I don't need your help."

"I have a lantern, and you can't hear out of one ear."

"Your point?"

"*I'm* not going to fly this ship when Ebba fixes it, and you need me."

"Like a headache," Kase mumbled.

He didn't follow as she strode past, but she turned, her eyes sparkling. "I'd rather you still be alive to have the headache. Come on."

Kase ground his teeth, and although every warning bell went off in his head, he followed. Turned out he'd found someone nearly as stubborn as he was.

Hallie

HALLIE REMEMBERED A TIME BEFORE electric lights. The dining room at her father's inn felt so cozy with chandeliers her mother stood on a ladder to light. She remembered the solitary candle she and her brother shared when they met Niels behind the butcher's cottage and stole a few drinks. She also remembered the wayward candle that started the fire at Niels' farmhouse. Afterward, all the Metzingers had were their lives and the Walkers' hospitality. This night felt much the same, though she held an electric lantern; the slight illumination was much too dim to conquer the overwhelming darkness of the strange forest she and Kase had stepped into.

In the distance, the storm roared, but the trees muffled its rage. The light radiating out only kissed the edges of the perpetually damp underbrush a few feet in front of them. She and Kase were mostly blind stumbling through the trees. Every now and then, they would hit a patch of Firstmoon's light breaking through the scattered limbs above. Those moments were few and far between.

Earlier, the trees were curious with their own sort of beauty, but now they watched her with unseen eyes.

She remembered reading a story like that once, about trees with watching eyes and creeping roots and grasping branches. She'd never read it again.

Kase stopped, and Hallie smacked into his back, her cheek hitting the cold leather of his jacket. Her shoulder throbbed.

"Watch where you're going," he muttered.

"I would have if you'd told me we were going to stop," she spat back, rubbing her injury. The pain lessened a little.

"Shh."

"What?"

"Hush."

Prat. "Why?"

He held up a hand. Hallie snapped her mouth closed.

"Shut off the lamp," Kase whispered.

"We won't be able to see!"

"Just do it."

The light wobbled as she obeyed, biting back a retort. It was hard to handle the lantern with one hand, but she spun the knob on the side. As she did, something on the bark of the nearest tree caught her eye. A smear of...something.

"I think I saw..." she began, but Kase held up his hand again. He strained forward with his good ear.

The sound was like breathing, but much louder. She froze. Kase pushed her behind him, hand on the grip of his electropistol. In the dim moonlight, she could just make out his movements.

Surely it was the wind whistling through the trees. Surely. It must've been the storm. Maybe they were nearing the other side of the eye?

But none of the branches moved.

"It's not too close," he whispered, "but we don't want it looking for us."

It? Hallie leaned forward slightly. "Do you know what's making that noise?"

"It could be the weather."

Right. "Then why are you worried about it finding us?"

He didn't answer, and after a few moments, the sound stopped. Hallie cleared her throat. "I'm turning up the lantern. Not too bright. I saw something on that tree before we heard the noise."

"Only enough for us to see what you're talking about."

Hallie set it on the forest floor and bent beside it. With the delicacy of a medic operating on a patient, she twisted the knob. She stopped once she had a dim light about the brightness of a dying candle. It wasn't much, but it would work for her purposes.

When Hallie stood, trying not to jostle her arm, she edged closer to the tree and held up the lantern. She found what she'd spotted earlier, and her stomach twisted. The rust-colored splotch was a few inches in diameter and smeared a little down the side of the trunk where the tree's bark was missing.

"Tell me that's not what I think it is."

He stepped up beside her and leaned toward the trunk, squinting in the faint light. "Is that...blood?"

"Possibly?"

"You think..."

She shrugged her good shoulder, the lantern light wobbling. "It could be. Let's see if we can find anything else of note. Just to be sure."

Kase nodded and knelt, fingers pushing aside bits of twigs and thick bramble-like bushes. His hand glittered with water droplets. "Can you shine that down here?"

She bent beside him. "Will you take the lantern? I can't hold it steady with my arm like this."

He grabbed it and examined the ground. Nothing of importance that Hallie could tell—no more blood, at least. Maybe it'd been from an animal, or not even blood at all. Even with all her knowledge, she knew barely anything about their location. The trees could've had ruby-red sap for all she knew.

Or maybe she didn't want to face the grim possibility it was Ben's blood.

"Look!"

Hallie peered at where Kase pointed. In the mud, plain as day, was a boot print. She gasped as Kase bent again to inspect the print further, holding the lantern close.

"Shocks," he whispered, "it's Skibs'. See? That's the pattern of the standard issue boots we have in the Crews. I lent him my extra pair because he messed up the soles of his climbing that tree."

Hallie brought a shaking hand to her mouth. "So that was his...on the trunk?"

She couldn't bring herself to say the word *blood* again.

"I don't know."

After handing back the lantern, Kase stood and started in the direction the boot pointed. They walked a little way before he stopped again and inspected the ground. He didn't say anything but took off once more in another direction.

"Kase, wait!"

"After crashing, you know he's hurt badly. Must be concussed or something to have wandered on his own."

Hallie caught up with him, and after a good five

minutes, they found nothing conclusive. No more boot prints. No more bloody smears on trees. It was comforting and disheartening all at once.

Kase pushed aside more leaves and limbs while Hallie peered into the surrounding darkness. To say it was eerie was an understatement. As the night went on, the darkness grew more so. Suffocating even. Like someone had stuffed her in cotton.

With every sound, every whisper of wind in the trees, the hair on the back of her neck stood straight up, but whenever she turned, only the forest watched. Nothing more.

Hallie held the lamp higher. Kase's dark curls reflected the golden light.

"Hold it closer and turn it up, I might've found something else," he said.

Hallie grabbed the knob and turned it, but as she did, a growl tore through the forest, and her hand slipped, pushing the knob to its full capacity. With a pop, sizzle, and pain in her arm, the lantern snuffed out like a candle.

She could just make out Kase as he stood. "And now you've burned out the light. *Wonderful*."

"What was that? It sounded like a... a wolf or something."

"I'm going to say yes."

"Can we go now?"

His voice quivered a little. "We'll come back tomorrow."

"Will Ben be okay?"

Kase ran a hand through his hair. Although Hallie couldn't see it well, she guessed it was probably messier than usual. "If he's survived this long on his own, he can survive one more night. Come on."

He strode off without waiting for her to follow. Her heart skipped a beat. "That's not the right direction."

His footsteps stopped, and soon, he walked back toward her. In the dim moonlight, she barely saw the outline of his jaw and cheekbones. "We came in over that way." He gestured wildly with his hand. "We turned right, then veered left. All we have to do is head *that* way, and we should find ourselves somewhere down the beach to where the hover is."

"Yes, but how do you know where you're going?"

"Trust me."

Like the stars I'd trust you.

Kase started off again, this time much slower. Hallie followed, gripping the handle of the useless lantern tightly in her fist. She saw him when he was directly in front of her, but that brought on other problems.

"For moons-sake, don't step on the back of my boots!" Kase growled. "You almost made me trip."

"Sorry," Hallie said. "But if you would just speed up—"

The words were lost when a quake shook the ground. Hallie screamed and lost her footing, falling into Kase, who somehow managed to keep his feet. The quaking didn't last long, but the following thud echoed for an eternity.

"What was that?" Kase asked.

Hallie straightened. "Earthquake?"

"Aren't you some kind of scholar?"

"We're on Tasava. It could...it could be anything. None of the explorers' accounts said much."

Kase brushed past her. "If you hadn't burned out the light, maybe we could go find out for sure."

"Wait! Why are you going back?"

"I want to see what that was."

"Have you lost your stars?"

"Nothing's attacked us yet, and I'm curious. Maybe it's some sort of animal I can take out with my pistol. That way we can have something else to eat besides that stars-awful beef stew you insist on making."

"Ungrateful prat," Hallie mumbled, glad the darkness hid her burning cheeks. Kase didn't seem to hear as he sped off.

She fumbled to catch up, praying the roots of the nearby trees didn't trip her. One got lucky. The root caught the tip of her left boot, and she flew forward, lantern flying and nailing something—Kase, judging by the shout.

"What's your *problem*, woman?"

Hallie held her tears at bay. She'd fallen on her uninjured shoulder, but that didn't mean it was a soft landing. "I tripped."

She blushed when her voice wobbled, but she lifted her head to see the outline of his hand. She pushed herself to her knees with her smarting left arm. "I can get up by myself, thanks."

Her voice didn't sound as confident as the words themselves.

"Just take my hand," Kase said, voice firm. "Let's go back to the ship. It's useless to be out here without a working lantern."

"You were the *dulkop* who was *curious*." She gritted her teeth but took his hand. It was rough, not at all like someone who'd been raised in high society, like Ellis. With Kase's help, she got to her feet without falling.

Hallie pulled her hand out of his as soon as she was on two feet again. She dusted the front of her trousers, but she couldn't see if she got all the dirt.

"Come on," Kase said. "Follow me."

Hallie went to do so, but as she did, she kicked the forgotten lantern. Pain shot through her toes, foot, and ankle. She cursed loudly as the broken lantern skidded over the ground to their left and fell off...something. The clanging and clacking echoed as it descended into whatever awaited in the darkness.

"Blast it, Hallie!" Kase spat.

She swallowed and limped over, trying to see where the lantern had gone, but Kase grabbed her arm.

"What're you doing?" His voice was pinched.

"I'm seeing where—"

But her words were cut off by a screech that shook the trees, the stars, and even her bones. And it came from the black abyss to their left...where she'd kicked the lantern.

She couldn't even scream as a roar rent the air, and Kase pulled her away from whatever she'd unwittingly awoken. They ran for their lives, and she held onto his rough hand for all she was worth, her shoulder and foot throbbing as another spine-tingling roar echoed off the trees.

As they sprinted, the forest thinned, and light from Firstmoon drizzled through openings above. Within a moment, they stumbled out onto a wide-open clearing with grass glowing in the pale light. Judging by Firstmoon's position at the tips of the trees, Secondmoon would be rising soon.

They made it to the other side where Kase slid to a stop, head whipping back and forth, trying to decide which way to go. In that split second of indecision, Hallie made the mistake of looking back the way they'd come.

What she saw chilled her to the bone.

The throbbing in her arm and foot disappeared in

the terror seizing the rest of her body. Nausea climbed up her throat like the ivy on the side of her father's inn, and she clamped her mouth tightly on a scream.

Its razor-sharp teeth and blue, iridescent scales gleamed in the moonlight. The creature was tall as the pines, with a head the size of two *Eudora Jaydes* side-by-side and two curled horns sprouting from just beside its pointed ears. Each arm ended in claws clenching and unclenching as it hunted. The monster's nostrils flared. Dark liquid seeped out of one like water. Something had cut it, and Hallie had the sinking feeling glass from a broken, burned-out lantern had been the culprit. It might have been a trick of the moonlight or her terror-riddled brain seeing things, but glittering dust floated around its long, serpentine body.

The creature was reminiscent of something she'd seen in a book. A *storybook*. All she had to go on were barely decipherable writings, legends, and that one explorer's account, nothing substantial, but a name still came to her. Except this one didn't have wings, and she prayed to whoever might've been listening it didn't breathe fire.

Dragon.

Its nostrils still searched out their scent in the air, and Hallie stood frozen as she watched the thick black blood from the cut under its nose drip over its skin and onto the ground below.

Kase moved in front of her, hand going to his pistol once again. What good was that going to do against a creature like *that*?

"Don't move," Kase whispered.

"Obviously," Hallie spat, hoping the bite in her words covered her fear. "What are we going to do?"

"I'm thinking. Give me a moment."

Hallie bit her lip as the beast sniffed the air a hundred feet away. "Kase, I think that's a dragon."

"*I know*. Now stop talking!"

No matter how slowly she breathed, the blood still pounded through her at a blistering rate. The monster seemed to stare at them, though Hallie couldn't see its eyes from her vantage point. Any moment, it would discern their location. Any moment, it would barrel toward them and snatch them up with a vicious chomp of its jaw, though Hallie still hadn't decided if it could roast them with flames or not.

They should run. They should use this time to escape, but neither she nor Kase could move.

"Kase, we have to—"

That was when the eye found them. If she hadn't been so terrified, she might have appreciated the beauty of it, but the glittering gold iris didn't stop the scream she let loose as it lunged forward.

With a swift click, Kase finally whipped out his electropistol and pulled the trigger. The bolt blasted from the barrel at a force surprising for such a small weapon. Its ball of electricity sped through the night air and smashed into one of the trees on the far-right side of the clearing, causing it to erupt with static. The various bolts of white light sputtered and sparked as it engulfed the tree. A few of the branches flickered with flames.

The creature halted and whipped its head toward the disturbance. Kase shot the electropistol again, this time hitting the beast near where Hallie guessed its stomach to be. It froze, the glittering dust in the air rushing to where the bolt struck, but what it did after, Hallie didn't know. Kase clasped her hand and tugged her through the underbrush. Small branches whipped around her, whacking her face, arms, and legs, but she didn't care. She just knew she needed to get as far as she could from that thing.

"Don't think it's...following us," Kase managed to huff.

"It—" Hallie breathed hard, sweat beading at her hairline. "Froze. When you struck...it with the bolt. Did you see the—did you see the dust?"

Kase stopped suddenly, and Hallie plowed into him, sending them both flying. Her adrenaline kicked in, blocking out any pain, and she got up and launched back into a sprint.

A roar split the air.

"Stars, oh stars," she panted. A few more minutes of running at top speed, and she miraculously found herself stumbling onto the beach. She looked behind her to see if Kase followed. A few seconds of furiously rustling leaves later, his tall form burst from the undergrowth.

"Come on!" he yelled.

He flashed past, and she tried to follow, but running in the sand made her infinitely slower. When they turned a corner, rushing past some trees, the sight of the *Eudora Jayde* almost made Hallie start weeping right then and there. Instead, her legs gave out and she crashed into the sand, the last furious dash finally catching up with her. Pain spiked through her shoulder.

She clawed at the sand, trying to pull herself along, but the grains slipped through her useless fingers. It was almost as if something had tried to saw her shoulder off with a knife wrapped in thorns. She couldn't help the tears pouring down her face as sand crunched in her mouth. Pulling herself forward inch by inch, the pain shot down her arm like an electrobolt. She felt herself slipping away.

No. She needed to make it to the ship.

"Kase," she cried, her voice weak. Black spots amassed at the corners of her eyes, but a pair of boots flew toward her, sand flying up every which way. Strong arms grabbed beneath hers. One went around her waist.

But the black dots grew, and she collapsed.

CHAPTER 12

YOU DON'T NEED ME

Hallie

SAND HAD BEEN PAINTED ONTO the back of Hallie's eyelids. She blinked. The light was even worse than the sand. It didn't scratch; it burned. As her senses woke up, two voices spoke words that were little more than jumbled syllables wading their way through the deep water in her mind. The pungent odor of rubbing alcohol wafted on the air and pierced through her haze. It was tangy and sharp and made her feel sick. She blinked again. Pain.

"Hallie?"

At last, she understood the voice. Her ears were improving. That or her brain switched on. She blinked again, this time with less pain. The shapes and colors were a blur.

"Slept long enough," said another voice, this one higher but throaty.

"Not her fault," said the first, strong and low.

Hallie blinked once more, and this time, everything came into focus. Two faces leaned over her, too close.

"Shocks and stars," Hallie croaked. "Let me breathe."

Both Zeke and Ebba left her field of vision, and a hand slid under her back and tried to lift her up. *Ebba.*

"Help me out, ya *dulkop*. I only have one working arm," Ebba grunted. Zeke's hand slipped underneath Hallie's injured shoulder as he bent over her. She winced. It wasn't nearly as bad as it was the night before when–when they–oh stars.

"The dragon, where is it?" Hallie gasped when they raised her to a sitting position. Brown Zuprium walls glinted under electric lighting. She was in her bedchamber.

"Since we're not breakfast or cowering in a corner somewhere, I'd say it's still frozen or too full after eating an electrified tree." Ebba grimaced. "How'd that happen, by the way? Not used to electricity?"

"Not sure, but I wish I could go back and study it. Well, I would if I was sure it wouldn't eat me. One explorer's account mentioned them, Belforte, I believe, and clearly he survived." Hallie brought her other hand up to her throat. Sand crunched in her teeth. "Is there any water?"

Zeke handed her a cup, and Hallie drank greedily. When she finished, he set it on top of the small table in front of the bed. "Not going to black out on us again any time soon?"

"I'll be fine."

"Good." He walked back over to her and leaned

close. "Now don't you ever, *ever* do that again. You and Kase can't do things like that!"

Hallie pressed herself against the wall, cringing at the pain in her arm. "Sorry."

"You'd just been in an airship crash, and you thought it was a good idea to stroll through unfamiliar territory? *At night*?"

"We wanted to find Ben."

"And did you find him?"

"No."

"Kase is foolhardy and blasted stupid sometimes, but you're smarter than that."

"I'm sorry, all right?" Hallie threw her uninjured arm in the air. "We wanted to make sure Ben was okay. But I knew better. Happy?"

Zeke nodded, his jaw tight.

"And I won't do it again unless I have your express permission, *Lieutenant Colonel* Shackley."

Zeke rubbed his eyes. "Ebba, make sure she takes another dose of the painkiller. She'll feel that shoulder again soon."

"Yes, Lieutenant Colonel Shackley." Ebba smirked.

Zeke ran a hand over his cheek. "I'll tell Kase you're awake. He's on watch for your *dragon*."

He left the room with a smart turn of his polished boots. Ebba watched him go and then laughed outright.

"It's as much Kase's fault as it is mine," Hallie muttered, tugging at the sling on her arm.

Ebba smirked. "Kase's dressing down was worse. I had to leave the room so they wouldn't hear me cackling. And then I got scolded because I could've been chomped by a dragon, which in some twisted way sounds like an exciting way to go."

"I'm certain Kase took it very well."

Ebba adjusted her own injured arm. "Very well."

Hallie laughed. "I still can't believe I saw an actual dragon. If I hadn't been so terrified, I might've sketched it right there. That's if I'd had a working right arm."

"I'm glad you ran instead. I couldn't stand being the only girl. Plus, you're a good roommate."

"I'm touched." Hallie looked around the room. "Any word on Ben?"

Ebba's face fell. She shook her head. "I'm sure we can have *Eudora* fixed by the end of the day if we work together. Or working enough to get us away from your beastie friend."

"But if we don't find him..."

Hallie cut herself off. She didn't want to think about that. Think about Ben alone in the forest. In pain. Dying. She remembered the bloodstain on the tree. He was out there somewhere. She and Kase had failed.

At that moment, a mop of curly hair peeked around the corner of the doorframe. Hallie jumped. Kase nodded, and she responded in turn. Then he disappeared.

Strange.

Ebba's eyebrows rose. "I guess that's better than a shouting match."

Kase

THANKFULLY, THE STORM HAD DISSIPATED completely by the morning. Remembering what Jove had said about the Bay of Storms, Kase hoped they fixed the ship and left the area before it returned with a fury.

Sweat dripped from his brow and into his eyes as

he and Zeke worked to repair the *Eudora*. Kase had left his jacket on the ship, but shocks, his linen shirt still clung to his back. The wrench in his hand was slick with sweat as he fit it onto a bolt on one of the ship's panels underneath the cockpit.

"No, loosen the other bolt, not *that* one," Ebba barked at him. He ground his teeth and obeyed, but he got it wrong again and she groaned. "Good *sterne*, how do you not know which one I'm pointing to?"

Kase had been chased by a monster only known to exist on Tasava *and* chewed out by his older brother in the last twenty-four hours. He did *not* need this girl ordering him around. Not now. Not ever. He knew she couldn't do it herself, as she still had a painful broken arm, but that didn't mean she needed to be rude about it.

"I can't tell which one you're pointing at from here!" He tried to hide the frustration in his voice. He wasn't successful, as evidenced by the frowns on everyone's faces.

He'd barely slept. After Zeke had made sure Hallie was alive and berated his brother for wandering the forest, he'd volunteered for watch duty to give Kase a few hours of rest. But being nearly eaten by a large, scaly beast threw a damper on his sleep schedule. He was just thankful the dragon was stupid and apparently hated electric bolts.

"Third one to the left," Ebba grunted.

"See? That was easy."

He found the correct one and popped it off. No disapproval came from the tiny girl, so he assumed he'd done it correctly. He moved to another one.

Ebba continued to direct him and Zeke, who hadn't suffered nearly as much feedback on his progress.

Everyone liked Zeke better between the two of them. Kase had gotten used to it. Of course, Ana had always been the favorite, even more than Zeke. The only girl.

Now it was Zeke.

"Hallie?" Ebba nodded at the toolkit beside Zeke. "Would you give Kase the pliers? I'd rather him not move."

A loose bolt spilled into his outstretched hand. "Do I need to take off this panel? And why did I need to remove the bolts in that order?"

Ebba nodded, brushing a hand over her chest. "The storm fried at least one wire inside. I've already cut the electricity, so you should be safe. And don't question the mechanic. I know what I'm doing."

He grumbled and stuffed the bolts in one of his trouser pockets. Hallie appeared beside him a moment later, holding out the pliers. Her arm was still in a sling, but it didn't seem to bother her too much. Kase would never admit how much it had scared him when she'd passed out the previous night. He thought he'd killed her.

Hallie held the tool out with a small smirk. "It's a good thing the power's off, because I'm not sure your hair could handle electrocution."

"Is that so?" Kase raised a brow. "I rather think it would look even better."

With that comment, he guessed she didn't hate him after what happened last night. A part of him was relieved, which was strange. Why did he care so much about what she thought of him?

The light reflecting off the metal pliers was nearly blinding. He squinted and ignored the weird tickling sensation in his chest.

As he went to grab the pliers, his fingers brushed

hers. She jumped, dropping the tool.

"Really?" Kase shook off his own shock. "I'll never get the sand off those."

Hallie's eyes flashed. "I didn't mean to drop them!"

"*Sure*, just pick them up, for moons-sake."

Her nostrils flared, and she kicked more sand on top of them. "Have fun getting the sand off now."

"Are you serious?" Kase growled. "You're the one who dropped them!"

"No, *you* dropped them!"

Ebba groaned. "For all the *sterne* twinkling in the sky, shut up. *One of you* pick up the pliers and get to work! Unless you want your beastie finding us."

Kase ground his teeth. He wanted to point out it was Hallie who had been the child, kicking sand, but he thought better of it. He grabbed the pliers and wiped them on his shirt. He hated sand, hated the way its crunchy granules found their way into every nook and cranny. But he'd be the bigger person this time.

Hallie stomped toward the stairs. Kase rolled his eyes. *So dramatic.*

He turned back to Ebba. "Now what?"

"Take off the panel."

Kase started to obey, but Zeke interrupted. "Go apologize first."

"What?"

"You heard me."

Kase pointed the pliers at his brother. "You've got to be kidding me."

Zeke trudged over. He was a little shorter than Kase, but much wider in the shoulders. Kase took a step back as Zeke crossed his arms over his chest. "We're on a highly important mission, and we have bigger problems to deal with than your ridiculous rivalry."

"But what about her? Why does she get the easy way out?"

Zeke poked him in the shoulder. "Because *you're* supposed to be the gentleman. And because you started it."

Kase bit the inside of his cheek and shoved the pliers into his brother's hand before climbing the ramp. Deep down, Kase knew he was being unreasonable, but there was something about Hallie that...well, if he was honest, he almost enjoyed their sparring. Not that he would ever admit that. Most girls catered to his every whim, but Hallie? She'd forged her will out of stone and blasted stardust.

He entered the ship and peeked in her room. Both beds were made, but the one to the right had its pillow all crooked. Ebba's, he guessed. With the clacking of boots and a bent posture, he made his way down the corridor and into the cockpit. Hallie was in Skibs' pilot seat, a book in her lap. Scratch that, two books. One was tucked into the other. While he couldn't make out the strange language on the top one, the one on the outside looked familiar.

The Odyssey once again. He couldn't fault her for her taste, at least.

He fell into his seat beside her. She didn't even look up, only moved so he couldn't see the smaller book tucked inside the epic poem. *Hiding something, are we?*

"Yes, Master Kase?" She asked in a flinty tone.

He took a deep breath, shoving the irritation down. "For the last time, it's just Kase. I came to say sorry."

"For what?"

Kase gripped the arms of the seat until it hurt.

Calm, calm, steady.

He gritted his teeth. "I'm sorry for

being...rude...earlier."

There, he'd said it.

Her eyes didn't follow along with the words on the page. At the agonizing pace of a far-off planet revolving around the sun, she took a scrap of paper from her lap and placed it in her book, closing both. At least she wasn't one of those terrible fools who folded the corners of pages. Mentally, he shuddered.

She looked up, her eyes narrowing. "Is this where I tell you to go blast off?"

Heat rose in his cheeks. Not anger this time, but shame. A surprising feeling for him. "Listen, about that, I..."

She held up a hand. "I'm not you."

Kase's anger licked at his insides like writhing snakes, but Zeke was right, as much as he hated to admit it. They needed to figure out how to get along, at least for the length of this mission. "I'm sorry, all right? I say stupid stuff sometimes."

The words burned like fire rolling off his tongue.

She set the books aside. "Thank you for the apology. I know how much it's costing you. Especially since Zeke forced you to come in here."

"What? He didn't—"

"Don't play dumb. I heard it all." She pointed to the missing windshield. They'd removed the parachute that morning to allow the dash and everything else to dry out properly.

"Oh." Kase's stomach plummeted to his toes. "Forgot about that."

"So don't be upset when I don't take your apology seriously." She got up from the seat and clutched the books to her chest.

Blood pulsing, Kase stood. He tightened his hands

into fists. "I still came in here, didn't I? I could've ignored him. Kept on banging around the underbellies of the ship trying to make sure we get up in the air soon. Instead, I'm here admitting that I was a stars-idiot."

"That's a first."

Kase stepped forward until their faces were inches apart. To Hallie's credit, she didn't step back. She looked up at him, square in the face, and he couldn't find a lick of fear in those eyes. Kase spoke low. "You don't know me."

"You don't let anyone try."

Kase could count the freckles dusting her nose. He blinked, trying to rid himself of the thought. "I..."

Her honey eyes were bright with anger. Soft pink lips pulled the corners into a scowl. Her fragrance, redolent of the mountain air, pulled at his senses. In the dim light from the sun floating into the empty, damaged cockpit, he leaned forward, tipping his head further. Her eyes widened, but she didn't move. Just sucked in a small breath.

Military-style boots clunked in the corridor, and Kase jumped. Hallie dropped her books with a smack. She bent to pick them up, but he beat her to it, almost knocking heads with her. Anything to cover up what had nearly happened. Her subtle scent swirled around him. He held his breath and grabbed both books. The smaller one had an archway etched into the cover. Curious. He was pretty sure the spiky symbols near the top were Yalven. The book looked familiar, but where would he have seen it?

As Zeke entered the cockpit, Kase straightened.

Stopping short, his brother schooled his face into one of indifference and pulled his shoulders taut. Kase winced.

"You should take better care of your books." Kase stacked the smaller one on top of *The Odyssey* but kept his eyes on the floor.

Hallie cleared her throat as she took them. "Of course. Thank you."

She clasped them to her chest and hurried past Zeke.

"You apologized?" Zeke pulled at the sleeves of his military style shirt. He rarely wore anything else. A muscle jumped in his jaw.

Kase ran a hand through his hair. "*Yes*. Happy?"

Zeke just nodded and left, his steps stiff and arms crossed.

What just happened? Shocks and stars, I need sleep.

THE REST OF THE REPAIRS didn't take too long. Kase and Zeke pushed the last panel on together and sealed it up. While the brothers made a decent team, they hadn't spoken since Zeke had nearly walked in on...well, on whatever had just happened in the cockpit.

Kase didn't want to think about what had flashed into his mind as he and Hallie stood there, inches away from each other in the dim light. No, he needed to focus, keep everyone alive, and find Skibs, who was still out wandering the forest, maybe even lying in a pool of blood, a blasted dragon looming over his decaying corpse.

A cold shudder ran down his spine. Yes, that visual helped him forget what had almost happened between him and Hallie.

"That's it?" Kase asked.

Ebba wiped a bit of sweat from her brow and ran a

hand through her hair, a few curls popping out of their place and falling into her eyes. "If you've done everything correctly, we can take off tomorrow...unless you'd risk flying tonight."

Zeke spoke up at that. "Let's get a little farther away from here if we can. The mysterious dragon hasn't shown himself yet, but it's only a matter of time before he finds us."

Kase tightened the last bolt with a fierce twist. "I'm not leaving Skibs."

"If the blood we saw on that tree is any indication, he's badly hurt," Hallie said from her chair, facing the forest, watching for anything suspicious. "Or worse."

"I know." Zeke wiped sweat from his brow. "We'll go scouting soon as we're done."

But it was Kase's fault they were in this mess. He was the one who'd been shock-headed enough to fly above the storm. He had to make it right.

Kase swallowed his guilt and focused on the puzzle of Skibs' disappearance instead. He gritted his teeth until they hurt. Why had Skibs gone off by himself? What put that thought into his mind? He'd hit his head hard enough to fall unconscious while they battled the storm, and the Cerl had knocked him out before that, but Zeke had strapped him into a seat before they crashed. Everyone else was hurt but alive. Still safely in the ship.

But Skibs had unbuckled himself and wandered into the forest, hurt and bleeding.

A tide of panic rose in his chest. His subconscious told him Skibs was gone, but Kase refused to listen. It was better to focus on the anger slowly simmering in his gut.

"If you'd have let me go looking the first day,

maybe we wouldn't be in this mess," Kase growled. "Who knows where he's wandered off to now."

Zeke turned toward him, hands on his hips and the handle of the wrench sticking out of his shirt pocket. "You weren't in any shape to go romping through the forest in your condition. None of us were. If you remember correctly, our airship crash-landed."

"And Ebba's broken arm is our worst injury. You have me to thank for that."

Zeke took the tool out of his pocket and threw it into the box at his feet. "Don't be so cocky. Sure it wasn't luck?"

Luck? Zeke didn't understand how much training Kase had undergone to make that landing. Granted, it'd never been on a beach, but...

"It wasn't all luck." Kase choked the grip of his own wrench.

Ebba looked back and forth between the two, wisely not interjecting her own opinion, but Kase knew she wanted to.

He ground his teeth. "Listen, just because you're older doesn't mean—"

Hallie stood up, the chair falling with a soft *thunk* in the sand from the force of her sudden movement. A chill zipped up his spine. Had the dragon found them at last? Something worse?

"What is it, Hallie?" He hurried toward her.

She pointed. "Something moved at the edge of the forest."

Kase squinted, trying to see what she saw. The forest was dark, even in the midday sun. The thick underbrush sat undisturbed. Nothing shook the trees, not even a breeze. Not the dragon.

"What is that?" Zeke raised his arm and pointed at—

"Skibs!"

Energy like Kase hadn't felt since running for his life the night before sang through his bones as a hunched form swayed on the edge of the treeline, collapsing into the sand. Kase sprinted toward him, working to keep his balance on the ever-shifting sand. The others followed, but his focus was on the body crumpled in the distance.

"Ben!"

The figure didn't respond.

Ice overtook the blood in Kase's veins. *No.*

Skibs had survived a rotten childhood, numerous Watch missions, and an airship crash. There was no way he'd die like this. Not here. Not now.

Kase skidded to a stop and fell to his knees beside the prone body. Blood splattered Skibs' torn clothing. Kase gritted his teeth against the emotions running through his mind. Skibs had to be okay. Kase wouldn't be able to live with himself if he died. The ex-pilot was one of the few people who understood him.

When Kase tried to grab his shoulder, Zeke stopped him. "Hold on, Kase. We don't know what injuries he has."

"I'll get the kit." Hallie ran back to the ship as Zeke knelt beside Kase, leaning over Skibs, inspecting his body carefully.

Gratitude stirred in his chest, but his fear nearly extinguished it. "Skibs. *Ben*, can you hear me?"

The crumpled form didn't reply. Zeke sat back, brushing a hand across his own forehead. He winced. Kase guessed he'd forgotten about his own cut with the impossibly neat stitches he'd done himself. "We can turn him over now. Nothing is broken besides his nose—not visibly, that is. Kase, you need to be careful."

"I get it."

Even in Kase's near-panicked state, Zeke reminded him of Jove for a moment as his older brother breathed sharply out his nose.

With Zeke's help, they turned Skibs over to lie on his back. Kase shuddered at the man's face. The dried blood covering most of it was telling enough. The broken nose was from when he'd hit the steering wheel during the storm. No one had cleaned up the blood, but the rest of his face seemed intact. As Kase put a shaking finger to Skibs' neck, he prayed he'd feel something. Anything.

"He's alive." Kase's voice broke a little as he pulled his hand back. Skibs was only unconscious. That, Zeke could work with.

Zeke rubbed his eyes. "He's also breathing, which is a great indicator he's not dead."

Kase glared but didn't say anything. It took a good bit for someone to wear Zeke down. He didn't feel like pushing him any further.

A minute or two later, Hallie settled beside Zeke, handing him the medical kit. She gasped, putting a hand to her mouth.

"He's alive," Kase told her. "Zeke will fix him up."

She looked up at him, and he bit the inside of his cheek. He remembered those eyes, close enough for him to see the sparkling bits of jade speckled in the pools of gold, but he broke eye contact and looked back at his brother, who dug through the medical kit.

"Blast, the tonic I need is in the other bag—no, it's okay, Hallie. Don't run and get it now. We can move him to the ship. He might have a broken rib or two, but I need to get him to his bed."

"So... we just pick him up?" Ebba scratched at her

arm in the sling.

He shook his head. "We need to be careful still. Do we have anything that can be used as a stretcher?"

"A mattress, maybe?" Hallie asked.

"That'll work. Kase, will you get one?"

Kase nodded and stood. Everything would be fine. Skibs would survive, and they could continue with this mission as planned.

Everything would be fine. It had to be.

CHAPTER 13

DON'T SPOIL IT

Hallie

SITTING IN THE COLD WOODEN chair she'd dragged into the room, Hallie read *The Odyssey* aloud to Ben. She used her best voice impressions, of course.

"They tried but didn't persuade my hero's heart—I was really angry—and called back to him..."

Her Odysseus was the best. When she and Jack were younger, her twin had said her voice was too low to be a girl's. She'd taken his legs out from under him, probably further proving his point, but he'd apologized in the end.

That had been nearly seven years ago. Stars.

Hallie blinked away the memory and shifted in the chair. As the men's chamber on the *Eudora Jayde* had three beds tucked inside, they didn't have the nice table and chair Hallie and Ebba's room had.

Thankfully, they'd fixed the ship enough to fly a little less than an hour before the sun set. It wasn't much, but Hallie was grateful they wouldn't run into the dragon. Still, if there was one, it stood to reason that there would be more. She shuddered, even if a bit of her longed to find its nest and sketch the babies.

It'd been a day and a half since Ben had emerged from the forest. Zeke had checked him again once they'd gotten him onto his bed. He'd also pulled out three syringes and plunged each into Ben's arm.

"What are those?" she'd asked.

Zeke had pulled the last needle out and wrapped it in a cloth. "Pain medication, along with my own modifications. It should help heal his brain, but I can't do much else until he wakes up."

Hallie might've been wary of what his "own modifications" were, but he was the expert, and Kase hadn't objected. Instead, the pilot had paced, raked a hand through his hair, and left the room altogether. She didn't blame him—it wasn't hard to read the helplessness in his eyes as he watched his friend. Not being able to help Ben was probably eating at him.

At the very least, his silence had delayed the potential fallout from their uncomfortable "close encounter" in the cockpit. Stars, she didn't think her heart had ever raced so fast. It still fluttered when she allowed her thoughts to wander down that trail—*not* in a good way. Because if she did, she'd remember the way that stupid hair fell into his stupid blue eyes.

Ahem.

The next night, though, Hallie had decided she needed to do something, anything to help Ben and get her mind off whatever was going on between her and

Kase.

"Cyclops, if anyone, if any mortal man asks you how you got your eye put out, tell him that Odysseus the marauder—"

Ebba walked in with a small plate of mostly dried beef and veggies. Only three weeks in, and they were already working toward the bottom of their supply. How long did the High Guardsman expect the mission to take?

The small woman held out the food for Hallie, so she marked her page and balanced the book on her lap.

"Thank you," she said as Ebba stepped past her, taking a seat on one of the other beds. Hallie figured it was Zeke's, as it was immaculately made. The one behind her was a mess of sheets—Kase's.

"Any change?" Ebba crossed her legs.

"Nothing." Hallie picked a little at a dried carrot. Not appetizing. "We need to do something about the food soon."

Ebba nodded. "I'm getting sick of dried beef."

"Do you think Kase or Zeke would hunt if we asked?"

"I guess?" Ebba shrugged. "Zeke would be good at it."

Hallie ripped off a chunk of beef with her teeth and chewed it. The too-salty flavor and coarse texture made her want to gag. "Kase wouldn't be able to stay quiet."

Ebba laughed. "If I knew how to use an electropistol or knife, I'd go myself." She leaned back on her good hand, her other still in the sling. "So, whatcha doing in here? I heard voices."

Hallie held up her book and swallowed another bit of food. "I'm reading to Ben."

"Reading to him?" Ebba tilted her head. "He can't

hear you."

Hallie set aside the beef, grabbed another carrot, and grimaced as she bit into it. She didn't care for carrots, whether they were dried or bathed in butter. But it was better than starving. "Jack told me people can still hear what's going on, even if they can't communicate."

"Who's Jack?"

Hallie choked on the carrot. "My twin brother."

"I didn't know you had a brother. I have five of 'em, all younger and crazier than the last, but the one who I collect rocks for, Eren, he's my favorite." She fell back and stared up at the ceiling. "Are you close with yours?"

"Um, yes, I was."

"Was?" Ebba raised her head off the immaculate coverlet.

Hallie slapped herself mentally. She shouldn't have brought him up. "Uh, yes. He, um...passed away a few years ago."

The look on Ebba's face made Hallie blush. She didn't want anyone's sympathy. Not anymore. Ebba sat up on her elbow, hand over her heart. "Hallie, I'm—"

"You didn't know." Hallie set her plate on the floor. "Anyway, I don't know if Jack was right, but Ben might appreciate hearing a story. I despise feeling useless."

"I'm sure he likes it." Ebba sat up with a small smile and adjusted her own sling.

"How's your arm?"

"Still hurts like exploding suns at times, but that stuff Zeke makes works wonders." Ebba tapped the fingers of her good hand on her knee. "I wouldn't mind listening to more of your story. It might help me forget about the pain, at least a tiny bit."

Hallie smiled and turned the page. "Sure."

Kase

AFTER GAGGING DOWN A MEAGER dinner of dried cardboard vegetables and beef, Kase knew he needed to sleep. But when he left Zeke outside on watch and entered his room, he groaned. Hallie was reading, both to Ebba and the unconscious Skibs.

"He can't even hear you," he grumbled as he flopped onto his bed behind her.

"It's rude to interrupt," Hallie hissed. She twisted around to glare at him.

"I just want to sleep."

"You can sleep when you're dead," Ebba said. "I wanna hear the story."

"Can't you do that in your own room?"

"No. Now shut up." Ebba blew a curl out of her face. "Hallie's voices are the best part."

"The voices are sort of the problem—"

"It's fine. We can leave. Sorry," Hallie huffed, hopping lightly to her feet. "I'm only trying to help."

"By reading to someone who can't—you know what? Stay. I'll go."

Hallie looked down at the book she held in her hands. "I'm reading *The Odyssey*, you know. You're welcome to stay."

Kase ran a hand through his hair and flopped back onto the bed. "*Fine.* But the voices better be good."

He wanted to sleep, needed to sleep, but it probably wouldn't come anyway. Maybe a bedtime story would help.

Pft. Who was he kidding? He laid an arm over his eyes.

A few seconds later, she began reading. "We came to the island of Aeolia, Home of Aeolus..."

Blast. Kase had missed the Cyclops part by minutes. Should he chance Hallie's rage and ask her to reread it? He peeked over at her from under his arm. Her hair looked redder in the electric light, and several tendrils had come loose from her ladies' bun. She wouldn't have passed his mother's thorough inspections, which Ana had despised.

Kase hardly cared. His hair looked worse.

Kase focused back on the story at hand. When Odysseus and his crew landed on his island, Aeolus promised to help them find their way home, but Poseidon, mighty god of the sea, always managed to find a way to thwart the hero's quest.

Kase closed his eyes once more.

Hallie's voice was raspy and a bit comical. She needed to work on her "man" voice, but teasing her about it now wouldn't help anything. He wished that was the only thing bothering him.

He was supposed to be able to handle anything. He'd been in a crash landing before in one of the smaller hovers. However, it hadn't been like the one with the *Eudora Jayde*. It wasn't until that morning when they'd flown an hour, only an hour, that he'd started to feel something again.

Unfortunately, he felt like he had the night of the bike fight. That wasn't any better. Because his mind would wander back across the ocean, over the Nardens, and through the city to where his father loomed, lording over his fate. He shuddered.

"He tied the bag down in the hold of my ship."

Holy moons, he needed to distract himself. All he saw was the lightning bolt, the rain, the beach. He sat up sharply.

"Should Odysseus have told his men what was in the bag?" It was a question that had bothered him immensely about the epic ever since he'd first read it. The perfect distraction.

Hallie stopped. Kase swung his legs around to hang off the bed, his hands gripping the side. He still had a little pain from his injuries, but he'd taken a bit of pain medication earlier, so it wasn't as bad as it could have been.

Hallie's eyes brightened, and their electrified moment the day before flashed through his mind. He blinked, trying to push it away.

"Why do you think he didn't?" Hallie asked, putting her bookmark in place and shutting the book.

What kind of question was that? She sounded like his old school mistress.

Ebba leaned forward from her perch on the edge of Zeke's bed, empty plate with scraps of dried beef beside her, and Kase bit the inside of his cheek.

"He didn't understand yet," he said.

"Understand what?"

Kase thrummed his fingers on the bedframe. "Well, Aeolus gave him simple instructions, but Odysseus had gone through so much he didn't think ahead."

"He should have told them." Hallie brushed hair out of her bright eyes. "Then they might've avoided all the successive chaos! People would've gotten to see their families and gone back to their old lives."

"If you've read this before, you know how selfish his men are. They're also stupid. Remember the golden cattle?"

"I wouldn't say they were stupid, just a little—"

"Don't spoil it!" Ebba cried, hands slapping over her

ears.

"But Odysseus was just as selfish," Hallie continued. "If he'd communicated more, he could've avoided all that."

"But there's also the whole ordeal with the Cyclops, and Odysseus made a fool out of himself. If he hadn't bragged, he might've gotten home in one piece."

Hallie snorted. "That's the whole point of the story, isn't it? That Odysseus had to overcome his pride?"

"Yeah, but he must have known better than to—"

Ebba leapt up from her place, sending her plate crashing to the floor. *"Ben!"*

Kase sucked in a painful breath as he turned toward Skibs' bed. His eyes were open. Kase bumped into Hallie as he knelt beside the bed.

"Get Zeke!" he commanded. Someone ran from the room as he grabbed his friend's arm. "How are you feeling?"

Skibs blinked once, twice more, a slight frown on his face. Kase remembered what it had been like when he'd woken after the crash, so he swallowed his impatience, giving his friend a chance to catch his bearings.

"What happened?" Skibs wheezed. Hallie shoved a canteen into Kase's hand.

"He needs water," she said, kneeling back down beside him.

His arm grazed hers, and the electric sensation was hard to ignore. Kase shook his head, his curls bouncing. *Focus, you dulkop.* Skibs was alive. And awake. Thank the stars.

Before Kase could position his friend to give him a drink, Zeke appeared in the doorway, eyes widening when he saw Skibs. "Bless the stars and heavens above," he whispered. Then, more loudly: "Ben, welcome back. I'll grab the supplies."

Kase and Hallie helped him sit up. It was a difficult task; Skibs could hardly move, and Hallie only had one good arm, but they managed it. She put another pillow behind his back.

"Thanks," Kase whispered.

Hallie gave him a small smile as Kase helped Skibs take a drink from the canteen. A bit dribbled down onto his shirt, but Skibs ignored it. He did wince once, but he brushed off both Hallie and Kase's attempt to fix whatever hurt. Hallie finally gave them room and leaned on the doorframe.

Ben finally spoke, his voice raspy from disuse. "Am I gonna survive?"

Kase looked away. Hallie answered instead. "You broke two ribs to match your nose, as far as we could tell. And there's the matter of your concussion, but..."

Zeke came back into the room, carrying the box of medical supplies. He set them on the chair Hallie had vacated. She moved her book before he could set the box on top of it, and Kase grinned at the gesture. When he realized what he was doing, he wiped the expression off his face.

Skibs, despite his rough condition, smirked. Kase glared back in warning.

"What hurts?" Zeke asked.

"Head." Skibs lifted a hand to rub it, wincing. "Arm, chest, everything. Got lost. Don't know... what..."

Skibs coughed, and Zeke bent down to prepare an injection. How many clean needles did they have left? This mission wasn't going to end any time soon, and they were burning through their med kit.

"I don't remember much of anything," Skibs

finished.

Zeke frowned. "This medicine helps repair any bruises on the brain."

"Are you sure?" Kase asked.

"I'm a medical specialist."

"But how do you know it won't make him worse?"

"It's the same medicine I gave him earlier, and he woke up, didn't he?"

Kase rubbed a hand down his face. Days-old stubble pricked his fingers. "Sorry. I'm just on edge."

Zeke lifted up Skibs' right sleeve, stuck the needle into his arm, and pushed in the plunger. Skibs gritted his teeth.

"I'm sorry, Skibs," Kase muttered.

"What do you mean?"

"I didn't find you sooner. I looked, but..."

Hallie laughed, and Kase glanced in her direction. She'd put a hand to her mouth.

"Sorry," she said. "I know it's not funny. It's just that Kase and I found a dragon instead."

Skibs' eyes widened. "You f-found a *what*?"

He stumbled over the word, and worry pinched Kase's stomach, but it might have been simple disbelief. Kase shrugged. "It's far away now. I hope. Anyway, it might have, you know, when Hallie and I couldn't find you..."

Skibs chuckled and coughed, his face scrunching with pain. "You two made nice long enough to look for me? I'm touched."

Zeke laughed. "Their truce didn't last, don't worry."

Hallie's cheeks went pink. "I'll check on Ebba. Glad you're awake, Ben."

She barely got the words out before she fled the room, clutching her book like a shield. Kase scratched the back of his neck. "We're doing better at the moment, actually."

Zeke snorted. "Only because I made you apologize."

Kase threw his hands in the air, and Skibs gave another pained and wheezing laugh. "Glad I'm back."

PART II: SWORDS

NO TIES INVOLVED

Jove

TRYING TO SMOOTH ANY WRINKLES, High Guardsman Jove Shackley pulled at the sleeves of his tight button-down shirt even though he'd ironed it to perfection already. He hated these meetings, but they came with the territory.

I'm making a difference.

That was his mantra, and one he repeated under his breath all too often.

The soft glow from the electric bulbs hanging from the ceiling reflected on his wife's black hair, numerous little braids tied up into a knot at the nape of her neck. She smiled at him, and surrounded by frock coats and slacks of his dressing room, she was like the sun shining amongst the gloom.

"I like this blue one." Clara held up a tie. "Brings out your eyes."

He groaned. "Must I?"

"Love, it's just a meeting." Clara chuckled. "You go to dozens of these a week."

"Yes, but this one is different." He couldn't say more than that. He hated keeping her in the dark, but being part of the High Council posed a security risk, naturally.

She wrapped the tie around his neck and pulled at it, tying it with quick, efficient brown fingers. "Heddie's going to be there, right?"

Heddie Koppen was his superior in the Watch, a veteran of the High Council. The group consisted of the elected Stradats, senior members of the Watch, and of course, the Lord Kapitan. It would almost be like a pleasant family dinner.

If by pleasant, one meant a meal on the frozen tundra of the highest peak in the Narden Range.

"You're right. I shouldn't be worried." He straightened the tie a little and looked at the effect in the mirror. It did bring out his eyes. Not that anyone at today's meeting would notice or care. Only his wife, but her opinion mattered most, anyway.

Clara ran her hands across his chest, straightening what she could. "If we end up with a boy, I'll be the one teaching him how to tie one of those."

He rolled his eyes. "I think I'd rather have a girl. Much easier to deal with. And no ties involved."

She pushed a loose braid behind her ear, the other hand going to her stomach. She was just starting to show. "You'll be sorely disappointed if you think girls are any less wild."

Jove cupped her chin and bent down to give her a swift kiss. "Whatever you say. I have to go."

He grabbed his jacket and bowler hat and left their small but luxurious townhouse filled with landscapes

Clara had painted. It wasn't much, but it was home. It pained him to think they'd probably need to find a bigger place before the baby came.

He considered ordering a motorcoach, but then he decided he'd much rather walk. He and Clara didn't live too far from the Jayde Center. As most of Kyvena was built on the largest hill in the basin between the Nardens and the Silver Coast, many city goers could see the center of the government from their own homes— even in the slums. Jove had always thought the building beautiful with its stunning white stone and large glass dome, and the arched front façade reminded him of the cathedrals in the religious sector dividing lower and upper Kyvena.

It was still a reminder of the work he had yet to do.

His hand itched to go to his pocket and grab the cigarettes and lighter he'd stashed there. Clara hated him smoking in the townhouse, and Kase hadn't touched a cigarette since Ana died, but it calmed Jove.

With a quick look around, he dug in his pocket, finding a thin smoke. He took it out and held it between his fingers. Not wanting to smell like smoke once he arrived, he only fiddled with it as he walked. Relief washed over him.

The early morning air was crisp with autumn slowly moving its way into winter. They'd soon have their first snow, but Jove wasn't sure how he felt about it. He'd loved it ever since he was a boy, but this year was different. On one hand, the snow already falling across the Narden Range meant the Cerls were unlikely to attack until spring. However, that also meant the mission he'd sent his brothers on...well, even the fancy airship wouldn't be able to cross the mountains. That meant no matter what happened, whether they succeeded or failed, Jove wouldn't know until spring.

His insides squirmed. As he ground the cigarette between his fingers, small bits of tobacco fell to the street. He tossed it aside.

He'd sent a few transmissions to them over the weeks they'd been gone, but he hadn't heard any response. The wireless telegraph technology was new, and he couldn't say anything too important lest it be intercepted, but he thought he would have heard something. Anything.

He hadn't told his mother or Clara any of that. It would only make them anxious and his mother more frustrated with him. He comforted himself by remembering they might not even have received his messages; perhaps the tech was faulty. That reasoning helped ease his conscience a bit. Panicking this early wouldn't do any good.

After flashing his identification papers, Jove nodded to the armed guard at one of the massive doors.

"High Guardsman," the man said with a salute. Jove returned it and slipped in through the door.

Entering the building, Jove took in the foyer. It was just as incredible as the outside—nearly all white with Jayde emblems. Those muted green symbols were the only true sources of color in the room. Sometimes they were in the form of the classic tree inside the sun— which could also be found on military uniforms. Others like the Lifeship were more of a historical symbol. Each showed strength and power. But with what Jove knew, he understood it to all be bluster.

He nodded to each guard as he climbed the grand staircase embellished with Zuprium accents. It'd been built ages ago, when the mines hadn't been compromised and the money had been flowing in.

When the stairs split into two at the first landing, Jove took the left staircase.

As he got off on the second floor and turned the corner, he nearly smacked into a tall man dressed immaculately in a stiff suit.

The Lord Kapitan. His father.

Harlan Shackley cut an impressive figure, the right side of his dark green coat weighed down with medals and ribbons. It wasn't as if the man's height, strong build, closely cropped gray hair and mustache were enough. The Lord Kapitan had worked his way up through the military, earning every promotion with literal blood and sweat. Jove had always been intimidated by him, and that hadn't changed as he'd grown up, not even when he'd become an important officer in the Watch. One sharp look from the Lord Kapitan's hazel eyes could still shoot an ice dagger into Jove's chest. He'd just gotten better at hiding it.

Zeke had clearly inherited Harlan's looks, but the Lord Kapitan's cold personality was another matter entirely. Thank the stars.

"High Guardsman," Harlan said, dismissing the aide he'd been conversing with.

"Lord Kapitan," Jove answered with a salute.

His father saluted back, and they walked down the corridor toward the Council Room side by side. Harlan stopped and gave quick instructions to the guards they passed. Say what you would about the man, but Jove had to give him credit. Harlan was good at his job. Each guard saluted and faded back into their near perfect posture, hands folded in front and electropistols waiting at their sides. Most even had swords hanging from belts, meant as a last resort.

"I trust Lady Clara is well," the Lord Kapitan said.

"Yes, Lord Kapitan." Jove kept his eyes trained forward on the tall Council Room doors at the end of the hallway. Had anyone told his father about the pregnancy? Jove decided the present moment wasn't the right time to tell him if not.

Harlan stopped just before the doors and dismissed the guards. Jove looked at him. What was he doing?

Once the guards were out of earshot, Harlan leaned in close. "And the mission?"

Jove shook his head. "Haven't heard anything."

The Lord Kapitan's lips thinned. "Sending Kase wasn't wise. After that stunt with the bikes—"

"He's the best, Lord Kapitan. You agreed with me on that." After several sharp words in the family drawing room. Thankfully, it hadn't come to blows.

"Yet his decision-making leaves something to be desired. Trainee Laurence Hixon still lacks the use of his legs."

Jove took a deep breath. "I sent the best team possible. Kase will prove you wrong."

The last word had unintended bite. Jove didn't take it back, though his stomach turned at his foolish gumption.

Harlan's eyes were daggers, but he merely worked his jaw. Jove hoped he wouldn't do anything here, in full view of the other soldiers. "You'll contact me when you hear anything."

Jove nodded, praying the relief that he'd avoided a shouting match wouldn't bleed onto his features. He straightened his tie and faced the entrance.

Harlan followed and knocked a pattern against the solid wooden doors, a code to tell the guards it was the Lord Kapitan who requested access. The entrance opened inward, and Jove cracked his neck as he followed his father inside.

The Council Room was sparse in décor. All four walls were covered with dark, portraitless tapestries. No windows. Electric lanterns lined the walls, and the only other source of light was the dewdrop chandelier hanging above the round table. Today's meeting wasn't a large one, but the number of chairs made it seem like they were expecting more.

Out of habit, Jove's eyes scanned the walls where armed guards stood at regular intervals, far enough away from the table so as not to crowd nor overhear the people sitting there. The other participants were already seated, which included the Stradats and Heddie. Jove walked over to the table and bowed to each.

He took a seat next to the graying Heddie, who nodded. She was a hawkish woman with a large, beak-like nose—as well as a fearsome, compassionate leader, one Jove was honored to serve under. In all her years in the Watch, she'd seen more than Jove probably ever would.

"Good morning." Stradat Richter smoothed out the papers in front of him. He was near the Lord Kapitan's age, but he wasn't wrinkled in the slightest, and blond streaks wove through his bright red hair. Jove had always figured his face was what had gotten him elected, rather than his pretentious politics.

Harlan took the seat to Jove's right, and Jove tried to relax his tense muscles. His father answered, "And to all of you."

Harlan hadn't even bothered to bow, of course. Jove knew what his father thought of how the country was run. He'd helped formulate the Eudora Jayde mission in the first place.

Heddie nodded to Harlan, leaning past Jove. "Good

of you to join us, Lord Kapitan."

Jove hid a smirk. His father might have intimidated the Stradats, but Heddie could hold her own.

"Now that you're both here, we'd like to get started." Stradat Sarson, the first ever elected woman to her station, tapped her fingers on the table. Her steel-gray hair pulled into a tight bun only enhanced the razor-thin scar jutting from the right corner of her mouth to her ear. She'd served under his father in the military for years, but Jove couldn't stand her.

At least that was one thing he and Harlan had in common.

"Loffler, why don't you start?" Sarson asked, fingering her scar.

The man on Heddie's other side jumped with a snort, and Jove bit back a smile. Loffler's voice was raspy as he began, "Yes, well, the infrastructure committee agreed to the changes in Lower Kyvena concerning the road to the outer gates..."

The final member of the High Council, Stradat Loffler, was a laggard old man whom Jove fully expected to fall over dead any day now. His memory was like a bucket riddled with holes, but a Stradat stayed in their position until death or retirement. Loffler was unlikely to do either, as Kase liked to joke. Jove didn't disagree. The man was pushing eighty-five at least.

As the man droned on, Jove found himself fading. Usually, he paid attention in important meetings such as this, but focusing today was nearly impossible. His mind wandered out into the city, toward home, toward the mountains, toward his brothers. Could he live with himself if something happened to them? Maybe he should've pondered on that more before assigning them to it.

Not that he'd forced them. They'd been given a choice—somewhat. Even so, he wished he'd sent someone else, or even turned Heddie and his father down when they'd dreamed up the mission. The fact they'd agreed had been strange in and of itself, but Heddie was half the brains behind it, and Jove trusted her.

"From my understanding, the Cerls have begun the process of mobilization. Please clarify, Lord Kapitan," Richter said, pushing his red hair back from his forehead. The mention of Cerulene brought Jove back to the present. "Does it simply have to do with our mines failing?"

Harlan nodded. "I have more than one intelligence report saying their foot soldiers have begun amassing at Sol Adrid."

"And do you expect movement other than that?" Sarson asked. A bit of light caught in the crevice of her scar.

Harlan shook his head. "They're no match for our hovers. Besides, it'll take them a month or more to reach the border by foot."

"But they have the technology," Sarson said, her voice chilly. "Surely, after nearly two decades since that traitor Ezekiel Fairchild sold them—"

Bringing up his mother's traitorous brother was a terrible idea. Especially since it was Harlan's orders that had led to his execution. Sarson only brought it up to be petty, Jove guessed, because the Lord Kapitan had refused to bow to her at the beginning of the meeting. Blasted politicians.

Jove cleared his throat. "The king isn't the one pulling the strings. It's his second-in-command—"

"Marcos Correa is a non-issue. Spineless." Sarson

waved her hand in dismissal.

Heddie's jaw clenched before she spoke. "Correa will attack before spring. Because, as you were saying, they have the technology. Our spies indicate they've been building a fleet of airships unlike anything we've seen before. Everyone here seems to be fond of forgetting that."

"Regardless if that information is true or not, they won't be able to traverse the passes in winter," Sarson tried to counter.

"Our outer villages are in danger. He'll take them first," Richter interrupted, rubbing his short-cropped amber beard. "They want our Zuprium."

Harlan slammed his fist on the table, causing Jove's pencil to clatter to the floor. "Of course they do. They're not all dulkops. If it'll keep your stars in your pocket, I'll send a couple squadrons to the border, but we're stretched thin as it is, seeing as enlistment is down."

"Lord Kapitan," Jove interjected, hoping the others ignored his father's jab. "As Stradat Sarson was saying, the passes are treacherous this time of year. We won't be able to get a sizable force through until spring."

Loffler woke up long enough to nod. Maybe he wasn't so bad after all. That or he had no clue what was said. Either way, Jove would take it.

"I can get our airships through." Harlan's fists were still clenched.

Richter leaned forward. "Is that our only option? I'd rather not risk any more of those, especially since the *Eudora Jayde* is out of commission. And we don't know when or if we'll ever be able to restore our mines."

"People will die if we don't," Jove said quietly.

"The mountains are our best protection against invasion." Stradat Sarson smoothed back her gray hair, her chest puffed out. "All things considered, maybe conceding a little ground would allow us time to prepare. It would give us a chance to search for more Zuprium, which could be a good bargaining chip when the time comes."

Heat rose in Jove's body. All those people left to the mercy of a foreign king? He gripped the arms of his chair. "You'd sacrifice our own people?"

Sarson straightened her papers with a firm tap. "We have a full company stationed at Fort Achilles. They can handle any advancing force, and if not, King Filip might be reasonable."

"Our agents in Sol Adrid say otherwise," Heddie said, her green eyes blazing. "Sacrificing a few for the whole is not a viable solution."

"What does Tev Rubika say?" Jove asked. "Can we count on their support if it comes to war?"

Richter rubbed his temples. "They have their own problems. I'd been hoping for more with my daughter Lavinia's betrothal. Their civil war wrecked them."

Jove ran a hand over his face. How were they going to come to a consensus? Sometimes he wished they only had one person making the decisions. That way there was an actual decision made, instead of all the posturing, but that didn't look so good in Cerulene. That was also the reason Tev Rubika was in such bad shape. Get one crazed, power-hungry dictator, and you could kiss your free will goodbye.

No wonder Heddie and his father were desperate to find the Yalvs and ally with them. Cerulene didn't need whatever weapon the ancient natives had.

"Let's table this and reconvene tomorrow morning." Sarson stood up. "Lord Kapitan, put together a plan to send soldiers across the passes in airships. I'll get my aides to pull stats about the outlying villages. Maybe there's something we can do."

"There is."

All eyes flew to Harlan. Jove tilted his head. What else was there besides sending troops?

"And that is?" Richter clenched his fist on top of the table.

Harlan smoothed his mustache and leaned back in his seat. "Use our spies and assassinate Filip, Correa, or whoever the stars you feel is most important. Kick 'em in the mouth."

CHAPTER 14

COLD TEA

Kase

AFTER CONFIRMING THAT KASE WOULD fly directly south until they found some river to follow to what Hallie called Haddon's Pass, the *Eudora Jayde* was in flight without her front windshield once more. Kase just hoped Jove's old map was accurate enough, because he didn't want to keep flying forever.

As he gripped the steering wheel in his clammy hands, he tried not to think about the storm or about the crash, but every ding of the control board thrust his heart into his throat. What if they hit something? Was their fuel too low? He'd switch it to all electric soon. Should he do that now? Yet doing that might overstrain the ship's recently repaired engines, and Ebba would flay him alive.

Kase cursed. What had gotten into him? Why couldn't he think straight?

"What's wrong?" Skibs asked. His eyes looked three sizes too big wearing his own goggles. He only kept Kase company at this point; his brain hadn't healed enough for flying. The dizzy spells were the worst—not to mention he still couldn't recall what had happened after the storm.

Kase barely heard his friend over the wind rushing past his ears. Checking the fuel gauge, he shook his head. "When do you want me to land? We need to refuel soon."

Skibs narrowed his eyes, but he pushed himself out of the seat, presumably to converse with Zeke back in their chamber, though Skibs was head of the mission. Kase kept his gaze straight ahead. All the people on the ship were counting on him. He could do this, but they needed to stop soon.

Skibs climbed back in his seat. "Land when you can."

"Will do." Kase hoped the wind hid the relief bleeding into his reply.

He scanned for anything remotely big enough for the ship. With any luck, they'd find something large enough for a runway, but the ship could use its hover capacities in a pinch. At that point, Kase didn't care which one he found first.

Sweat beaded at his hairline, dripping and pooling on top of his goggles. He jerked, using his left hand to wipe his forehead. Surely he looked normal enough, right?

With the ship flying much lower due to the missing windshield, anything past the carpet of treetops was difficult to see, but after a few more minutes, the trees thinned and opened onto a spotted, shining expanse. Little fingers and splotches of land interrupted the water below like one of the abstract art pieces his mother hated. A bog was not an ideal place to set down the ship, but they were known to have an abundance of yalvar fuel beneath the surface, and the *Eudora* needed fuel. He scanned the horizon for anything past the water-laden ground only to discover that for the next several days, they'd be flying over the bog. The distant mountains Hallie had shown him on the map were barely perceptible on the horizon, only peaks like daggers shrouded in blue mist. Haddon's Pass would be somewhere there, and beyond that, Myrrai.

And in Myrrai, they'd find the Yalvs. Once they found them, they could establish a Zuprium trade and an alliance.

I can do this.

To his left, the forest ended as well, most trees giving way to shrubbery. *Blast.* And they hadn't passed anything suitable for hours. "Think we could find a big enough stretch of dry ground down there to land without sinking the ship?"

Ben looked out and shrugged. "Sure, but maybe near the trees? That way we aren't completely out in the open?"

Slowing the engines and switching on the hover capacities, Kase turned the ship. Even the greenie would approve of such a sluggish turn, but the boy was probably still in the city infirmary trying to recover the use of his legs.

His hands shook, but just outside where the forest ended, he spotted a good swath of brush and grass that didn't glisten with water.

Even with his shaking hands, he managed to set the

craft down better than he had in training. He thrust his hands into his pockets once he'd landed and shut off the ship's engines.

"Okay," Skibs said, once everyone joined them in the cockpit a minute or two later. "Let's go ahead and start preparations for camp tonight. Ebba, will you take a look at the ship? Hallie, will you start prepping to cook..."

Kase couldn't take his eyes away from the ground outside, from the watery puddles, from the shrubbery laced with tall, waving grasses, though his vision blurred further as his heart raced higher.

What in the stars had gotten into him? If he didn't get it together soon, he might as well tell the crew to leave him there to die.

"Kase? Can you hear me?" Zeke asked.

Kase shook his head to clear it. "I heard you."

"Then come on. You're helping me secure the area."

Kase grumbled under his breath and pushed himself out of his seat.

"What was that?" Zeke put a hand on his shoulder.

"Do you have my pistol?"

Zeke grabbed a weapon from the copilot seat. "Here."

By Kase's estimation of the sun, it was mid-afternoon, with only a few clouds dotting the sky. If he was in Kyvena, he might've begged his Hover Captain to train through the midday meal, where he could pretend he was all alone. Instead, he was miles away from the capital, and the Lord Kapitan would kick him off the Crews if he wasn't successful on this mission. Of course, none of that would matter if the thought of flying made him want to hurl.

Stop being a stars-idiot.

He and his brother left the ship, their boots squelching on the sodden ground. Kase looked back at Ebba, whose untucked trousers were soaked nearly to her knees as she tinkered with a panel. The *Eudora Jayde* didn't seem to be sinking into the ground, but Kase didn't think it'd be wise to stay here for long. What if it rained and flooded the already struggling engines?

Zeke waved to Ebba, and she saluted with a wrench in hand. Kase knew the ship wasn't in the best shape, but how much more could she work on it?

Once the uninterrupted view of the sky vanished with the trees, Kase relaxed. He didn't hate it, but the blasted blue mocked him with each cloud winking back.

Every so often, Zeke would stop and break a twig on a smaller tree or bush. Moss covered most of the trees and what open ground the brush didn't conceal. A dull chill waited in the wings, felt with every other breath. Bits of frost clung to the edges of a few of the leafy bushes. Kase shivered.

He kept a tight grip on the handle of his electropistol. According to the map and Hallie, they were still days if not weeks away from finding the Yalven city. An uneasy feeling like stone weighed heavy in Kase's stomach. This continent was mainly uninhabited by people, but apparently, other terrifying creatures haunted the dark spaces between the trees. Kase really didn't fancy running into another dragon. What mythological monster was next? Goblins? Or maybe a Cyclops like the one Odysseus had encountered? Shocks and stars, walking through the woods like this with the goal of "securing the area" wouldn't help against any of those.

Unless the Cerls had somehow followed them over

the ocean.

"You don't know anything about the Battle at Sashiera, do you?" Zeke asked suddenly. He turned off his pistol and stuffed it in the holster attached to his right leg.

Kase ran a hand through his hair, trying to shake the mental image of himself as Odysseus hiding under a sheep to escape a cyclops' cave. "No."

"I'll never forget it." Zeke crossed his arms and inspected the canopy of leaves above.

Kase tilted his head. "Okay?"

"I wasn't supposed to be in any real fighting for months, but the Cerls attacked a border village. I didn't think anyone outside of the military had been told about it."

"And your point?"

His brother met his eyes once more. Kase avoided the hazel depths. The serious tone and lack of spark reminded him of their father.

"The point," Zeke said with a deep breath, "is I killed my first man as I made a tourniquet for another's leg. I heard someone behind me, unsheathed my sword, and swung for all I was worth. The sights, the sounds...everything still haunts me."

With a pristine military-grade boot, Zeke traced small swirling patterns in the dirt. The soft mud ate away at its previous polished shine. "You're scared to fly."

"No, I'm not." Kase gripped his pistol firmly.

Zeke's stare pinned him in place. "*You are,* but before you get upset, know this has happened to billions of people since the beginning of time. Some call it Battle Fright."

"But I've never been in a battle."

Zeke shook his head. "You crash-landed an airship in the middle of a storm. Only the moons know how you did it. You don't have to kill a man to experience something like it."

Kase struggled not to roll his eyes. "Fine, say I have this...thing. What am I supposed to do? Hypothetically."

Zeke took his pistol back out and cocked it. He started off, gesturing for Kase to follow. "First, acknowledge you're scared to fly."

"I'm not."

"Hypothetically, of course."

"Fine, I first have to *acknowledge* I'm scared to fly if I have this Battle Fright. What's next? Anything useful?"

They walked for a quarter mile before Zeke stopped to inspect the ground. In the mud clear of moss and other plants, a hoofprint appeared.

"Looks like we might be able to find some bigger game here. That should make everyone happy." Zeke bent over and broke a few branches on a neighboring bush before standing once more. "After you acknowledge the problem, you can go through the reasons why. This doesn't work for all types of Battle Fright, but it helps if you understand your fear."

"We almost died in a crash. That's the why," Kase grumbled.

Zeke smiled. "And we have you past the first step."

"What? No, I—" Kase stopped when Zeke didn't break eye contact. "Fine, I'm scared to fly. I don't think anyone else would be better off."

"I don't doubt it. Anyway, then you use logic to combat the fear. For example, if I hadn't killed that man, he would've killed me." Zeke's fingers left a muddy streak on his uniform jacket as he brushed them off and continued forward. "I had no choice. Looking at it that way helps."

"But that doesn't help *me* at all."

Zeke spun. "For stars sake, think it through. You crash-landed a hover in a storm. That's why you're nervous about flying. Now, use logic. Try it."

Kase walked a bit further. "If I had been a worse pilot, we wouldn't be having this conversation."

"Very true. Now keep going."

"And if we didn't continue the mission because we were dead, everyone back home would be upset. Not Father, but Mother would be a wreck. Of course, we'd probably lose the war...and that would be even worse."

If Zeke had a problem with Kase talking about Harlan that way, he didn't say anything. Instead, he prodded Kase even more. "What else?"

"If I hadn't been a pilot, someone else would have gone on this mission, and they couldn't handle what I did."

Zeke shrugged. "Okay, next step. You've explored what you're struggling with, why, and the logic behind it. Now, you have to force yourself to face it. Or at least, that's what I did."

"So we fly again?"

"Tomorrow, but it's up to Ben, technically. It'll be too dark tonight, and we should refuel before taking off again."

"Yeah."

"It's not going to be easy, but it'll get better over time. At least in your case. Killing someone, even if he's trying to kill you, is never easy, but it helps knowing you're doing it because everyone is depending on you to keep them safe."

"Is that how you cope?"

Zeke nodded. "I'm sure there's something else I

could do, something healthier, but I don't have the time nor the energy. I'm always on duty, and what I'm doing works fine for now. Perhaps when I'm done, I can do something further. I have insomnia from time to time, but it's better than the nightmares."

The lightning flashed in Kase's mind, and he shook his head to rid himself of the memory. To entirely forget what had happened would be near impossible. But he had to live with it...and figure out how to get them all home.

He stood a little straighter. The crew needed him.

"What do you think that is?"

Kase looked over at his brother and followed his gaze. Off to the right and half-hidden behind trees and under moss stood...something. It wasn't a tree or a bush. It wasn't a dragon—at least, Kase didn't think it was. Zeke cocked his pistol, and Kase followed suit. "Do you think it's an animal or something? Or just a weird...plant? It's not moving."

His brother shook his head. "No, it looks...well, it looks human. See?" He stepped toward the thing, Kase right behind him. "That one bit looks like an arm, but it looks like nature's taken it over."

Zeke held his pistol up, ready to fire. Kase agreed as they got closer, Zeke was right; the thing's arm was out in front as if at one point it had dangled something from its corroding fingers.

It was a statue of a man or had been in a previous life. Moss grew from its cracks, bits of its face were missing, and rain and time had smoothed folds in its stone cloak wrapped around the statue's broad shoulders. Kase reached out and brushed a hand over its surface. Bits of craggy rock caught on the pads of his fingers.

Zeke holstered his electropistol. "I know we're a good way from Myrrai, but I think this is a positive sign at least we're on the right track."

Kase shrugged. "Except no one's probably been out this way for who knows how long. Don't know how much it'll help us." He took his eyes off the statue and spotted another one through the trees. "Look, there's more."

"We should probably go back and get Hallie. She would want to see this."

Kase ignored his brother and strode toward the other statue. "Let's do a little investigating first. Wouldn't want her to be disappointed."

Zeke followed, and once they reached the next statue, they discovered another; each one was in a state of ruin like the first. Kase and Zeke moved through the trees, following the path of statues until finally, it led to a small clearing and towering cliff face.

But it was the structure carved into the stone that stopped them in their tracks.

Bits of Zuprium adorning the stones and the archway into the small courtyard reflected the late afternoon light. The metal wasn't structural from what Kase could tell but added as accents, rimming the bricks and molded into letters decorating the archway.

"Okay, you were right," Kase breathed as he stepped up to the opening, "Hallie should've come with us."

Zeke pulled out his electropistol. "She'll have to come inspect it tomorrow. By the time we get back to camp and then trek back here, it'll be too dark, and after your escapade with the dragon..."

Kase rolled his eyes and stepped through the archway. "Yes, it was terrifying. Yes, it might have burned us to a crisp, but the electropistol worked against it. None of that stars-blasted trash about the dragon's hide being too thick for magic or whatever to get through was true."

"What're you going on about?" Zeke asked as he stepped through the archway. The sparks at the end of his pistol fizzled out. He uncocked it and set it in the holster.

Odd.

"You know, the old stories about knights and mages fighting—" Kase paused at his brother's blank stare. "They're mostly novels from First Earth."

"You know I don't read."

Kase shrugged and turned back toward the courtyard. Cracked and weed-ridden stone covered the floor and led to an even larger archway and decaying wooden door. He crept across the stone and grasped the handle.

But the door didn't budge. Kase tugged, grunted, and tugged again. A light breeze like whispers tousled his curls. "Blast it. It's locked."

He released the handle and kicked the door for good measure.

"Don't do that!"

Kase crossed his arms and turned. "Didn't hurt anything."

"You're impossible sometimes, you know that, right?" Zeke stepped up next to him and put a hand to the door. "It feels like stone, but my eyes tell me it's wood."

Kase snorted. "Must be that Yalven magic. That writing above the entrance definitely looks like what was on the cover of that book Hallie was reading the other day."

"Yalven magic..." Zeke rubbed his chin. "I don't

know much about the Yalvs myself, but I doubt it. If they supposedly had all that power, why run away to Tasava? Why not blast us with fire or turn us all into rodents?"

"You really should read more," Kase said with a laugh. "But maybe Hallie can tell us what all this is. We should head back."

"We'll finish our route." Zeke led him out of the courtyard and into the forest once more. At the edge of the trees, Kase chanced a look back. The structure hadn't changed, but the breeze picked up again. A breeze that nearly sounded like words in his ears.

Kase shivered. While the Bay of Storms and dragon had been terrifying enough, he had a feeling whatever the structure was, it would be worse.

After they covered their assigned territory with no other incidents or signs of danger, the duo headed toward the ship, using bits of broken branches and twigs Zeke had left behind to mark their path.

Coming out of the trees, the *Eudora* loomed in front of them, its exterior gleaming. Even with the crash, the outside was still in pretty good shape. The marvels of technology, Kase supposed.

Ebba appeared, a grease-streaked rag in hand, the sun's dying red glow making her skin appear even darker. "Everything seems to be okay. Nothing loose, missing, or busted. We're running low on fuel, though. You were right. And this bog will have some of the best fuel if you can somehow avoid mixing too much water with it."

Zeke raised a brow, walking past her to enter the ship. Kase nodded. "I'll do that tomorrow."

Ebba smiled at the ship. "She's just beautiful. *Eudora* is gonna spoil me."

Kase shrugged.

Footsteps came from the staircase ramp, and Hallie waved. "Would one of you get the fire going?"

Kase looked at Ebba, then back at Hallie. He dreaded another night of her cooking, but he wasn't up to volunteering. And judging by the silence, neither was anyone else. He sighed. "Did you ask Skibs if it'd be okay? We don't want to alert anyone to our position. And using more of our reserved wood might be costly later on."

"He found some dry wood at the edge of the forest and said it was fine as long as we started it now, so hurry!" Hallie scrambled back up the steps. She tripped on the last one but caught herself before she fell off. Zeke said something about her being careful and followed her inside.

He turned to Ebba. "So, how are you at..."

"The wood's over there." She stretched and pointed.

"Why didn't Skibs start it?"

"Said he had a headache." She shrugged. "Here's the flint. You should be able to use some of that thick brush for kindling. It's mostly dry now."

"No, I can't—" Kase protested as Ebba shoved the bit of flint into his hand.

"Bye!" Ebba scurried off toward the ship before he could protest.

Blast it.

Kase looked down at the offending rock in his hand. Scars from pocketknives used to light fires marred its dark surface. Most blades wouldn't dent even the weakest Zuprium. The near-mystical metal was a boon of a find for the descendants of First Earth after living centuries without any way to make their technology work properly. It was amazing how many leaps and bounds Jayde's Engineer Corps had made.

Kase ran his thumb over the marks marring the flint. His knife weighed a thousand pounds in his pocket. He could do this. The First Settlers and their descendants dealt with worse hardships, and they'd brought humanity from the brink of extinction—slowly and over the course of a millennium, but they'd done it. Kase Shackley could light a fire. It wasn't difficult. He'd watched Ben and his brother start one dozens of times in the past few weeks.

He stuffed the flint in his jacket pocket and looked around for the wood Ebba had pointed to. The wet earth beneath him dampened the knees of his trousers as Kase used one of the sturdier bits of wood to dig a small pit. The bottom of the shallow hole filled with water from the ground.

"Blasting shocks."

He moved over a bit, didn't dig a hole, and stacked the wood in what he thought was a good formation, all coming to a point without the pit underneath and tucked the kindling in the spaces between. Maybe if he simply tried to light it that way? The wet ground would prevent the fire from spreading, and he only needed it to last long enough to make dinner, right?

Fishing the flint and his knife from his pockets, he gripped them loosely in his hands. His breaths came faster. He tightened his hold on the flint as he flicked open the knife.

"You can do this," he whispered to himself. "If you don't, you'll have to eat something cold and probably wet."

Yet as he scraped the knife across the surface of the flint, screams echoed in his mind. Flames grew at the corners of his eyes. Blood coated his hands in a memory he could never forget.

It's your fault.

Kase blinked hard, bringing himself back to the present. The damp, earthy smell assaulted his senses, and a breeze chilled the sweat on his face. He stood, dropping the flint and pocketing his knife.

Where was Zeke? He could light the fire, couldn't he?

As he climbed into the ship, voices filtered from the food storage. Hallie laughed at something his brother said, each peal like a soft bell. With a scowl, Kase peeked in. He coughed when they didn't notice him. "Zeke? Come here a sec?"

"Sure." Zeke turned back to Hallie, a crooked grin on his face that Kase had never seen before. "Don't get any wise ideas about those potatoes, now."

She grinned. "Wouldn't dream of it, Sir Lieutenant Colonel."

Instead of waiting for him to follow, Kase strode into the corridor, not liking the feeling in his chest. What were they thinking? Now was hardly the right time to be *flirting*, moons above.

After a few seconds, Zeke joined him, still smiling in a way that made Kase's stomach churn. "What is it?"

Kase relaxed his fists, trying to control his tone. "Would you start the fire? I've set up the wood, and the flint is out there beside it."

Zeke stared at him for a moment, confusion darkening his brow. After a moment, his eyes dropped to Ana's ring on Kase's hand and softened in understanding. "Remember what we talked about today?"

Kase looked down at his boots. He stopped fiddling

with the ring—stars, he hadn't even realized he'd started.

"You need to acknowledge the problem," Zeke whispered.

He was right, but Kase didn't have an issue with acknowledging it. He ran a hand down the smooth metal wall of the *Eudora*. "I can't get through this one."

"It might help to at least—"

"It *won't*." Kase's ears burned. "The flying thing, sure. But this? You don't get it. Just start the fire, will you?"

Zeke chewed on the inside of his cheek before squeezing Kase's shoulder lightly. "All right."

Kase nodded in thanks as he left, the pit in his stomach growing. Zeke was just trying to help, he knew that, but this was one fear he couldn't face just yet.

KASE KNEW HALLIE WOULD BE too excited to eat dinner after hearing about the discovery that afternoon. Light from the fire only enhanced her overly large grin.

"Oh my blessed stars!" she squealed. "Are you sure they were genuine ruins?"

Kase shrugged. "The building didn't seem too old, but the statues leading to it on the other hand might have been."

Hallie stood, bits of potato and dried carrots flinging from the plate held loosely in her hand. "Do you think we have enough light now? I really want to go inspect! Oh stars, I can't believe we've found—"

"Not tonight," Zeke interrupted. "You and Kase lost that privilege."

Hallie sat down with a grumble, but she eventually sighed. "All right, but I'll go first thing in the morning."

"I'll go with you," Skibs spoke up. "Kase and Ebba can handle the refuel. Zeke can keep watch here. But remember, we can't waste too much time here if we want to finish this mission before winter sets in. I'm well enough to shoot a pistol." He threw the unsalvageable scraps of his dinner into the fire. It crackled and spat a few sparks before returning to normal.

Even though Kase hadn't lit the fire himself, he didn't appreciate the mocking flames.

Using Zeke's method, he found that once he put his mind to it, he could easily work through the crash. Maybe it was because he'd been able to put his superior skills to the test? Maybe it was because no one had died? In any case, he tried to do the same with the fire, but as soon as flames began to flicker in his mind, his heart drummed too loudly against his ribcage. Trying to calm himself, he focused on the forest surrounding them. It didn't work. Like he'd told Zeke, he didn't have a problem acknowledging what had happened. It was just everything else.

"Well, if that's all settled..." Ebba's curls escaped from her bun and bounced as she stood abruptly, spinning a length of twine around the fingers of her uninjured hand. Her voice echoed loudly off the nearby trees: "Any of you wanna challenge the sling master?"

Kase shook his head. He'd completely zoned out again. Stars, Zeke was right. Whatever this "Battle Fright" stuff was, it could really knock a person down. He peeked over at his brother.

Zeke chuckled as he finished the last of his dinner and dusted his fingers on his trousers. "Us Shackley boys used to have slinging contests out in our courtyard. Kase here busted one of the Manor's windows."

"I still won," Kase huffed, but he stood, glad for the distraction. "And if I remember correctly, Jove took the blame for it."

"Mother's face was nearly purple."

Kase grinned, relief bleeding into every muscle. "In other words, we'll take you up on your challenge. Skibs?"

His friend shook his head. "Nah, never tried and never will. An electropistol is good enough for me."

"Will someone teach me?" Hallie brushed off her trousers with one hand. Kase smirked. He'd win this one no problem.

"Come on." Zeke grabbed Skibs' shoulder. "Kase isn't a bad teacher, believe it or not."

Ebba laughed, and Kase glared at her. "I won nearly every time my brothers challenged me."

She raised a dark brow. "Fine then. Prove your worth, *city boy*."

He took the twine sling from Ebba and picked out a stone from under a nearby tree. It was the size of his palm and relatively smooth. While it had a few crags along the side, it would work. He walked back to the fire, ignoring Ebba's smirk and Hallie's too-excited grin.

He cracked his neck and stretched his arms out, loosening his shoulders. Years had passed since those sunny afternoons in the Manor courtyard with his brothers, Ana cheering on from the side if she managed to escape their mother's latest tea of overly dignified ladies in corsets. He swallowed hard and shook out his arms a little, the rock and sling still in his hands.

"Stop stalling," Ebba barked, laughter lacing her voice. "I know my skills are intimidating, but there's no harm in admitting you're scared."

"If you had any real *skills*, you'd know you have to get loose first," Kase threw back at her. He pushed the small loop over his pointer finger and grasped the knot on the other side of the twine. "Now, what's my target?"

Zeke dug in his pocket and pulled out his pocketknife. "Can we borrow a piece of parchment from your sketchpad, Hallie?"

She nodded and rummaged through her book, finally ripping a page free. "I messed up this sketch the other day when I tried drawing that dragon."

Sure enough, a rough outline of what Kase and Hallie had fled from in the forest was scrawled across the page. It wasn't the best, but not terrible considering her shoulder still hadn't fully healed. "You might have a little trouble slinging with your shoulder."

She shrugged. "I can use my other arm."

"Your left?"

"Sure."

"Whatever you say." Kase placed the rock in the sling's split pouch as Zeke stuck the drawing of the dragon in a tree about fifteen yards away. Once his brother finished, Kase whipped the sling in a figure eight motion. It was well-made; he personally preferred a leather pouch and sturdier cord, but it still felt good with the weight at the end.

When he was certain of his target, he let the rock fly. It smacked the tree with a soft thump just below the dragon's gaping mouth.

He put his hands on his hips. "That's how you sling a rock, my friends."

Hallie's eyebrows rose, and Zeke shook his head, a small smile spiriting across his features. Skibs rolled his eyes, but Ebba scowled. "I could've hit the thing square in the eye."

Kase picked up another rock. "Let's see who's best, then."

She stalked up and snatched the sling from his fingers. Kase turned back to the others. "You in?"

Zeke held up a stone. "I'll go after Ebba. Hallie, find the smoothest stone you can."

She nodded and headed toward the far side of the ship while Ebba warmed up her uninjured limb. Kase looked at Skibs. "You sure you don't want to try?"

He pushed his blond waves from his eyes. "I'd rather heckle."

"You're a terrible heckler."

"Not true."

Kase raised a single brow. "Then why aren't you commenting on how Ebba looks like she's drowning with that terrible warm-up? Especially troubling as she's only doing it with one arm."

"I heard that, you *sterning* oaf."

Skibs let out a small laugh. "I was planning on only heckling you. You're an easy target."

Kase narrowed his eyes. "Unfortunately for you, I'm an excellent shot, as you saw."

"Sure." Skibs rolled his eyes.

Ebba, it turned out, was just as good as Kase even with one arm broken. She hit the target a little to the right of Kase's mark and puffed out her chest for a full minute while Zeke warmed up. Kase's brother was a little worse, hitting the edge of the parchment tacked to the tree, and Skibs broke his only-heckle-Kase rule and ribbed on Zeke for being the soldier with the worst aim. His brother only laughed.

And then there was Hallie.

Her face scrunched with concentration. If it wasn't

chilly that evening, she probably would have been sweating, too. Kase hid a small smile behind his hand.

With a violent swing of her left arm, she loosed the rock at the worst time. The stone flew backward and clattered into the empty cockpit.

Ebba cackled. "*Sterne*, you're worse than my brother Eren. And he's *bad*. Couldn't hit a wheat field at harvest."

Kase caught the scholar's blush, and he chewed the inside of his cheek. *Not bad for her off hand.* Skibs was silent, but Zeke had a bit of encouragement. "You have decent aim landing it in the cockpit like that. Next time, you should—"

Kase stepped forward, drowning out his brother's next words. "His advice will probably be crap. Sorry, Zeke."

His brother waved a hand and went about trying to find another rock for Hallie, while Ebba inspected the target to make sure it was still secure to the tree. Skibs poked a stick at the fire, sparks flying up in the air and disappearing into the dusky sky.

"You're better off learning from an expert," Kase continued, if only to break the awkward silence.

Hallie shrugged and handed him the sling. He took the small loop and tightened it around his finger. "Make sure you get it wound up properly without tangling the string. Plus, you're too tense. Relax a little and keep both eyes open. You closed both last time."

"Did not!"

"Did too."

She tapped her foot. "Anything else?"

Kase looked back at the cockpit, then back to her. "What were you aiming at?"

"The target, obviously!" She waved her hand in the

air.

Still holding the sling in his fingers, Kase walked to the tree and jammed a finger in the center of the target. "You don't aim for the entire thing. *Focus here.*"

"But that's so small! There's no way I'll hit that."

Zeke ambled back, offering her another stone. "Listen to him. He's right."

She took in a loud breath through her nose before turning to Kase. He straightened his shoulders and pointed again at the center of the target. "Focus on this little area with his eye. Even if you miss, you'll still hit the target as a whole."

"I guess that makes sense."

He picked up another rock and strode back to her. "Relax, keep both eyes open, aim for the center of the target. And remember, you're a beginner, so don't try to get too fancy with the sling. Here, do this."

Kase placed his rock in the pouch and held it, pointing it directly at the target. "Put your off foot slightly in front of the other and square your shoulders. Once you're ready, pull the sling back." He slung the rock back and rolled his shoulder forward, the ammunition following his movements a second behind. "Then release just above the target while your hand is still in motion."

The rock hit the target with a smack—just below the dragon's eye, according to Ebba's groan. "I guess that was decent."

He grinned and held out the sling to Hallie. "Got it?"

She bit her lip but nodded, taking the twine from him. She looped the ring around her middle finger, and Kase quickly grabbed her hand, pulling the twine off. While cold, her skin was soft without the callouses of Kase's own. "Not that way. Put it around your index finger."

"Oh." Her voice was strained as he tightened the loop on her other finger.

He let go and handed her the other end, pointing to the knot. "Hold this between your index and thumb. Not too tightly, just enough so it doesn't fling the rock before you're ready."

She nodded again, setting the rock into the pouch. "Then what?"

He pointed to her feet. "If you're slinging with your left hand, put your right foot forward. Good. Now hold the rock away from you and aim it at the center of the target."

Hallie still looked skeptical, but she followed his instructions, the tip of her tongue peeking out the corner of her mouth. Zeke walked up beside Kase, staying out of harm's way. "Don't forget to keep both eyes open."

Kase bit his tongue on a retort. "When you're ready, hold onto it tightly. Sling it back and then forward, letting go just above your target."

After taking a few deep breaths, Hallie slung her arm back, her tongue still poking out.

The smack on the tree was lost in Hallie's jubilant shout. "I did it!"

Ebba gasped. "You hit the eye!"

Hallie bounced on the balls of her feet. She turned to Kase. "Did you see that?"

"Great shocks, I saw it." It was beginner's luck, but she'd beaten them all with that shot. He couldn't help but smile. "Think what you'll be able to do if you keep practicing."

Hallie beamed as she raced over to the parchment and inspected her handiwork. Kase watched her go, a hint of pride bubbling up in his chest. Zeke put a hand on his shoulder. "I knew you were a good teacher."

"Maybe there's hope for me yet."

Hallie

SETTLED WITH HER SKETCHPAD, HALLIE was on watch that night for the first few hours. Part of her was glad the rest of the crew trusted her enough to do the task, but the bigger half was uneasy. She was pitiful with the electropistol at best, so hopefully her shouts would be enough to get the others to come running if she needed help. However, she still had Ebba's sling beside her and a stone, so maybe she'd have another stroke of luck if she was forced to fight something.

The lighthearted moments of a few hours ago had disappeared with the sun. No matter how hard she wished they wouldn't—even the thought of exploring a potential Yalven ruin in the morning didn't banish her memories.

Tomorrow would mark three years since Jack's death. The twenty-third of October. Three years, and she still felt a deep sting in her chest. A thousand years wouldn't be long enough for her to get over it.

Sometimes, she wondered about the different life she would have led if Jack had survived. She usually didn't let it bother her too much, but the anniversary...well, she was only human.

If Jack hadn't died, she wouldn't have attended the University. She would have stayed home, her brother taking the savings and heading to school. If Jack hadn't died, her parents wouldn't have hidden away in their inn, happy to let their daughter do whatever she wanted out in the world without a care. That seemed backward to Hallie, but she supposed she should be grateful. If they'd known about the *Eudora* mission beforehand, they might have argued with her about it, if they'd cared enough to try.

But the other thought, the worst of them all, flashed in her mind. Like it did most times when she let her guard down.

If Jack hadn't died, she would've been perfectly content running the inn. She would've been married to Niels. She never would have known an entirely new world awaited her in Kyvena. And when she thought about that, a part of her was relieved her brother was dead.

She was a horrible excuse for a sister...maybe even the worst kind of person for even thinking that. She shivered.

Leaning forward to turn up the lantern, Hallie pulled her jacket closer around her. Thankfully they'd found a spare in one of the compartments, as the other one had woken the dragon. Too bad they couldn't leave the fire burning through the night. Ben's reasons made sense, but she doubted the Cerls had made it through the Bay of Storms. They didn't have Kase to fly them.

Unless they'd figured out another way through.

Trying to focus on her sketch of the *Eudora* she'd started a few days ago, she bit her lip, hoping to tame the sloppy lines into something coherent. Her fingers shook from the cold; her breaths puffed out, a crystalline mist above her lips. The moonlight fell in fractures through the clouds above and onto the page, waltzing with the lantern light.

Gracious day. She growled and ripped out the page. Crumpling it, she tossed it over her shoulder onto the open walkway of the ship. When would her shoulder heal enough for her to sketch again? All her lines looked as if inebriated ants had trampled across her page.

"What'd that parchment ever do to you?"

Zeke stood in the doorway, two steaming cups in his hands. She forced a smile, even as her teeth chattered. "It doesn't want to be properly sketched on. I had to punish it."

"Ah," Zeke said, handing her a cup and squeezing past. "Makes perfect sense."

Hallie curled her hands around the hot drink. She breathed in the bittersweet tang of tea. "Thank you. I forgot my gloves inside. But where did you get the hot water?"

The tall soldier pulled up a mossy log they'd used as a seat earlier and sat below her. "We appreciate you sacrificing your hands for our safety, but it's okay if you fetch them. As for the hot water, I found a small burner buried in the storage closet. It's not large enough to do much more than a couple cups of tea, but . . ."

Hallie took a sip. "I'm not complaining. Thank you, again. I didn't expect anyone else to be awake."

Zeke ruffled his hand through his caramel-colored hair. Hallie had to blink for a moment to make sure it wasn't Kase sitting in front of her, and she hoped the unexpected heat on her cheeks wasn't visible in the dim light of the lantern. Kase was probably deeply asleep, unaware his snores could wake the dead. Not out here being thoughtful for once.

Zeke rested his head on his fist. "I had a weird dream and couldn't get back to sleep. Figured you'd appreciate the hot drink."

"Oh, I do. I feel particularly privileged for being gifted one of the coveted tea bags."

Zeke laughed. "True. This was a good occasion for it...since I went ahead and made myself a cup."

"So, you gave me one because you didn't want to be the only one in trouble?"

"And it's appropriate that the slinging master receive some sort of prize." Zeke took a sip of his tea. The daintiness of the cup didn't match his strong demeanor.

Setting hers on the stair, she stood, stretching her legs. She cursed as the pencil and sketchpad hit the ground with a muffled thump.

"Why do I always do that?" She bent to pick them up the same time Zeke did. He got up to help, but she held up a hand. "It's okay. I've got it."

"Sorry." He smiled. "Just trying to be a gentleman."

Hallie laughed. "Oh, do I long for the days of polite society."

She set the drawing utensils next to her cup and jogged in place to warm herself up. They were getting closer and closer to winter by the day, and that made her nervous. How much further did they have before they reached Myrrai? If they were to broker an alliance and secure a Zuprium trade, would they reach home before winter raged? Would they even be able to make it back through the Nardens?

"So," Zeke started, "as you're the scholar, what're your thoughts about the mission so far? Have you found anything interesting other than the dragon? I feel like I should be more shocked than I am about that whole ordeal, but everyone knows Tasava isn't anything like our own continent."

He said it so matter-of-factly, as if it were an everyday occurrence. Hallie shook her head. "Nothing. I wish I could tell you more, but none of my classes ever covered this part of the world. I did that reading on my own with the records we have, which aren't incredibly forthcoming. Only the Jaydian government knew the Yalvs went into hiding over here." She scuffed the tip of one boot in the dirt. "Aren't you worried we won't be able to get back?"

Zeke took a long sip of tea. "I have to believe we will. Jove has faith in us, or he wouldn't have picked us. There's a reason Kase is on this mission despite being...well, Kase. He's one of the best pilots there is."

"No kidding. I still can't believe we survived not only the storm, but the landing, too. And when that Cerl shot at us?"

Zeke nodded. "I could hardly believe it either, but here we are, and we have Kase to thank for it."

"I already did. I'm sure it went straight to his head." Hallie rolled her eyes.

"He's not so bad once you get to know him. He's just terrible at making new friends. Being the Lord Kapitan's son doesn't help much."

She wouldn't say Kase's treatment of her in the beginning was simply *terrible at making new friends*. Although Zeke's tone was light, Hallie still blushed, but she pressed on. "But you're also the Lord Kapitan's son, so..."

Zeke's smile was wry. "Kase has had it rougher than me, especially since Ana died. He took it hard. The press was all over it because she was a Shackley. Don't get me wrong, Kase can be a stars-idiot, but he does have a softer side."

Hallie didn't know how to respond. Of course, she didn't understand how his life was. She wasn't anyone of importance, but that still didn't mean he could treat someone like dirt.

"He's a good pilot, and he taught me how to use the sling. I'm thankful he's here," Hallie said by way of apology.

"Me, too. Ebba's also a whiz at fixing this ship. She's truly a genius." Zeke stood.

"Exactly. I'm amazed she was able to do what she did after we landed on the beach." She played with the chain holding Jack's pocket watch and looked out at the darkness surrounding them. She stood. "I'm going to do a quick loop around the ship and then get back to sketching. I still have a little while until I need to wake you."

Zeke raised his cup to her. "I'll try to get back to sleep then. You should probably finish your tea before it gets cold. And I'd suggest taking the electropistol when you do your loop. Or at least the sling."

"Oh, right." She grabbed the cup and took a sip. Already lukewarm. She coughed.

"What's wrong?"

She shook her head. "I hate cold tea."

He laughed and took it from her. Holding the string of the tea bag with his thumb, he poured the liquid out to the side of the staircase ramp. He tipped his head. "See you in a few hours."

She nodded as he walked up the stairs and out of sight. Blowing out through her lips, she grabbed the pistol and cocked it. It was probably a safer bet than the sling, though she put the latter in her jacket pocket. The electric sparks at the end of the pistol provided a little light, too. She began her slow circuit.

When she came back to the steps, she smiled. At the top sat a pair of men's gloves.

CHAPTER 15

NOTHING BUT DUST

Hallie

FROST LACED THE GRASSES AND underbrush the next morning, and with each step Hallie and Ben took through the trees, a pleasant crunching followed. It was the loudest sound. For Hallie, the memories of that day three years ago kept her mouth closed. She didn't know why Ben was so quiet, but ever since he'd woken up after falling onto the beach, he hadn't had much to say.

They'd been traveling along the route Zeke had given them for at least a quarter of an hour, though that was an estimate on Hallie's part. Sometimes she wished she'd bought herself an actual working pocket watch, but that was only in times such as these. She rubbed her thumb over the cover of her broken one.

Her mind reviewed the last passage from the *Gate*

of Time book as they walked. It kept her busy, at least.

"The Gate of Time for which this book is aptly named is something I still find curious. Having studied it from a distance, I was able to discern very little about its power and purpose here on this planet. The Yalvs are also less willing to speak of the object as it has something to do with their religion, though not all Yalvs follow their god's edicts and bylaws fastidiously regarding the Gate."

Hallie found Jasper Morgan's words just as curious as he found whatever the Gate was. She'd read about the Essences, or what little there was about them in the University library, but not a single text referenced the Gate.

"The most I can get out of the current Lord Elder is: 'Anoheme caraten amha Toro.' While I'm well-versed in their language, I am unable to translate anything except for the god's name, Toro. The same can be said about the inscription upon the Gate's stones: 'Anora Yas Ess Vanaktr.' I believe it has something to do with the Essences, but those beings, like the Gate, are a mystery to myself at this time."

It was the words even Morgan was unable to translate that intrigued her most. The language predated the Landing for certain, but if Morgan had no idea what the words meant, how could Hallie hope to figure them out? And then there was the bit about how he believed the Gate and Essences were connected.

Stars. She wished they were in Myrrai already. Then she could ask all the questions she pleased.

It'd taken her hours to translate those paragraphs the previous evening once Zeke had gone to bed. She still wondered why Professor Christie had tasked her with this if even she couldn't decipher some of the words. How was this supposed to help her with the Yalvs?

As she and Ben continued to search, sunlight peeked through the trees and caught on the crystallized flora around them.

"Such a pretty flower," Hallie cooed at the red and gold plant in front of her. It looked like two different stars piled on top of one another, the gold underneath. She paused and fished out her sketchpad and pencil as Ben halted and looked back.

"This place is something out of a dream, isn't it?" Ben mused as he holstered his electropistol. He reached out and touched the flower in question. "Makes you wonder why we haven't explored this continent more."

Turning to a new page, she gave him a smile. "I'd say the Bay of Storms and dragons might deter the weak of heart."

He laughed. "True. I still can't believe you and Kase ran into something like that and lived. I wonder how the Yalvs deal with them."

She held her tongue to the side of her mouth as she sketched a sloppy outline of the star-shaped flower before her. Jack always teased she'd bite off her tongue one day.

She shook the memory of his laughter out of her mind. *Focus on the flower. Focus on the petals.*

She wished she knew what type it was. After she sketched it, she'd grab a few to take with her. They would be nice to put in a cup to brighten up the lavatory. Kase would probably think it silly, but he was busy fueling up the ship with Ebba at present anyway.

"I'm still just as shocked as you are." Hallie finished her quick sketch and returned her supplies to her satchel before snatching a few of the flowers. "But the Yalvs have their power, whatever that might be. Probably comes in handy from time to time."

"True," Ben said with a shrug. "Guess we'll find out soon."

They continued walking a bit further and finally found one of the statues Zeke and Kase had described. Hallie sketched it on the same sheet as the flower before they continued on, finding more statues.

They'd finished inspecting one more corroded than the last when Hallie saw something out of the corner of her eye: a glimmer of light through the trees, like a reflection.

"I think that's it!" She pointed to the gleam.

As they inched through the trees, the sight unfolding in front of them made her stomach tighten and her eyes mist over. The structure was carved out of the cliff face, just as the others had said. The glimmer of light, though, was the Zuprium accents reflecting the early morning light.

"Oh stars," Hallie whispered. "I can't believe I'm actually seeing—I'm actually seeing this with my own eyes. A real Yalven temple."

Crack.

Hallie whipped her head around, eyes scanning the ground and surrounding trees. Nothing. No animals, no crashing trees. Ben pulled out his pistol, sparks flying from the tip.

"What was that?" he asked, finger hovering over the trigger.

A bird the color of rubies flew past and landed on a limb near the tree line. They waited a beat, two, three, but nothing else moved.

She breathed out slowly, the soft exhale joining the light breeze across her cheeks. "Probably just a branch falling?"

They turned back toward the structure, and Hallie

caught the words etched into the first archway. "Stars, this really is amazing. Just look at this. This dialect probably dates back to...well, much further than mankind's first landing on Yalvara."

Each letter stood about a hand's breadth in height, some of the edges eroded with time.

Ben hadn't released his grip on the pistol. "What does it say?"

Hallie shrugged and pulled out her supplies. "I could probably give you a rough translation, but it's better if I copy it down and reference one of the books I brought to be sure."

As her pencil whisked across the page, a faint whispering tickled her ears. She whipped her head around again, trying to find the source. Nothing. "Did you hear that?

Ben, who'd been running his fingers over the stone bricks, turned. "What?"

She shook her head. "Never mind."

The whispering still tickling her ears, she finished copying the roughly carved letters and put away her supplies. She was probably just tired. Last night hadn't been very restful.

"From my research, this courtyard would've been used for cleansing oneself," she said as she stood and followed Ben through the archway. "The ancient Yalvs believed these places to be sacred, and if they wanted to use the temple, they needed to present a clean body and heart."

Ben prowled the edges of the small courtyard and stopped at the door. "Amazing, really, my ancestors built this..."

His words were whispered and barely audible above the wind, but Hallie had caught them. Her heart stammered in her chest, cool shock tingling her limbs. "Your...your what?"

Ben spun, his pistol flinging sparks. Hallie leapt out of the way, falling to the rough stone ground and scraping her palm. Fresh blood bubbled up through the small punctures.

Ben put away his weapon and bent down beside her. "Oh stars, Hallie. I'm sorry. I thought I heard something, and then, I just reacted. I'm glad you're okay."

Hallie wiped her hands on her trousers and pushed herself up. "It's all right, but what you said..."

She trailed off as Ben straightened and fiddled with the end of his untucked shirt beneath his Watch uniform jacket. The morning sunlight made his hair and eyes practically glow as he looked at her, his lips pressed together. Finally, he sighed. "I'm part Yalven. Through my mother's side. That's one of the reasons I was so keen on heading this mission."

Hallie's heart beat in her chest as excitement thrummed through her veins. "*Really?* I can't believe you haven't said something before. I have so many questions. But of course, if you'd rather keep that private...I'm sorry. You probably don't want to talk about it."

"It's all right," Ben said with a shrug. "I don't know much. My mother died when I was young, and Father never liked talking about her."

"That's...that's awful." Hallie swallowed the words aching to climb out her mouth. She wanted to know more. She'd always wanted to meet someone who had any connection to the Yalvs, just so she could ask them all sorts of questions.

She'd been only sixteen when she'd found the

painting of a woman as pale as Firstmoon with midnight hair and glowing golden eyes in the attic of her family's inn. Her father had said it was someone her great grandmother had known, but Hallie found the blush in her father's cheeks suspicious. Jack had dismissed it, and Hallie had nearly forgotten about it until she'd gotten to the University.

In her required history course, a nearly identical portrait graced a page in the Yalven culture section of the textbook. That's when she knew she had to change her focus to Yalven Studies. Her great grandmother had known one of them, and by the stars, Hallie had to know more.

Crack.

The sound echoed against the cliff face, and Hallie flinched. "Gracious day, good thing we aren't standing under that tree—"

Louder whispers took her breath away as the wind picked up.

"We can go a little deeper," Jack laughed. *"The strange light was a bit further. Right, Niels?"*

Hallie shook her head. She could almost see Niels' flashing smile in return and smell the bit of sweat he'd worked up trekking through the cave. She inhaled the gritty dust as it floated from the ceiling of the old mine. Their words echoed in the darkness looming ahead.

Her own voice was a shadow of what it had been then. *"But Papa said the mines aren't stable."*

Niels' voice joined the others. *"Come on, Hal. Where's your sense of adventure?"*

"Yeah!" Jack added. *"If you wanna turn back, go ahead, but you can't have any gold then."*

Except what they found was far from gold.

She blinked. What was going on? Why did it feel

like she was there, back in the mountains? Was her mind playing tricks on her? Because of what today was?

Hallie looked over at Ben. "Did you hear…"

But he simply stumbled toward the door, his face as white as the snow topping the Nardens. She followed, her footsteps muffled with the foliage covering the courtyard floor.

Vines grew through the cracks in the arched doorway carved into the cliff face. Brushing her hand against the vines, she frowned at the rough touch of the plant itself. She pulled a bit away, and her breath caught in her chest. All the unease from the past few minutes melted away.

Carvings decorated the stone, each one telling an ancient story. Bits of her own blood speckled the stone as she continued to inspect the artwork. The story engraved on the one in front of her told her of a battle with an enormous lizard-like creature. The wings on the monster spread toward the heavens, and miniature carvings of people waved swords.

"A dragon," she breathed. She peeked over at Ben, who stared blankly at the door itself.

When he noticed her looking, pink colored his cheeks. He ran a hand over the surface of the rotting wood. "I just can't believe they're actually real."

"I know."

Hallie gripped the unadorned Zuprium handle and pulled. The door creaked and got caught on the courtyard's overgrowth, but with Ben's help, she tugged it open.

Holy stars and heavens, if only Professor Christie could've been here with me.

As she and Ben stepped over the threshold, a soft sobbing reached her ears, the cries jagged and gaining in pitch.

"Hello?" Her voice shook.

Ben looked at her funny, his eyes boring into hers. "You heard that too, then?"

In the dim light coming through the slats in the massive door, she could just see the back of the room. It was barely larger than the cockpit on the *Eudora*, smelling of dust. It reminded her of something else, but the cries got louder, drowning out every other sense. She spun in the small space, searching wildly for the source of the voice, but there was no one else there. Only...

Swords?

The arched and crumbling room was full of all kinds. Intricate carvings decorated the blades. On most, they looked to be some form of Yalven, but there were too many unfamiliar letters and figures to be sure. Each pommel had a gemstone square in the center. They winked at her like stars.

"It's an armory," Ben said, bending down to inspect one. "The archway stone had carved battle scenes. It has to be."

As suddenly as it began, the crying fell away. She barely heard it now, almost like it'd been smothered in cotton.

Or like it had never been there at all.

Grunting from the effort, she picked up one of the blades. The grip was warm, and it must've weighed nearly fifteen or twenty pounds. The blade was a silvery metal, mixed with tell-tale bronze colored Zuprium. "Guess you're right."

She glanced at the others. All the same, except for the jewels in the pommels. Each one was a different sort; the sword she'd chosen had a deep green one. The gem's color reminded her of mazelberry leaves in her mother's garden. It wasn't jade, but it might've been an emerald.

"There's no way we can carry them all back," she said, "but we'll bring Kase and Zeke next time. They'll be excited to use those impressive muscles of theirs for once."

Ben laughed. "Zeke, maybe. Kase, on the other hand..."

He grabbed a sword with a ruby pommel and gave it an experimental swing. The metal screeched and sparked on the stone as it met the wall.

"Be careful!"

Ben held the edge up to his eyes. "Didn't even leave a scratch. Let's head back, shall we?"

She'd just stepped on the threshold of the doorway and pushed the rotting wood aside when someone *screamed*—an unholy, otherworldly death scream. It rent the air and stuck into her very being, like she'd fallen on one of those beautiful swords. She stumbled out of the armory, nearly losing her footing.

She'd heard that scream before. Three years ago. Her heart nearly leapt out of her chest.

"Jack? Niels?"

Was it a ghost? Her imagination?

Another scream—but not one she knew. This one came from the direction of the forest.

"That's Kase!" Ben yelled. He sprinted for the trees, sword held at his side.

Holding tightly to her own sword with her good arm, she ran. She probably shouldn't run with a sharp weapon, lest she trip, but she didn't stop. She wouldn't let anyone else die. Not today.

Please, please *let everything be okay.*

Dirt and leaves kicked up and floated past her as she stumbled back toward the ship. She ignored the frosted branches and vines licking her face and the sting of thorns catching on her trousers, the crisp air biting at the open seam.

More screaming and shouting met her ears. Even with complete terror flooding her veins, she couldn't mistake that for anything but Kase's voice. Heart pounding, lungs wheezing, she rolled her ankle in the sprint. Blast the too-soft boggy ground. Her ankle burned like fire and embers and shocks and bolts, but she ignored it as she righted herself, still clasping the sword in one hand, limping faster than a shooting star.

"The pistols aren't working!" Kase shouted, his voice strained.

Hallie burst through the last of the underbrush and stopped dead in her tracks. Standing at nearly seven feet tall, a form seemingly carved from rough stone loomed over Kase, his curls peeking out from beyond the thing's monstrous arm.

The thing Kase fought was missing part of its nose.

Hallie's breath froze in her chest.

Its honed arms and legs swung at Kase, who ducked and rolled out of the way. Hallie's mouth opened in a silent scream, like her larynx was made from simple cloth as she took in the thing's face. The stone statue was even more beautiful in its own way, now that it was moving. The carver must have taken years to put in every detail of the stoneman's face with its handsomely shaped features, its straight brow and determined mouth. Animated, it almost looked as if it was a human trapped within stone skin, the veins laced with gold. All the moss and mold had fallen away.

It was also a born fighter, complete with rippling

muscles. And there were more of them. Thundering footfalls echoed in her ears as three others smashed through the underbrush to her left.

"Hallie!" Kase shot a bolt of electricity, dodging the stone arm swiping at his head. Hadn't the stars-idiot just screamed the pistols didn't work? "Ship! Go!"

But she couldn't move. All she could do was watch in frozen horror as Zeke wielded the machete from the ship's storeroom, joining Ben fighting two stonemen. When the soldier hit one of their faces, only a little sliver of rock chipped away from his foe's cheekbone. With his wild swipes, Ben clearly didn't know how to use the sword he'd chosen, but a chunk of the statue's hand flew off and hit Zeke's arm, ripping his uniform, blood spewing forth. The soldier hollered, pulling that arm to his chest, but he kept fighting with the other.

Crashing, burning stars.

"Hallie! Go!" Kase flung the useless pistol in the direction of his monster. It hit, but it only stopped the creature for a breath. It seemed more confused than injured.

Kase scooped up a few rocks from the ground and threw them. Again, the monster seemed surprised for only a moment, but it was enough for Kase to spot Hallie over the thing's shoulder. "*Get to the blasted ship!*"

He wasn't looking as the creature pulled back an arm to swing again. *Oh stars, oh stars.* It was going to knock his head clean off his shoulders. Her thoughts raced faster than a motorcoach, faster even than the *Eudora Jayde* before the storm. In her mind's eye, she imagined the blood, saw it soak Kase's curls as his head rolled upon the gore-streaked grass.

Just like the blood had coated Jack's face when the rescue crew had freed his body from the rubble.

The corners of her eyes burned. She couldn't stop the stoneman, she didn't have any sort of weapon to—

The sword.

The weapon she carried. She rushed forward as Kase turned. He opened his mouth to make what Hallie presumed would be his final roar in the face of death.

With all her strength, she swung the sword gripped in both her hands, nailing the creature right in its neck. It cracked all the way through. Heavy with momentum, the head slid from the monster's shoulders.

It didn't scream. No blood spewed forth.

Hallie stumbled and nearly impaled herself, but strong arms gripped her waist. *She* did scream, her voice finally working once more, fighting the thing's grip with all her might. The stoneman had grabbed her; it didn't have a *head*, but it had still grabbed her—

"Hallie! Snap out of it!"

Kase. Those were Kase's arms around her waist, Kase's voice in her ear.

She whipped her head between the dead stoneman, Kase, and the sword stuck in the ground beside its rocky corpse. "Is it dead?"

"It's dead. Now *get on the ship*."

Still breathing hard, she nodded and obeyed, pulling away to run for the steps. Kase grabbed her fallen weapon and went to hack a third monster joining Zeke and Ben's battle.

"Let's go!" he yelled. "Come on!"

Hallie didn't look, only flung herself up the steps and onto the ship. Ebba was at a cockpit side window, her jagged breaths audible over the stonemen trying to climb the side of the ship. A few moments later, the stairway slammed shut, footsteps pounding down the corridor. Skibs abandoned his sword on a seat and lunged for the pilot controls.

"Lift off, now, Skibs! Ebba! The electrobomb!" Kase shoved Hallie's strange sword and a bleeding Zeke into her arms. Ripped from forearm to wrist, his uniform sleeve clung to the blood gushing from a cut just below his elbow. She helped the man to a chair and laid the sword beside him, her head whirling with adrenaline and terror.

"Blow them to the stars!" Kase shouted as the *Eudora Jayde* jerked into the air. Hallie barely caught herself on the back of one of the seats as wind rushed into the cockpit.

"The code won't work!" Ebba pounded the dash.

Kase flung himself out of his seat, and Hallie leapt out of his way. His voice was harsh, guttural—scared. "Why'd they put this *blasted* thing all the way over here?"

He smashed a sequence of buttons as the ship lurched to one side. Hallie dug her fingernails into the soft material of the seat. Ben tugged on the steering control, and Zeke moaned.

"One's grabbed onto the engine!" Ebba's terrified sob was muffled by her good hand.

Kase cursed and pounded another button as Hallie's stomach lurched into her chest.

They're going to take us down. They'll pulverize our bones until we're nothing but dust.

But then the air crackled.

The ship rocked when the stonemen released their prize, and as the *Eudora* rose higher, the ground exploded below them.

CHAPTER 16

JUST IN CASE

Kase

AFTER A THOROUGH SEARCH AROUND the new campsite well to the east of the statues, Kase wasn't the only one avoiding the usual dinner of dried beef and vegetables. He and Skibs hadn't found any statues or any remnant of the Yalvs in this part of the forest on the edge of that same endless bog. Shocks, how far did it extend? Kase was just lucky they found a rather dry stretch not drowning in a foot deep of murky water.

When Skibs got up to go stir the fire, Zeke volunteered to go hunting the next morning for something else to eat, insisting he was more than capable of trapping or shooting something with one arm. Always the soldier, never admitting defeat in the face of pain.

When Hallie had finished sloppily stitching Zeke's gash, she'd volunteered to gather some edible plants, but Ebba and Skibs hadn't said much other than to agree with the others. Those two went to bed soon as night fell, and Kase couldn't blame them. He hadn't thought anything could be as terrifying as the crash in the storm. Or the dragon. But nothing could have prepared him for deadly stone statues.

He played with the bandage wrapped around his left wrist, staring into the campfire until his eyes began to burn. He'd only acquired a small scratch, thank the moons. It could have been so much worse. If Hallie hadn't swung that sword...

"Kase?" His brother had a foot on the bottom stair, holding his injured arm to his chest.

"Yeah?"

"Will you take first watch? You're the least injured out of all of us."

Kase waved his hand. "Fine."

"Thank you." Zeke limped up the stairs. At the top, he turned to Hallie, who sat against a tree at the edge of the firelight, her injured ankle wrapped tightly. Not broken—only twisted. "Hallie? You coming in?"

The girl flinched, turning toward Zeke slowly, as if in a dream. She shook her head, a few loose strands of hair floating around her face.

She gripped that sword again. The weapon that had saved him. She hadn't let it out of her sight since the fight. The one Skibs had grabbed still lay on the floor of the cockpit. They'd inspect it more thoroughly in the morning. Kase looked back toward Hallie.

Though he'd only known her a little over a month, Kase had learned she would draw whenever she could, but especially when she was nervous. Much like when he ruffled his already messy curls. But tonight, the sketchpad was nowhere in sight.

Maybe Hallie could take first watch. She didn't look like she'd be moving any time soon, much less sleeping. This side of her made him pause. He'd only seen the fiery or the quirky Hallie. This one was new. He didn't know what to call it. Maybe it was a little like Zeke's Battle Fright.

"Hallie?"

Her grip tightened on the sword hilt.

"Do you want to take...you know what, I'll be right back. Can you keep an eye out for a minute?"

She tilted her head but nodded. Bounding up the steps, he whisked down the hallway, ducking into the room he shared with his brother and Skibs.

"Kase? What're you..."

He ignored Zeke. Skibs was already asleep, which wasn't surprising; he'd been more or less like that since he stumbled onto the beach. Zeke said he was still healing, but Kase thought it was more likely that his brother's medical cocktail wasn't as effective as he'd hoped it would be.

"You're supposed to be keeping watch." Zeke sat up in his bed.

Kase threw open his trunk and pulled out the pilot's jacket he'd stuffed there earlier. He went over to his bed and stuck his hand underneath the pillow for the book wedged between the mattress and the wall, then left the room, Zeke's mutterings floating in the air.

Before he made it out onto the stairs, a strong hand gripped his shoulder and spun him around. Zeke. His bandage would need to be changed soon, based on the small red blots leaking through the cloth. He narrowed his sharp hazel eyes, and he looked so much like their father in that moment Kase had to do a double take.

"What do you want?" Kase asked, still pulling.

Zeke squeezed until Kase winced. "You can't leave your post. Especially after what happened today."

Kase fought the urge to roll his eyes. "Hallie's out there, remember?" he hissed. "She might want to read."

Zeke's eyebrows lifted as Kase held up the book. "Make sure she doesn't stay out there too long."

When his brother headed back to their room, Kase turned toward the exit. As he left the ship, he leapt down the last few stairs and strode toward Hallie. He was only doing this because she'd saved his life earlier that day, and the look on her face told him she needed something to distract her.

Kase slowed as he approached. She didn't move, didn't even acknowledge him. Her eyes were fine-spun glass, staring straight ahead at something unseen.

He cleared his throat. "Hallie?"

Not even a twitch. He lowered himself to the ground opposite the sword, trying to quell the flame of anger itching to catch his kindling thoughts. He set the book and jacket down beside him to give him time. She'd saved his life today, and it'd probably been the first time she'd ever fought anything like that, let alone killed something. Hallie seemed like the kind of person to spare a spider—probably so she could sketch it.

He faced her, knees pulled up to his chest, and picked up the jacket with one hand, holding it out. "Here, at least take this. You'll freeze to death without it."

The sword twitched as the glaze melted from her eyes, and she turned at last. Kase ached to run a hand through his hair, but she still hadn't taken the jacket from him. He decided he didn't know how to deal with this Hallie. He enjoyed arguing with her, that he could do well, but this was something else entirely.

"Come on. It's the least I can do." Kase tossed the leather into her lap. She looked down at it, then back up at him.

"I'm fine." Her voice was raspy from disuse. She coughed.

Kase's fingers curled into fists. "Why don't you go in and sleep?"

Hallie's eyes flashed for a moment, then softened. She gathered the leather close with her free hand, hugging it to her chest like a child with a teddy bear. "I can't."

"If your shoulder hurts too much, I can..." He could what? Help her put it on? She wasn't five, for moonssake.

The tip of the sword moved in the dry grass as she threw the jacket at his feet. It landed with a soft thump. "I don't need it."

We've all been through a lot today. Keep your temper.

"Look," Kase tried again. "I'm sitting here because you carved a blasted monster up with that sword. Take the jacket. It's warm."

Her mouth quirked. "I did keep it from knocking those curls off your head."

Progress. His lips pulled up at one end, just a little. He handed the jacket back to her, and she took it, laying it across her knees. She still wouldn't take her hand off the sword.

"You like Marisee, right?"

Hallie tilted her head. "Yes, but what does that have to—"

He picked up *The Odyssey* and held it out. She halted when she saw the cover. Instead of taking it from him, smiling, or even acknowledging it, she stared.

Kase's arm ached. Marisee loved his thorough analyses of ancient texts in addition to the translation itself, which made for great reading material, but it wasn't exactly light—on the mind or the arm. Was she not going to take it?

After another agonizing few seconds, he set the book down beside her and prayed the soggy ground wasn't *too* soggy. "I thought you might want to read my copy. As thanks...for today."

She didn't say anything, so he pushed himself to his feet. Maybe if he left her alone, she'd take the hint and go inside. As soon as he stepped toward the fire, she choked out a sob.

"Thank you." Her voice cracked.

He froze. Crying women weren't a strong suit of his. But blast, he couldn't leave her there. He slowly turned back, going over their conversation in his mind. He hadn't said anything offensive, had he? Even if he had, why would she thank him for that?

Streams of tears dampened her cheeks as she met his eyes. She swiped at them with the cuff of her dirt-streaked sleeve. "Thank you, but I don't want it. Not today. Jack..."

She sniffled and finally let go of the sword as she buried her face in her hands. Kase shifted his weight from foot to foot. What was he supposed to do? Ana had been the only girl he'd cared about enough to comfort when she cried, but that hadn't been often. And he'd been terrible at it, besides. She'd said so herself.

Hallie lifted her wet face, her nose crinkling as she sniffled hard. "I'm—I'm sorry. I didn't mean to..."

Kase chewed on his lip and crouched down in front of her, putting a hand on the laces of her boot. That seemed safe. "Hey, it's okay. I didn't mean to upset you. For once."

She shook her head. "Not your fault. For once."

Her small smile mirrored his. *There we go. Almost back to normal. Maybe.*

"It won't hurt my feelings if you don't want to read the book. Thought you'd like it, that's all. Didn't realize it'd make you cry."

She laughed, but the tears didn't stop. He resisted the urge to wipe them from her cheeks with his fingertips. She wouldn't appreciate that. But the thought of her soft skin made his stomach clench. Where had *that* feeling come from? This was *Hallie*.

She gripped the leather jacket. "No, it's just that— actually, will you sit here with me?"

"You're not going to slap me again, are you?"

Hallie shook her head and bit her lip. "I don't want to be alone. Not tonight." She took a breath. "You can sit on the other side of the tree...if you want. Just in case."

He was uncomfortably aware of an icy burning in his chest. A new feeling. He didn't know if he liked it or not. "In case of what?"

"Just in case I *do* have the urge to slap you. That'll give you time to run."

A laugh bubbled in his throat, but he sat to her left, facing the other side of the campsite.

Toward the bog, the light from the fire stretched and yawned, the flickering creating shapes in the darkness. Kase shivered.

He didn't know how long the silence stretched out, but the soft creaking of burning wood eased the tension in his shoulders. Just a little bit.

"Did we make a mistake coming out here?" she

asked.

Kase turned so he could see her out of the corner of his eye. Yet, instead of seeing her, he could almost feel the rain fall on his cheeks and watch the greenie's body slide off the hangar roof. Stone bit into his knees as he caught the boy. He smelled the metallic tang of blood as it soaked his trousers and heard the desperation in his own voice as he shouted for someone to get a medic.

I've lost count of all my mistakes. Why not add this one to the pile?

When he didn't answer, she continued, "I didn't agree to this blindly. But all I left behind was a stupid letter. Just ink on paper."

Kase's fingers gripped the stiff material of his pants. He blinked away the shadows of bloodstains, of a cheek stinging from his father's backhand. "Me, too."

It might not have been the most eloquent answer, but Hallie accepted it all the same. Kase knew his motivation for coming out here. He didn't have a choice. It was fly to who blasting knew where, or face charges.

But what had motivated her? What had motivated anyone? Why had Zeke gone blindly along with Jove's plan? What made Skibs leave Lucy behind? And Ebba? What had she to lose by saying no to this insanity?

Hallie didn't say anything for a long while. So long that Kase thought she'd fallen asleep against the tree.

"Today is the third anniversary of...of..."

Kase whipped his head toward her. The fire laced her profile with golden light, highlighting the tears dampening her cheeks. He hadn't realized she'd started crying once more. Did that make him a bad person?

"Third anniversary of what?"

"My brother's death," she choked. "Jack was my

twin. He died. And now my parents probably think *I'm* dead, too."

His stomach felt like the stoneman had come back and punched it. "I'm...I'm sorry."

She shook her head. "I hate when people say that. You didn't kill him."

Kase chewed the inside of his cheek. He knew exactly what she meant. He'd felt the same way after Ana died.

Hallie sniffed. "That was rude of me. You were...I can never shut up when I need to."

"Me either."

Hallie wiped away the ghost of a tear. "Our favorite story, Jack's and mine, was *The Odyssey*. I didn't mean to...thank you for letting me borrow your book."

Kase ran a hand through his hair. "You're welcome." Although he was a blasted stars-idiot for bringing up terrible memories, accidentally or not.

He didn't know what to say. For once, he didn't want to break the soft truce they'd found. But then again, he selfishly wanted to ask her about it. He knew he shouldn't. He didn't like anyone nosing in his own situation, but for the first time, he might have found someone who understood. Other than his brothers, anyway.

Hallie sniffed again. "It's odd. You don't just lose a person when they die. You lose a laugh, a look, a touch. You lose a past, a present, and a future."

Kase traced a seam on his trousers. "I guess."

Her shirt scraped against the trunk as she turned toward him. His eyes stayed fixed to the seam he fiddled with.

"You lose an entire lifetime, and you'll never get it back. I don't know how—" Hallie's voice softened even further as she cut herself off. "Sorry, I'm just sitting here babbling."

His hand froze in place as he looked into her red-rimmed eyes.

"You're not babbling." His stomach clenched. "You're right."

His heart climbed into his throat, and tears pricked the corner of his eyes. Memories of happier times, of laughter, of singing in the rain, of a tiny hand held fast in his, flashed in his mind. His words were choked, clawing to reach the air. "I lost...I lost my sister. A few years back."

Hallie's hand clenched as she said, "Oh."

"Yeah."

She brushed her fingers across the sleeve of his jacket and gave a low, coarse chuckle. "We're not so different after all."

Kase didn't respond.

After a moment, Hallie cleared her throat. "What was her name?"

Kase grasped his curls, but he still answered, "Ana."

"A pretty name," Hallie murmured, but it seemed more to be a comment to herself. Silence fell over them for a moment before she spoke up again.

"It's not fair." Hallie shifted, reaching around the trunk and grasping his shoulder. She looked him straight in the eye. Her watery gaze was bright gold in the firelight. "It's not fair the only thing we can do now is believe both Jack and Ana found their way among the stars. Not that it helps us feel any better. It's a stupid thought, anyway, thinking that our souls travel in the heavens after a Burning..."

She trailed off, but Kase didn't have anything else to add. For once, he and Hallie were of one mind. He understood Burnings were a way of making the living feel like there was something else after this life.

At a Burning, mourners gazed into the sky above, watching the smoke of the deceased make their final journey. He knew that back on First Earth, many cultures buried their dead. But after landing on Yalvara, the ritual of funeral pyres made a resurgence—maybe because this wasn't their native planet. The people of Jayde belonged elsewhere.

The spirits of the departed would soar among the stars and find their way back to humanity's true home—that was what some people believed, anyway. It might be easier than accepting the truth, that those who died never returned to the realm of the living.

Because Hallie was right, you didn't just lose a person, you lost a lifetime.

After stars knew how long, Hallie pushed herself to her feet. "Thank you for the jacket, and listening, but I'll try to get some...I think I'll go inside now."

Kase watched her climb the stairs, wishing she wouldn't but unable to think of anything to make her stay.

STILL RECOVERING FROM THE STONEMEN attack, the crew of the *Eudora Jayde* stayed one more night at the same campsite. The next morning, Zeke trapped a few squirrels with purple streaks in their tails, which were much tastier than Kase expected, and Hallie found a kyanberry bush. The combination of the squirrel meat and the berries was intriguing, and Kase ate it with gusto. He didn't know if Hallie's cooking had improved or if he simply didn't care any longer. It was better than stars-awful beef stew no matter which way he looked at it.

While the crew ate more of their dinner than they had the previous night, conversation still lacked. The near-death experience replayed on loop in Kase's head, and with each successive sound in the trees, he cricked his neck, praying it wasn't the stonemen back for revenge. He just hoped they wouldn't follow them across the bog and to Myrrai.

Firstmoon had finally made an appearance by the time Ebba's voice, soft and barely above a whisper, shattered the delicate silence. "I know you probably don't care, but I feel like I need to tell you all before...before anything..." She took a deep breath. "My brother Eren has an incurable heart disease, and the money from this mission was supposed to help my parents with the financial burden. Made a deal with the Medic's Guild. They'll go to debtor's prison without it." She sniffed a little and wiped her eyes. "Didn't realize I might die even when the High Guardsman said it was dangerous. I'm a *sterning* fool because I thought this was an easy way to fix it all."

Her last words thickened with emotion and broke off. The fire reflected in her dark eyes, and she pushed her hair back from her face. With a soft sniff, she wiped again at the tears dribbling down her cheek. "Thought you should know."

Zeke sat straight up. "Did they not file for aid with the Guild? Surely, they would understand."

Ebba shrugged. "They didn't qualify."

Zeke heaved a sigh, but he didn't add anything else. Hallie, who sat beside her, squeezed her shoulder and let go.

An incurable disease? A wave of shame washed over

Kase's body. He remembered how he'd rejected her request to be on his ground crew, thinking she was just a kid. He gritted his teeth. What a blasted *helviter* he was. But the words he needed to say jammed in his throat. Apologizing now wouldn't make a difference.

The silence lasted until Zeke snapped bits of a stick and threw each piece into the fire with swift precision. As the flames licked the new wood, the soft crackling echoed in the clearing. Once he finished, he said, "Well, I'm here because Jove asked me. I trusted he knew what he was doing, but even he couldn't have predicted this."

Kase chewed on the inside of his cheek, fiddling with his ring. He knew why he'd come along, and selfishly, he knew he couldn't return to Kyvena without a successful mission. By the stars, he wasn't even close to a decent human being. "If we aren't successful, there's a chance I...I..."

He dug his heel in the dirt as four pairs of eyes burrowed into the top of his head. "I made a mistake. A terrible one, and I thought coming on this mission would fix it. But what's even more ridiculous is that I just wanted to get out of that blasted city. *I hated it.*" He deepened the furrow his boot had made.

The partial truth rolled off his tongue like fire. He peeked up and caught Zeke's sad smile. He swallowed.

Ebba nodded. "I never liked it much either. We moved there because of Eren, though Pa says it was for his art, but things are worse off for my family. Now I'd give nearly anything to be back there in that sloping mess of a cottage in the lower city with my brothers."

That's not exactly what I meant. Did she not hear the first part of my botched confession?

"You don't need to worry." Zeke dusted his hands on his trousers and winced as he moved his injured arm. "Jove will make sure they're taken care of."

"Lucy's pregnant."

Skibs' choked words were a lightning bolt in a summer storm, but instead of electricity burning through Kase, his breath froze in his chest. *"What?"*

Skibs' laugh was wry and jarring, opposite of his tone moments before. "We were gonna use the money to run away and start over. How stupid of me to think I could do this. I can't remember hours on end, and my head hurts like bursting suns for the others. I told her I'd come home, but I don't think I'll..."

He cut himself off. After a few more moments of complete silence, he stood. "I need to—I need to go."

"Ben!" Kase's words were lost in the clacking of his boots on the metal stairs.

He clenched his jaw. He should get up and try to talk to him, but his feet wouldn't move, shock rooting them in place.

It all made sense now, why he was so defensive about Lucy, and it left a bitter aftertaste in Kase's mouth, like acidic bile and the burning smell of yalvar fuel. He understood the desperation at wanting to escape. He understood the desire. But how could Skibs have been so reckless? What did he think would happen once her parents discovered she was pregnant out of wedlock? She'd be tossed out of any respectable social circles, and she was the sole heiress to her family's fortune.

But what I did was worse. The greenie's paralyzed because of me.

As egregious as that was, it wasn't the only thing bothering him. The minutes waned away in silence, and in those moments when no one else made a sound save for the fire, something deep down in Kase sparked and grew into an angry, roaring blaze. The strength of it caught him by surprise; maybe it was his own childhood rearing its ugly head, the abandonment he'd felt, or the pain and abuse he'd endured. But whatever it was, it flooded him with rage. Kase didn't know how much money Jove had promised Skibs, but if their situations were reversed, there wasn't anything in heaven or hell that would tempt Kase to leave his unborn child or almost-fiancé, much less leave them to the mercy of the bloodthirsty Jaydian elites.

Kase's eyes burned as he stared into the flames, willing his blood to stop boiling. Because if it didn't, he might do something stupid and knock his friend senseless for the third time. His chest heaved even as he tried to calm himself.

The only thing Kase could do was make sure they made it home in one piece. And calm down. And breathe. And not lose his temper.

That list was entirely too long.

Hallie tucked her knees to her chin, wrapping her arms around them. She hadn't said a word during the whole exchange. The only sign she'd acknowledged any of it was her silent shoulder squeeze at the beginning of it all.

The anger drained out of him like water through fingers as he watched her. He was a wreck every year on the anniversary of Ana's death, and he wished he could do or say something else to comfort her, but even *The Odyssey* hadn't helped the previous night.

It wasn't long before both Zeke and Ebba headed inside, Kase volunteering for first watch once more. Not only did the horrors of their last weeks haunt his thoughts, but the evening's conversation played in his head on repeat. With each successive run-through, shame and anger rolled over him like waves of the sea, each one dragging him under harder than the last.

He'd thought leaving Kyvena would cure him of the past, but he was wrong. So very wrong. And he had no one to blame but himself. Maybe his father was right. Maybe he wasn't mature enough to make the decisions in his life. Whenever given leave to do so, he screwed up worse than the last time.

"Kase?" Hallie's voice snapped him out of the vicious cycle. He took in her form at the foot of the stairs. Her jacket nearly reached her knees, where thick brown trousers were tucked into her boots that were peeling at the heels. She fiddled with a button on her jacket, her hair falling out of a loose braid and casting shadows on her face, but she didn't push the strands away. "I'm only here for the money. For myself. Because I'm too much of a coward to face my past. That's it. So if *you're* ridiculous, I must be a stars-blasted fool."

She disappeared up the stairs, each step ringing in the silence, and her words joined the cacophony in his head.

CHAPTER 17

BREATHE SLOWLY

Kase

PULLING HIS GOGGLES OVER HIS eyes, Kase readied the *Eudora* for takeoff. Today was the day. After Cerls, storms, dragons, stonemen, and three nights spent in a bog praying the ship didn't sink, they would reach Haddon's Pass. They'd determined the river that would lead them to the pass had become the bog they'd been in, taken over with time. It was the only thing that made sense with the mountains in the distance.

With each passing day, those towering giants had grown larger and darker. If Jove's map and Hallie's assumptions were correct, Kase would be flying the ship through the Pass and into the Yalven city of Myrrai by dinner.

Maybe it was the thought of the blasted mission

finally ending, but for the first time in ages, Kase's hands didn't shake as he gripped the steering control.

Skibs silently followed his pre-flight protocol, and with his help, the ship was in the air within minutes. Through the missing front window, Kase studied the mountains and forest before them.

When they passed the hour-and-five-minute mark and only a mild sense of unease nibbled at his gut, Kase smirked. He'd beaten his record of consistent flying time since the crash. It was the only good thing he could say about the last few days.

Stars, how much further was this pass? The range didn't end, and each peak merged into the next without a break. How would he even know where the Pass was? What did it look like? He should probably ask Hallie.

Or maybe he wouldn't ask.

Things were still a little awkward after their fireside confessions. Kase didn't know what to say, and apparently, she didn't either. It was strange not having anything to fight about. He didn't think her ridiculous at all; if he'd been in her shoes, he'd have done the same thing. Actually, he *was* doing the same thing. He wasn't on this mission for some noble cause. Yet, Kase was the worst of them all, no matter what Hallie thought.

To his right, a bit of sky opened between two peaks. Was that the pass? He steered toward it. The space grew and filled with light the further they flew. That had to be Haddon's Pass. It was closer than the map said, but then again, he hadn't been able to pinpoint exactly where they even were.

"I'm sorry I didn't tell you earlier," Skibs said, his voice ringing out above the air whistling past Kase's ears.

Kase's gaze didn't leave the growing gap in front of

them. "About what?"

"You know what."

He knew exactly what Skibs was talking about, but now wasn't the time to discuss Skibs' problems and Kase's thoughts about them. They had an airship to fly. His heartrate picked up. *Don't lose your temper. Don't do something stupid while you're flying this hover.*

"Kase?"

He stared straight ahead. He didn't trust his mouth to follow his mind's orders. While the last few days had been tense, Kase had been able to keep his temper in check. It wouldn't do to ruin it all now. All he needed to do was take a deep breath or five. He needed to focus. He couldn't lose himself to his anger...or his fear.

"You think I'm a platinum-class stars-idiot, so spit it out."

Breathe. Breathe slowly.

"Just be honest with me, please."

"Fine. You're a platinum-class stars-idiot," Kase spat. "Happy?"

Skibs was silent.

Kase steered the ship into the gap and saw several trees rising above the rest. They were oddly shaped, skinny and branchless, but nothing surprised him on Tasava anymore.

"That's it?" Skibs asked.

"You want me to elaborate on your stupidity?"

No response.

"It's not even that you knocked her up," Kase continued, his temper swelling, words leaking out like water breaking a weakened dam. "It's that you *abandoned* her afterward, and for what? A handful of gold hunders?"

"You don't—"

Kase cut him off, whipping his head toward him, his face on fire. His fear disappeared, burned up by the anger. "I don't care that you came from a poor family. *I never blasted cared!* But you think it means you aren't worthy or something equally stars-ridiculous. If this is you trying to buy your way into deserving her—"

"Kase, my steering control—"

"No, you don't get to speak. You don't get to talk. You wanted me to say something, so I will. You wanted to know what I think? *What I really think?*"

Kase gripped the steering control so hard, he was sure his knuckles would start bleeding any moment. "You're a blasted *helviter* for leaving Lucy and your kid behind to go on this suicide mission. Blast the money. You're a worthless piece of trash if you—"

"*Kase! Watch out!*"

Kase whipped his head around to see them heading straight for a column of shining brown stone above the treetops. The strange trees he'd noticed before. Every single organ below his collarbone soared into his throat, choking him as he yanked the steering control up.

But it wasn't enough. The left side of the *Eudora Jayde* scraped against the column, and screams echoed down the corridor. He gritted his teeth as the ship ricocheted off another nearby column on the right side.

"*Blast!*" Kase yelled as he overcorrected to the other side. "Press the hover buttons! Now!"

Skibs pounded them, but the ship didn't level them out. The blond cursed. "It's not working!"

"*What?*" The ship jerked under Kase and listed to the right. The right engine had gone out.

Not again.

"Bring it down!" Skibs kept smashing the hover buttons, and while they flickered once, they refused to stay on.

Kase scanned the ground for any clearing large enough to accommodate a crash-landing, but the sea of gold and red didn't falter. In the trees, then. He hit the button for the mechanical parachute, praying it would still work. With a whoosh and a swift crack, it deployed.

As the left engine sputtered out and the ship's nose turned downward, the air caught the parachute, slowing the ship's descent into the tree canopies. With a lurch that strained the limits of his safety belt, the ship caught in the branches, groaning to a halt. His heart pounded, tears welling up in his eyes.

I almost killed us. Because I lost my temper.

He cursed, but the bulbous plops of vomit hitting the floor of the cockpit cut the rest of the words off. A branch nearly as thick as his entire torso impaled the seat beside him.

"Ben!"

Another plop. "I'm—I'm fine."

Kase's vision blurred again as he ripped off his goggles and slung them toward the dash. They skipped across the buttons and knobs, the lens cracking before they fell out of the cockpit window; the sharp taps grew fainter as they fell from the tree. He undid his buckles and stood, his hand grasping the back of his pilot's chair. His shoulder burned from where the belt had dug into it.

"Kase? *Kase!*" His brother's voice was three octaves too high.

Footsteps. The ship lurched, and Kase caught himself on his steering control. He hugged his body to it, his feet slipping and trying to find a foothold. Holy moons and shocks, the ship was going to fall. Something cracked. Whether it was the tree or something within the ship, Kase didn't know, nor did he truly want to find out.

"Stop!" he gasped as the ship rocked back toward the tree.

Think. *Think.*

"Get some rope and everyone else into the cockpit, now! Hurry!" His feet finally found solid footing.

"Got it!" Zeke called back.

Kase turned to the limb impaling the seat, and Skibs, who'd crawled under it. Kase's throat tightened. "I'm—I'm—"

Skibs shook his head. "No, it's not your fault."

"We're in a blasted tree because I couldn't keep my temper."

Skibs wiped his mouth and shook his head. "I deserved it. Not the tree thing, but—you're right."

Kase swiped at the tears escaping his tight hold. He didn't trust himself to say anything else, so he just nodded. They were alive. He needed to focus on that.

He got on his knees, joining Skibs, and faced the entrance. The others arrived, unhurt except for a few bruises and scratches. Hallie's arm seemed to be the worst, a sloppy bandage wrapped around the upper part. She'd also grabbed her satchel. *Mother of ash, does she go anywhere without that thing?*

"Just...just a scratch," she squeaked when she noticed him looking.

Ebba's eyes widened to the size of his mother's fanciest tea saucers when she spotted the giant limb stuck through the back of the co-pilot's chair. "What in the *sterning* suns happened?"

Kase glanced at Skibs.

"I distracted him." His friend's face was stoic. "Our engines went out, electricity and all, when we hit some sort of metal column thing in the trees. Kase's quick reflexes saved us."

"What do you mean her engines went out?" Ebba growled. "I checked those myself this morning."

Kase shook his head. "I don't know what happened. But we have to get off *now*. Before it falls with us in it."

Zeke nodded and crawled forward. "I'll go first and help people out on the other side."

With each movement, the ship creaked, and Kase winced. "Carefully."

After Zeke inched his way over, he squeezed Kase's shoulder. "Thank you."

Kase didn't look him in the eye. He couldn't.

With the precision of a practiced thief, Zeke made his way onto the sturdy branch of the tree, one of the swords tied on his back.

"You had time to grab that?"

"*Kase.* Focus, please."

He nodded and sucked in a breath as the ship creaked once more. "Ebba?"

"On it."

Like an acrobat, she gracefully crossed the space from the entrance to the dash. Quite a feat, as she still had one arm in a sling. In a moment, she was through the cockpit window and on the limb with his brother. He turned back to Hallie. "Come on, you next."

She shook her head. "No, no. Ben can go."

Kase's already high blood pressure flared, but he bit back his retort. *Now's not the time to argue.* "Fine."

Still pale from his near-death experience, Skibs followed the path the others had tread. Zeke helped him out and onto a separate branch. When Kase was sure Skibs was stable, he turned back to Hallie. "Your turn."

She bit her lip and played with the edge of the bandage on her arm. "What if I fall?"

Kase closed his eyes. *Calm. Getting angry is what got us into this mess.* "Listen, I'd rather not do this either, but we have to. The ship could fall any second, and we need to get into the tree before it does."

See? He could be calm and collected.

When Hallie didn't move, Kase swallowed his frustration and held out his hand. "Do you trust me?"

Tears formed in the corner of Hallie's eyes. She stared at his hand, then back at him. "I'm scared."

Kase took his hand back and shouted to Zeke. "Tie the rope to the tree and toss it to me." Zeke grunted his reply, and Kase looked back at Hallie. "I'll tie the rope around you as a fail-safe. Will that help?"

A barely imperceptible nod.

As Kase stood to grab the rope, the ship lurched once more, and the crack of a tree branch echoed through his skull.

The floor tilted.

Kase fought to grab the rope and pull himself to safety, but in a single moment, he found Hallie's widened, terrified eyes.

He let go, diving for her as the *Eudora Jayde* plummeted to the ground below.

CHAPTER 18

AN INVISIBLE BEAT

Hallie

COLD WETNESS WAS THE FIRST thing Hallie felt when she opened her eyes. That, and—*ow*.

She grimaced, but that only worsened the pounding ache in her head, as did the raindrops pelting her eyes. The ground was soft beneath her back.

"Hold still. I'm almost done bandaging your head," a deep voice said. Zeke, possibly.

Hallie blinked again, and the world came into clearer focus. Zeke indeed hovered above her, tying off the last bit. He sat back, his hair damp and messy for once. "You had me scared for a moment there. What else hurts?"

Sitting up, she put a hand to her throat. It felt raw, like she'd been screaming for hours. She wiped the raindrops from her face and inspected her hand. It wasn't until she saw the blood mixed with the water that she felt the pain of it. "What—what happened?"

"We survived falling out of a tree. Barely," someone groaned near her.

Kase swam into focus sitting beside her, flinching every time he rubbed a dirty rag across his blood-streaked face, his curls matted with red. Hallie gasped. "Kase, how are you—all that blood!"

"Looks worse than it is. Not that it doesn't hurt. But we got lucky."

A sharp something smacked against metal, and Hallie jumped, groaning as pain spiked through her skull. Searching for the source of the sound, she put a hand to her head.

A little way behind her lay the remains of the once great airship. One blackened engine, the one closest to her and bent at the wrong angle, was barely connected to the ship's core. Ebba ran a hand through her hair and gave the thing another kick. It gave off a tiny spark but went dark almost immediately. She explained something to the nearby Ben, who shrugged and picked up a scrap near his feet. A string of Ebba's down-country curses followed.

Hallie swallowed, biting her lip to keep herself from crying. They'd survived. Somehow. She vaguely recalled the ship tilting and Kase lunging for her, but she must have hit her head after that. She didn't remember anything else.

"How long have I been out?"

Zeke shrugged. "Not too long. I haven't been back inside the ship to grab anything. It looks stable enough to use as shelter for at least one night, but Ebba still hasn't figured out why the engines died."

Hallie chewed her lip. She'd have to trust Ebba and her assertion she could fix anything. Stars. Hallie remembered thinking the woman was conceited for saying something along those lines in Professor Christie's office, but she had yet to let them down.

Closing her eyes, she ran a hand over the spot where her pocket watch should've rested against her chest, but only sodden lace met her fingers. She gasped, eyes snapping open. "My pocket watch! Where is it?"

Kase groaned and reached into his jacket pocket. "Is this it?" In his hand, the small, rounded trinket sat. The chain that kept it around her neck fell down the sides and in two pieces. He held it out to her. "It probably snapped when we fell."

She reached forward and took it from his palm. When her fingers kissed cool metal, relief warmed her chest. The outside was the same as ever with its smoothed ridges. Jack's voice rang in her ears as she inspected every inch for scratches.

"Papa gave it to me, said I could wear it on a chain to school. Wonder if I can fix it?"

The ends of her lips tipped up as she remembered her brother attempting to open the back. It'd been sealed shut with no visible seams to fix the broken cogs. With each unsuccessful attempt, Jack's boyish face had grown redder and redder. He didn't seem to mind much after that—only proud to carry around such a precious heirloom.

She popped open the cover. The watch was simple, dust and age fogging the edges of the glass. Numbers laced in gold rimmed the edges of the face, and long, elegant hands ticked along with an invisible beat.

The hands ticked along with an invisible beat.

Hallie gasped and blinked. Hard. Her vision

blurred. Another blink. Her hand shook as she smoothed a finger over the face. So all the watch needed was a good whacking to work? That didn't make a lick of sense.

The minute hand slid to the next miniature hash as the second hand reached the twelve.

"What is it?" Zeke asked, his eyes searching for any other injuries. Kase, who had resumed mopping the blood at his hairline, froze.

Hallie shook her head and closed the cover. "Nothing. It's…just later in the day than I thought."

Kase narrowed his eyes, but he didn't comment. He saw straight through her lie. She glanced away.

"It's late afternoon, but that's only by my estimate. These rain clouds came out of nowhere." Zeke stood, dusting his trousers off. He glanced back toward the *Eudora.* "When we saw the ship fall…" He waited a moment, as if trying to gather his thoughts. "I've never been so relieved than when Kase crawled out the window with you in his arms. It's a miracle you both survived."

Hallie looked down and then at Kase, who was too intent on cleaning his already clear face. In fact, a bit of dirt and blood from the rag streaked his forehead with the last swipe.

He'd saved her? She thought back once more to the last few moments before the ship fell. Kase had grabbed the rope. He'd been about to pull himself out, but he'd gone back for her instead.

Her voice wobbled as she inspected the muddy ground littered with autumn's last leafy remnants, her now working pocket watch still clutched in her fist. "Thank you."

She wanted to add *for saving my life*, but she couldn't

form the words. Instead, she found Kase's blue eyes. He held her gaze for once, an understanding smile on his face, like he heard what she wasn't saying. He rested a hand on her boot and squeezed softly. "You're welcome."

Zeke cleared his throat, and Hallie broke eye contact with Kase. The soldier straightened the sleeves of his dirt-streaked uniform. "I'm going to inspect those tower things Ben said you crashed into, Kase. Will you lead me?"

Hallie's heart sped up a little. "Can I go too? With us being in the Pass, I assume they're Yalven-made."

Zeke shrugged as Kase stood. Hallie stashed her watch in a trouser pocket and pushed herself to her feet, but her head gave a painful throb as she did, throwing her off balance. Within seconds, Kase's hand was at her back.

"Thanks," she mumbled.

"You probably shouldn't stand."

Hallie gritted her teeth as another painful throb pounded against her skull. "I think you're right."

"I'm always right."

Hallie snorted and instantly brought a hand to her head, cursing herself silently. "I'll be fine as long as we walk slowly."

Zeke cleared his throat again, and Kase's hand fell away from the small of her back. She hadn't realized it was still there. "So, where are these structures?"

Ben ambled over a second later. He took one look at Kase's head and grimaced. "Don't think that improves your looks, mate."

Kase grumbled something under his breath, but Hallie didn't catch it. She smiled at Ben instead. "We're off to inspect the towers or whatever you all saw."

"I'll come along, too."

Zeke turned to Ebba and shouted. "You want to come inspect what Kase hit with the ship?"

A loud curse followed along with another kick to the ship. "I'm staying here with *Eudora*, or don't you want her fixed up?"

Zeke sighed. "I'll stay behind. She won't be able to keep watch. You all go on ahead since it isn't too far. Don't push yourselves."

With that, Ben led them through the trees. Hallie's legs groaned at the exercise, but she kept pace as best she could. Not that it was easier when Kase walked just at her elbow, ready to catch her lest she fall.

A month ago, it would have annoyed her. But with her head throbbing with each step she took, she was grateful for his presence. Funny how things changed so quickly.

After at least a quarter hour of walking, a brown shape came into view: a pillar of solid stone soaring above the trees, its slick surface shimmering in the light peeking through the clouds. Like the ship. And the sword. And the dust that had always settled in Niels' blond hair. Stars, if this was Yalven, they sure had a good bit of Zuprium to spare. Hallie's brain might have hurt, but her thoughts dashed a mile a minute.

Could it be another type of temple? Maybe a shrine? It wasn't natural, and the ship hitting it had caused the engines and electricity to go out...interesting. Intriguing, actually. And then there was the subject of her dormant pocket watch coming to life. Through pain and even a little fear, a flicker of curiosity ignited in her chest. She *was* a scholar, after all.

She thought back to the High Guardsman's words about their intelligence on the Yalvs. No contact in twenty years. Could this tower be part of the reason? Or maybe it had something to do with the Essences? How else would something be able to knock out the airship's power? The texts Jayde possessed on the topic never went into detail about what exactly the Essences could do, only that they were something to be feared.

Not helpful at the moment.

Ben circled the structure, but Kase stood at a distance. "All I know is that I scraped it, and the engines shut off. I wouldn't get too close."

"Nonsense." Hallie stumbled toward it, ignoring Kase's protests. She grinned. "It's most certainly Yalven. It has to be."

Ben stopped his circling and rejoined Kase. "It's not emitting any heat or light. Just plain Zuprium. Except for the carvings."

Standing at the bottom of the pillar, Hallie looked up as rain fell, just a small sputtering. She inspected the stone with narrowed eyes.

Ben was right. The massive bricks were carved with tiny patterns. No, not a pattern—*words.*

She went to grab her sketchbook from her satchel only for her hand to find the soaked canvas of her trousers. "Blast it, my satchel...is it still on the ship?"

Kase shrugged. "I only grabbed the watch because it seemed valuable. Sorry."

"What do you need?" Ben asked, stepping toward her, hand going into his jacket pocket.

Hallie looked back at the towering column and then turned. "I need to copy this and check it against my..."

Her words trailed off as Ben took something from his pocket. A small, red-leathered something with Yalven scrawled across the front. Her heart picked up in pace, beating against her throat.

"Found this on the floor of the cockpit when I went in to make sure the structure was stable. This particular book has been banned for nearly twenty years, yet somehow a copy shows up on our ship."

Hallie swallowed her unease. "I found that in the bookshop I used to work in before I decided to come along on this mission and thought it might help us. Didn't realize it was banned! Jess has never been one to look at the books he sells too closely."

Ben held it out to her, and she took it. Kase frowned. "What's that on the cover?"

Hallie brushed away a few stray drops from the leather. The rain had simmered to a heavy mist. "Not sure, but the title says *The Gate of Time*."

Ben smiled. "You really are a good suns-blasted scholar. Glad Jove found you. Even I wouldn't have been able to read that title if I hadn't known what the cover looked like."

"Shocks and bolts." Kase fingered his electropistol and sighed. "While I would never want to stop a book discussion, I think we should hurry and head back. Blasted things are giving me bad vibes."

Hallie tucked the book under her arm and leaned in closer to the column. The writing was as old as the inscription above the archway back at the temple armory. Yet, a few words stood out to her.

Essence. Gate. Time.

Had the Yalvs simply scrawled their history upon the metal? She glanced down at the book. With so much going on, she hadn't gotten to read much. She really hadn't felt like it with the translating of each word taking time. Professor Christie's words echoed in her mind.

There's a reason no one's been able to contact the Yalvs in two decades, and there's a reason why that book in the package has been banned everywhere.

She shook her head to clear it, though pain spiked at the back. She stumbled, dropping the book and throwing out her hand to break her fall.

Metal, slick and cool with rain and the promise of winter, met her hand. Carvings bit into her palm. A sense of calm fell upon her.

"Hallie!" Kase's voice was lost in the wind picking up the edges of her head bandage and hair, swirling, twirling, ripping out the ribbon she'd used to tie it up. She gasped, and Kase shouted her name again.

She tried to pull away, but she couldn't move her hand from the column. Pain like golden lightning spiked throughout her entire body.

Without anything else keeping her upright, she collapsed to the ground, and the world went dark.

Kase

KASE HAD ONLY WHITTLED AWAY badly at the wet stick for a short time before Hallie woke. He was surprised by how relieved he was when she did. He told himself it was because he didn't know how to whittle, and she'd saved him from probably slicing himself with the knife, but it was more than that. He'd been worried when she'd blacked out after running from the dragon, sure, but that paled in comparison to the way she'd crumpled after catching herself with the strange pillar. Despite his best efforts, they'd finally reached a good place, so she wasn't allowed to die on him now.

Her eyes were bright in the dim light filtering through the busted window of the women's chamber.

When he and Ben had gotten her back to camp, his brother had settled her in here, and Kase hadn't left her side since.

He couldn't. Not after everything.

She blinked again as she took in Kase, sitting by her bed in the little wooden chair. It was almost too small for him. While he wasn't as broad-shouldered as his brothers, he was tall, and the back of the chair only reached the middle of his spine. He'd inherited his mother's build but his father's height. His mother had told him he favored her older brother, but Kase despised the comparison. Thinking about him only brought up terrible memories of what the man had done.

Hallie finally spoke, her rasping voice dragging him out of that place. "What happened?"

Kase helped her sit up and handed her a canteen, which she sipped from daintily, her lips perched about the edge like a proper lady. Stars, no, why was he thinking of her *lips*?

He took the vessel back from her and screwed the top back on. "What do you remember?"

Hallie winced, putting a hand to her head as she adjusted her position, but she waved off his offer to help. "I touched the pillar?"

"Yeah, you decided to fall into it."

"Whatever." Hallie reached down and snagged her satchel from where it lay at the end of her bed, searching through it. Kase had gathered the supplies and brought it into the room, thinking it might help her wake up. Probably stupid, but he didn't know what else to do. Hallie continued, "Guess I'll have to sketch it and do research when we get...when we get..."

Her words choked off, but Kase finished them for

her. "We'll find a way."

A bitter, empty promise, but he didn't know what else to say. Stars-idiot. They were all screwed if they stayed; *he* was screwed if they made it home. And they didn't even have a functioning ship.

Hallie chewed on her lip. "With what airship? Not that I'd ever get on one again."

"At least you're still alive." Kase threw his poor, misshapen stick through the jagged hole in the window. It smacked against a nearby tree trunk. Whittling was useless.

"Thank you, again." Hallie played with the edges of her notebook, not meeting his eye. "Most people don't make it to crash-landing number two, much less live through it. Nor survive the ship falling out of a tree."

The pressure in his chest only swelled as she flipped through the pages in her notebook, the soft whisking of her fingers across the parchment getting louder with each second that passed. "It was my fault," he said. He didn't know why, but he did. "Skibs lied to cover up the fact I messed up."

Hallie's fingers paused.

Kase couldn't stop now he'd started. "I tore into him about the whole Lucy thing. About how much of a piece of blasted trash he was for leaving her and coming out here. I wasn't paying attention. That's when we hit the column. *It's my fault.* My fault we're stranded with no way...with no way..."

He stopped when her slender fingers grasped his hand and squeezed it. He looked up to find her eyes boring into his. They were like pools of gold, the brown and jade specks glowing in the little light they had left in the day.

She didn't say anything for several moments. He

wanted to cower, wanted to pull his hand out of her grasp, but her eyes were the only thing keeping him from falling apart.

"Kase, it's okay."

"But—"

She brushed her thumb across his knuckles. He stifled a shiver. "At this point, we have no option but to make it to Myrrai and pray the Yalvs can get us home. That, or hope Ebba can pull a miracle out of her back pocket. Both are viable. I've decided to put my faith in that."

"How can you go from...how can you be so confident..."

"Because I don't have a choice, Kase. Neither do you." She gave his fingers one last squeeze before going back to her notebook.

Kase stared at the floor, sifting through her words. What did they have to lose now? Maybe Ebba *could* do something to fix up the ship. He didn't know how long that would take, but she was the best mechanic he'd ever known. He'd rather put his confidence in her than the Yalvs, but at this point, Hallie was right. There wasn't another option, and Kase was never one to roll over without a fight.

The memory of Harlan's fist flashed in his mind. He shut his eyes and took a deep breath. No, Kase had never backed down from a fight. No matter what the outcome might've been for him.

Closing his eyes, Kase listened to the strokes as Hallie sketched. While the noise might have irked him a month ago, it calmed him now. The same could be said of Hallie herself. She no longer antagonized him at every turn.

He opened his eyes and peeked over at her

notepad. She *was* talented. Whenever Kase tried anything like that, not even he could tell what it was supposed to be. Maybe if they all survived, he'd bully Hallie into teaching him.

"How long was I out this time?" Hallie wouldn't look at him.

"Don't you have a pocket watch?"

"Oh, yeah. Right." She dug around in her satchel, pulling it out. Peering at it, she frowned. "I don't think I trust it, says it's nine. I think the crash did something to it."

Kase ran a hand down his face and grimaced at the prickly stubble. "We've been back twenty minutes or so, but that's a guess."

She added a few more touches to her drawing and held it up. "What do you think?"

He took it from her and inspected it. Her skill shone through, even if it was a rough sketch. His eyes widened. "You said you only remember touching the pillar, but this—this is so detailed!"

"Huh?" Hallie took it back. "Hmm...I guess I remember more than I thought. That's ancient Yalven writing. It's similar to what I've studied in my classes."

"Can you read it?"

"Not easily. I could study it for a bit and figure it out, but the Yalven language has evolved immensely in the millennium, and only bits and pieces of the original tongue are the same. A few of the words are familiar enough."

"This reminds me of that place with the swords." Kase looked in the direction of the pillar, though the forest hid it from their view.

"Me too. That's why I think they're connected." Hallie took her notebook back and stashed it in her satchel. "I want to go closer again to see if I can figure out what it says."

"That's a terrible idea."

"I won't touch it."

"Forgive me if I'm skeptical."

She rolled her eyes. "I *promise* not to touch the scary pillar thing, lest I black out for the five hundredth time on this mission. Is that good enough for you?"

Kase answered her smile with one of his own. "Thank you. Now, if you're up to it, let's go eat. Skibs was trying to pull something together last I heard. He's terrible at it, but I'm sure anything he comes up with will be better than any of your meals."

She glared at him for a second before laughing softly. "You're not wrong."

She swung her feet over the side of the bed and stood. They were possibly stuck here without a way back home, but a strange thought flitted across his exhausted mind:

There isn't anyone else I'd rather be stranded with, I don't think.

CHAPTER 19

LET GO

Hallie

AS IT TURNED OUT, THE evening only brought more rain—meaning no fire for the night or the hot dinner Ben had been assembling—but Hallie wasn't too upset, because her head ached from where she'd hit it in the fall. The only problem was that with the onset of night and her previous run-in with the pillar, no one would let her inspect it once more.

Instead, she rummaged through her trunk trying to find *The Gate of Time*. Kase said he'd carried her back from the pillar and put it in her trunk as she slept.

But it wasn't there.

She didn't think Kase would lie about something like that, but then again, where was the book?

Instead of finding her quarry, she did discover the

bag of caramels she'd stuffed there the first day. The bag was crinkled and slightly torn, but it was in better shape than the airship. Even with the light rain outside the broken window, Ebba's occasional curse still filtered in. She'd refused to come out from under the ship for nearly an hour after the precipitation doused Ben's budding campfire. And she was still at work.

Gracious day, was she ever going to admit defeat?

Hallie had to give her credit for perseverance, but at this point, the *Eudora Jayde* was a lost cause. The crew's only chance of getting home once more was through the Yalvs' help if they chose to give it.

Her chest tightened, and she squeezed the bag of caramels, the brown paper crinkling. They were never getting home, and all she'd left her parents was a blasted letter. That wouldn't make up for the loss of a child, even one they hadn't seen since she'd said goodbye over two years prior.

Deep breaths. I'm on this mission to treaty with the Yalvs. If anyone can do it, I can.

If she told herself that enough, maybe she would believe it.

She'd just set aside the caramels when she was thrown sideways. A loud boom deafened her momentarily, followed by curses from Ebba outside the window and shouts from the corridor.

"What in the blazes are you doing?" Zeke's voice echoed off the walls. More footsteps joined his.

Ebba's voice was even higher. "Were you trying to kill me? I was underneath *Eudora* trying to fix whatever *you* did to her!"

Someone answered, and Hallie left her room. Up the corridor, the raised voices came from the food closet. She peeked around the frame to find the rest of the crew. Grease and soot covered much of Ebba's skin and clothing. Zeke's arms were crossed.

It was Ben and Kase who looked worse for wear. The Watch agent's face was stained black, his eyebrows missing, and Kase, well, his hair was messier than normal. He still had both eyebrows. Beside Ben sat the ruins of some contraption or another. With it being burnt, busted, and otherwise destroyed, Hallie had no clue what it had been in its previous life.

"We found this burner to help make dinner," Kase said, pointing to the ruined device. "Skibs thought he could do something to the wires to make it work, because it runs on electricity, but obviously..."

Zeke's eyes turned cold. "If the blasted ship doesn't work, why did you think this would?"

Kase glanced at Ben, who wiped what he could off his face with the sleeve of his jacket. The blond spoke up. "I might've had one of my...moments...when working with the wires. Ever since I hit my head during the storm...I should've known better than to try. Sorry, Zeke, Ebba."

Her gaze caught on Kase, his blue eyes flashing and contrasting with Zeke's level stare. Did the latter ever lose his temper? She'd always assumed it was the military training, but now it bothered her. He didn't need to be like Kase, with every emotion spilling over like wine on a white tablecloth, but keeping the emotion in must have been draining him—especially on this terrible mission.

Both Ebba and Ben left, the former grumbling obscenities under her breath as she passed. Hallie turned to follow them out when Kase spoke again, his voice low and dangerous. "What exactly did you give Skibs to heal him?" His right hand gripped the edge of the counter. "Because it isn't working."

Zeke's tone matched his brother's. "What he needed."

"*Then why isn't it working?*" Kase grabbed the lapels of his brother's shirt. "Did you mix medicines or something? What did you give him?"

Zeke pried his brother's hands off him. "There's no need to lose your head over a standard military medical practice."

"*Tell me what you gave him.*" Kase straightened his own shirt as Zeke did his.

"Yes, please explain," Hallie said.

Kase turned. "You don't need to get involved."

"This concerns all of us. Of course I need to get involved."

Kase looked like he wanted to say something more but thought better of it. She filed that away for later examination. "Please. Just tell us."

Zeke cleared his throat. "With his condition, I did what I had to, so I gave him a standard pain reliever as well as a few other medicines to heal his internal injuries."

"Like what exactly?" Kase growled.

"Like scerotaine, almimferjen, and of course, getasol invatmine."

Hallie blinked. She'd never heard of any of those, but she stepped up beside the two instead of lingering by the door. She peeked back toward where Ben had left and looked up at Zeke. "I don't know much about medicines or how to mix them, but I'm not sure whatever you gave him was a good idea. It seemed to make him worse."

Kase tugged his arm free. "You should've thought it through before you just up and gave him—"

"I would never do something so *stupid* as mixing medicines that don't work well together." Zeke's nostrils flared. Huh, so there was emotion tucked somewhere inside. "And no one wants or needs your blasted opinion, Kase. You're only on this mission because of Jove's pity. Because you *shocking* nearly killed someone, and you're too cowardly to face the consequences. *I* had something worthy to contribute."

Kase had nearly *killed* someone?

Kase snarled, lunging for his brother. She grabbed his arm and tugged hard, snapping, "Stop! This isn't helping anything!"

"Just because you're jealous of Jove doesn't mean you get to play god!" Kase shouted, his breaths coming out in sharp bursts.

Hallie's eyes widened as she stepped back, wishing she'd never left her room. Kase had been right. This wasn't her fight.

"Have you lost your ever-twinkling mind?" Zeke spat. "You don't get to spout off ridiculous accusations."

"You know I'm right. That's why you joined the military, isn't it? So you could be the favorite son? You hated living in Jove's shadow, and you didn't have the balls to call out Father when he lost his mind at Ana for trying to run away."

"*Shut. Your. Mouth.*" Rage lit Zeke's gaze. "You have no blasted idea what you're talking about."

Hallie's breath caught. She should do something. She scanned the room, looking for anything she could use to help diffuse the situation, but how would old potatoes or dried beef help?

"Enough," a low voice said from the doorway, and both brothers froze. "Whatever the moons you're fighting about has to stop. *Now.*"

Hallie turned to find a mostly cleaned Ben. His eyebrows were indeed singed off. "Fighting like this won't accomplish anything. Now both of you, *grow up!*"

Kase's breaths were ragged as he pushed past the others, making sure to knock Zeke in the shoulder before heading up the corridor toward his chamber. Hallie bit her lip and took a step after him before she stopped. She was probably the last person he wanted to see. And Zeke's words still rang in her ears.

"...because you shocking nearly killed someone, and you're too cowardly to face the consequences..."

Her heart pounded. While the first half of the accusation was a shock, it was the latter half that struck true. Her face grew hot. Hadn't she done the same back in Stoneset?

Zeke ran a hand through his hair and over his face. "I'm sorry, Hallie, Ben. I didn't mean to—I haven't lost my temper in so long. Kase has a way...sorry. Everything with the ship, this mission...just give me a moment to compose myself."

Without anything to do, Hallie scampered back to her bedchamber. Ebba wasn't there, probably outside. She stared at her plain bed wrapped in a dull brown blanket, the caramels sitting on top. She schooled her face into one of indifference, desperately trying to compose herself. Tensions were clearly high, and another breakdown wouldn't help anyone, least of all her.

She replayed Zeke and Kase's words in her mind once more. Passion and frustration drenched each syllable. It was so unexpected of Zeke—another blow-up between her and Kase had been far more likely, not one between him and the ever-calm soldier. *Stars.*

She stared at the caramels as both Ben and Zeke

headed out of the ship, their footsteps too loud in her head. Sitting down on her coverlet, she pulled her knees up to her chest. What a terrible, blasted mess they were in. They might never get home. They might die out here in the wilds of Tasava, and no one would ever know their story.

Another loud bang crashed her melancholy thoughts. Without any curses filtering through her window from Ebba, nor footsteps, it could only be one person—the one with a temper to rival her own.

Making her way into the corridor and peeking around the frame to the men's chamber, Hallie frowned when she found Kase lying on his back, arm stretched over his eyes.

He'd nearly killed someone.

She flinched when he hit the wall again with his fist. She took a hesitant step forward but pulled back and hid before she even made it over the threshold. She pressed her back against the cool metal, squeezing her eyes shut. He didn't need her barging in on his misery. When he hit the wall again, she pushed herself off and headed straight for her own chamber.

Better to let him simmer in silence. She was sure he had an explanation for everything. The Kase she'd come to know through bits and pieces wasn't someone who'd...who'd...

Ignoring another fist to metal from Kase, she tossed her coat on her bed and dug through her trunk.

Her search was fruitless yet again. *The Gate of Time* was most definitely not in her trunk. Kase must have remembered wrong. The book was probably ruined with rain beside the pillar.

She sighed, turning her attention back to the caramels. If there ever was a time to eat them, it was now. She'd barely touched them, even at her hungriest. Sitting on her bed, she untied the string holding the bag closed and played with one of the candies.

That fight had been bad. Worse than anything she or Kase had ever argued over. What if Zeke had seriously hurt Ben with those medicines? What if he never recovered? Was that essentially Zeke's fault? He was a trained medic, but...

A small clatter interrupted her thoughts. Hallie tossed the caramel back into the bag and turned to where she'd heard the sound. Jack's pocket watch had fallen from where she'd laid it on the edge of the bed frame.

Hallie picked it up and inspected it. The ridges of the front calmed her, and she opened it. She half expected the thing to quit working once more, but the hand still moved. It said it was only one o'clock, which was incorrect. With a shrug, she stuffed it into her trouser pocket. She'd worry about it later.

Another bang reverberated throughout the ship.

I can't fault him for being upset, at least, though if he keeps it up, he might damage the ship further.

Eyeing the paper bag at the end of the bed, she had an idea. Possibly a laughable one, but concentration was out the window if Kase kept the noise up. She grabbed the bag of caramels and walked toward the men's chamber. Just outside, she squared her shoulders, then knocked lightly on the doorframe.

"Go away, Zeke." Kase punctuated his words with another slammed fist.

Right. Dumb idea. "Um, it's Hallie." She twisted a strand of hair from her braid and moved into his view. She hadn't had the will to do it in a ladies' bun after the crash. "I have something for you. I'll leave it, um, I'll leave it on the bed. Sorry to bother."

Kase let his arm fall away from his face, tilting his head up to frown at her. "A paper bag? Is that supposed to help?"

He's not mad at me. Hallie stepped into the room. "You like caramels? That's what's in here. If you don't, no worries, and I'll just go back to my..." She cleared her throat. "Sorry. I'll go now."

Before she turned away, Kase sat up and swung his legs off the side of the bed, pushing the mess of blankets aside. "You brought me caramels?"

She nodded, flushing under Kase's discerning gaze. She gripped the bag harder. "I haven't eaten many of them. You can have the rest."

He stared at her several seconds too long, and she swallowed. Her mind told her to leave, but her feet wouldn't obey. Zeke's accusation rang in her ears.

"Kase? Did you...um, did you really almost...what Zeke said about you, and . . ."

Just go. Drop the caramels and leave.

Kase worked his jaw for a moment. Hallie's stomach tightened.

"It wasn't my fault. Not really." She didn't move. He ran both hands over his face and leaned back against the wall. "It's complicated. The Crews have an unofficial induction ritual. The last one ended with a greenie paralyzed from the waist down, and I volunteered to take the blame for it, thinking the Shackley name would protect me. Conceited, I know."

She swallowed, tightening her grip on the bag. "Is that all?"

One of his blue eyes peeked out. "If our mission isn't successful, meaning I don't prove my worth as a pilot, I'll be...my father's kicking me off the Crews.

And..." he hid behind his fingers once more, "I'll end up facing charges, and if I somehow escape punishment from that, I'll probably be forced to join the army. Probably only to die in that blasted war Jove hinted at."

"Oh," she whispered. For a moment, she considered turning around and leaving again, but as she did, Kase's moment of indecision right before the *Eudora* fell flashed in her mind. She'd been so terrified by that look, seeing how badly he wanted to pull himself to safety. Thinking she'd die alone because she wasn't important enough to save. Not to the Lord Pilot, not to anyone.

But then he'd let go.

Let go. Jack's voice echoed in her mind. The corners of her eyes burned, and she blinked away the water clouding her vision. *Let go.*

Even though her stomach was wrenched tighter than her mother's twisted bun, she padded over and took a seat next to Kase, bag still in her fist. She held it out and mumbled, "They'll make you feel better. Promise."

Taking it from her, he snorted softly. "I guess it's as good a try as any. I do love caramels." He pulled one out and handed it to her.

She shook her head. "No, it's fine, really. They're for you."

Kase raised an eyebrow. "You brought an entire bag of sweets on this mission, only to eat..." He peeked inside. "You haven't eaten any of these, have you?"

"I did! I've had two!"

"I don't believe that one bit. Not that I'm complaining. You know this wouldn't have lasted the day if it'd been in our room. Regardless, you can't let me eat them alone."

She plucked it from his fingers. The knots in her stomach finally relaxed, and she leaned back against the wall. "If you insist."

Let go.

She unwrapped the candy, the cellophane crinkling, and popped it into her mouth. She moaned as sweet, sugary goodness exploded across her tongue. "Oh good stars, I should've had more of these."

Kase ate one of his own. "This is the best thing I've ever eaten. By lightyears."

Hallie grinned and took another, unable to stop herself now. She unwrapped it and tossed it in the air, trying to catch it in her mouth. It hit her cheek instead, dropping onto the floor.

"Oh, please, I can do better than that."

"Prove it, Lord Pilot."

Kase threw it up and leaned backward to catch it, but the effort was for naught. It hit him in the eye. "Ouch! That nearly blinded me!"

Hallie laughed and grabbed another caramel. "Someone needs to practice."

"If you had shared these earlier, I could've been proficient by now. This is your fault, really."

She threw the wadded wrapper at him and chewed the candy, savoring every bit of it. Once she'd swallowed, she smiled. "Well, maybe I would've shared them earlier if you hadn't been such a *dulkop*."

Kase quirked his eyebrow. "Strong word for a gentlelady such as yourself."

Hallie snorted in a rather unladylike fashion. "*Me?* A gentlelady? You must have me confused with another Hallie Walker."

"Because I know so many."

"Of course. But for the record, I'm the best one."

"I don't doubt it."

Hallie grinned and took another. Enjoying the sugary treat and the camaraderie they'd found, she chewed for a moment. Kase unwrapped another and tossed it up in the air; this time, he caught it with a satisfied grin.

"I believe the win goes to me," he said through sticky teeth.

Hallie rolled her eyes. "You do know Odysseus paid for his excessive pride. With our luck, you just unleashed a horde of dragons upon us."

"I do what I can."

"You're impossible."

"It's true. I won't deny it." He took out another candy and held it in his fingers. "Thank you."

She pushed a bit of hair out of her face. "For what?"

"For this. And for..." He held up the bag. "You didn't run or anything when I was...well, when I told you what happened."

She fiddled with the hem of her shirt. The lace pattern, a line of aster flowers, was one of her favorites. It had been one of her first purchases upon arriving in the capital. "You're not the only one who's done terrible things. You don't have to shoulder that burden alone."

Kase's eyes were shadowed, but his words were strong. "Thank you."

A beat of silence, and like always, Hallie couldn't stand more than that.

She took another caramel. "Tell me. If you've read Marisee, you must have heard of Kaylor. He specializes in other ancient literature, particularly Shakespeare, but he's wrong about some of his analysis of *Julius Caesar*, particularly when he goes through Brutus' speech..."

It wasn't until Hallie was tucked into her bed hours later, after discussing all sorts of books and authors and eating so many candies her stomach was fit to burst, that she realized not once did they discuss the fact they might never return home. Not a single time did it cross her mind.

She smiled into the pillow as she rolled over, content to listen to the soft nighttime sounds and murmured voices of Ben and Zeke outside her broken window. It wasn't long before she fell asleep, the smile never leaving her face.

PART III: GATE

INTERLUDE II

SHATTERED STARS

Jove

THE TRIUMVIRATE ARGUED FOR A week after the Lord Kapitan's suggestion to assassinate the Cerulene Commander, Marcos Correa. Jove was sure he'd gained at least five gray hairs from these past few days alone, and they weren't his first. Clara teased him about them, saying his hair looked like someone had sprinkled salt on the side of his head. For stars sake, he wasn't even thirty.

"Don't worry about your hair, love," Clara soothed as Jove tried to pull his hat down to cover the gray strands. They rode through the city on their way to dinner at Shackley Manor. Mother had insisted, saying she wanted to talk with Clara about the baby. He wouldn't have cared so much about going if his brothers were also attending, or even some important dignitary. But no, it would just be Jove, Clara, and his parents—a private, cozy family affair. *Wonderful.*

Jove quit fiddling with his bowler hat and peeked at his wife. "You're just saying that because you're younger."

Clara's laugh was like a songbird in spring. "Be thankful. Not everyone is given the gift of growing old."

Jove snorted. "I guess you're right."

"Always am. Should've learned that these past few years."

What had he done to deserve her?

Jove smiled, his first real one in days. His hand engulfed hers as he took it and pulled it onto his lap. "It'll sink in eventually."

She squeezed his hand. They didn't talk much the rest of the way, which allowed Jove to look out the window as the driver took them to the manor. Even though he usually preferred walking everywhere, Jove didn't want Clara to walk that far, especially at night. Besides, what was the point of having a prestigious name like Shackley if it didn't come with certain perks? Having a chauffeured motorcoach was one of the best.

As the evening mealtime approached, well-to-do families were already in their own spiraling estates, leaving many of the roadways clear. Several of the wealthiest had homes outside the city, but many of the buildings in Upper Kyvena were built higher instead of wider due to the space restriction. That didn't mean they weren't any less garish than their country estates. Probably more so.

Jove liked his and Clara's little townhouse. Simple and practical. It felt more like home than anywhere else.

Around this time in the lower city, people of all

sorts would still be wandering around trying to find the best deals in the market, seeing a show at the public theater, or going to local taverns. Jove didn't enjoy going down to that part of the city; it was too dirty for him. But at that moment, he would have eaten in one of the dirtiest establishments of them all. Instead, he headed for one of the cleanest, most prominent estates in the city: his childhood home.

"Jove?"

He grunted as he turned to his wife. She was biting her lip—she only did that when she was nervous.

"Yes, love?" He rubbed a thumb across the back of her hand.

"Will you try not to fight with your father tonight?"

Jove stiffened, pulling back his hand. "He's the one who usually starts it."

She put her hands on her growing stomach. "I know, but your mother's been under a lot of stress with your brothers gone. Please? No matter what he says?"

Jove clenched his fist as he leaned his clean-shaven cheek against it, his elbow propped up on the door. He tried to blink back the memory of another fight so many years ago. It had been Kase who started it with their father, Jove only jumping in when Harlan's fist had—

He shook his head to clear his thoughts. "I'll do my best."

"Thank you."

They rode the rest of the way in silence, but Clara took his free hand in hers once more. He didn't stop her. He knew she was always on his side, something he didn't want to take for granted. Once the motorcoach pulled through the front gates, he pulled it away and tried to wipe off the sweat gathering in his palms.

"Here we go," Jove muttered as a serving man came to the door, opening it for them. Jove got out first and turned toward his wife, grasping her fingers to ease her onto the cobblestones below.

With a nod to the servant and the driver, Jove led Clara up to the front door and knocked. Taking a deep breath and smoothing the front of his jacket, Jove prepared to enter the lion's den.

"OH LES, YOUR COOK MUST give me the recipe for this canapé," Clara gushed as the group, including both Jove and Harlan, sat in the formal drawing room just before dinner would be served. "I haven't been able to eat much since, you know, the baby..."

Jove's mother grinned, her soft blue eyes alight. "Of course, and don't you worry about that. I remember I couldn't stand the smell of fish the entirety of my pregnancy with Kase. Well, that's not saying much, is it? No one really likes the smell of fish."

Jove grimaced at his mother's attempt at a joke, even if Clara laughed outright. She tried so hard to get into his mother's good graces. Marrying Zeke would have given her a better chance as he was everyone's favorite. Never caused problems. *The perfect son.*

The room overflowed with wealth, as evidenced by the mahogany bookshelves framing the fireplace and the decadent glass figurines his mother loved to collect dotting the exposed surfaces. Each one twinkled in the light from the chandelier. Jove's favorite was the one of King Arthur on the side table. It was the only story he'd ever liked—well, if it was read to him. He wasn't like Kase, always content to sit around getting lost in a dusty tome.

Jove brought the brandy to his lips, the ice clinking against the fine-spun glass. His father echoed his movements.

All Harlan had said upon learning of the impending birth of his first grandchild was, "Thank you."

Nothing else. Not a smile. No congratulations. Just *thank you.*

Jove still hadn't quite pieced together what that meant. No one else had understood either, it seemed. His mother had laughed it away in her nervous manner and peppered Clara with other questions, which his wife was happy to answer. Jove hadn't paid much attention, focusing more on his drink than anything else and ignoring the canapé appetizers. At least if Kase had been there, he would have said something outrageous or embarrassing. Jove would have welcomed a sparring match against his youngest brother with open arms if it'd kept Harlan's silence at bay.

Really, Harlan's response shouldn't have been that surprising. What else would Jove have expected? A smile? Popping a bottle of champagne?

Nope. Just: "Thank you."

"Lord Kapitan, High Guardsman, Ladies Seleste and Clara, dinner is served," the maid announced, punctuating her words with a deep curtsy.

"Thank you, maid," Harlan said. At least he'd added another word to his response. Even if he apparently didn't know or care to know what the maid's name was. Nevermind that Zurie had been with them since Jove was in grammar school. Jove set his glass down on the side table before heading into the dining hall.

Dinner was tolerable, if only for the women's

chatter. He could never be truly comfortable in the room with the long table, towering ceiling, and candlelit chandelier. No electricity in this sacred hall. He knew his mother had wanted to put the new technology in here, but Harlan had refused. Jove had a sneaking suspicion it was because of Uncle Ezekiel's treason having to do with electricity, but he wasn't sure.

As Jove picked at his roast and traced the gilded swirls on the tablecloth with his index finger, he attempted to listen to Clara's conversation. At least his wife and mother were ignoring the wall of silence that was Harlan. Their chattering made the dinner slightly less unpleasant than he'd imagined it would be. And he'd kept his word to Clara, no fighting with the Lord Kapitan. If he could make it another hour, he could go to sleep without a guilty conscience.

But one bite into the decadent chocolate pie Jove would have never been able to pronounce the name of, Harlan struck the first blow.

"I don't appreciate you challenging me in our meetings." Harlan used a knife to cut the tip of his own dessert. He placed the morsel in his mouth with grace a swan would kill to achieve.

Jove gripped his utensils tight enough that he thought he might have bent them. Slowly, he set them down, lest he be tempted to stab the table or the pie. The women's conversation ground to a halt as he folded his expensive cloth napkin beside his dainty plate, lamented the thought of not finishing the final course, and sent Clara a silent apology.

"I'm sorry you feel that way." Jove stared at his father. "However, I would suspect the High Council would frown upon us discussing sensitive information outside meetings."

"What I say in my own home need not be censored."

Jove glanced at Clara's pleading eyes and stood up from his chair. "Perhaps we can have a civil conversation about this in the drawing room?"

Harlan set his knife and fork down along with his own napkin before standing up. The servant rushed forward to push the chair back in after Harlan strode away from the table.

Jove followed, running his tongue along his teeth. They couldn't even get through one night—one that was supposed to be joyful. Celebratory. Jove and Clara were going to have a child. But no, Harlan had to make it about himself.

As Jove closed the door on the two women, he barely heard his mother tell Zurie to put the rest of the pie in the icebox. The Lord Kapitan led him into the drawing room, and Jove spotted his abandoned brandy glass before Harlan turned on him.

"Now, let's have what you call a *civil* conversation, shall we?" Harlan crossed his arms. His mustache twitched. "You are not to contradict me in meetings."

"I'm High Guardsman, Lord Kapitan. I'm there for a reason." Jove tried to keep his tone even. And he was about as successful as he would have been at dragging a twelve-ton boulder up a mountain. "I was only stating facts. Facts that the Stradats needed to know."

Harlan narrowed his eyes. "Sarson is waiting for any chance she can to depose me, and she's now got Richter on her side."

Jove bit his tongue. He'd promised Clara. He and Harlan were having a simple conversation, nothing more. His earlier tone could be excused. Usually, Harlan was all bluster in the beginning of any argument, and more often than not, Jove took the bait, but not this time.

"And then today, you had the blasted nerve to go against my plan."

Because he'd wanted to slaughter innocent people. Using what special operation forces and spies Jayde already had on the other side of the Nardens, the Lord Kapitan wanted to destroy the city of Sol Adrid itself after Correa was dead. To show Cerulene who really held power on Yalvara.

Jove swiped at his brandy glass and drank the watery dregs. He swallowed, breathing heavily out of his nose. He needed more alcohol. "I need to look impartial. Family ties can't get in the way of our jobs. I thought you'd understand that."

Harlan slammed his fist against the wall near the bookshelf, rattling its contents. His hazel eyes blazed. "Don't you dare give me that! You and the others would sit idly by and do nothing while Cerulene gains all that power. I'm the only one who would do anything about it!"

He didn't stop there. His father spat onto the green carpet, his spittle darkening the precious wool. "That Yalv mission was my idea, too. But apparently, I have not one, but three useless sons who take after their blasted uncle."

Red filled his vision as Jove hurled his glass at the fireplace, where it smashed into a thousand pieces. "*Useless*? I made a name for myself. That was all me. I run the Watch!"

Any restraint he might have had broke along with the glass. He pushed into Harlan's face. "You made me send them! I was insane enough to go along with it, thinking it all for the survival of Jayde. But they might be *dead* for all we know, and you don't care! You've never cared. If my brothers never come back, their deaths are on your hands. Just like Ana's is. Just like Uncle Ezekiel's is. You only care about that stupid uniform and your own blasted pride."

"I refuse to be talked to that way in my own house. I am your father." Harlan shoved him into the side table, the sparkling King Arthur figurine toppling over and crashing to the floor. Shards of glass like shattered stars winked in the light from the chandelier above.

Jove stared at the pieces, working his jaw to hold back tears as anger and frustration coursed through his veins. His voice cracked as he spat, "I don't have a father."

He picked himself up and fled into the hallway where Clara and his mother waited. Before he could do anything rash, he strode toward the front door, yanking his coat from the hook. "Apologies for the glass, Mother."

Clara's footsteps tapped softly against the hand painted tile as his mother called for the car. He calmed himself as best he could before turning. "Sorry I didn't keep my promise."

She didn't say anything, only took his hand in hers. A minute later, the motorcoach rumbled around to the front, and Jove helped her inside. He slid in and dug into his pocket, pulling out a cigarette and his lighter. Clara gave him a dark look.

Just as he was about to tell the driver to head to the apartment, someone rapped at his window. He probably would have punched the feeble glass if it had been Harlan, but it wasn't—only an exhausted messenger. Jove opened the door.

"Sorry to disturb you, High Guardsman. I was

tasked with delivering this to you." He bowed, handing Jove an envelope. Jove took it and turned it over. It was emblazoned with Heddie's personal seal, an owl against Firstmoon.

The messenger headed up the stairs to the manor. Jove squinted. It must have something to do with the High Council, then, if the man was taking a message to the Lord Kapitan as well.

"What is it, love?"

Jove shrugged. "It's from Heddie." He closed the door with a snap. "To the townhouse, Avery, please."

The driver nodded, and the coach jerked into motion. The stench of yalvar fuel tickled Jove's senses as he stuffed the cigarette and lighter back into his pocket. It didn't help the fury still pulsing through his veins. He broke the seal and fished out the parchment inside.

It was a short missive in Heddie's precise hand.

Stradat Forrest Richter is dead. Foul play suspected.

CHAPTER 20

THE LAST TRUE PROMISE

Hallie

HALLIE WOKE TO THE STINGING, sputtering whiz of an electropistol bolt. As she sprang out of bed, her answering gasp was lost in unintelligible shouts.

She looked over at Ebba's sleeping form in the bed beside her. Only a solitary curl moved in the wind of slow and steady breaths. Stars, how'd she stay asleep?

More shouts. Another electropistol blast. Footsteps on metal.

Hallie thrust her feet into her boots, not bothering to tie them nor twist her hair up into a ladies' bun. Strands of auburn stung her eyes as she stumbled into the corridor.

"Kase!"

He stopped in the doorway of the ship and flicked

a glance her way. He held an electropistol aloft, his eyes burning brightly in the light from the sparking end of the weapon. "Zeke caught someone sneaking around our campsite."

Hallie's leaden legs followed Kase out of the ship and down the stairs to find both Zeke and Ben beside a man with a shining bald head, his features contorted as his arms and legs jerked and twitched against rope bindings, an electropistol bolt's energy still thrumming through his body. The man lay on his side, a wad of cloth stuffed in his mouth.

But all Hallie could do was stare at the tattoo inked onto the man's pale neck.

Three intertwined blue diamonds watched her in the pale predawn light. It was a mark Hallie knew and had learned to fear living so close to the Cerulene border. Its meaning was terror and pain.

"Cerl soldier," Hallie whispered as the man attempted to spit the wad of filthy cloth out of his mouth.

Zeke looked up from where he knelt, his eyebrows raised. "You know that?"

"Of course she does," Kase said, kicking the Cerl in the side. "She's a scholar and grew up near the border."

Ben cocked his pistol and held it to the man's forehead. His voice took on a chill Hallie had never heard before as he spoke. His words and tone froze the early morning air in her lungs. "No matter who he is, he won't survive an electrobolt to the brain." He looked up, keeping his weapon to the man's head. "You've got his pistol, right?"

Zeke gestured with his other hand; a small firearm was clasped in his fingers. While it resembled the sleek look of an electropistol in size and general feel, the barrel was jagged and frayed like an overused rope, and the metal had a subtle blue hue.

"Don't kill him," Hallie squeaked. Her hands and shoulders shook against her efforts to still them.

But if Zeke hadn't caught him...

The Cerl jerked and fought his restraints but stilled as Ben removed the end of the barrel from his head and clocked him with the butt of the electropistol. Hallie recoiled, her hands covering her eyes as blood spewed from the man's temple and ran down his cheek, dripping off his long nose.

"Why in the blazes did you do that?" Zeke shouted. "We need answers from him! You of all people know that."

But Ben never got to respond.

A blast like a cannon echoed off the trees and the ruins of the *Eudora Jayde*. Brilliant blue light blinded Hallie even though her fingers still covered her eyes. A scream rent the air. Her own.

A massive weight collided with her chest, and both she and the weight slammed onto the cold, hard ground. Roots and rocks bit like knives and teeth into her back, her shoulder. She still hadn't opened her eyes.

"Hallie!"

She blinked to Kase's face swimming above her. Her recently healed shoulder twinged painfully, and she gasped. "What—"

He pulled her up by her other arm. "Get Ebba and hide. Now."

"Why..."

But she finally took in the destruction around her. Trees sheared midway up their trunks bent backward. Ben, Zeke, and the Cerl lay on the ground motionless.

Another scream bubbled in her chest. Its release

ravaged her aching throat as four silhouettes materialized at the edge of the broken treeline. Three carried the curious pistol Zeke had taken from the other Cerl, but the one on the far left heaved a larger gun onto his shoulder. Its end still leaked ethereal blue smoke.

Kase dove for the electropistol he'd dropped and within nearly one motion, fired several bolts in a matter of seconds. "RUN, HALLIE!"

Most shots flew wide, but one nailed the Cerl on the far left in the leg. The man screamed and stumbled forward, his massive weapon falling from his shoulder. Golden static sparks grew from where the bolt had hit and engulfed the rest of his body. He twitched and jerked all the while screeching against the pain.

His companions cocked their weapons, taking aim at Kase, who'd risen from his knees, his finger pressing the trigger once more.

Jagged blue fire shot from the end of three Cerl pistols. One hit the *Eudora*, one hit a broken tree to Hallie's right, but the final collided with the electrobolt.

A crackling like lightning and thunder deafened Hallie as the two forces of energy exploded. Electricity and fire burned her retinas as she covered her ears and fell to the ground beside Kase.

Darkness, light, ice, and fire.

All raged through her body.

Someone grabbed her arm, and fingers felt along her wrist, finding the soft spot. Her heartbeat stuttered.

"Hallie! Can you hear me?"

Kase.

She opened her eyes to flames. The trunks and ripped branches burned; sparks like stars licked the sky above. Kase dropped her wrist and grabbed both sides of her face. His hands were rough yet slick. She prayed it wasn't blood.

"The Cerls aren't moving. Get Ebba and start down the mountain."

Tears stung her eyes and panic pierced her chest like talons. "But Zeke...Ben..."

He dropped his hands and turned. "I'll get them. That second blast didn't hit them, I don't think. Don't know how we're not dead...just go, we don't have time!"

Bones aching, lungs straining, Hallie pushed herself to her feet and sprinted up the ship's stairs. Miraculously, neither the first blast nor the second had ravaged it, only marring its side with scrawling black marks like grasping fingers. *That* was why Jayde needed more Zuprium. It was a blasted indestructible metal.

Before she reached their bedchamber, Ebba stumbled out, good hand to the side of her head. Blood leaked from between her fingers.

"Good stars!" Hallie gasped. She ran toward the woman, but pain shot through her ankle, and she tripped, catching herself on the wall.

"Worse than it looks...I think." Ebba didn't move her hand. "Woke up when something rocked *Eudora* and tossed me from my bed. It's a miracle I didn't also bloody my nose."

Hallie righted herself and limped forward. "Cerls. Have to get out of here."

Ebba's hand fell from her head. Blood matted her hair and streaked across her temple and cheek. "What? Are you blasting serious?"

Hallie nodded and moved past her. She scanned her room and grabbed two things: her satchel and jacket. Jack's watch was already in her pocket.

"I don't want to leave *Eudora*." Ebba put her hand

back to her head as she followed Hallie inside. "I need more time."

Hallie retied the end of her braid and turned. Her chest burned, and her breathing hitched. "If that map is correct, the Yalvs are less than a day's hike down the mountain, and we don't know if any more Cerls are coming."

Tears glittered in Ebba's big brown eyes. "I don't care. I can't leave him. Not now."

"Who's him?"

Ebba ran a hand through her sleep-adled curls, messing them further. "*Her*. I can't leave her, the ship."

Hallie grabbed the woman's shoulders and squeezed lightly. "Our mission here is to find the Yalvs. Now, grab what you need. We have to go."

Ebba didn't say anything, only jerked out of Hallie's grasp and wiped a tear, smearing blood across her cheek. She made quick work of her valuables, only grabbing her wool coat and stuffing the pyrite rock in the pocket.

"Let's go." Her voice was gruff as she shoved past Hallie.

With one last look at their home for the past couple of months, Hallie followed. It was just a ship, a hunk of metal. But in that moment, it really did feel like she was leaving a friend. Her blanket was rumpled, her trunk laid bare. Rays of the rising sun and reflections from the burning trees made the broken window glass glow. She shook her head and limped out of the room.

Heat assaulted her as she stepped out the ship door. Blast, what if they set the whole mountain afire? Would they be able to outrun the flames? What if the inferno reached Myrrai?

Even with her panic, a wave of relief hit Hallie when

she looked at the others. Zeke and Ben were up and moving, both inspecting the Cerls. Ben examined the large weapon. While dirt and gore covered one side of his face, he looked to be all right.

"It's one of those blasted hand cannon prototypes," he said as he heaved it up. "Not sure how far we can make it with one of these, but better us throw it off a cliff than leave it here."

Zeke checked the pulse of one of the others. Soot and dried blood coated his fingers. "They're not dead, but killing them now is out of the question."

"What—" Kase started. He'd been facing the forest with his electropistol cocked and ready to fire.

Zeke stood. "They're defenseless, and we don't need to invite retribution."

"But they nearly blasted us to the stars!"

Hallie tangled her fingers in the strap of her satchel. "Let's just go. Before someone else finds us, please?"

Kase met her gaze from across the small clearing and nodded. Holstering his pistol, he jogged over. Zeke and Ben followed. Ebba rested a hand on the side of the ship, tears streaming down her face. "I'm sorry I couldn't fix you."

As they passed her, Zeke put a hand on her shoulder. "Let's go."

Ben hefted the cannon higher on his shoulder and led them into the burning forest.

Kase

EVEN THOUGH THEY'D WALKED FOR miles, the smoke in the air burned Kase's nose. It was in every breath and every step. The crew had outpaced the flames thus far, and he prayed for rain. It wouldn't do for the entire forest to burn. What if it reached Myrrai? What if the Yalvs rejected them because Kase had burned their homes?

Because Kase's shot colliding with the other started it.

His grip on the electropistol tightened, and his own sweat beaded on his brow. He wiped it with a shaking hand.

As the crew trekked out of Haddon's Pass and into the valley, the trees became thicker and more diverse. Evergreens now wove in between various other species of trees Kase didn't care two stars about. Even with it being so late in the year, they still hadn't lost most of their leaves. That only meant it was harder to see what lay in wait before them and what followed from behind.

No one talked much on their hike down. Kase didn't care. The early morning attack was on repeat in his mind.

It was only when they reached a small creek that Skibs called a halt. "I don't know how far we are from Myrrai, but the Yalvs won't appreciate us showing up with a Cerl weapon. Let's rest while I go find a place to stash this."

He hefted the thing higher on his shoulder and started to walk off when Zeke's words stopped him. "Hallie can explain to the Yalvs what happened."

"I'll be fine." A muscle twitched in Skibs' whiskered jaw. "Trust me, we don't want to show up armed with this."

Kase looked around at the others. Hallie had slid down one of the tree trunks and rummaged through her satchel. Ebba on the other hand stared out toward the creek away from the rest of them. The blood from her head wound had dried on her cheek, down her neck, and onto her shirt, yet she hadn't bothered to wipe it.

It was up to him to keep his best friend and his brother in check.

He stepped up between the two as Zeke said, "You stay here. I'll do a quick patrol to make sure no one's following us, and then we can figure out what to do about that cannon."

"It's my call, Lieutenant Colonel Shackley, not yours," Ben spat. "I'm in charge of this mission. The Head Guardsman appointed me himself."

I crashed the ship. I started the fire. This is my fault.

Kase waved his pistol in the air, sparks flying. "Shut it! The both of you! Zeke, you go make sure the stars-blasted Cerls haven't caught up with us. Skibs, go dump that thing, but watch your back. We don't need to be fighting over stupid things like that now."

Calm down. Follow your own advice.

Zeke shrugged, but Skibs gave him a hard stare before hiking up the creek. Kase holstered his electropistol and ran a hand through his hair. "Shocks and bolts."

"You don't get to act all high and mighty," Ebba said, her voice taking on a tired, waspish tone. "It's your *sterning* fault we're in this mess to begin with. You're the one who crashed *Eudora*."

Kase's face heated as he turned. "It's not like I meant for the engines to go out."

But she's right.

"You hit that pillar."

"Ebba," Zeke said, holding up his hands. "Calm down."

Kase pulled at his hair. "You're the mechanic! Why

wasn't the ship working? Huh?"

Ebba lunged, her teeth bared. "I just wanted to save him!"

"Kase," Zeke hissed as he caught Ebba's good arm and held her back.

"What's it to you if my parents end up in debtor's prison?" Ebba screamed. "What's it to you if we never get back? I heard the talk on the airfield. If you show your face in Kyvena, you're gonna end up in front of a judge for what you did to that pilot!"

Hallie stopped rummaging through her bag and stood. "You're not the only one worried about getting home, Ebba."

Ebba glared at her, but instead of retorting, she turned on her heel and stomped off the opposite way Ben had gone moments earlier.

Zeke's shoulders relaxed. "I'm going to patrol. Try to be civil while I'm gone."

And then he left too. Kase's skin still burned from the argument and his own shame. If he hadn't hit that column, the ship might've been fine. Everything would've been okay. They wouldn't have run into the Cerls either. They might already be on their way home.

Great shocks.

He stumbled over to the creek and fell to his knees. Scooping up a bit of water, he washed his face. He needed to calm his nerves if he was to keep his composure. While the Yalvs were still very much an unknown, they were their only hope. Kase had to find them. Kase had to make this right. Ebba wasn't wrong.

He had just scooped up another handful of water when sniffling met his ears. The water draining from his fingers, he turned. Hallie hadn't moved from her spot, but her shoulders shook, and her hands tried to hide the tears.

"Hallie?" He wiped his wet hands on his trousers. "Hallie, what's wrong?"

She swiped at her eyes and pressed the heels of her palms into them as she crouched down. A soft breeze blew through the trees and picked up wayward strands of her hair. "The Yalvs, for all their power, can't do anything to fix our ship, and I doubt they'll have anything of the sort to loan us. What are we going to do? My parents...now they'll have lost both their children. I'll never get to open a school. I'll never get to live out the rest of my life. I never should've left home. This is all my fault."

Her words were a flaming arrow straight to his heart. It hurt. It burned. It caught the rest of him in a blaze. Without any way of getting back, what had Kase lost out here? What would he miss out on?

Nothing. Because he'd already lost everything that mattered.

But looking at Hallie now, he realized that was selfish. Not everyone was as messed up as he was. Not everyone had endured his trauma. There were those whom this mission was costing them everything, even when he had nothing else to lose.

He chewed on the inside of his cheek and stepped up to her. She hadn't moved, only still sobbed into her hands while crouched on the leaf-laden ground. "I promised you yesterday we'd find a way back, and we will."

She didn't look up. "How?"

Kase squatted beside her. "I don't know, but we don't have a choice *but* to believe that. Isn't that what you told me?"

She finally peeked over at him. Her eyes were like

glittering jewels in the sunlight filtering through the trees. "Yes, but...with the Cerls, and even Ebba couldn't..."

Kase took her hands in his. They were wet from her tears, cold from the autumn air, and delicate in his calloused fingers. "I know, but when I make promises, I always keep them."

The lie burned his tongue. The last true promise he'd ever made had ended with Kyvena in flames.

She sniffed again, turning away slightly. She took her hands from his and stood, wiping the remnants of tears. "You're right. If I'm to convince the Yalvs of anything, I need to be at my best. We'll...we'll worry about getting home later.

CHAPTER 21

STARLIGHT

Kase

WITH THE SUNSET'S RAYS ALIGHT in the trees, the crew fumbled through the last vestiges of the forest and tangled underbrush. Kase tucked his jacket closer around his shoulders and gripped his electropistol in one hand. He'd probably have permanent marks on his palm.

According to Jove's map and Hallie's calculations, their destination should lay on the horizon now they'd made it out of the Pass and into the valley. The journey would be over at last. All Hallie had to do was convince the Yalvs to join their side. Easy. He hoped.

After a quick break to drink the little water left in the canteen Hallie had stuffed in her satchel, Kase followed the others up the next hill. He waved the pistol with each peek back at the forest behind them. No sounds other than the ones they made in their trek met his ears. Nothing moved the trees other than the wind. Maybe the Cerls at the crash site were the only ones, or maybe they were still incapacitated?

Once they crested the hill's peak, Kase found it didn't matter. None of that mattered.

"No," Hallie gasped. "No, no, no..."

Cold like the blistering winter wind started in Kase's heart and flowed out to his hands, his feet.

Instead of a shining city bustling with people, torn and marred heaps of metal and stone lay before them. Moss, vines, and other plant life had overtaken the unoccupied spaces. A lone deer near the city gate darted into the maze of ruins.

Crashing, burning stars.

They were never making it home.

Hair streaming behind her like fire in the late afternoon light, Hallie sprinted toward the city despite her limp. Kase and Skibs took after her.

"Hallie!" Kase yelled. "Wait!"

But she didn't listen, didn't stop until she'd reached the city gate and fell to her knees before it. He and Skibs slowed as they approached.

"You can't just run off like that," Skibs said, each of his breaths coming out in pained huffs. "We need to assess the situation."

Kase only nodded, too out of breath to say anything else. Eyes full of desperation and a little pain, Hallie looked up. "There must be some explanation. There must be someone left in the city. I'm supposed to...supposed to..."

"It's not your fault." Kase pushed back his sweaty curls. "We had bad information."

Was it Jove's fault, then?

He couldn't have predicted this, surely. Kase swallowed the stinging, burning bile rising in his throat. Jove had admitted the government had lied about the Yalvs dying out. Had this all been another lie? How much was the Watch covering up?

Kase squatted next to her and put a hand on her shoulder. "Maybe this is a different city? We know the map was old. It could be that Myrrai is somewhere..."

But he trailed off when Hallie pointed to the archway that made up the city gate. The structure towered above his head and connected to a crumbling wall on either side. The builders had constructed the archway itself out of Zuprium, recognizable by the bronze sheen in the light. Each brick stood solid and silent as they grew to a point. Spiked symbols Kase vaguely recognized as Yalven were scrawled across the keystone. Hallie's voice was tight as she spoke, "Starlight. The gate says this is...*was* Myrrai."

The sliver of hope he might've had vanished. Footsteps behind them made Kase clench his electropistol, but it was only Ebba and his brother. The mechanic spoke first. "So, this was all a waste?"

Kase holstered his weapon and helped Hallie to her feet. She hid her face behind bits of auburn hair that had come loose from her braid. She didn't bother to fix it.

Ebba continued, "I'm going back to *Eudora*."

"No." Skibs rubbed a hand down his haggard face. "Let's see if we can find shelter for the night. Tomorrow we'll search for anything that might help us repair the ship."

Ebba muttered something under her breath, but she followed as the rest of the crew entered the city.

In the dying light of day, each shadow and crevice was vast and reaching. Kase shivered. Many of the buildings, while made of stone and Zuprium, had toppled or eroded, leaving half walls in their place. Rubble littered the streets. Time, wind, and rain had weathered the stone, but the Zuprium looked the same. The miracle metal. Didn't mean it couldn't be twisted and contorted like the bits to Kase's right as they passed through the archway.

Skibs turned, and Hallie nearly stumbled into him. She was on the verge of tears judging by the water accumulating in her eyes. Kase understood. To have come this far only to find they failed? Heartbreaking. To know that their one hope of getting home was gone? Devastating. Yet a part of him was relieved. The selfish part of him.

For once in his life, he was *free*.

"Let's split up." Skibs said, his fingers tapping the electropistol strapped to his leg. "Just two groups."

Hallie nodded, wiping her eyes, but Ebba crossed her arms. "I'm staying put. You go search."

"Ebba..." Zeke started.

Skibs held up a hand. "No. We don't know the situation. As lead on this mission, it's my job to make sure everyone is safe. You go with one of the groups, understood?"

She rolled her eyes and stomped off without waiting on anyone. Hallie sighed. "I'll go with her."

Kase stepped up. "Me, too."

Skibs furrowed his brow, but he nodded. "Zeke and I will explore that way." He pointed in the opposite direction Ebba had gone. "Meet back in an hour. Got it?"

Kase unholstered his electropistol and followed Ebba into the desolation that had been the Yalven city of Myrrai. He had only heard tales of it, and even then, he barely remembered much about them. The buildings held little clue as to what they might've been an age past. Hallie probably knew, as with each ruined doorway, spiked symbols were just visible on the remaining Zuprium bricks. He didn't ask what they meant. He didn't want to know or feel for the long-dead Yalvs who used to live there. He didn't want to feel anything.

"Where in the stars did she go?" Hallie asked, her voice thick.

"If we listen closely, we might catch her cursing Skibs."

Hallie looked back, wisps of hair blowing in the soft yet chilling breeze. "Don't blame her. Her job was to fix the ship, and that's been taken from her."

"It's the Cerls' fault, not Skibs," Kase retorted. *That's not true either.* He slumped his shoulders. "Well, actually, it's mine, I guess. I'm the one who crashed."

Hallie put her right hand on his forearm. Not saying a word, she simply squeezed it and let go.

They didn't speak as they continued their search. They peeked into houses and shops, not finding anything of note under the rubble they could move. Sadly, nothing in Myrrai would help them repair the ship, though Kase wasn't sure what they were even looking for. How could they repair something if they didn't know what was wrong?

It's my fault. His new mantra. Kase swallowed hard and continued the search.

Close to their meet up time, they still hadn't found Ebba, but Kase didn't care. She was probably off hiding somewhere, maybe even heading back to the ship. With each subsequent building free of anything useful, he found he cared about nothing at all.

"Gracious day, what do you think that is?" Hallie whispered, her voice filled with amazement and awe.

Kase looked up from where he'd inspected the remains of some sort of decaying crate. He imagined the building behind it had been a butcher's shop based on the cleavers laced with rust still hanging from their perches through the busted window.

Even with the devastation, the building was beautiful. In fact, the crumbling stone and missing roof made the structure more entrancing. At twilight, the Zuprium bricks and accents glowed, giving off their own sort of light. Creeping, snake-like plants that hadn't yet died out for the year crawled up the sides and invaded glassless windows. If Kase had been back in Kyvena, he would've called it a cathedral. With its gothic archways and weathered façade carved with statues of people Kase couldn't identify, the building must have been important back in its prime. It reminded him of a more lavish version of the structure they'd found in the woods before the stonemen attacked.

"Oh stars, this must be it. This must've been the...the Gate temple," Hallie gasped as they reached the overgrown courtyard in front of the building.

"What?"

She half turned. "It's from the book. I still have a few of the translated pages in my..." She rummaged through her satchel and pulled out her sketchbook. Flipping through the pages, she smiled to herself. "Yes, Jasper Morgan's description is almost—"

What the description was almost like, Kase would never know because a scream interrupted Hallie.

Before he could fire his holstered electropistol or

even move to grab it, a voice spoke. It was a man, judging by the deep baritone, but that wasn't what chilled Kase to his core. The voice was silky, the 's' sounds a beat too long. "I wouldn't grab that unless you want a bullet in your skull."

Kase swallowed hard. Hallie's breathing came fast beside him, and Kase tried to think. But the Cerl wasn't patient. "Drop the weapons. You and your *shilka* are no match for us."

He didn't know what a *shilka* was, but he gripped his pistol tighter, still not turning. "I think you're bluffing."

"Kase," Hallie's voice squeaked a little, and he glanced at her. Her eyes were wide, and she was paler than Firstmoon. He needed to come up with a plan, and he needed to come up with it thirty seconds ago.

A choked gasp. Not Hallie.

Who or what was that?

He took his hand off the electropistol. "I honestly thought that blasted unnatural storm would do you in. It almost did us."

Silence. Kase pressed his luck. "I'm not sure what you want. We're stuck on this stars-forsaken side of the world same as you."

A pit opened in his stomach at the Cerl's next words. "I said drop the weapons. If you don't, your friend here will suffer. As will you."

He did as he was told as he unholstered his electropistol and laid it at his feet. He and Hallie turned.

Think. How can you get out of this? Blast. Are Zeke and the others okay?

But that thought disintegrated when he saw who the Cerls had caught. A blonde woman with the tell-tale diamond tattoo on her neck held a bleeding Ebba in a crushing headlock, a pistol pressed to her temple. The Cerl woman's hair was tied back with braids, all twisting up into a knot on top of her head.

"Ebba!" Hallie squeaked.

The other Cerl was a tall, windswept man with the same yellow hair and braids. He and the woman shared a long, thin nose and matching tattoos. His too-deep voice didn't match the way his body looked, like a subtle summer breeze could blow it over. His pistol, however, spoke volumes. It was the same jagged-barrel kind Zeke had taken from the others. He waved it between them. Ebba clawed at the woman's arm with one hand, the other in a fist at her side. The woman clenched her throat tighter, and Ebba's arm fell, her eyes filling with tears.

"Please." Hallie's voice shook slightly, and Kase glimpsed her clenched fists. "We're travelers from Tev Rubika, and we're here studying the plant life. That's all. Our friend was supposed to be looking for the acasia moss that grows uniquely on Zuprium."

If lives hadn't been on the line, Kase might've snorted. What a terrible lie.

"We know you're with the Jaydian government. We've been following you as this *jiro* surmised."

"Seeing as he figured out you've been following us, I'd say he's not a *jiro*," Hallie said, her voice growing stronger with each word. "Now, release our friend, and we'll be on our way."

Kase winced as the Cerl aimed the barrel of his pistol at her heart. "*Hallie...*"

She narrowed her eyes at the Cerl. All the fear she might have shown earlier had vanished. Jaw clenched, she stood with her feet apart, ready to leap into action at any moment. "If you've followed us this far and not done anything, you must want something from us now. So please, tell us what you want, and we can both be on our way."

"The Gate is ours to take." The man's pistol didn't waver. "Jayde has no Essences."

Hallie's face drained of what little blood it had left. Under her breath, she whispered, "That's what Jasper was trying to say. The Gate needs Essences."

"Say it louder," the woman growled. She took her own weapon from her belt and held it to Ebba's head.

"Hallie," Kase said, still cognizant of the danger they were in. "What are they talking about?"

No one was supposed to know about this mission. Only a handful of people. And most of those people were part of the *Eudora Jayde* crew. As much as he hated his father, Harlan would never betray Jayde, and neither would Jove. Head Guardswoman Heddie Koppen probably knew. Was it her? Was she a traitor?

Hallie thought for a moment before she spoke again, "We aren't here for the Gate, whatever that might be." She shifted, the two Cerls tensed, and Ebba whimpered. Her head wound had reopened, and blood trickled down her face and onto her captor's arm. Hallie continued, "The city's been abandoned for quite some time. Therefore, arguing with us over whatever you might've traveled all this way for is fruitless. I suggest you let my friend go, and then we'll be off."

"No."

The word froze in the wind as the last bit of light disappeared from the horizon. All they were left with were faint glows from cocked pistols and pale fractals of rising Firstmoon.

Come up with a plan, blast it!

But that was all Kase could think of in that moment. He needed time he didn't have. *Stars blast it all.* He should just lunge for his weapon and fire.

"Then let's make a trade," Hallie said, her voice as icy as the man's rejection. "You and I both know you've been stealing Zuprium, or at least tampered with our mines."

No response.

"I assume you're willing to listen, then."

"Hallie—"

She cut Kase off with a sharp look as she dug into her pocket. She pulled out the pocket watch she'd been wearing around her neck since the day he'd met her. It was small, and the etchings on the front had faded with time. Its Zuprium casing was pale in the budding moonlight, almost ghastly.

Hallie held it out. "From what I know, you're getting the better bargain with this. Please, let us go in peace. Take this back to your commander as proof there is no Myrrai."

"Hallie, what are you—" But Kase was too late.

Everything happened in slow motion. Hallie turned at his voice, holding out the watch as a blast of electric blue zipped through the air and nailed Hallie's hand. Her mouth gaped open as she screamed, the trinket falling to the ground. She stumbled as shouts and more pistol fire joined the first.

Golden blasts joined those of blue.

Ebba screamed as a jet of blue light hit her chest. She crumpled in her captor's arms. Everything slowed down to a crawl as Kase's heart thumped painfully in his throat. The Cerl woman jerked as golden bullets peppered her body, some hitting Ebba in the process. Both faces shone with the golden glow.

Blood soaked Ebba's trousers and shirt as both lay on the street. Kase lunged for his electropistol and fired back to where the Cerl man had stood seconds ago. He caught him in the chest, and it exploded with electricity. He fell backward from the impact, his weapon tumbling from his hand. A direct shock to the heart.

More electric blue light flew through the air as did the golden fire. It zinged above them in small pulses and struck targets judging by the cries. He hadn't realized there were more Cerls. Or was that Ben's scream? Zeke's shouting?

Ebba went limp, a craggy stone peeking out of her previously clenched fist. Kase scuttled over and checked her pulse.

With each still and silent second, the fight he might have had leaked out of him. She was dead. He eyed the rock loosely clasped in her cooling fingers and grabbed it. It was important to her for some reason, and it seemed a crime to leave it here. He stuffed it into his jacket pocket.

"Retreat!" Someone yelled in Common.

That must have been a Cerl, but more words followed in a language Kase didn't recognize. Though he might not have understood the words themselves, the shouts were guttural and vicious, the anger behind them apparent.

He glanced away from the blood pooling around the bodies. The size of the one near the Cerl was too big. There was no hope for her.

"Kase!" someone sobbed.

Hallie.

The golden and blue lights stopped whizzing above them, and Kase whipped his head around to find her gasping for air and clutching her hand. Her shirt, trousers, everything was splattered with dark red blood. It matched her hastily tied maiden sash. Her voice was shrill through her tears. "My hand...it burns...and my fingers..."

She turned and heaved, though nothing came out.

Bile rose in Kase's throat as he scrambled over. He took Hallie's hand. Two of her fingers, the middle and ring, clung to the rest by a sliver of skin, but the pinky was missing entirely. Kase shut his eyes and wished the nausea would go away. Ebba was unconscious, maybe dead, but Hallie would be the latter soon if he didn't do something. After three deep breaths, he opened his eyes. Her index and thumb were still intact, if soaked in slippery, metallic smelling blood. But how to stop the bleeding? Without knowing what else to do, he pressed hard where he thought the blood was coming out. Hallie screamed.

"I have to stop the bleeding!" His words came out like the wind as he pressed harder.

He looked around, hoping to find a solution, but nothing but the varied shouting and thundering footsteps surrounded them.

Still, the bleeding didn't stop. His drenched fingers slipped on her skin. *What do I do? I promised...I promised...*

Tears burned at the corners of his eyes as he let go of her hand and ripped off his jacket. "I don't know if this will work, but I'm going to try it anyway."

She looked up at him with her honey eyes. They stood out even more against her even paler face. She was losing too much blood. Kase cursed, and he pulled his once fine linen shirt over his head and grabbed one of the Cerls' pistols. The bite from the evening chill nipped at his bare skin, but he hardly felt it. "This is going to hurt like the sun, but it's the only way..."

Using the jagged edge, he ripped a long, uneven strip from his shirt and before measuring a few centimeters above where blood continued to spurt out of Hallie's hand. Best to tie it off at the wrist, maybe? Elbow? Shocks, where was Zeke when you needed him?

Should he cauterize it instead? No, he didn't have time to build a fire even if he could. Blast it. Any medical knowledge he'd learned in training evaporated. He could only recall what he'd read in stories. Fictional stories.

Trying to keep his own breathing even, he tied a knot just below her elbow with the strip. He set the barrel of the Cerl gun on top of that and twisted the other bits of shirt around it until Hallie jerked and screamed.

Kase caught her arm. "I know! But if I don't, you'll bleed out!"

Blood soaked the front of his trousers and splattered his abdomen, but he made sure the tourniquet was tight. Hallie moaned and cried, and each one sent a fresh dagger into his chest. He had no choice. *Shocks and bolts.*

"Kase! Hallie!" the familiar voice rang through the air. Kase whipped his head around to see Zeke sprinting toward him.

But he wasn't alone.

A horde of cloaked figures preceded him, and more joined, falling into line as they seemed to appear out of the beams of Firstmoon. They were tall and too skinny. One of them carried what looked like the swords Hallie and Ben had found when the stonemen attacked.

Kase leapt to his feet, blood-soaked hand fumbling to fire the electropistol, but no bolt shot from the barrel as he pulled the trigger. In seconds, a cloaked figure wrenched it from his hands.

How did it get here so fast? Why didn't the pistol work?

"What do you think—" He stopped when the figure pointed its own weapon at him. It was much like the electropistol and the Cerl gun, but this one radiated soft golden light like the sun. It put the static at the end of electropistols to shame. Kase remembered the golden blasts from minutes ago.

Zeke finally caught up. "Stop! He's—he's my brother!"

Blood ran down his older brother's face from where he'd acquired yet another cut to match the other he'd gotten in the first airship crash. His left arm hung loosely beneath a curtain of blood soaking his shoulder. "Mother of ash! Ebba!"

Zeke fell on his knees beside her as the cloaked figure lowered his weapon and pushed back his hood. The man's shiny black hair hung down in a single braid over his shoulder. His face was paler than parchment, but his eerie golden eyes shone like stars in the night sky.

"I am sorry," the man said in heavily accented Common. "I did not realize you were with this one."

He pointed down to Zeke, whose face was nearly as pale as Hallie's. His brother turned from inspecting Ebba. "I don't think...she's not..." He swallowed and looked back down at the girl's form, dwarfed by both Zeke and the Cerl woman. "I can't find...I can't find a pulse. And all this blood..."

"She got hit...the Cerls captured her, and...and then glowing bullets hit her." Tears streaked down Hallie's face. "She needs to get back to her family!"

The golden eyed man shook his head and gestured

to one of the other cloaked figures who had joined them. "Search the city for others. The Lord Elder will need at least one of them alive."

The other figure nodded and whisked away. Kase could only stare, unsure of what was going on before his eyes, but then Hallie moaned, and his eyes snapped back to her. "The bleeding wouldn't stop, and I think they hit an artery, and I didn't know what else to do besides the tourniquet, and..."

But the man held up a hand. "I will do what I can here, but she needs the attention of an experienced healer."

Kase slid his shirt over his head and his jacket on as the man knelt next to Hallie. He unearthed the Cerl pistol from the wrapping and with practiced hands, untied Kase's sloppy knot. Hallie's blood splattered onto his dark cloak.

"You're—you're Yalven," Hallie whispered as the man stuck his hand in a pouch at his waist and pulled out glittering dust. He smeared it on the bits of torn flesh and murmured a few words.

"Wait, you're—" Kase stared at the man, his mouth and brain not connecting. "What happened to this city—what in the blazes did you just—"

He sounded like a child who didn't know how to string two words together. The Yalv simply put up a hand.

"The Vasa needs time."

Hallie moaned again, but in seconds, her face was awash with light from the glittering dust. Before Kase's eyes, the skin stitched up along where the bullet had entered. The skin at her two fingers barely hanging on knit together, though they hung at a grotesque angle.

Had Kase gotten hit in the fray? Had the Cerl shot

him in the head and Kase found himself in a nightmare of an afterlife? How could he just knit her skin back together like that? He'd known the Yalvs had power, but hadn't Hallie said they'd died out or something because of some treaty? What had she called them again?

"That's impossible." Kase shook his head. "What about Ebba—couldn't you..."

"I cannot save the other girl. She must make the final journey." The Yalv looked up at him. His eyes were alight in the night. "As for this one, I don't have the skill to fix the bone, but she won't bleed out. We need to get her to the city."

Zeke stood. "I need to find our other crew member. He was fighting with a Cerl over near what I thought might've been a market square."

Skibs.

"Where is he?" Kase shouted as he whirled his head around. "Is he okay, is he..."

The Yalven man stood, wiping his hands. Remnants of gold dust clung to the cloak in bloody streaks. "Vanktr will find any survivors. But for now, we must take you to Myrrai."

Hallie shook her head. "But I thought this was...are you saying...did something...what happened to this one?"

It must've been the blood loss, because Kase had never seen her fumbling for words like that. Granted, Kase wasn't sure what to say either.

But they didn't have to speak a word.

With a whisk of his hand, the Yalv threw whatever the dust was over all three of them, Zeke included. Kase sucked in a breath to shout, scream, or maybe simply argue, but the dust clogged in his throat.

The last thing he saw before the darkness overtook

him was a pair of bright golden eyes.

CHAPTER 22

WHEN MORNING BREAKS

Kase

DARKNESS SURROUNDED KASE WHEN HE opened his eyes again. He jerked, cursing as some sort of rope dug into his wrists and ankles. His clothing scraped damp stone with each movement.

"Kase?" a deep voice asked.

He still couldn't see anything. He wasn't sure if he'd gone blind, or if there simply wasn't any light. His wrists burned as he tugged on them again. "Zeke?"

"And Hallie," came a soft voice near him.

"Skibs?" The silence was too long. "Where is he?"

Zeke's voice was too soft. "Dunno. The Yalvs didn't bring him in."

Kase's heart pounded. "What do you mean?"

"We're the only ones the Yalvs brought here. All the

Cerls that attacked escaped or were killed."

Hallie's voice trembled. "And Ebba, her body is still there. She's...she's..."

Dead.

A pounding began in Kase's ears as he tugged on his bonds. "So the Cerls might have Skibs?" The silence was answer enough. He cursed. Loudly. "They'll torture him for information."

"There's nothing we can do." Hallie's voice was tiny. "We're stuck. And he's star-knows-where."

Kase's chest hurt badly, worse than his burning wrists. Was this how it ended? Executed by the very people they'd been searching for? Shocks. If the Yalvs had healed Hallie and helped them fight the Cerls, why were they here now?

He tested the restraints on his ankles, but the rope was too tight. *Wonderful.* However, he managed to haul himself into an uncomfortable sitting position. Between being tied up and the beginning of a pounding headache, he ended up falling back with a thump that reverberated through his skull. Kase groaned.

"Are you all right?" Hallie asked.

"My head feels like I was hit by a brick, and we're being held prisoner. What do you think?"

Her sniffle was like a punch to his gut. He cleared his throat. "Sorry. Didn't mean for that to...will you explain what's going on? I thought the Yalvs were on our side."

Hallie shuffled nearby, like she was trying to find a better position. Zeke, wherever he was, was silent. "The Yalv who healed me wasn't in charge, and when another one of his party saw they were taking us in, that one got angry. Thinks we're Cerls if my translation was correct. But the dust knocked you out," she said. "It only temporarily paralyzed us, yet I don't remember how we got here."

"Paralyzed?"

"The Yalv who healed me did say he would take care of Ebba's...body, though."

"And where is he? Couldn't he explain?"

His brother's voice was raspy. "Not here. Apparently, they're still trying to decide if we're friendly or not."

Kase wished he could see better. As his eyes slowly adjusted, he saw a faint light fifteen feet or so in front of him. Not blind, then, thank the moons. He guessed it was a door, but the light was so soft, he couldn't tell for sure. Were they in some kind of dungeon? "So. We're stuck, and the Cerls have Skibs. Shocks. Hallie, can't you do something? Talk to them?"

"They won't listen. We're being held here until we meet with the Lord Elder. I think."

Stars. They had finally found the Yalvs, yet it was nothing like he'd imagined. "And when is that going to be? I don't know how long—"

He was interrupted by a noise in the direction of the faint light, and in seconds, the door swung open, the torchlight burning Kase's eyes from being in the dark. He blinked away the water blurring his vision and took in the form at the door.

The light flickered across a pale face.

"The Lord Elder will see you now." It wasn't the same Yalv from before, but he had the same black braid and long face as the healer.

"Great. Is he coming here?" Kase grunted. "I'm a little tied up at the moment."

The Yalv's form flickered. In a blink, he was in front of Kase, driving his foot into Kase's stomach. Kase doubled up, the breath whooshing out of his lungs all at once.

"Kick a man while he's down, why don't you?"

"Shut up, Kase!" Hallie squeaked.

Another kick. He coughed, and his vision went black for a moment. As he tried to catch the breath that had been knocked out of him, he squinted over in Hallie's direction. She didn't look hurt.

Lucky for the Yalvs, then.

"I'll untie your feet, but any attempt to run or attack will result in punishment, Earther," the Yalv growled.

When Kase didn't say anything, the Yalv moved to untie Hallie's ankle bonds, his form flickering and reappearing again.

What in the moons were they dealing with?

Kase's blood caught fire when he finally saw his brother. A mixture of fresh and dried blood covered half of his face and soaked most of his uniform near his shoulder. He looked worse than he had earlier. He blinked slowly like it took too much strength to do so.

"Will you rein in that tongue, or do I need to remove it?" The Yalv bent down to Kase.

He tried to push himself up. *Stars*, that kick had been hard. "My brother needs a healer's attention."

"We will wait for the Lord Elder to pass judgment. I'll not injure you unless you provoke me, Earther." He untied the ropes on Kase's feet.

"My name is Kase, not Earther," Kase growled, but that was all he did. He wasn't foolish enough to test whether this Yalv would make good on his threat. Not yet.

Kase pulled himself to his feet, his bruised stomach smarting, and the Yalv grabbed his shoulder and squeezed. "For what your people did to mine, I will call you what I want. Now, follow your friends before I lose my temper."

"What my people did to—"

"Kase! Come on!" Hallie interrupted.

Blasted monster. He gritted his teeth and joined Hallie and his brother. Kase knew they were supposed to make friends with them, but he hadn't expected to be taken prisoner.

The Yalv led them out into the night. Was it still the same day they'd been captured? Surely he hadn't been out any longer than an hour or two. Another Yalv filed behind the prisoners, and three others appeared on either side of their group.

How dangerous did they think he, Hallie, and Zeke were? Holy moons, if they thought they were Cerls...Kase swallowed hard. What were the Cerls doing to Skibs? He needed to find him, save him. He had a fiancé and child waiting at home. Skibs had to get back.

Or was he dead? Was his body strewn, bloody and rent apart, next to the rubble of Myrrai?

Kase swallowed hard.

Their guards led them through a few shadowed paths before they turned the corner onto what must have been the main lane. Hallie sucked in a breath, and Kase turned immediately, expecting to find her being yanked out of line and beaten. Instead, she stared up and to the right. He followed her gaze.

Starlight radiated against the pitch-black sky like a thousand candles in the night. He'd never seen anything so beautiful. They walked at the base of one of the mountains so high he couldn't see the peak. Currently, they were on a winding path lit with flame lanterns held by stone statues, not unlike the stonemen they'd fought in the forest.

These didn't move. For the moment.

Along the path, structures grew up from the rock below in jagged shapes. In the daylight, Kase might describe it differently, but with the lanterns, the shadows made them look like an impossibility of gravity. Each level stuck out at a different angle, as if someone tried and failed to knock over a stack of blocks. Some buildings were more complex than others, but each had the same box shape as a base and a sloping roof that pierced the air like the edge of a sword.

Hallie shook her head, her eyes wide. "Your architecture is exquisite! How do you build the roofs at such an angle?"

One of their guards answered, his voice like a fluted melody. "With the secrets of our ancestors."

What an odd way of speaking. And now that his eyes had adjusted, Kase could make out their clothing, also strange. Each had a brown cloak, but underneath, the guards wore a long garment clasped at the shoulders and embroidered with colored thread at the hems in varying patterns. The guard closest to Kase had swords on his. Swordsman?

The woman on Kase's other side had a scene out of the night sky. He couldn't guess what that said about her. Either way, the dress itself reminded Kase of what those living in ancient Greece or Rome wore on First Earth. He couldn't remember what they were called. He'd ask Hallie later.

On and on they wove through the city at a steady incline. Kase didn't see many other Yalvs, and he assumed it was late, meaning everyone was likely getting ready to sleep. That, or they were wary of outsiders.

As they walked, small, intricately-carved stumps

stood at regular intervals in between the stone statues. They looked like miniature versions of the pillars in the Pass. Were they one and the same? A creeping suspicion they had something to do with the *Eudora Jayde* losing electrical power tickled his senses. It was a vague inclination, but there was something strange about the stones.

More than once while they walked, Hallie's hand twitched as though itching to grab her sketchbook. Like good captors, they'd relieved their prisoners of their possessions. Zeke, however, merely trudged forward, never taking his eyes from the road in front of him. That rattled Kase more than anything. He'd never seen his brother so beaten down. Even when Ana had died, Zeke hadn't shown any emotion deeper than the initial shock.

Kase was shivering and nearly wheezing by the time they reached the end of their hike. He couldn't see far in the night, but looking back the way they'd come made him feel incredibly dizzy with the height and the sea of lights. The castle in front of him was something else entirely.

Each turret was built in the style of the structures below, with their askew architecture and blade-thin roofs. The walls gleamed like jewels; the Yalvs had built them out of polished Zuprium.

There you go, Jove. There's plenty of Zuprium on this side of the world.

Where a gate should have been, there was only a pointed archway, with other long-robed men standing to each side, swords at their waists. The rest of the structure was like something out of a decaying storybook from First Earth complete with towers, parapets, and walkways. Light from Firstmoon glinted off each shining surface.

Breathtaking was the only word for it.

To his right, the path veered, coming to an end at a giant door carved in the same pointed fashion as the castle archway. The door opened right into the mountain itself.

"What's in there?" he asked.

"Only with the Lord Elder's permission do you learn the secrets of our ancestors," the guard with the embroidered swords answered.

"Then can we get to him already?" he mumbled under his breath. Hallie jerked her head toward him, shooting him a deadly glare.

Right. If he didn't behave, he'd get his tongue ripped from his head. Thankfully, the guards didn't seem to hear or care. His stomach still twinged with pain as he walked.

When they passed under the arch, the light disappeared, and a wave of heat blasted them. It was made worse by the fact they were all shivering from the climb in the near-winter temperatures.

Before Kase could yell, the sensation disappeared as quickly as it had come. "What in the moons?"

"Only with the Lord Elder's permission do you learn the secrets of our ancestors."

Kase fought the urge to roll his eyes. He shouldn't bother asking anything else. Hallie slowed to walk beside him, keeping a wary eye on their guards. She didn't look nearly as pale nor did she seem to be in pain from her ordeal earlier. Thank the moons.

"I know this has something to do with the *Eudora* losing power." Her eyes darted to the guards. "Like a defense system."

Zeke flashed a look back, the side of his face crusted

with blood, but he didn't say anything. *Blasted Cerls. Blasted Yalvs.*

"Are you sure?" Kase asked.

She rolled her shoulders, trying to adjust the bonds on her wrists. The gnarled fingers of her right hand made Kase's stomach turn, and a bit of raw skin peeked above the rope. *Calm. You want to keep your tongue.* She didn't notice the tension in his shoulders. "I think it's all connected. Somehow."

"What do we do?"

"Leave it to me."

Kase tugged on his bonds again, grimacing at the burning in his own wrists as they entered the castle. The main door was another archway, greeting them with the same heat blast. Beyond was a long hallway, lit with flame lanterns like the road, except they hung from the gleaming ceiling instead of the hands of inanimate stonemen.

"But if they don't believe us? What if they lock us up again?"

"I'm on this mission for a reason, remember?" She moved in front of him once more. The fingers of her injured hand twitched.

"Yes, and you're doing such a stars-fantastic job so far."

She glowered. "Keep your mouth shut and *leave it to me.*"

The flickering memory of the meeting in Professor Christie's office flashed in Kase's mind. Yes, that was why Jove had insisted she come along, even if Kase had argued with his brother afterward. If he'd been the kind to blush, he would've at that moment.

"Good luck, then." Kase straightened. "Don't get us killed, please."

Hallie

FINALLY REACHING THE PALACE MADE Hallie feel like she was coming home. She'd studied the Yalvs for so long, been a little bit obsessed, and now...she was in their presence, in their city.

Was this also called Myrrai, city of starlight? Maybe that was one thing she could ask if she cemented an alliance.

After a walk through another corridor, their guards led them through a door that must have been at least two stories high and climaxed in the center at a point, similar to the house roofs in the city. An image of the sun peeking over the mountain tops graced the Zuprium of the doors, and they opened outward. The group stepped inside.

The meeting chamber competed with Grieg's Theater, in Hallie's much-valued opinion. The ceiling rocketed upward three stories, capped with a dome on which someone had painted the warm glow of Firstmoon and sparkling stars. Hallie wished to be so gifted. Sketching she could do, but painting was another thing entirely. With her hand the way it was...

She tried to move it, but the disfigured bits left behind ached. She should be awed by the fact the Yalv used magic to seal the skin shut. She should be brimming with excitement. She should be taking notes.

But all she felt was numb. The fiery bullet hit Ebba again and again. Pain spiked in her hand.

At least that was better than the numbness.

She sucked in a small breath. She should focus on the paintings and the fact she was actually here, in a real

Yalven city. Hallie had a job to do.

Don't focus on your hand. Don't focus on what the Cerls might be doing to Ben. Don't focus on the memory of Ebba's cold and bloody body draped in a Yalven cloak.

Deep breath in. Deep breath out.

Zuprium columns dotted the perimeter of the vast circular room, each with a torch in an unadorned sconce. The torches themselves were made of ivory and carved with strange pictures Hallie couldn't quite make out. She wished she could draw them. Did they have something to do with the unexplained Yalven powers? But alas, her satchel was probably still in the ruins...along with Jack's pocket watch, now mangled by the bullet that hit her hand. She swallowed.

On the other side of the circle, a Yalven man with palms on his crossed knees sat on a scarlet pillow. His coloring matched that of his race, but there was something unnerving about his eyes. Their bright golden irises burned right through her. They looked so familiar to hers, yet so different. Did the power the Yalvs possessed cause their eyes to glow? What had the Essences' eyes looked like? The same?

The man hadn't taken his gaze off of her, and Hallie repressed a shiver. In that one solitary look, it was almost as if he knew all of her, the best and the worst.

Stitched sunbeams decorated the hem of his robe. Hallie tried to remember what it meant; she thought it had something to do with their occupation. The Yalvs chose their profession early on and never wavered. While she should be terrified, she ached to know more. She'd been fascinated by their culture even before heading to University, an interest her father had unwittingly instilled in her.

Stars, get your head together. If you mess up, they'll not only kill you, but Kase and Zeke, too.

She had a job to do: convince the people who'd nearly been destroyed twenty years ago to join Jayde in yet another war. Except the Yalvs presumably thought she, Kase, and Zeke were with the Cerls. The odds weren't great, to say the least.

Professor Christie wouldn't have recommended me for this if I wasn't capable, right? And that book, The Gate of Time...

"Kneel." The Yalven man's voice was like a whispering wind. If the room hadn't been silent, Hallie wouldn't have heard him.

The guards gestured for the prisoners to sit roughly ten feet away from the Lord Elder. Who else could he possibly be? The floor was cool to the touch—also made from Zuprium, like everything else. Gracious day, there was so much of it.

If Kase held his tongue, she might be able to accomplish this mission on her own. Playing her cards right might mean they returned home with allies and wealth; they'd be heroes.

"May the stars rise upon you, Lord Elder," Hallie said in Yalven, sitting on her knees and bending so far forward her forehead touched the floor. Awkward, with her hands tied behind her. *Stars,* that hurt.

"And may they not fall when morning breaks. I see you're accustomed with our ways and our language, child." The man tilted his head, answering her in his native tongue.

She welcomed the compliment, but she wasn't a child.

"My name is Hallie Walker." She tried to offer him a smile, but she was sure it came out as more of a grimace. She nodded to the two men at her sides. "This is Pilot Kase Shackley and Lieutenant Colonel Zeke Shackley. Would you mind if we spoke in Common, so they also understand our conversation?"

No response, but he didn't seem to mind when she switched. Hallie hoped she honored him enough with the Yalven she spoke. "My companions and I have traveled a long way to meet with your esteemed personage."

Kase would probably scoff at her pretty words later, saying she'd laid it on too thick, but the overkill might work in their favor. The Yalvs were proud people, according to the mysterious Jasper Morgan.

"You have a honeyed tongue." The man barely moved his lips.

"I'm simply in awe we have finally found you, Lord Elder."

Now that *was probably too thick.*

"Child," the man said again, his eyes staring unblinking. "Your kind has gone to great lengths to rid the hallowed world of our race. Why should I listen to your flowery words to persuade me otherwise?"

"Please don't mistake us for citizens of Cerulene. We're Jaydian."

"Does it matter? Were you not both trespassing in our holy city?"

Hallie bit her lip. And this was why she never intended to run for political office. She hated the intricacies of holding your cards to your chest and not saying what you meant. "High Guardsman Jove Shackley sent us on this mission to meet with you because Cerulene is...well, we think they're preparing for war. We need your help."

And the Cerls are after the Gate. They're also possibly in possession of an Essence. And please believe me.

The Lord Elder gestured around the hall. "Does it appear we want to join you? Do you not realize what the last conflict of man nearly did to us?"

"The Great War was terrible. Everyone suffered...is still suffering." Hallie knew she must've had that desperate look in her eyes, because for a moment, the Lord Elder's own gaze softened. The War's lingering effects haunted Jayde. Even Stoneset bore scars in one way or another, whether it was the fletcher's missing leg or the increased patrols from Achilles. Another conflict on that scale might just set the world ablaze. It was up to Hallie to prevent that. Somehow.

Holy blasted stars.

Hallie took in the flickering torches, the only light in the room. Their flames gave her strength. "We're here trying to stop another. Jayde's offering to help before it comes to a head."

The Lord Elder's look made Hallie feel small. His mouth hardened at the edges, his slim lips forming a downward slope. His brow furrowed, deepening the shadows on his face, yet his eyes were as bright as ever, like two stars against the winter's night. As the Lord Elder stared, Hallie felt like a child once more, like her mother had berated her for once again leaving the back door open during a rainstorm.

No one else moved. No one else breathed. Finally, the Yalv spoke. "Humanity sought to exterminate us for control of the Gate. I will not allow anyone to endanger my people, no matter how much Yalven they speak. I have decided."

Failure.

The thought was sour on her tongue, yet it slid down her throat like newly fallen snow.

Hallie blinked.

No.

She would not take no for an answer. She would not die here. Not now. She straightened her back and threw back her shoulders best she could. Her wrists burned once more, and her mangled hand throbbed. "You are *already* in danger from our enemies! They found Myrrai. They'll find this hideaway, too."

Swords scraped out of their scabbards, and Hallie flinched. Kase's shoulder bumped into hers as he squirmed. "Let her finish!"

Good moons, he was going to get his tongue ripped out. Hallie shot him a glare, and his struggling stopped. The weapons went back into their scabbards at the Lord Elder's raised hand. His slender fingers were too long and skeletal, like they would break with only a slight breeze.

Hallie's eyes fell to the floor. The muddled reflection of the dome's detailed painting above mocked her.

Deep breath in. Now out. In. Out. You can do this.

The Lord Elder's voice was as calm as ever when he spoke. "Continue, child."

Hallie gave him a hesitant smile. It didn't elicit one in response. "Cerulene attacked Lieutenant Colonel Shackley and our other companion, Ben Reiss. They attacked us and killed...killed..." she took a deep breath. "They killed Ebba. I can assure you; they'll attack soon." She looked directly into the man's unnerving golden eyes. She still felt small, but she spoke anyway. "Jayde aims to ally with you in the coming fight against Cerulene."

The Lord Elder stared her down. Her heart beat against her ribs in time with Zeke's labored breaths. Stars, he needed a healer. *She* needed a healer.

"I could believe you, child." His fingers tightened on his knees. "But I know you are only after the Gate."

That Gate again. The weapon the Cerls sought to wield.

Jasper's words came back to her. *I believe it has something to do with the Essences...*

Hallie'd never truly believed in magic, but these last months had taught her otherwise. Her research told her it existed with the Yalvs, though scholars didn't quite understand. There was also the fact the highly advanced technology of the First Settlers had failed upon landing on Yalvara. All evidence pointed to some sort of supernatural power on this planet, and that power rested with the very people who now held her captive.

One careless word might have her at the receiving end of whatever that magic was.

Swords and the strange pistols each Yalven guard also carried were at her back. She was wholly in their power, and her next words might condemn not only her but Kase and Zeke as well. Yet, they might be their only chance of surviving this whole ordeal.

She took a deep breath, focused on those ageless golden eyes, and spoke. "I do know about the Gate, though not what it does or what even it is, only that it exists and the Cerls want to use it. I know you've had to protect yourselves in the past from us—your power is the reason Jayde has worked a millennium to untangle the mysteries of our lost technology. You were frightened. You still are. We come from a world you have only heard of with a different sort of power."

Only a slight twitch from Kase, but he kept his mouth shut even if he hadn't come to this realization himself. The Lord Elder hadn't moved. Not even to blink.

Hallie wet her lips. "Regardless, I know the power of the Essences hasn't died out. Jasper Morgan theorized that was true, and according to our own intelligence agents, the Cerls have found one. Jasper also says he'll be in touch, though even I'm unsure how that'll happen seeing as he lived hundreds of years ago...well, maybe it's a different one and..."

She cleared her throat. *Stay on topic.*

"What I mean to say, again, is that Jayde wants to help. All Yalvara is in danger if we don't work together."

A flicker of shock registered on the man's ageless face. It was present in his furrowed brow and the subtle blink. "How do you know Jasper, child?"

"I don't," Hallie said, looking down at her knees and the too shiny floor. "I was just told to pass on the message."

Blast me for losing that book.

The Lord Elder sat silently. Each breath Hallie took made her hand hurt more. Finally, with the flickering torches playing across his features, he spoke again. "And that's why I cannot let you leave."

Hallie's stomach flew into her throat. Kase started to shout something, but she cut him off. "With all due respect, Lord Elder, I don't know what Jasper wanted, and we hope to return to Jayde with your help due to our ship no longer being serviceable. However, I understand you are wary of us, and rightly so, seeing how we have treated you in the past. Our alliance would be beneficial to both sides. We will be happy to escort a representative back to our leaders in Jayde before you make a final decision."

"And I am to trust that you won't hold my chosen ambassador hostage?"

"Respectfully, with your power and that dust your

guard threw on us, I doubt we could do anything to harm whoever you choose." Hallie shifted again. Blast these floors. She needed to get him to agree soon.

She met the man's golden eyes and held his stare. For several moments, he didn't say anything, only gazed into her soul. Those ageless eyes.

She understood his hesitation. She might've been the same way if she was the leader of a hunted nation.

"Yalven Lords, escort them to the southern wing's quarters, and allow them to dine and rest." The Lord Elder looked to the men near the door. "I will think on your words. For tonight, you'll be kept under guard."

Kase mumbled something, and Zeke groaned. Hallie cleared her throat. "Thank you for your hospitality. I hope you hear the sincerity in my words and our offer. Rest assured these bonds are unnecessary; we will do whatever you ask. My companion and I are also in grave need of a healer."

His stare was unnerving, especially with those pointed canines poking out over his bottom lip. After a few moments, he sighed. "We still have much to discuss, but I'll allow you and your companions to rest and heal."

Hallie offered him a small smile of thanks. However, the Lord Elder spoke again: "In the event you decide to go against your word, the Mountain will decide your fate."

Hallie didn't want to find out what *that* meant. Her knees ached; her fingers throbbed. "We understand."

He gave a nod of dismissal, and the guards helped the three of them to their feet. When they left the chamber, Hallie's body nearly sagged with relief.

She'd done it. Or had almost done it, at any rate.

"Thank you," Zeke whispered as they walked. The

fact that they hadn't been killed seemed to have given him a little more energy, but new blood stained his shirt.

Kase was silent the entire trip, and Hallie couldn't blame him. Her mind buzzed with what had occurred in the Lord Elder's chamber. She hoped she'd done enough.

They'd find out in the morning. Hopefully.

Chapter 23

FINISH WHAT WE STARTED

Kase

KASE ONLY HAD MINOR BRUISES and scrapes, but the mysterious gold dust still cleared them all up. It'd been at least an hour since a strict Yalven woman had smeared it on his, Hallie's, and Zeke's injuries and murmured—or really sung—a few words in her language.

The healing hadn't felt like anything at all itself. There was an almost phantom-like burn, but by the time Kase had determined how to describe it, his wounds, small as they were, had vanished. All that was left behind was the blood, dirt, and gore to be washed away. He'd then asked about his previously busted ear drum, and low and behold the woman had healed that in a matter of seconds.

He glanced over at Zeke. His brother lay on a bed too long for his tall frame, the firelight from the hearth in the common area peeking through the cracked door and falling onto his tensed face. Even in sleep, Zeke looked to be in pain, though the woman had healed him as well. The adrenaline from the fight had been thoroughly drained as the Cerl-inflicted wound in his shoulder continued to ooze blood. It was a miracle he hadn't bled out on the ruins' streets.

Kase shivered even now an hour later. Everything had been a blur, and the thought of losing his brother was unthinkable. He'd probably lost Skibs, and Ebba was gone. Those were tough enough, but Zeke...

He swallowed hard and blinked back emotions and memories of happier times with Skibs—flying out in the country underneath an uninterrupted blue sky, sharing drinks and dreams in a rousing tavern at the edge of the upper city. He pushed back flashes of Ebba mocking them as they climbed the tree or her shocked face when he'd beaten her at the slinging contest.

He wasn't going to be able to sleep a wink.

Kase looked out toward the common room. He remembered seeing a few leather books on metal shelves flanking the fireplace when they'd come in earlier. Maybe they were written in Common? A good book would be the only thing to help him now.

Before he stepped into the room, a soft noise met his ears. He looked back at Zeke, and while his brother slept fitfully, his breaths coming in huffs, it wasn't him. Kase looked back at the door. The noise was soft, like a breath but labored. Was it Hallie?

Without making a sound himself, he peeked through the crack. A form with narrow shoulders and long, braided hair huddled in a chair near the fire. He stepped into the small parlor.

"Hallie?"

She spun around, wiping her eyes. "Yes?"

"Didn't realize you were awake."

She smoothed out wrinkles in her bloodstained blouse. "I couldn't sleep." She sniffled and wiped more tears from her face with her shirtsleeve. "Sorry. I didn't mean to wake you."

"You didn't wake me. I...I couldn't sleep either." He glanced down at his stockinged feet. The wool had worn away in spots, leaving near holes in the toes. It was an inopportune time to wish he'd packed more socks, and he hoped Hallie didn't notice. He wasn't sure why that mattered now.

He tore his eyes away. They landed on her face.

Hallie turned back toward the fire, where the flames licked the logs and stretched toward the far reaches of the visible stone laced with designs made of Zuprium. The bricks reminded him of those that had decorated that temple near the stonemen.

She buried her head in her hands. "I don't know what to do. I didn't know Ebba as well as I should, but now she's gone. She'll never go home. Her parents...they'll be thrown into the debtor's prison, and I can't do anything about it. I failed to convince the Lord Elder, and...and..."

Her shoulders shook as she sobbed. She said a few other things, but Kase couldn't make out what they might've been. Instead, he didn't think, only strode over and pulled her out of her seat and into his arms.

He held her there as her tears soaked what was left of his shirt. Unbidden, the memory of that terrible night after they'd fought the stonemen, when she'd told him about her brother, popped into his mind. He hadn't known what to do then either, but with his arms wrapped around her shoulders now, he realized how much he needed her there with him. His heart thumped too loudly, and he hoped she didn't notice.

Hesitantly, he pressed his cheek to her hair. It was soft, like some sort of...cloth? Silk? His brain wasn't working right. He was exhausted, mentally, emotionally, and physically. His body ached from the night's events. Skibs was missing; Ebba was dead. The Lord Elder hadn't agreed to an alliance yet. Would they be allowed to go home? And if they did without accomplishing their objectives, he'd face charges.

None of that mattered. He needed to be present, in the moment. Still, he held her tightly for a good while, because it was the only thing that felt right when everything else around them was so wrong.

Her body was warm tucked next to his, and as terrible as it sounded, he didn't want to let her go. But her sobbing had stopped. "Come on," he whispered reluctantly into her hair. "Shall we read a book from that shelf there? Maybe it'll help to think about something else."

Stars, that sounded callous.

Hallie pulled back and sniffed. "I think I need a few moments."

"Don't blame yourself for this."

She shook her head. "Maybe I could have—could have stayed with her when she stormed off. Maybe I could have done something other than just stand there."

"There wasn't anything you could have done better. None of us could."

Hallie put her face in her hands once more, but Kase pulled her wrists away. "We still have a job to do."

Hallie avoided his eyes, tugging her wrists back and

fiddling with the lace at her throat. Kase had never noticed its intricate floral pattern. He blinked. *Focus.*

Digging in his pocket, Kase brought out the stone he'd taken from Ebba. He held it out. "Not sure what this is, but Ebba had it in her hand when...well, I thought you might know what to do with it?"

She looked at it curiously for a moment before her eyes lit with recognition—then darkened. "It was for her brother. She was taking it home to him, but now..." she swallowed hard and took the rock from Kase's outstretched hand. "I'll deliver it. It's what she would've wanted."

Kase nodded. "She'd also want us to take care of the ship, yet that's not going to happen."

Hallie's laugh lacked mirth. "And she'd be mad if we didn't finish what we started."

"Exactly."

Neither said anything for a moment. Then he blurted, "I need to—"

"I think I'll—" Hallie said at the same time. They both stopped.

Kase cleared his throat. "I really do think reading one of those books will help. Join me?"

Hallie bit the inside of her cheek and nodded. "Except I'll need to translate them for you. They're all in Yalven."

Kase smiled as she grabbed a book from one of the shelves. They spent most of the rest of the night in the cozy chairs, Hallie reading aloud some Yalven folk tales Kase could hardly understand even after she translated them, but he didn't mind. It was just nice to sit there for once and not worry about the fire in the grate behind him, nor the mission...nor what might await them when morning broke.

Hallie

THE MATTRESS IN THE YALVEN castle was a definite upgrade to Hallie's on the *Eudora*, but she longed for the day she could sleep in her own bed and have a decent night's rest.

She woke up to sunlight warming her eyelids. She hadn't bothered to close the shutters on the window the previous night after she and Kase finally said goodnight. For the first time on this trip, she woke feeling refreshed even if she'd only had a few hours of sleep, her spirits lifting with the rising sun.

She would convince the Lord Elder to ally with them. If only to honor Ebba.

Hallie swallowed hard and pushed the terrible memories from the previous night to the back of her mind. She needed to be strong. Tears for a fallen comrade showed weakness she couldn't afford. Instead, she focused on her surroundings.

The room she'd slept in was about as spacious as her bed chamber in Kyvena, minus the books. Under the large window sat a sturdy trunk. With the Zuprium walls, she could almost imagine she was back on the *Eudora*. Her heart throbbed again. It had been her home for the past two months, and now it was a heap of metal somewhere out in the forest.

She almost laughed at herself for feeling sorry for a ship, but . . . well. Ebba would have appreciated it. She hoped that wherever her friend was, she'd somehow heard her thoughts.

Hallie pushed off the too-soft blanket and swung her legs over the side of the bed. Hopefully, the Lord

Elder would decide today, and they could go home. The thought made her smile. *Home.*

She understood the fears of the Yalvs if they allied with Jayde, but surely the Lord Elder would find the benefits outweighed the risks, and all would be well.

Except for Ben.

After a healer fixed her hand with more of that mysterious dust, Hallie had been so exhausted the previous night she'd fallen into a dreamless sleep without any trouble, but now that she'd awoken, the thought of Ben...it was like she'd gotten a rock stuck in her shoe, but she couldn't figure out how to extract it. A silly analogy, but it bothered her nonetheless. Hopefully she could coerce the Lord Elder into helping get Ben back.

That would at least make up for the fact they'd lost their other comrade, right?

Hallie blinked and took a deep breath in. She should get out of bed and get ready for the day. That would keep her mind busy.

Attached to her small chamber was a tiny bathing room, and Hallie spent way too long inside. The water in the tub was delightfully hot, steam rising like smoke from the surface. Her eyelids fluttered shut, her muscles practically groaning in relief.

It'd been a while since she'd soaked properly. The bathing chamber on the ship had been functional, but nothing like this. She stayed in until her fingertips wrinkled, and only then did it occur to her that she hadn't heard anyone come in to fill the tub this morning, and though she stayed in for far longer than she should have, the water never turned cold. Maybe they'd let her sketch whatever supplied the water and kept it warm.

"Miss Walker?" a feminine voice said from the other side of the door.

Hallie jumped, splashing water onto the floor. She gripped the sides of the slick tub. "Yes?"

"The Lord Elder requires you and your companions to dine with him," the voice said. Though Hallie could tell the woman was the same as the Yalven woman who'd healed them last night, it still made her uncomfortable knowing she was naked with a near stranger on the other side of a door only a few inches thick.

"But I only have my filthy clothes I wore yesterday." Hallie got out of the tub and grabbed the drying cloth.

"We've provided you with more appropriate clothing. You can find it in your trunk."

Would she get to wear one of those robes the Yalven Lords wore?

"I will wait in the common area with the others, but hasten with your preparations. The Lord Elder expects you soon."

Water from her still-wet hair ran down her back, and she shivered. With the towel wrapped around her, she nudged the door open and peeked around it. Her room was empty, but she hadn't heard the door open, nor had she heard it close.

After finding a toga without embroidery at the hem, Hallie left the room and entered the parlor. A few comfortable chairs like the ones she and Kase had used last night dotted the room, as well as a sturdy wooden table set before a brick hearth. If she didn't know she was on the other side of the world, she would've thought she was in Ellis' small city manor.

The others waited, Kase and Zeke in two chairs and

the Yalven woman standing near the door. She was willowy and paler than the mountain snow, her golden eyes glowing beneath a heavy brow. Hallie wouldn't necessarily describe her as gorgeous, but there was a strange, ethereal beauty about her. She nodded to the woman as the men got up from their seats. Immediately, she tried to clamp down on a laugh. She failed miserably.

It was traditional Yalven clothing, she knew that, but there was no getting around the fact Kase wore a dress. One identical to hers. Zeke was a natural in his, but Kase...

"You look ridiculous!" she said through her tears, trying to get her laughter under control.

Kase crossed his arms, eyes blazing. "I didn't have much of a choice."

Zeke chuckled, but the Yalv spoke, her voice as hard as Hallie's drawing pencils. "This is our customary dress. Is there a problem?"

Hallie swallowed her laughter. "No, honored one."

The woman's mouth thinned, but she said nothing more as she left through the door. Hallie choked back another laugh as Kase and Zeke passed her to follow.

Kase

IF SOMEONE HAD SERVED KASE purple food back in Kyvena, he would have refused to eat it. However, after weeks of dried beef jerky and the occasional rabbit or squirrel, the purple mush dotted with some salty nut was the greatest thing he'd ever put in his mouth. It had the consistency of oatmeal, but a distinctly fruity taste. Before they went home, he'd have to steal some of this, or at least ask for the recipe.

He wasn't the only one enjoying the meal. Hallie had already finished a bowl and taken a second. If he wasn't so invested in his own feast, he might have laughed.

Zeke barely touched his. The elder Shackley brother didn't have much of an appetite. While a Yalven healer had visited and healed the injuries on the outside, Kase knew some went deeper than anyone knew.

Skibs' and Ebba's absences were weights on Kase's shoulders, like he'd taken on too many G's in his old hover. He scooped more purple mush into his mouth and focused on the fresh sweetness of the meal.

But then it soured at his next thought.

He didn't trust these people...and felt incredibly foolish for scarfing down the food. He'd let his stomach get ahead of his mind. In fact, he hadn't even entertained the possibility one of the Yalvs might have poisoned it before that moment. What a stars-idiot he was.

He put a hand on Hallie's arm next to him and whispered, "What if it's poisoned?"

She swallowed her bite and wiped her mouth with a cloth napkin. "The chicken we ate last night wasn't."

"But if it's poisoned—"

"Why refrain from killing us last night only to do so now? That doesn't make sense. And why would they heal us just to poison us?" She scraped her spoon around the bowl to fish out the last dregs. "Besides, we don't have any other options. Now eat your purple mush."

"Yes, *Mother*."

"I'm rolling my eyes at you." Hallie finished her last

spoonful with a sigh. Whether it was one of contentment or frustration, Kase didn't know, but if he hadn't been enjoying the possibly poisoned mush so much, he would have flung a spoonful at her. Childish? Yes. But it would have made him feel better.

"Stop bickering, you two." Zeke sounded like he needed at least three more hours of sleep.

Kase hadn't had time to talk to his brother at all yet. The rude Yalv had woken him much too early and forced him to wear a dress—well, toga, but still—saying his old clothes needed to be cleaned.

He reluctantly pushed away the rest of his porridge and crossed his arms. "Wasn't the old guy supposed to be here?"

Silence, and then—

"*Ouch*, woman!" he hissed at Hallie's pinch on his arm.

"If you don't shut up, I'll let that Yalven Lord rip out your tongue," Hallie growled under her breath. "Go along with whatever they want us to do. I can convince them to let us go home. Don't ruin it."

Kase pressed his lips together. He wouldn't compromise that, no matter what he felt. He'd promised to get her home, hadn't he?

While they waited, Kase took in the dining hall. Instead of sitting in chairs around a great wooden table like the one his family had at the Manor, they knelt on plush pillows at a low metal one spanning the length of the elongated room. Above them, windows allowed sunlight to filter through gauzy curtains. Kase wished he could look out and down at the city below, but the bottom of each window was about five feet above his head. The walls themselves were barren other than the torches, which were lit even in the daytime.

A soft melody hit his ears. He turned to find Hallie absentmindedly twirling her spoon and humming the tune. It was soft and soothing like a lullaby, and it was one Kase nearly recognized but couldn't recall the words. "What is that?"

She shrugged. "It's whatever that Yalven healer was singing when she healed us last night."

"Oh."

"It's stuck in my head," Hallie said, still fiddling with the spoon. "I wonder if the Yalvs could've healed Jack..."

Kase had been thinking the same thing, but before he could say anything, the Lord Elder appeared on the other side of the table, and both Kase and Hallie jumped, her bowl clattering as she dropped her spoon into it.

"Mother of ash," Kase breathed, trying to calm his heart, "will you stop doing that?"

The Lord Elder's pointed teeth peeked through his smile. "I apologize. I forget Earthers are not used to our way of travel."

"Do all Yalvs blink in and out of existence like that?" Hallie set her bowl aside.

The Lord Elder didn't show any emotion. "You have yet to earn my trust."

Kase tried not to roll his eyes at the response.

"Will we be discussing our potential alliance this morning?" Hallie asked.

"I have decided."

He didn't say anything else.

"And your decision is?" Kase asked, unable to keep silent. Hallie's arm twitched, and he knew she probably wanted to pinch him again.

The Yalv's golden eyes bore into Kase's own for a solid thirty seconds before he answered, "You must *earn* my trust by staying with us for a time. If you cannot do so, we'll leave you to the justice of the mountains."

"You mean you'll kill us." Kase would be dead three times over if Hallie's looks could do damage.

"I would advise you to keep a tight hold on your tongue and temper, human."

"My tongue and temper are fine."

"We understand, Lord Elder," Hallie said. "Are there any other parameters to our agreement? My companions and I would love to learn more about your culture while we're guests here."

Guests, my foot. Why won't he tell us how *to earn his trust?*

"I'll allow it. However, you'll be under careful watch the entirety of your stay."

"Yes, Lord Elder. Thank you." Hallie gave a slight bow.

Kase cleared his throat. "Lord Elder, I have a request."

"Do you, hot-headed one?"

Kase dug his fingernails into his palms. *Stay shocking calm.* "We think the Cerls captured our companion. I would like to search for him. With a guard, of course."

There. That was reasonable.

"I cannot allow that—"

"They might be torturing him—" Kase started.

"—But I'll send a contingent to search for your comrade. My warriors are well-equipped to handle any danger your friend might be in."

"I . . . thank you." Kase swallowed. It was better than nothing at all.

Hallie shifted in her seat. "And our other companion, a young girl. She was...killed in the attack. Is there a way to...what I mean to say is...her body, where is it? We wanted to take it back to her family when we leave, if that's possible."

"All those slain at Myrrai were honored by the flame, as is our custom."

"Oh, well," Hallie said, fidgeting with the end of her braid. "Is there...anything we can take back? At all?"

"I will have Lord Saldr see if that is possible." The Yalv looked at each of them before standing. "I take my leave. Remember: we will be watching."

Before Kase could process that or Hallie could argue more, he was gone.

C H A P T E R 2 4

THE BEAST CALLS

Kase

FOR TWO AGONIZING DAYS, THE guards led Kase and Hallie around the great Yalven city. Zeke opted to stay in their quarters, and Kase tried not to read into it.

The city buildings were pristine, gleaming like new steel in the early winter sunlight, but they couldn't distract Kase from the fact the Lord Elder's contingent of warriors hadn't found Skibs yet. With each passing hour, Kase worried even more. However, on the second day, Hallie convinced the Yalvs to show them the library.

They were still stuck in this city, had to gain the elusive trust of the blasted Lord Elder, and Skibs was missing, but Kase couldn't deny being surrounded by dust and parchment for hours made him feel a smidge better. It even made him a little sad he hadn't attended the University. But then he remembered the sky. He remembered his first flight in a hover after wasting all that time on the bikes learning something he knew instinctively, and the feeling passed.

Kase had just bathed and dressed in his cleaned, old clothes for another day of reading when a smart rap sounded on the door. As he tied off the laces of his boots, Kase peeked at Zeke's slumbering form. He hadn't even stirred.

Kase swallowed the bile in his throat as whoever was outside rapped on the door once more. He grabbed his pilot's jacket and headed out into the common area to find Hallie opening the door. She was dressed in her lacy blouse with her usual trousers tucked into her boots, a few rebellious strands of her russet-red braid falling around her face. Stubborn, just like she was.

Outside in the hallway, a Yalv stood in a toga with swords embroidered along the hem and a dark blue gemstone tied around his throat like a choker. Hallie moved out of the way, and the man walked in and bowed.

Kase narrowed his eyes. He resembled the one who'd threatened to cut out his tongue if he'd kept mouthing off the night they were captured. When the man's golden eyes found his, Kase's muscles tensed. It *was* him. He had the same rounded tip to his nose and thin lips.

"May the stars rise upon you. I am Lord Rodr, head huntsman of Myrrai."

Hallie's smile was tight, but it didn't affect her manners. "May they not fall when morning breaks, Lord Rodr."

He bowed once more. "I've come to collect Master

Shackley."

Kase's nostrils flared even as his stomach flew into his throat. "Why?"

"It's a tradition here in Myrrai. If you pass this test, the Lord Elder might consider you trustworthy enough for an alliance. That *is* what you want, correct?"

Kase swallowed, catching Hallie's gaze. She widened her eyes and pinched her lips together, silently pleading with him: *Go along with it.*

Under normal circumstances, he'd have probably blown the Yalven Lord off, moons hang him, but Hallie had yet to lead him astray where the Yalvs were concerned. "And what's this tradition?"

"A hunting expedition."

"I've never been hunting in my life."

"Fear not. It's a relatively easy task. I'll be instructing your every move."

The gleam in his golden eyes told Kase it would be anything but enjoyable. Unfortunately, he didn't have much of a choice. Besides, this might mean he could search for Skibs. He looked back at Hallie and nodded. Her shoulders relaxed. "I'll let you know if I learn anything interesting at the library."

He turned back to the Yalv, Rodr. "I don't have to wear a toga—er, robe, do I?"

Rodr's face and voice remained neutral as he responded, "You've yet to earn the proper attire for the hunt, but if you're successful today, you may yet earn the honor."

Perfect. He'd just fail, then. Hallie gave him an exasperated look as if she could read his mind, and he rolled his eyes. "Lead on, Lord Rodr."

NEARLY AN HOUR LATER, KASE rode a horse out of the city and into the surrounding forest. He thought it strange that something as simple as a horse existed on this continent, seeing as many things he'd seen were not what he considered normal. After meeting a dragon earlier, he quite expected this horse to have wings.

It didn't.

Regardless, Kase's knuckles were white from gripping the reins as Rodr led the group past the city gates and into the wilds of the surrounding forest.

His horse jerked unexpectedly, and Kase nearly slid off his mount. He caught himself just in time, and the horse whinnied in return. Rodr looked back with a raised brow before continuing ahead of him with the others in their party.

How could he be so good at flying an airship and controlling a hover bike, yet this was nearly impossible? Kase blamed the animal, who he could've sworn knew he wasn't a seasoned rider.

Kase tried to listen in on the chatter amongst the others. There were five Yalvs in the hunting party, each with swords embroidered on their hems, and each spoke in their Yalven tongue so quickly Kase couldn't keep up, even knowing the few words Hallie had taught him over the last two days. His heart picked up in speed a little as Rodr slowed his mount to ride beside him, pulling something from the saddle bag attached to the back of his own steed. Hopefully it wasn't something with which to cut out Kase's tongue.

Rodr handed a sleek metallic pistol over and addressed Kase in heavily accented Common. "Use this to take down the beast, but if you shoot one of my hunters, you'll feel the Mountain's wrath."

Kase leveled a glare at the man, trying not to hint at

the fear coursing through his veins at whatever the Mountain's wrath might mean. He took the pistol anyway and inspected it while trying to stay atop his horse. The metal of the weapon was brown and shiny like the *Eudora Jayde*—Zuprium. What else would it have been? Great shocks, where did they find all of it? He hadn't seen any mines on his tour of the city.

Kase held it loosely in his free hand, the other still holding tightly to the reins. "So, what're we hunting?"

Zeke was the better hunter; he would've been more suited to dealing with this Yalv. Rodr clicked his tongue between his teeth, and both his steed and Kase's sped up. Kase nearly lost his seat, but a hand from Rodr steadied him. The Yalv gave a derisive laugh. "As we feast tonight in celebration of Toro, our god, it's only fitting we slay a dragonar. This one has come too close to the city and has forfeited the right to live."

"Oh." He didn't like the sound of whatever this *dragonar* was. "But why me? My brother's the soldier." Rodr laughed again, and the others joined in. Kase's neck burned. "I don't understand what's so blasted hilarious."

His riding partner grinned once more. "The one who slays the dragonar can claim the maiden he so chooses at the feast tonight, and Saldr tells us you and your brother both compete for the same woman."

"*What?*"

Rodr clicked his tongue again, but this time the horses slowed, and they stopped on the edge of a meadow the size of the Kyvena airfields. "We did not think you had a chance, but my older brother was insistent."

Kase's face was aflame. Which one was Saldr again? *Stars*, the guards all blended together. They all hated him, but that wasn't even the worst part. The Yalvs thought he and Zeke were *competing* for Hallie? His heart sped up even more, her face flashing in his mind. "We're not *competing* over anything. And I thought this whole thing was about earning the Lord Elder's trust."

But the others just laughed. Another Yalv slowed down and patted him on the shoulder, his voice breezy, surprisingly playful. "Rodr didn't think you'd come if you didn't believe you had to participate in our tradition here. He doesn't like losing bets—especially with the esteemed Lord Saldr. To your other point, this is how we choose our wives. No one denies the results of the Hunt!"

Kase shook his head. "No, no, you've got it all wrong, I—"

But at that moment, a roar ripped through the forest.

An eerily familiar roar.

"The beast calls!" shouted another Yalv, raising his weapon in the air and firing it. A golden blast burst from the barrel and exploded fifty feet up; smoke glittered in the air. The weapon reminded Kase of the old flashpistols the military had used back before electricity.

Rodr pulled another pistol from his bag for himself. "The best way to take down a dragonar is to hit its eye, unless you stun it with its own Vasa. Anything else will enrage it further."

"Vasa? I don't know what that is." Kase gulped as the dragonar roared again, this time rattling his bones. "I don't think—"

"Don't you want to prove to your potential wife that you're the better choice?"

Another roar split the air as Kase stumbled over his

words. "I don't think—you don't know—"

But before he could come up with a coherent response, the trees across from him parted like the clouds. Parted like grass. Because what tore through them was . . . was a . . .

"*Dragon!*" Kase fumbled with the pistol in his grip. The words were a wheeze in his throat as he stared up at the monstrosity. Somehow it was even more terrifying in the daylight, almost identical to the one he and Hallie had stumbled across. Except Kase was certain this one's teeth were sharper. And longer. And about to chomp his body in half. Shimmering dust floated around its body just like the one in the forest, though Kase wasn't sure if it was the same or if it was something from the pistol fire.

The other Yalvs whooped and circled, waving their weapons in the air. But Kase could only curse himself for agreeing to this, the heartbeats hammering in his ears muffling all other noise.

"Shoot it now!" Rodr shouted from his right. The Yalv waved toward the beast, who was confused by so many targets, their weapons blasting out golden bullets and glittering smoke. They were distracting it so Kase could take the kill shot.

He swallowed hard and tugged on the reins of his steed, leading it to the side so he could get a good look at the thing's eye. The hand holding the Yalven pistol shook as he held it up and aimed for the large, liquid black orb perched in the folds of sapphire-colored skin.

Kase's breath caught in his throat. Time ticked by in slow motion as the beast's iris and pupil moved, trying to focus on its attackers, until it finally locked gazes with Kase.

It charged.

Kase's scream was lost in another roar. He pulled the trigger on the weapon.

No bullet exploded from the barrel. No glittering smoke. Nothing.

Kase cursed loudly and fumbled to cock the thing with his free hand. The dragon was too close, its jaws opening to devour him. He fired blindly, but his bullet only shattered one of the monster's sword-like teeth. A yell and a flash from his left came at the same moment, the golden bullet lancing the dragon in the eye. The monster's breath was hotter than the sun as Kase yanked his steed away from its gaping maw.

The dragon shrieked in unfathomable pain as it collapsed, shaking the earth with its fall. Kase's steed reared back on two legs, tossing Kase from its back. He fell hard, pain exploding in his shoulder; fifteen feet to his right, the dragon's claw sprayed him with dirt, rocks, and other debris as it dug into the soil. Its bottom jaw snapped, the sickening pop and crunch echoing across the meadow as the full weight of its body followed and pressed its open mouth into the ground.

When the thing didn't move, its eye staring sightlessly ahead, Kase turned over on his knees, shaking all over. He wiped the large beads of sweat rolling down his forehead as a sword-embroidered hem swished into view.

"You are the worst hunter I have ever seen."

Sweat still ran down Kase's face in rivulets, landing in the soft dirt. He took several deep, shuddering breaths. "I tried to tell you that."

Rodr laughed and held out a hand. Kase took it, and the Yalv helped him to his feet. He dusted off Kase's shoulders, bits of earth flinging to the ground with each sweep. "I'm impressed. You didn't run when the dragonar charged you. I'll tell Saldr you slew it anyway...I might even speak to the Lord Elder."

Kase struggled to breathe properly. The Yalv's eyes were bright, and the others brought their steeds close. Kase swallowed, pushing his sweaty curls from his face. "Thanks, I guess."

The others laughed, and one brought Kase's runaway horse to his side. Pulling himself onto its back, Kase tried not to glance at the dragon. Its size made it look like a small mountain, but the scaly skin told a different story. The other Yalvs clapped him on the back, and Rodr led them away.

Kase urged his mount to follow. "Are we going to leave it there?"

Rodr waved his hand. "Another team will carve the meat for tonight's feast. Our only job was to bring it down."

Kase shivered but didn't say anything more. The Yalvs were crazy if they thought he was going to eat the meat from that monster.

Hallie

ONCE ZEKE WOKE NEARLY AN hour after Kase left, guards escorted him and Hallie down to breakfast, which was just as delicious as it had been that first day. She did everything in her power not to stick her face full in the bowl and lap the fruity mush like a sheepdog. It was *that* good. Even her mother couldn't have pulled off a delicacy such as that.

After breakfast, the Yalven man named Saldr came for them. He was the one who'd healed her the night Ebba died and was part of their usual guard, and though he had yet to smile, his eyes told her he thought Hallie and her companions were fascinating. He didn't even mind when Kase begged to visit the guardhouse at the end of the day to check if Ben's scouting party had returned. He led him without complaint.

None of the visits had yielded success, each passing day chiseling away at Hallie's hope. She saw the same in the slump to Kase's shoulders when he returned without Ben in tow.

Hallie had just finished her last spoonful of the purple mush when Saldr strode into the dining chamber. Zeke pushed his food around in his bowl and set aside his spoon before looking up at the Yalv. Chewing her lip, Hallie stared a second too long at Zeke's uneaten food.

Zeke had claimed he was only there because the High Guardsman had asked him to go. He wasn't one to lie, but what sane person would agree to a mission he might not return from just because someone asked him to? Everyone else, save Kase, had been in it for the money—altruistic or not. She wasn't privy to what charges Kase could be facing, but he'd be giving up his freedom if they weren't successful. That still left her with the question of Zeke. What was his *why*?

His fight with Kase echoed in her mind. He'd said something about Zeke wanting to play god, and how he wasn't like his brothers. Hallie bit her lip.

She blinked away her thoughts as Saldr stopped next to the table and bowed, the ruby tied around his neck glittering. Hallie shook herself out of her reverie, rose from the table, and bowed back. "The stars rise upon you, Lord Saldr."

"And may they not fall when morning breaks." He clasped his hands behind his back and looked up toward the sunlight streaming in through one of the high windows. "Am I to escort you to the library again, Miss Walker?"

Hallie played with the ends of her hair. "Yes, I want to keep researching the ancient languages and the comparisons to modern day..." She trailed off and cleared her throat. No one cared what she was researching. *Stars.* "Of course, I could get there on my own, Lord Saldr. I hate forcing you to go down there with me."

He shook his head. "It is not an inconvenience, and the Lord Elder wishes it." He bowed to Zeke. "Will you be staying in your quarters again, Master Shackley?"

The soldier's hazel eyes were dark, and his voice crackled from disuse. "I'll go to the library today."

Lord Saldr nodded. "As you wish. Shall we go now?"

Hallie took in Zeke's broad-shouldered form. He used to stand tall and straight, but now he sat hunched over his bowl of uneaten mush. If only there was something she could do, but she didn't even know what was wrong. And she was terrified to ask. Zeke had been a stalwart figure throughout the entire mission, but now, all he did was sleep.

She could tell Kase was also worried by the way his eyes flickered to Zeke every few minutes. She'd been around grief enough to know the soldier was working through something of the sort, but she didn't have the courage to ask for specifics.

At least the fact he was going to join her in the library was a good sign.

Slinging her satchel over her shoulder, she nodded to Saldr, and the Yalv led them from the hall. For each one of Saldr's strides, Hallie took three. She pulled her jacket tighter around her shoulders and shivered a little as they left the palace and traversed into the crisp mountain air.

After a brisk ten-minute walk, the elegant library building came into view. While all the houses looked clean yet jagged, the library was the shining bit of jade in a cave full of coal. Its columns and sparkling glass windows brought a smile to her face as she followed Saldr up the steep stone steps.

Back in the extensive library at the University of Jayde, Hallie had spent countless hours buried beneath tomes and parchment researching, writing, and reading. She enjoyed curling up by the enormous fireplace on the first floor and staying there until the old bat of a librarian kicked her out. It was one of her most favorite places in the world—or it had been, until she'd seen this one.

Lugging open the arched wooden doors, Saldr led them through the Zuprium-gilded lobby and into the three-story room with ivory-colored shelves and towering windows filled with daylight tucked between each row. As she took a seat at a table near one of those windows, Hallie glanced out at the shining Zuprium palace with its background of snowy mountain caps. Another perfect day full of dust, books, and that gorgeous view.

Zeke fell into the seat beside her. "No wonder Kase has come here every day. All these books."

Hallie shrugged off her satchel and hung it on the back of her chair while Saldr grabbed a book from a nearby shelf and took a seat a few tables away. Maybe he liked reading as much as she did, so he used her as an excuse to get out of his regular duties. "I can't believe all this knowledge is at the Yalvs' fingertips. I know there's a plethora of research at the University library, but I've found so much more here. I wish I could read everything."

Zeke propped his chin on his left hand and drew circles on the table with his right. "I never liked reading. Never found anything I was interested in."

Hallie froze, her fingers searching for her sketchpad and pencil. "What do you mean you never found anything you were interested in?"

Zeke avoided her eyes. "I was never good at it, so I didn't try."

Hallie bit her lip and set her supplies down. Her pencil rolled across the tabletop, but she caught it before it fell. She stuck it in her hair for safekeeping. "I used to be the same way, until the right teacher came along. Mistress Jules showed up when I was twelve, and she changed everything."

"This Mistress Jules is the reason you've become a scholar?"

Hallie smiled a little. "If it wasn't for her, I might never have considered University."

It'd been her suggestion to leave Stoneset after everything. All because Hallie couldn't face Niels after what he did. After what she didn't do to save Jack. That mine accident was going to haunt her for the rest of her life.

The corner of Zeke's mouth turned up slightly. His smile drove the darker thoughts from her mind. It was his first since Ebba's death, and something in Hallie's chest relaxed. She'd have to tell Kase about it when he got back.

"I'm glad you did." Zeke clasped his hands in front of him on the table. "Is there anything you'd recommend?"

"You just asked a dangerous question."

"I have nothing else to do today, so I might as well try to enjoy my time here."

Hallie stuck her hand in her satchel and pulled out her copy of *The Odyssey*. She ran a hand over its cover. "You'll like this one, being a soldier and all. It's also my favorite."

He peeked over at the title. "I think that's one of Kase's, too."

She nodded. "That's one thing I like about...I mean, I didn't expect him to be into the arts. Or ancient literature. Or anything I was interested in. But the other night, we started talking..."

And I'm word vomiting. She knew her face was brighter than fire, but Zeke chuckled. "I told you he wasn't so bad once you got to know him."

Hallie's cheeks burned even hotter. "It's not what you think. I didn't mean to..."

What's that Shakespeare line? The lady doth protest too much, methinks? Great. Now he probably believes...oh stars.

She swallowed and tried to smile as Zeke said, "Mother would like you. She's obsessed with books, too."

How she didn't combust right then and there was a miracle. She cleared her throat and opened the book. "Then I'd love to meet her one day." She flipped toward the end. *Move on. Change the topic. Hurry.* "I know you haven't read the rest of it, but you'll like this particular scene at the end."

Her fingers finally found the page. Zeke looked over. "You're going to have me start reading from the end? Isn't that against the rules or something?"

Hallie shrugged. "But it's my favorite part. It's the reason I started to love reading, and it would be perfect for you. I'll give you some context before I start, so you won't be lost." She paused, finger on her page. "If you don't mind being read to, of course. I do a wonderful Odysseus voice."

Zeke laughed and waved her on. "Yes, Mother would love you."

Hallie chewed her lip, and she turned back to the page. She explained how Odysseus suffered from an exorbitant amount of pride after the Trojan War, and how it had cost him everything. She explained that Poseidon, Greek god of the sea, cursed him for blinding his Cyclops son, and how nearly twenty years after Odysseus left for Troy, he returned alone and broken only to find his home overrun by greedy suitors vying to take his place as king.

"And so, he smuggled himself into the palace under the guise of an old man with the help of his son Telemachus. His wife, Penelope, finally agreed to entertain the suitors, and said she'll marry whoever can string Odysseus' bow and shoot an arrow through twelve ax heads. But she knows it won't work. Only Odysseus can do it."

"But if he's right there, why does this matter? Why can't he just reveal himself instead of going through all that? Is he going to have to fight the suitors?" Zeke trailed off at Hallie's severe look.

She clucked her tongue. "Quit thinking like a soldier and relax."

She found her place in the text and read, "Owl-eyed Athena now prompted Penelope to set before the suitors Odysseus' bow and the grey iron, implements of the contest and of their death..."

On and on she read, Zeke listening at attention, drinking in every word. With a brother like Kase who loved this story, she was confused as to how he would have missed reading it, but the surprise in his face when she got to the part where Odysseus strung his own bow and shot the arrow straight through the ax heads made her heart leap. Then he laughed when the suitors realized who stood before them. She couldn't wait to tell Kase.

She turned the page to continue, ready to regale him with the bloodbath that was the suitors' deaths, when she found a piece of folded parchment stuck in the pages. She paused and took out the paper, frowning. Where had that come from?

She was about to open it when a soft cough interrupted her. She looked up to find Zeke waiting patiently, but he gestured behind her. Stuffing the parchment down in her satchel, she turned and found she had an audience.

Where all the Yalven children had come from, she didn't know, but each had an expectant look on their face and a glimmer in their golden eyes. Near the front of the group, a girl with soft, curling hair stood, her hem boasting embroidered books, scrolls, and quills. She looked about twelve, but it was hard to tell with the Yalvs. She bowed slightly. "Please continue, Miss."

Hallie's chest warmed. She'd found kindred spirits on this side of the world. "I can start from the beginning if you'd like!"

The girl looked down at her companions. *Stars,* there were nearly fifteen of them. The girl beamed. "We want to know what happens to the suitors, Miss. But after, we would like you to keep reading."

Out of the corner of Hallie's eye, a smile pulled at Saldr's thin lips as he set his book aside and leaned in.

With gusto, she launched back into the story, reading right up until Saldr said they needed to head to the evening's feast. She walked back with a little hop in her step, old dreams spinning a new hope in her head. Hopefully upon their successful return to Kyvena, she'd have more of these days, reading to all the children in the new school she wanted to open.

Soon. They would be home soon.

CHAPTER 25

ONLY JASPER

Hallie

UPON ARRIVING BACK AT THE palace, Hallie didn't get a chance to change, nor put her satchel away, but she didn't mind. She wanted to sketch the feast with her charcoal pencil. When else would she get a chance to witness something so spectacular?

Saldr led them into the palace and once more into the dining hall from that morning. However, it'd been decorated for the occasion. In addition to the torches along the walls, the table held tall, bone-colored candelabras down its center. The light from the skinny candles on each arm of the candelabras reflected on the metal. So many Yalvs surrounded the table that Hallie couldn't possibly count them all without looking like a fool standing on the threshold for too long. Each wore their traditional robes, and Hallie wished she could study all their hems to decipher what their occupations might be. But alas, Saldr led her and Zeke over to sit next to Kase. He looked out of place with his curls and non-toga-ed attire. He mustn't have been successful in whatever he'd been forced to do for the Lord Elder.

Hallie knelt on the floor pillow next to him, with Zeke on her other side. Saldr took a seat across from them and next to the Yalv who'd collected Kase that morning, Rodr. Rodr sat next to a pretty woman with ruby-red lips. Hallie slung off her satchel and set it behind her, keeping it within reach for the moment she needed to sketch something important.

Before she could ask Kase about his day, the Lord Elder stood, and the room hushed as if the curtain at Grieg's Theater had risen. Hallie leaned forward, her elbow knocking the Zuprium plate in front of her. She caught it before it knocked into the candelabra. Kase shook his head with a small smile before turning toward the Lord Elder.

"We bless this feast as Toro blesses us. Our lives glorify Toro, and let us remember thus which he bestowed upon us at the beginning of time, our duty as Chronals. May he guide us on our way to the Mountains at this life's end."

Oh, how she wished she could write down every word. She would have to do her best to remember it all when she had time to pull out her sketchpad. Once she returned home, she would publish a book about her findings and dealings with the Yalvs.

While she'd been engrossed in her thoughts, Yalvs with smoky swirls on their hems came into the hall bearing large plates full of steaming meat and green, leafy vegetables. Her mouth watered as soon as she caught the aroma. It smelled like steak dripping in melted butter. *Oh stars.*

The smoky-hemmed Yalvs set the platters along the table in between the candelabras. As they sat there on their knees around the table, Hallie noticed the others were using their own forks to grab food for their plates. She followed suit. As she went to pile on what looked like a cousin to asparagus and the steaming brown meat, she paused at Kase's face. He was nearly as green as the vegetable she was about to grab.

"Kase?" she whispered, setting aside her fork. Everyone was chatting, but she didn't want to draw attention, because Kase looked like he was about to hurl. "Aren't you hungry?"

He tapped his fork on his empty plate. He'd devoured everything the Yalvs had fed them thus far, but not tonight. She tried again. "What's wrong?"

He shrugged. Hallie grabbed a hunk of meat and piled it on his plate. "You like steak, don't you?"

Still, he hesitated, and she followed his gaze to find both Rodr and Saldr watching them with interest. Hallie tilted her head. "Is there something wrong?"

Kase shook his head. "I'm not hungry. That's all."

"I find that hard to believe," she muttered.

"Master Shackley." Rodr sawed off a chunk of meat and held it out. "You have earned this feast and the benefits of slaying the dragonar, have you not?"

If possible, Kase's face became an even darker shade of green. *Oh stars, he's going to puke right here on the table.* "Kase, if you need to—"

"I'm fine," he hissed. He glanced at Rodr. "I didn't slay the...the..."

He shut his mouth abruptly. Hallie raised an eyebrow, and Zeke caught the end of the conversation.

"What didn't you slay? You didn't tell us what you ended up doing."

Rodr grinned, his pointed teeth showing. "Master Shackley hunted today, and he slew a dragonar, meaning he gets to—"

"Nothing!" Kase's face was as red as the morning sun. It didn't mix well with the green already present. "I don't get to do anything. Nothing at all."

Saldr raised his glass to Kase. "When you finally do claim your right of the Hunt, I will support your decision."

Hallie caught sight of Kase's fists under the table. While she smiled pleasantly at the Yalvs, who conversed about whatever a dragonar was and the implications of one skirting too close to the city, she turned to Kase. "Did you offend them somehow? You were supposed to help make the Lord Elder trust us!"

Zeke leaned across Hallie. "Yeah, and why'd they choose *you* to go hunting? You've never been."

Kase ran both hands over his face. "I told them that." He caught Hallie's eye. "They took me out to hunt the...the...it was a dragon, all right? Like the one we saw in the forest. It's for some ritual of theirs, and I almost didn't make it back in one piece."

"You saw another dragon?" Hallie squealed. She slapped a hand across her mouth when several Yalvs turned toward her. She gave them an embarrassed smile. "Was it similar to the one we ran into? Are there more? Can they take me on their next hunt? I believe they had them on First Earth for a time before they went extinct. If you look at the right texts, you'll find that almost all ancient cultures had lore concerning them and..."

She trailed off when the Yalvs, plus Kase and Zeke,

all stopped to stare at her, slack jawed. A sheepish blush warmed her face. "I read a lot."

They returned to their meals, and Hallie lowered her voice. "So...back to the dragon. You didn't answer my questions."

Kase looked down at her. "It's not something I want to relive, thank you very much." He paused and quirked a brow. "Is that a pencil in your hair?"

"Huh?"

Kase pulled it out. With a smirk, he held it up. His face had regained some of its normal color. "Because you never know when you're going to need to draw something?"

She narrowed her eyes. "You say that like it's a bad thing."

He chuckled a little as she grabbed her satchel and stuffed the pencil inside, but when she did, her fingers hit something rough and crinkled. The parchment. The one she'd found in *The Odyssey* earlier.

She looked around, but no one seemed to care what she was doing. Saldr and Rodr were speaking in Yalven about some sort of ritual involving the dragonar. Zeke took a bite or two of his meat, and Kase pushed bits of his food around his plate. She snuck the parchment out and hid it under the table. With careful hands, she unfolded it, smoothing it out.

The writing was sloppy with some letters half-finished or smeared, but the message was clear.

Only Jasper can work the Gate.

Hallie didn't have to see her own face to know every single blood cell she possessed had fled her cheeks. Her head felt entirely too light, and her stomach too heavy, like a sack of stones inhabited its depths.

What in the blasted, burning stars? Jasper? Hadn't he

been confused by what the Gate did? How did...

Then it clicked in her mind. Jasper was an Essence. He might not have been when he'd written the book, but somehow, someway, he'd taken on one of the Essences. But why did this matter now? How had this note gotten into her copy of *The Odyssey?* If the Cerls were after the Gate, did that mean they truly did possess the Essence to work it? They'd somehow captured Jasper?

That didn't make much sense either. Jasper Morgan lived and died centuries ago, yet Professor Christie did say Jasper would be in contact with the Lord Elder soon.

Stars, it doesn't make any sense. What am I missing?

Kase's hand found her shoulder. "Shouldn't have eaten the meat. It's from that dragon...Hallie, what's wrong?"

Her forehead beaded with sweat as she tried to calm her racing heart.

Zeke looked over, concern etched across his features. "Do you need to go lie down? I'm sure the Yalvs won't mind."

She gripped the note so tightly it felt like it might combust at any moment.

Only Jasper can work the Gate.

"Lord Saldr," she whispered as she leaned forward. Kase's hand fell away. She clutched her queasy stomach with one hand and the note in the other. The Yalv looked up, and Rodr did as well. She continued, "Please, I don't mean to breach your trust, but is the Gate being protected? I have reason to believe the Cerls..." she trailed off and looked around. Most of the other Yalvs were busy devouring the meal or conversing. A few had gotten up from their seats and begun to sing and dance in celebration of their god. Kase and Zeke were the only other ones listening.

"I have reason to believe the Cerls possess the Essence that works the Gate."

Saldr's golden eyes flicked to where the Lord Elder sat drinking and conversing with the surrounding Yalvs. Rodr set his own drink down too hard, water sloshing out the side. "You've not earned—"

Saldr cut him off with a hand on his arm. He held Hallie's gaze and seemed to choose his words with extreme care. "The Essences died out centuries ago. Your treaty hasn't been broken."

Hallie gripped the edge of the table so hard she felt like her fingers were glued to it permanently. She kept her voice low. "Please, Lord Saldr." She looked down at the note, then back into his golden eyes. "I have reason to believe the Cerls indeed have a—"

The doors to the feast hall banged open. Silence fell as a Yalven man with swords and shields on the hem of his toga sprinted inside, his braided midnight hair coming loose and sticking to his sweaty face.

It was strange, as most Yalvs would blink in and out of existence rather than run, but Hallie didn't get to dwell on that oddity long. His words stole whatever thoughts she'd been thinking straight from her head.

The cryptic note slipped from her fingers and fluttered to the floor. The Yalv spoke in a slightly older Yalven dialect, but Hallie could still understand his words.

"Invaders! Invaders at the gates!"

The room erupted in chaos.

CHAPTER 26

FOR ONCE, WILL YOU JUST LISTEN

Kase

IN MOST SITUATIONS OF UTTER panic, Kase never had a clear head. He was decent at split-second decision-making, no matter what his father thought, but that didn't mean those choices were always the best. One of those decisions had sent him to blasted Tasava.

Yet now, when the entire feast hall erupted, cold calm washed over him. He glanced at Hallie's frozen scream and Zeke's flared nostrils, but neither of them affected him in that glimpse in time. Not a flicker of fear, shock, or even surprise.

This was something he could work with. If the city was under attack, he, Zeke, and Hallie could slip out through the chaos and find Skibs. He could steal a few of those Yalven pistols, and they would be off in a matter of minutes. He leaned around Hallie to get his brother's attention. "Hey Zeke, do you know how to work one of—"

Before he could finish, Saldr appeared behind him in a blink, grabbing his shoulder.

"I will take you to your quarters." The Yalv's grip was too tight, the grimace on his face dark and uncompromising.

Kase pulled free. "But what if we don't want to go to our quarters?"

Hallie's voice was too high. "The Cerls are after the Gate, Lord Saldr."

Kase whipped his head toward her. "The Cerls? The Cerls are the ones invading?"

Hallie nodded, and Kase cursed. Zeke stood, almost tripping a Yalven man running from the room, shouting orders about the west gate into the city. Zeke's voice was the strongest it had been in days. "Allow us to help, Lord Saldr. Kase and I can fight."

But Saldr shook his head, his eyes shadowed. "I cannot take any chances. After this is over, we can speak, but right now, I must get you back to your quarters. Please follow me. I do not want to force you."

Kase gritted his teeth but leapt to his feet. He held out a hand to help Hallie, but she stood on her own. She grabbed her satchel and slung it over her shoulder with a shaking hand, the one miraculously healed. "Then let's go, Lord Saldr. I know you want to help the others."

He led them into the hallway, but before they left the room, Kase heard the Lord Elder's orders booming above the voices. "I will need Kainadr. His soul has been lost these thousand years, and it is time I free him."

Any other words were cut off by the door slamming and Hallie's tug on his arm. What was that? How did a soul get lost for a millennium?

"Did you hear what he said?" Kase whispered as they sped down the corridor after the Yalv.

Hallie's jaw was tight, but she nodded. Zeke kept stride beside Kase. "What did he mean by freeing him?"

Hallie shook her head. "Not now." She looked toward Saldr, who sped through the palace like a storm wind. Was he trying to lose them? *Great shocks.*

The Yalv was also muttering to himself, and every so often, his form would flicker. Each time he reappeared, his soft cry of pain grew louder.

"Lord Saldr," Hallie finally said after the fifth reappearance.

He stumbled to a halt and swiveled. His eyes whipped to the sides of the corridor and back down at the three of them. Kase's stomach tightened. This behavior wasn't like the Yalv he'd come to know, but then again, Kase had only learned his name because he hadn't thought Hallie and Kase would be good together.

Hallie spoke once more. "*Lord Saldr.* I'll make sure we get to our quarters and stay there."

He looked at her hard. "I cannot allow that."

"I know you'd rather be protecting your people," she said. "Trust me, please."

"Miss Walker, I cannot allow that."

Hallie took his hand. He flinched a little before relaxing, and she continued, "If it is indeed the Cerls, they're after the Gate, and you and I both know what they're capable of."

Kase glanced at his brother, who hadn't moved a muscle. If Hallie could convince Saldr to leave them, then maybe...maybe they could pull this off and get out of there. Hallie was good.

"Thank you," Saldr whispered. And before Kase

could blink, he disappeared.

He shook his head. "I still don't understand how they do that."

Hallie didn't offer any of her Yalven knowledge. Instead she said, "We need to get to the temple."

Zeke shook his head. "Angering them is the worst thing we could possibly do. The palace should be the most well-defended structure, and with my skill, we might be able to help keep anyone from entering through the front archway."

"Have you both lost your blasted minds?" Kase ran both hands through his curls and pulled. "This might be our only chance to get out of here! We'll steal some supplies and a few weapons, then we can go find Skibs. It's perfect."

Hallie's eyes softened at the mention of Skibs, but she plowed on. "You're both wrong. If the Cerls get a hold of this Gate...and with us preparing to go to war...if we don't protect it, everyone in Jayde will have to face however the Cerls try to use that. They need an Essence to work it, and I believe they have one. I can't—I *won't* let them get their hands on something that should be left well-enough alone."

She choked on her words, and Kase gritted his teeth. "*To the stars with Jayde.* If Skibs is still out there, we need to help him!"

"Stop thinking of yourself, will you?" Zeke interjected, his eyes blazing. He glanced at Hallie, then back to Kase. "We're under attack, and all you can think about is—"

"How is wanting to save Skibs selfish?" Kase took a step forward, but Hallie put herself between them.

"This isn't helping!"

Zeke stepped around Hallie and got right in Kase's

face. His breath was hot. "*Ben is dead.* You can't save him, Kase. You can't. This obsession you have with saving everyone has to stop. It's not healthy, and it puts everyone around you in danger."

Kase's vision blurred with burning, angry tears. "That's a bunch of *stars-blasted* crap and you know it."

Zeke's finger needled him in the chest. "You couldn't save Ana, and you've been blaming yourself ever since."

"*Shut up!*" Kase shouted, his voice echoing off the corridor walls and slamming against his eardrums. He shoved Zeke, and his brother stumbled. "I'm not going to fight with you right now!"

Hallie's voice rang out, silencing them both. "*Stop it!* Fighting about whatever the stars you're talking about is getting us nowhere. If we don't protect the Gate, we're screwed!"

Kase's breaths came hard as he blinked back tears of frustration. He glanced at his brother and found him doing the same. But within a moment, the soldier mask was back on. "Of course. I apologize. This is no time to lose our tempers."

Kase didn't say a thing. He couldn't. Because if he opened his mouth, he didn't know what would spew forth. Instead, he stormed past them both and headed up the corridor to their quarters.

He was halfway down the final hall when the other two caught up. Hallie spoke first. "What're you doing? We have to get to the temple."

He didn't turn. "If we're going outside, I need my jacket. And I have a pocketknife. I don't know if we can get our hands on one of their pistols, so I'm going to need something."

After visiting their quarters, the trio sprinted down

empty hallways and staircases until they found themselves at the front archway. Kase flipped open his pocketknife, missing the reassuring weight of an electropistol at his side. He hoped they could find something better to use or that they wouldn't have to fight at all. Maybe the Yalvs would take care of it before the invaders got as far as the palace.

However, as soon as they stepped through the archway with its strange heat wave, shouts met their ears and the metallic tang of blood flooded his nose. He coughed and put a hand to his mouth.

Bodies littered the stone beneath his feet outside the palace entrance. Empty-eyed Yalvs with blood bleeding into their dark hair stared up at him. They weren't the only casualties. Others lay among them like leaves scattered along the forest floor, except these bodies had diamond neck tattoos.

Cerls. Hallie was right.

Her face had turned the same shade of white as Firstmoon, and Kase wasn't faring much better. Shouts came from his right, and he looked down into the fray where the fighting raged on. The Yalvs had beaten the Cerls back from the palace steps. Golden light and sparkling bullets zinged from their pistols, but the Cerls answered with their own. Their bullets were blue lights flashing across the sky like shooting stars.

Kase also spotted the stone statues that lined the main road up to the palace. Instead of staying frozen and holding the lanterns like they'd been before, they fought alongside the Yalvs, their chiseled arms deflecting as many of the blue bullets as they could. However, unlike the electropistol, the Cerl weapons worked—each time blue light struck a stoneman, large chunks of rock flew through the air.

If that wasn't bad enough, Kase could only watch in horror as one of those bullets hit a Yalv. His chest exploded with blue fire, and he fell, silent.

Holy shocks.

Kase glanced down at the pocketknife clasped in his fingers. What a joke. He inspected the bodies in front of them. Some still held pistols loosely in their hands. He didn't think, only moved, dodging a glowing blue bullet and grabbing three pistols. All Yalven. He shoved one into Zeke's hands, the other into Hallie's.

He ignored more screams coming from the right. "These work exactly like electropistols. Cock it and pull the trigger."

When both Zeke and Hallie nodded, Kase turned back to the fighting. "If we find cover over that way," he pointed to a collection of buildings nearby, "we might be able to hold off some..."

He stopped. A few Cerls had snuck around the outside, sprinting toward the giant door in the mountain. One of them lugged the great cannon weapon like the one Skibs had disposed of in the forest.

Hallie's words were nearly lost in the battle sounds. "That's the temple! The Gate! It's in there!" Her eyes were wild. "We have to stop them!"

Kase still didn't understand what the *Gate* was, but he knew it was important, and it was time he trusted Hallie once more. He cocked his gun and aimed at the Cerl with the cannon. He missed.

Instead, the Cerl turned and aimed the cannon right at Kase.

"MOVE!"

He, Hallie, and Zeke dove just as the cannon's blue-flamed blast hit the archway behind them. However, instead of exploding or disintegrating, the archway shook, shone with a blinding light, and absorbed the blast.

There really was magic on this side of the world.

Zeke recovered first and shot toward the Cerls still making their way up the path to the temple. But the others lucked out, Zeke's bullets missing. Kase didn't know where the guards had gone. The Cerls reached the massive door and shot the cannon at it. The metal reacted the same way the palace archway had, but the Cerls weren't deterred. One dragged forward a struggling body—a Yalv.

No, not any Yalv. Rodr.

Zeke stopped shooting, and Kase turned. Cerls were trying to break off from the main fight. Kase fired again at the ones near the doors, but the weapon clicked, empty of its mysterious bullets. He stuffed it in the back of his pants and looked around, trying to find another weapon.

"No!" Hallie shouted. He whipped his head up to find her running toward the mountain door.

He caught the edge of her jacket. Her shout didn't stop the Cerl from blasting Rodr's arm off at the elbow, nor did it prevent blood splattering on the metal door, lighting up like the sun as the door opened. Rodr's scream echoed in Kase's skull.

The small group of hooded Cerls fled through the opening and slammed the door shut, taking the screaming Rodr with them. Hallie pulled herself out of his grip, taking off toward the door. Kase cursed, but he followed. When they reached it, Kase grabbed the edge and tugged. There was no obvious handle, and it didn't budge.

He glanced back at Zeke twenty feet away, facing down another wave of Cerls. His brother fired relentlessly, but it was like swimming upstream.

Hallie tugged on the door with Kase again. Nothing. Tears laced her voice as she said, "We have to get in! Why won't it work?"

Kase grabbed Hallie and pulled her down as a blue flash of light burst over their heads. The pistol she'd been holding clattered to the ground. Her whole body shook as she looked up at him, her eyes wide. "The blood. We have to use the blood."

Golden bursts headed their way, but the Yalvs wouldn't make it in time to help. Kase spun, looking for another Yalv to use. "But we don't have a Yalv to open it for us!"

"The arm!" Zeke sprinted toward them.

"But isn't that disrespectful?" Hallie asked at the same time Kase leapt toward Rodr's mangled arm. With a silent apology and a grimace, he smeared the Yalv's blood across the cool metal.

Zeke fired more shots, and Kase and Hallie ducked as more blue fire flew past them.

When they looked up, the blood glowed, turning from red to gold. The door opened, and Kase shoved Hallie inside. He glanced at Zeke.

"Go!" his brother shouted, still trying to hold back the others.

"Not without you," Kase growled, grabbing the back of Zeke's shirt.

Zeke yanked away and kept firing. "I'll hold them off!"

"Zeke, get *in here*!" Kase yanked at his brother's shirt once more.

Zeke turned, pulling out of Kase's grip, and shoved him through the opening. "For once, will you just listen—"

Moments like that were always strange. The first time had been three years ago, when Ana had run into the furious flames engulfing the small cottage in the lower city. The second was only two months earlier, when the greenie pilot slid from a hangar roof slick with rain.

It was something Kase would never be able to fully explain. It was like his heart beat in time with the clicking of a malfunctioning mechanical clock. Each second, each movement, each breath lasted for an eternity.

Before Zeke finished his sentence, a burst of blue hit him in the leg, and he fell to one knee. Zeke roared and fired his own weapon. Blood and blue fire gushed out of the wound and pooled on the ground.

Kase's eyes widened as another glowing bullet smashed into his brother's chest, and Zeke crumpled. But before Kase could leap back through the small opening, his brother used the last of his strength to shut the door. The metal creaked and slammed as cool air froze in Kase's lungs.

And then the screaming began.

CHAPTER 27

I DO REMEMBER

Hallie

THE FIGHTING ON THE OTHER side of the door threatened to drown Hallie, but that was nothing compared to the screaming in her head. She shut her eyes and willed it to go away, willed herself to wake up from the terrible nightmare she'd found herself in.

But Kase's shouts only proved she wasn't asleep.

"Zeke, no, *no no no you can't—*"

Hallie's vision blurred, and she choked on the sob stuck in her throat. Zeke. Brave, sturdy, trusting Zeke. Her fingers quaked as she brought them up to her mouth.

She'd seen the blood, seen the final shot as Zeke's body convulsed and crumpled to the ground. Just like a lifetime ago when the beam, the entire section of the abandoned mine, had crashed down from the ceiling. She should have screamed. She should have grabbed Jack's hand, but she didn't. Because she and Niels were nothing but cowards.

Jack, Ebba, and now Zeke. How many deaths would she have to witness before her own?

Her knees gave out, and she fell to the ground of the rough-hewn, torchlit tunnel. Kase's grief echoed off the stone walls. She clawed at her ears, willing the noise to stop, but it didn't. There was no blocking it out.

I can't fall apart now.

She lowered her hands and inhaled as deep as she could. Her lungs ached with the effort, but that helped ground her and clear her head. The Cerls. They were somewhere in this temple. They were trying to find the Gate, and Hallie didn't want to find out what they would do with it. If they could hold them off long enough for the Yalvs to get there, they might stand a chance of saving Jayde—all Yalvara—from whatever would happen. She pushed herself to her feet.

Kase knelt in front of the door, weakly pounding on it, his voice growing hoarse.

"Zeke...don't...leave," he gasped as Hallie dropped beside him.

He didn't acknowledge her, and she had to blink away the memories. It hurt. It hurt like a knife in her heart, but they had to keep moving.

"Kase."

His fist hit the door again and came away bloody. He'd scraped it raw.

"Kase."

Another bloody fist on the metal.

"Kase!" she shouted as she grabbed his sweaty face in her hands and forced him to look at her.

His dark blue eyes were wild, wilder than his hair, and streaming with tears. He choked, "I can't leave him. Ana, the greenie, Ben, all those people, the fire—"

Hallie's fingers tightened on the sides of his face as she pushed her own pain aside. "Don't waste Zeke's sacrifice."

"But he's just on the other side!"

"Listen to me!" Hallie shouted through a sob she let escape, but she didn't let go of Kase. "You can't save him. He did this so we could live, so we could save Jayde. We *have to go*."

"I *won't* leave him!" His voice rose, pitching toward hysteria.

"Kase!"

He clawed at the door once more. "I can't. I won't. *Zeke!*"

"You can, and you will."

"*No!*" Kase shook her off, pounding on the door again, still shouting through his tears for his brother.

So, Hallie did the only thing she thought would shock him out of it.

She slapped him.

All those weeks ago, she'd promised herself she wouldn't again, but he'd left her no choice. She couldn't go on without him. His eyes blazed as he raised a hand to his cheek.

"Why did you—"

"We can grieve later," she whispered, "but right now, we have to stop the Cerls from using the Gate. Kase, I need you here. I—I need you. Please."

His eyes cleared, but he didn't say anything.

"We might be the only hope Jayde has. So please, *please*..." She dropped her hands to her lap as her voice cracked.

Kase ran a hand down the door once more. The shouts, screams, and clashes on the other side were parts of a grotesque symphony. The Yalvs had joined the battle in front of the doors.

None of the voices were Zeke's.

Kase sniffed, wiping away the last of his tears with his palms. "I'm sorry."

She swallowed the lump rising in her throat. "Let's go."

He nodded, and they got to their feet. Kase gritted his teeth as he turned away from the door. "Do we have any weapons other than my useless pistol?"

Hallie bit her lip and shook her head. "Do you still have your pocketknife?"

He took it out and flipped it open. "This is it, I guess."

"Sorry."

He shook his head and closed the knife, stuffing it back into his pocket. "It'll have to work. What—what now?"

She grabbed his hand and pulled him toward what might be their last moments on Yalvara.

Kase

THE DARK STONE TUNNEL WAS long and winding, lit with only a few torches, and it was silent like the calm before the storm. Once they reached the first chamber, Kase nearly lost what tenuous grip on reality he had left. Blood pools glinted in the flickering torchlight, revealing a splattering of corpses, both Yalven and Cerl.

"Are any of them still alive?" Hallie's eyes were shut tight.

He squeezed her hand, although his chest was too tight and the smell of stale metal too pungent. He nudged an arm with the toe of his boot. Blood seeped into the leather, and his stomach lurched when he saw the nearest body without a face.

"I'll check. Don't look."

Anything that might have been useful was a blob of melted gunk next to their owner's corpse. So it was the useless Yalven pistol and a pocketknife to take on the monstrosities that had mutilated the corpses.

"Which way now?" Hallie opened her eyes just a sliver, looking at the two hallways in front of them, avoiding the bodies below.

Kase peeked down the left corridor. It was darker than the one they'd come out of, and eyeing the torches in the chamber, he couldn't reach them in their sconces. "How much do you know about this place?"

"Not much."

Kase walked back toward her, avoiding a pool of blood. "If this Gate thing is so important, it must be down the largest hallway."

"Your deductive reasoning is impeccable."

"I can't tell if you're being serious or not."

Hallie shrugged. "Doesn't matter. I would say we should try down—"

Shouts echoed off the stone walls of the right corridor. Hallie and Kase jumped, Hallie grabbing the lace at her throat. "I guess we know which way to go?"

Kase nodded and took her hand in his once more, leading her down the passage. It wasn't lit nearly as well, but feeling his way along, they finally reached another chamber much like the last.

After searching through it only to find more dead bodies and melted hunks of weapons, they traveled down the only available tunnel. The sole illumination in this one was a simple torch, which cast long shadows along the walls, and the silence gave way to his terrifying thoughts. Had they chosen the wrong corridor? What if they killed Hallie like they'd killed Zeke?

Holy moons.

They'd killed Zeke.

Kase's breaths came fast as he tried to swallow hysteria wedging its way into his mind. Zeke had died to save them. He was dead. He was never coming back. If that happened to Hallie, he would never—

She squeezed his hand. "Kase. We'll figure out something. We only need to stall until the Yalvs can get in."

He clenched his jaw and blinked back his emotions. They had an impossible job to do, and if he went down, he would go down fighting, hoping it would be enough. He would be a hero, not a coward.

His words echoed. "I'd feel better if you hid down one of the other tunnels until the Yalvs get here."

She ripped her hand from his and crossed her arms. The faint flickering of the lone torch danced across her face. "I'm not leaving you."

He shook his head. "I don't want whatever made that mess...please, I don't think I can handle it if something..." He swallowed, but his throat was tight. "I've already lost Zeke. I can't...I'm not going to lose you, too."

Blasted emotions. He couldn't even get a sentence out.

With a brief hesitation and a slight quivering of her hand, she cupped his cheek. Her dark golden eyes met his, and something in his heart constricted at the determination reflected in their depths. "Kase...you won't lose me. I promise."

And then she stood on tiptoe and kissed him on his stubbled cheek. It was as light as a breeze, but Kase's heart nearly stopped and leapt out of his chest all at once. "What was that for?"

Her cheeks turned a lovely shade of pink as she forced a smile. "There's no one else I'd rather be here with at the end than you."

The city was under attack, his brother had just died, and he and Hallie were scrambling to stop whatever the Cerls were doing in these caves. But Hallie's eyes were bright and bold and...

He stopped thinking and placed his fingers underneath her chin, lifting her face toward his. But before he followed through, the distant slam of a metal door echoed off the corridor's rock walls. They jumped, bumping heads.

"Shocks," Kase moaned, holding a hand to his forehead.

At the same time Hallie grumbled, "Your head is harder than I thought."

"If you hadn't jumped out of your skin, this wouldn't have happened."

"So it's my fault? If you hadn't leaned in to...to..." She covered her cheeks with her hands.

"I don't remember you turning away," Kase whispered. The heat crept into his own face. "We need to keep going."

As he took a step, he caught Hallie's muttered curse. "Blasted door."

His stomach leapt as a grin crept onto his face. He held out his hand. With a small smile of her own, she laced her fingers through his.

He squeezed softly. "Let's go, Hals."

As they walked down the corridor together, Kase almost forgot the dark thoughts clawing at the edge of his mind. Almost. "Promise me you'll do what I say when we find the Cerls. Deal?"

Hallie took a minute before she squeezed his hand. "Only if I don't have a better idea."

Kase rolled his eyes and chuckled. "Fine."

They continued down the corridor and stopped when they faced a door identical to the one at the entrance. Kase pushed and pulled at it, but it didn't budge.

He cursed. "Should I go back and drag one of the bodies down here?"

Hallie bit her lip as he saw the smear on the side of the door where a normal handle should have been. The Cerls hadn't left anything of Rodr. If Kase went back to grab one of the dead ones, they might be too late. But it might be his only choice. He pulled on her hand. "Come on. It'll be quick if you help."

She stared at the door, unblinking, her breathing picking up in pace.

Kase groaned. He tugged again. "We have to hurry."

"Give me your knife."

Huh? "That won't work."

"Just hand it over."

He pulled it out of his pocket and held it out. "What're you going to do with it?"

She flicked it open and sliced the tip of her left index finger. She sucked in a quick breath at the pain.

What is she...wait, how would that—

She smeared the bubbling blood on the metal.

"What makes you—" The golden glow snatched the words from his mouth, and the door creaked open.

Holy blasted stars.

"Hallie, what did you—are you—"

She wiped the blade on her trousers and handed it back to him. As he stuffed it into his pocket, she wound her finger up into the hem of her shirt to stop the bleeding. "No time to explain. Let's go."

The grip of the Yalven pistol was slick with his sweat as Kase pulled it from the back of his pants, but he clutched it as he pushed the door open and stepped inside, Hallie behind him. Kase wracked his brain, reeling over her revelation, as he crossed the threshold. He didn't have time to ask the millions of questions he now had as a wave of heat flooded over him, just like when they'd entered the palace.

"No, no, no," Hallie gasped.

Two people stood before a glowing archway, and a third lay at their feet groaning in pain. Rodr. The archway was the only light in the cavern room, but it shone as bright as a dozen lanterns. Carved metal blocks not unlike the pillars in the forest made up the arch itself. The two Cerls inspected the space between the stones, where images flashed by too fast for Kase to grasp what they were. One of them held the cannon prototype.

"That's the Gate, isn't it?" he whispered. "What'd you say about it? It's a weapon?"

Hallie grabbed a fistful of his jacket and pulled him close, trying not to attract the men's attention. "I found a note. In my book. I didn't understand...I still don't...but the Cerls have an Essence...and...and Kase..."

A sound from the archway made Kase glance up toward the men, and his heart leapt into his throat.

Crashing, burning, and blasted stars.

At first, the flashing images and light coming from

the Gate distracted him from taking stock of the men in front of it, but the one on the right stood with his arms crossed and hood fallen back, his blond hair backlit by the Gate's light, making it appear like a crown.

There was no question, even from behind.

Every nerve in his body tingled as he jerked out of Hallie's grip. "*Skibs!*"

His friend's features had always reminded him of a fox with his sharp nose and clever eyes, but now they took on a more sinister feel. It was clear where his nose had been broken and reset after the initial crash. Hallie grabbed Kase again.

"Wait," she hissed. Her breath tickled his ear. "Something's not right."

Skibs blinked hard and stumbled forward, catching himself before he made it five steps. "Kase? Is that you? Hallie got my note?"

"It was you? What did you mean only Jasper can work the Gate? He's dead." Hallie's fingers gripped tighter.

Kase tugged out of her grip. "What're you doing? I thought you were—I thought you were dead."

A grimace skittered across Skibs' face. The other man wore a bloodstained blue uniform. A Cerl. Had he been the one to mutilate those bodies in the previous chambers? Skibs' voice was sharp. "Tell General Correa we found the Gate."

"Yes, Agent Reiss, but what about these two?" The man spoke with an accent, his 's' sounds drawn out.

Kase held the pistol in front of him and pulled back the hammer, ready to fire. His finger trembled on the trigger, though he knew it wouldn't work.

The grimace never left Skibs' face. "I can handle them. Now go!"

The man nodded and ran off, towing the cannon on his shoulder. He didn't stop and try to hurt him or Hallie, but something was wrong. Kase focused on his friend. "What in the *blasted shocks* is wrong with you?"

Skibs ran a shaking hand down his face. "I didn't have a choice."

Kase blinked sweat out of his eyes, his arm never falling from its position with the pistol. "I thought they kidnapped you, but you...are you..."

He couldn't get the words out. He couldn't say what he was thinking. Couldn't say what this was because it wasn't real. It wasn't. Soon, he'd wake up from this *stars-blasted* world he'd found himself in where his brother was dead and his best friend a traitor. Pain squeezed his lungs.

Skibs bent to where Rodr still moaned. In the light of the Gate, a sparkling rope bound his feet. Blood from his missing arm seeped across the stone. Skibs' voice was low and thick. "If I didn't lead them here, if I didn't do exactly as they asked..."

Hallie stepped forward, her hands in fists. Her satchel knocked into Kase as she stood beside him. "How? How did you...Jasper is dead. That book. He wrote it centuries ago."

Skibs' eyes were soft when he turned, his face was pained. He stared at Hallie a moment too long before he looked toward the flickering images of the Gate. "Jasper isn't dead, yet he's not truly alive either." He paused and cleared his throat. "But none of that matters. Not now."

Kase gritted his teeth. "What is going on?"

His voice was low, close to a feral growl. Hallie stiffened beside him.

Skibs stood. He opened his mouth to say something

else when his right eye twitched, then his shoulders. Kase stumbled back, but he didn't let go of his weapon.

In seconds, Skibs' face changed to one he didn't recognize. It was the same blond hair, the same blue eyes, but it was like a new person had taken up residence behind them. Kase didn't know how to describe it any better than that.

"Of course..." Hallie gasped. "The Essence...you...and Jasper...you're the Essence. You took on whatever Essence he possessed."

"I did what needed to be done." Ben narrowed his eyes at her. "And when I discovered that you had *The Gate of Time*, I knew I had to do something. Ben didn't want to, but he's not in control. He's weak, unlike Jasper."

He jerked again, and his eyes changed. He fell to his knees, shaking so badly that his next words were barely audible. "No. No, please, don't."

His moan broke the sting of betrayal coursing through Kase. He didn't know what was happening, but that pain lacing his friend's voice was real. Kase still didn't have a blasted clue what was going on, but he didn't care. He dropped the pistol and fell beside his friend.

Skibs pushed him away. "No, you don't understand. I can't control—argh!"

His whole body convulsed as his eyes went blank. After a moment, Skibs shuddered, vomiting onto the ground. He wiped his mouth with a shaking hand.

"Give me your notebook. Please. And then get out of here."

Kase flinched away and looked toward Hallie, who hovered near the door. He turned back to Skibs. "I don't understand. Clearly you need help—"

Skibs swung his arm at Kase, and he barely missed knocking him in the side of the head. "Leave the notebook and get out! If I don't...if I don't do this, they'll kill Lucy. *I don't have a choice*. Please. I don't want it to kill you too!"

Hallie fell to her knees on Kase's other side. "Why? Why do you need my notebook? Whatever the Cerls want, it's only going to hurt Jayde."

Sweat slid down Skibs' face like rain. "For the Gate. I already destroyed the book, but you wrote what you know about it in the notebook. Maybe they'll be lenient, maybe they won't...and they want her, but I told them she wouldn't...you wouldn't cooperate..."

Her?

His body convulsed once more, and Kase shot up, grabbing the pistol and dragging Hallie with him. This time, Skibs didn't regain control after the blank stare. Because when he stood, something else gazed out of Ben Reiss' eyes, and whatever it was chilled Kase to his core.

Skibs. Not you, too.

Ben reached down and grabbed the now-unconscious Rodr by the collar of his blood-spattered toga. "I'm sure Ben would prefer you make this easy, but he's always been weak."

Kase's hands shook as Ben tossed Rodr into the Gate. Hallie screamed, but Kase could only stare as whatever had possessed his friend's body stuck his own hand into the images and mumbled words Kase didn't understand. His hand slipped through, the images reforming around his arm. They didn't slow in the slightest, and Kase's eyes burned trying to make out each one.

"I'll give you the notebook!" Hallie yelled,

stumbling forward. "Just bring him back!"

Ben shut his eyes and breathed deeply. "The Chronal served his life's purpose, and he'll finish you both off. It's what Ben would want. To save you from the pain of seeing what Cerulene will do and what will happen if we don't collect the Essences in time. You are both worthless to me now."

Kase swallowed hard, his heart pounding in his ears. He fingered his forgotten pistol and held it in front of him. Ben pulled his hand from the Gate at last. In it, a shimmering sword followed, a dark blue gemstone in the pommel. The same gemstone Rodr wore around his neck. What in the *blasted suns* was going on? The sword was nearly identical to the ones Hallie and Ben had found just before the stonemen attacked.

"What did you do?" Kase grabbed Hallie's arm and pulled her back with him toward the entrance. "What did you mean about collecting the Essences in time?"

"Doesn't matter. You won't be here." Ben took an experimental swing with the sword. "My Essence controls the Gate, and this sword is its key."

Hallie's voice squeaked. "There's a reason the Yalvs agreed to the treaty. The Essences are dangerous to take into oneself."

Ben shook his head, stalking closer. Kase met his eyes. They were the same clear blue he knew so well, but Skibs was gone. Kase didn't understand it, but he was gone.

He couldn't feel his hands nor his legs. He didn't know how or why, but Skibs was dead.

"You're smart, Miss Walker, but you don't see the bigger picture, do you? I thought you were smart. I thought you *knew*."

Trying to distance himself from the memories and

laughter of days past, Kase took aim at his friend as his finger trembled on the trigger even though he knew it was out of bullets.

"Knew what?" Hallie asked.

"It doesn't matter now. We'll find someone else."

"Someone else?"

Ben lunged.

Kase chucked the pistol at him just before he and Hallie jumped to the side. The thing that had been Skibs batted the weapon away with ease.

"That was stupid," Hallie hissed as she righted herself.

"There was a chance it'd hit him in the eye."

What could he do? Kase needed to distract him long enough so Hallie could get away. He refused to lose her, too.

"Do you trust me?" Kase whispered as they edged back further.

When she didn't answer, he caught her wide eyes tracing the sword's movements as Ben stalked toward them.

"Hallie. *Do you trust me?*"

A breath.

"Yes."

Ben didn't stop his progression with the sword, held it out with one arm, and pointed it directly at Kase's heart. Kase didn't know how to do it himself, but even he knew there was a better way to handle a sword. If he could get Ben off balance, he might have a chance of disarming him.

Putting one hand in his pocket, Kase pulled out the knife, snapping it open, and stopped a few feet from what he hoped was the door.

Kase would go down fighting.

Like Zeke.

Don't waste my sacrifice either, Hallie.

When the sword was in striking distance, he took a deep breath. "*Run.*"

The sound of her footsteps sprinting away lifted the weight from his shoulders as he flung his knife at Ben's face. It sliced across his cheek, taking a sliver of skin with it.

Blast. I missed.

Ben staggered and roared, lunging for the door. Kase spun to the side and kicked the hand holding the sword, but the weapon didn't fall. He grabbed the sword hand and tried to force Ben backward, away from the entrance.

"I guess I'll deal with you first," Ben grunted. He was too strong. He shoved Kase off and swung the sword at eye level. Kase barely ducked in time, rolling to the side and coming up on one knee. His body throbbed from where he'd tumbled across the craggy floor, but if he hadn't been terrified, he might have congratulated himself on such a move.

Ben tried to slash, but Kase went in low and tackled him before he could do much more than raise the weapon in the air. Kase groaned as they landed, rolling away when the sword swung toward him.

He lunged to his feet and faced his foe. They were closer to the Gate now, but it wouldn't help. It only illuminated the shadows on Ben's face.

Are you still in there, Skibs?

Ben climbed to his feet with a wicked sneer, sword gripped in both hands. Kase breathed heavily as he used his shirt to wipe the sweat dripping from his chin.

"You're quick," Ben said. "But I will kill you."

Kase fell into a stance he'd seen hand fighters take,

a slight bend to his knees, hands up and ready to punch and block. Not that either would stop a sword.

"You were my friend. My best friend." Kase choked on the words. Ben's eye twitched. Kase continued, "Don't you remember? We always had each other's backs. Always. Remember!"

Ben twitched again, his head jerking to the side. Kase powered on. "We got so drunk after our induction into the Crews, you had to carry me home while I sang 'Tovo Bless the Wenches' at the top of my lungs."

Another twitch.

"Don't you remember all those training flights together? When we'd stolen that electric gramophone and hooked it up to the hover? My favorite song was that flowery, stringy one that sounded like...sounded like..." Kase barely got his words out now that the memories inundated him. His tears were salty in his mouth and mixed with the sweat. "Just remember, Skibs. Remember!"

Ben twitched violently, the sword scraping the ground, but he caught himself. He looked up at Kase. Tears budded in his blue eyes. "I do remember."

Kase didn't leave his stance, his breathing all the more labored from his tears. "Then fight whatever's controlling you! Please!"

Skibs wiped his eyes with his sleeve, still stained with blood, probably from Rodr. He shook his head, gasping, "I can't. I *can't*. I've tried, I'm trying—"

Ben lunged, thrusting the sword at a blazing speed. Kase dove to the right, but he wasn't fast enough—the sword pierced his left side, just beneath his ribs, and he fell. His head cracked against the stone floor, but he barely felt it.

A labored breath. Two. And then pain like he'd

never experienced in his life exploded throughout his body. It was as if someone had lit a fire where the sword tip had gone in, and it caught the rest of him in the blaze. He screamed his throat raw.

His vision clouded as he looked up through white-hot pain to see Skibs, sword raised, tears streaming down his own face. "I'm sorry. I'm sorry, but I can't, I can't..."

The pain. It was too much.

I tried. See you soon, Zeke. Ana.

Ana.

CHAPTER 28

A GIFT FROM THE GODS

Hallie

FOR ONCE, HALLIE LISTENED TO Kase, and when he gave the word, she ran. The other Cerl hadn't bothered to close the door, to Hallie's relief. The first thing to go right. But when she was halfway up the tunnel, voices up ahead echoed off the walls.

"Kase?" She whipped around, breathing hard. "Is Ben following..."

Kase wasn't behind her.

Torchlight flickered. No curly-haired pilot followed. The tunnel was empty.

He was going to sacrifice himself. For her.

No. No. I can't do this without you.

Her boots slapped the stone floor as she sprinted back to the Gate room. Words, shouts met her ears as she approached the door, but she didn't register what they meant because all she saw in her mind was Kase bleeding and faceless like the corpses in the tunnel.

Barreling into the room, Hallie slammed the door just as Kase screamed.

She looked up to see him fall to the ground writhing in pain.

Please, no.

Anguish seized her heart in its talons as Ben staggered over to his friend and raised the sword high above his head. Tears streamed down his face, but his words were chilling to Hallie's ears, "I'm sorry. I'm sorry, but I can't, I can't..."

Oh stars. Oh blasted, burning stars.

She didn't have anything in her satchel. Her notebook might throw him off balance, but then she'd be giving him exactly what he wanted. It was half the reason they were in this mess.

She stuck her hand in her pocket, and her fingers clasped around the rough texture of Ebba's twine sling and the pyrite rock she was going to give her brother, still bloodstained from when the Cerls had shot her down. It would have to work. She'd been lucky once, and maybe she would be lucky again. Lucky enough to distract Ben, lucky enough to save Kase.

Thank you, Ebba.

Hallie pulled the sling out, thrust the loop on her finger, and fit the stone in the pouch like Kase had taught her all those weeks ago.

Aim and hold tight.

She focused in on Ben's face. It was the only place where the rock might do enough damage to catch him off guard. With nothing but a prayer, she slung it back and loosed it just above her target.

The rock soared through the air and nailed Ben in the eye. He shouted and jerked back.

Hallie screamed as she rushed forward and slammed into his legs, the move she used to pull on her brother when they were younger. Ben didn't expect it, and she knocked him off his feet. He stumbled over Kase's body, kicking Hallie in the face, and fell headfirst into the glowing Gate. Except his hand snatched her satchel, ripping it from her shoulder.

Hallie lunged for it, but Ben disappeared through the light.

Gone. All her sketches, notes, her copy of *The Odyssey*...all had disappeared through the flashing images of the Gate.

She looked about for the stone only to find it lying in a pool of blood next to Kase.

"No, no, no!"

Hallie stumbled backward over to him. He was still as the grave if only for the barely perceptible rise and fall of his chest. Her heart pounded in her ears as she let loose a silent scream.

I saved him! I stopped Ben!

"Kase!" She found her voice at last as she crawled to his head. The blood pooled around the left side of his body and soaked the knees of her trousers. His breaths were scattered, and his face scrunched against the agonizing pain. At least he was no longer screaming.

"What do I do? What do I do?" She fumbled around for anything to put pressure on the wound, but there was nothing except that sword and the rock. Ben hadn't taken that through with him, at least. She looked at Kase's blood-drenched shirt and whispered a quick apology before pushing aside his jacket and gripping the tear where he'd done so to make the tourniquet for her days ago. He'd refused to wear the togas, and that was all the Yalvs had. She ripped his shirt all the way to his neck, revealing his chest. She tore off a good chunk of the linen and wadded it, pressing it onto the still oozing wound. Blood pulsed in her ears.

Kase shuddered as voices grew louder from the other side of the door. Hallie choked on the tears flowing freely down her face. What was the use? She'd be dead in minutes once those monsters made it through the door. The images of the mutilated bodies from the previous chambers flashed in her mind. She squeezed her eyes shut against them.

"Don't let me face them alone, please. I don't know what to do," she pleaded, her fingers slick with the blood soaking the shirt scrap. "Wake up. Tell me I'm being stupid. Call me names. Anything."

Her tears changed to wracking sobs, and she leaned her forehead to his chest. "Please. I promise I won't yell at you or slap you again. Just don't—don't—"

His breaths had faded to whining wheezes nearly drowned by her tears when the door burst open. She screamed and scrambled to where Ben had dropped the sword sticking partway out of the Gate. Before she could get the weapon up to defend herself, a Yalv blinked into existence before her. The weapon clanged as it hit the floor, barely missing Kase's arm.

"Move, Miss," the Yalv said. It was Saldr. Grimacing from pain, his face was streaked in blood; a gash on his cheek needed to be stitched. He removed the bloody shirt wad and shoved his hand inside a small pouch hanging from his belt. As he pulled out golden dust, he pushed Hallie out of the way with his other hand and smeared the contents onto Kase's wound. The dust's color bled to red.

He murmured words she didn't understand, and the wound glowed softly. Kase's entire body jerked as he let out a whimper.

Hallie tried to shove Saldr aside, but someone gripped her arm, stilling her. "Lord Saldr will do what he can."

The Lord Elder stood above her. When she stopped fighting, he let her go, and she collapsed to her knees and hid her face in her hands. An image of her brother flashed before her eyes. Zeke fell again, followed by Ebba's serene face as she breathed her last. When would it end?

Don't die. Don't die. Don't die. She rocked back and forth, hugging herself. Saldr's humming was a faint whisper in her ears. It was the same as the one the healer had used on them days earlier.

"It is up to him now," Saldr said.

Hallie stopped her rocking. "What do you mean? Don't you have more of that *blasted* dust?"

The Lord Elder put a hand on her shoulder. "Vasa can only manipulate time so much. A gift from the gods, not meant to be used by man. We are limited in our knowledge of its use."

Hallie crawled forward and grabbed Kase's hand, the one with the ring he never took off. Why was his skin so cold? The calluses on his fingers were rough, the ring chilled as she brought his hand to her cheek. His handsome features were soft, if streaked with blood and dirt. He looked only to be sleeping. Her stomach lurched.

"There's nothing more you can do?"

"The Vasa may yet work." Saldr climbed to his feet. "His body must accept the gift."

"How does it work? You said it manipulated time?"

"Time holds many answers."

"That doesn't tell me *anything*."

Stupid cryptic Yalvs.

His silence pressed down on her, but Kase's breathing drew her attention. He sucked in a great gust of air and let it out slowly. He groaned, and his eyelids fluttered.

"Kase?" Hallie dropped his hand and grabbed the sides of his face. "Kase? Can you hear me?"

His chest stilled.

"No, Kase! *Kase!*" She laid her forehead on his chest once more, her tears coursing onto his skin and mixing with the bloody dust smeared on his wound. "You promised to get me home. I can't go without you. Come on, you *promised,* you blasted *dulkop!*"

She waited for the scowl, for an insult to one-up hers, *anything*.

Nothing. He was too still. Did that mean...did that mean he was...dead?

She found his hand again and squeezed it as tight as she could. Past scenes played out in her head like the moving picture shows she'd read about on First Earth. They flitted and fluttered in her mind's eye as the tears spewed forth even harder with each memory.

Kase's tangled hair the first time he'd come into the bookshop, telling her to organize the shelves.

Fussing at her because she'd messed with the ship's controls.

The Odyssey *held out before him in an attempt to comfort her.*

His soft smile after she'd kissed his cheek not a half hour before.

"Why is it always me?" She lightly pounded her fist on his silent chest. He didn't react, didn't move.

And now I've lost you, too.

The tragedy Hallie was doomed to repeat. No one stayed long. Kase was no exception. A fresh wave of tears flooded her eyes. Each one dripped down and mixed with the dust.

"Child?"

When she didn't answer, the Lord Elder put a hand on her shoulder. "I am sorry. It seems Toro has spoken."

Hallie's vision blurred further. "Why didn't your magic work? You have all this power, hiding like cowards on this blasted side of the planet, and you can't save one single human? *Why?*"

The Lord Elder looked down. "Man does not govern the Vasa. Sometimes, Toro's answer is no."

Hallie laid her head back down onto Kase's cold chest.

"Saldr will stay until you're ready to accept Toro's judgment. Master Shackley fought bravely. He died a hero. Take heart in that, my child."

He left, and Hallie's chest ached as the rest of her body faded into numbness. She sat back and gripped his hand tightly in hers, trying to feel anything at all.

Silence.

Looking into his face, death had erased the pain, leaving his forehead unwrinkled, his mouth relaxed. She brought his hand to her cheek and leaned into it, closing her eyes. His ring rubbed her skin.

She sat there in silence for who knew how long. The gentle hum of the nearby Gate and her own soft sobs echoed against the stone walls. Saldr didn't move, didn't make a sound. She wished he would leave.

Why am I always the one who survives?

She focused on the rough calluses of his fingers and how they caressed her skin. She never did get to ask where he'd gotten them. She'd never gotten to ask him much of anything, because of her blasted prejudice and his stubborn pride. All those arguments. All those wasted words.

They'd cost her so much time.

Maybe it was a desperate plea or just something to comfort herself, but the words of the melody the healer and Saldr had used came to her unbidden. She whispered them into the silence, the tune coming in gasping bursts.

"Anoheme ana hoiseh li Valihanora. Jir dremu hiasa li grer mara..."

Protection and healing, oh Creator of Time. We humbly ask you grant us this gift...

She took a rattling breath, and as she did, his finger twitched beneath her cheek. She flinched, her eyes snapping open as she clenched his fingers tighter. Out of the corner of her eye, the dust in his wound glowed again, and the jagged cut resealed itself in seconds.

Was he...was he...did the song actually...was she really Yalven, then?

That picture in the attic...the pocket watch working after the crash...

Kase coughed. Eyes flying to his face, Hallie gripped his hand tighter. "Wake up. Please. Open your eyes!"

At the sound of her voice, he blinked, and blessed slivers of blue peeked out.

"Kase?" Her voice choked on his name. How was that possible? He'd been dead. He'd been *dead.*

Blast it. She didn't care how it worked, only that it *had worked.*

Kase blinked again, and this time, he managed to open his eyes all the way. A sob escaped as she dropped his hand to wipe her streaming eyes.

"Hallie?" His voice was raspy from screaming as he tried to sit up. "What's going on? Everything hurts."

Hallie went to help, but he shook his head. He brought a hand to his temple and groaned. Had he hit his head, too? No matter. He was alive.

Holy heavens, he's alive.

Electricity zipped through her body, to her fingers and toes, and sunlight burst from her smile. Inundated by tears, for the first time in her life, Hallie Walker couldn't find any words at all—even broken, incoherent ones.

Before she could do something reckless like kiss Kase senseless or collapse into a blubbering mess, Saldr spoke up.

"Toro blessed you this day. I was not sure your body would take the Vasa." Saldr stepped toward them. "I do not have enough Vasa for your head, Master Shackley. Allow me to take you to the healing wing."

Ignoring Kase's weak protests, Saldr picked him up as if he weighed no more than a child. Hallie carried the sword in one hand, holding Kase's with the other, and followed all the way back to the palace, her breathing ragged and uneven as she tried to calm herself.

By the time they made it to the entrance, she'd gotten it under control. But she flinched, pulling her hand out of Kase's grasp, when she noticed a specific pool of drying blood outside the door. Bile burned in her throat. She swallowed it down hard.

Saldr gestured toward the palace. "I will take you to the Lord Elder. He needs to know what happened."

She nodded. They said no more until they reached the palace. Saldr led her through the corridors until they found the Lord Elder in the healer's wing, attending the other wounded packed into the room. Once the man saw Saldr, his shoulders relaxed. "Praise Toro."

Saldr nodded, still holding Kase, who mumbled something incoherent.

The Lord Elder strode over. "As you can see, we are full here. Lord Saldr, please take Master Shackley to his rooms, and Healer Jera will attend him with more Vasa."

A Yalven woman with dark red lips joined them. It was the one she thought might've been Rodr's wife. Hallie felt something akin to a punch in the gut. *Rodr.* She looked away.

Saldr bowed his head slightly. "Miss Walker is ready to speak with you, Lord Elder."

With that, the man swept from the room, not waiting for Hallie. She took one last look at Kase, who still hung limply in Saldr's arms as the Yalv followed the woman back toward their quarters. She had to sprint to catch up with the Lord Elder, but he only led her to the same receiving hall she'd visited before. As he took a seat on his usual pillow, Hallie knelt, the sword across her lap.

"If you will, please tell me what happened in the Temple this evening."

She gripped the sword tightly in her fist. "Explain how Cerulene had an Essence, and I'll tell you what I know." Her words were strong, but her voice shook from fatigue and emotion.

The Lord Elder's eyes pierced hers, but she didn't squirm. It was a minute before he finally spoke. "Those secrets are only for those who have earned trust."

Hallie fingered the handle of the sword, taking in the blue gemstone. The same one that had been on

Rodr's necklace. She couldn't help the flinty tone of her next words. "Zeke is dead for your cause, and Kase nearly gave his life for it as well. We've more than earned your trust, *Lord Elder*."

"Your words may yet lead you to the Mountain's judgment." When she didn't respond, he sighed. "It is our holy right to protect the Gate. We Chronals are a sect set apart from our race and chosen as Essences and Keys. It is our holy duty."

"But what does that mean?" She tightened her grip on the sword in her lap. "That doesn't explain why you broke the treaty...or are there other Essences not under your control?"

The Lord Elder straightened his long tunic, much of which was splattered with blood from the enemies he'd fought. "Captain, will you please bring a pillow for our guest?"

Hallie spun. She hadn't realized anyone else was in the room. *Stars.* The captain had silky thick eyebrows that furrowed as he left the room to follow orders.

After the other man left, the Lord Elder turned back to her. "I'll answer as much as I am able, but I have many others to attend, so I'll not tarry here long."

"Fine," Hallie huffed as she sat on the pillow the soldier brought in for her.

"The Gate is the intersection of not just our timelines, but only Toro knows how many. The minor gates in the other temple corridors can be used to travel between parts of our own world, but this Gate is the most important. That is why it is our duty to protect it."

Timelines? "What would happen if an Essence went through it?"

The Lord Elder's eyes bore into her own. "Did someone enter the Gate?"

"The man Kase fought, he—he fell through it. When I pushed him. He said he was the Essence that controlled the Gate."

The Lord Elder's silence deafened her. "It is impossible. The Essence of Keys...died nearly a century ago."

"But he was able to create this sword." She inspected it. Zuprium, judging from its coloring, but it must have been the purest form; it was nearly blinding in its shine. "Ben threw Rodr into the Gate and pulled this out."

No emotion crossed the Lord Elder's face as he stood and took the sword from her. He inspected it as a scientist would an interesting new specimen. He set it beside his own pillow. "Even if the Essence has returned, the Gate holds many worlds too terrifying to even imagine, and he doesn't have this key." He rubbed his eyes—a very human-like gesture that took Hallie aback for a moment. He continued, "It hails from a land full of beasts deadlier than those roaming this side of Yalvara. One we closed off a century ago." He looked down at the floor before finding her gaze once more. "Do not speak of this unless I give you permission. If you break your oath, you will face the Mountain's judgment."

Hallie tried to keep her growing terror under control, breathing as slowly and evenly as she could. She didn't quite understand how Essences were passed down, but she knew she wouldn't get any further answers from the Lord Elder. Hopefully, what she'd learned would satisfy the High Guardsman.

Besides, Ben was never coming back this side of the sun because she still had the sword. Cerulene would be unable to use the Gate as a weapon against Jayde. She took another deep breath. "I understand, and I'll agree to keep it a secret *if* you help us get back to Kyvena. And if possible, we would like to take back Zeke Shackley's body for our own ritual Burning."

He held out his hand, palm up. Hallie got up, placed hers on top of his, and bowed until her forehead touched her own hand. It was the traditional way of sealing agreements in Yalven culture. He copied her movements. "We will preserve his body. We lost too many good soldiers this day. If you have no more questions or information for me, I must get back to the healing wing."

Hallie paused. She wanted to ask him about her own history, but something in the back of her mind told her not to. What would happen if anyone found out? Kase was the only one who knew, and she could get him to keep quiet about it. If the Lord Elder knew she had Yalven blood, he might not let her leave. Another question, then. "Why would Cerulene want to collect all the Essences? And would every Essence *possess* their...um, host?"

"I cannot answer."

"But—"

"I have told you everything I am able to tell an unbeliever." The Lord Elder gestured toward the door. "But rest assured, Toro is in control, not those blasphemists of Cerulene."

Hallie chewed on her lip. She wanted to ask more, but the look in the Yalv's eyes told her he grew impatient. "Thank you for your confidence."

He dipped his head. "Now, go check on your comrade and rest. We will speak again soon."

Hallie nodded and rushed from the room. She would try and research all the information she'd just learned later, maybe when they returned home if she wasn't able to go back to the Yalven library. After a silent walk through the corridors, she finally reached the guest quarters she, Kase, and Zeke had been assigned to.

Oh, Zeke...

She blinked back the tears. Not the time. Not yet.

With a heavy heart, she entered the common area. She eyed the food on the table briefly, then turned away. Someone must have left it for Kase when he awoke. Just thinking of food made her sick. Besides, her jaw ached from Ben kicking it before he fell through the Gate.

Holy moons and heavens, this day was...

She made her way to the room Kase and Zeke had shared and pushed the door open a crack. The soft light of Firstmoon coming from the small window laced Kase's curls. He slept, but he didn't snore for once. From time to time, she and Ebba had been able to hear him from their room on the *Eudora Jayde*.

Trying her best not to disturb him, she pushed the door open all the way. When he didn't wake, she grabbed one of the wooden chairs from the common area and set it down beside Kase's bed. She left the door open for light—and for propriety's sake—and sat down.

His breathing was a soft breeze, a curl rustling with each exhale. He'd lost his brother and nearly died himself, but sleep erased those painful memories for a time. Someone had cleaned his face and dressed him in a new shirt. With a deep breath of her own, Hallie covered his hand with hers.

A lone tear traced its way down her cheek. "I'm sorry I didn't listen to you, but I'm glad I went back."

She didn't know how long she sat there watching him, but she didn't think he'd mind if she laid her head on the edge of the bed. *Just for a moment.*

Just a moment.
Just...

Kase

WHEN KASE'S DREAMS FADED AWAY, he tried to snatch them from the air, but his left arm collided with something on the way up. Someone gasped, and he opened his eyes. It was dark, but as he blinked away the remnants of sleep, torchlight streamed through the open doorway. The soft gray glow of early morning glinted off the metal ceiling. Was it time to get up already? Maybe he could find out more about Yalven fighting techniques in the library that day. Their complicated use of swords was intriguing, and...

"Ow," a voice whined from his left. He turned his head, though it felt like he'd been hit with a ton of bricks. Hallie was there, rubbing her jaw.

What was she doing in his room?

His head throbbed again, and his entire body ached. Why did he hurt so badly?

"Hallie?" His voice was hoarse, like he'd been screaming for hours. "What're you doing in here?"

She jerked and looked over at him. *Stars,* she was a mess. Bits of hair flew every which way from her face. She must've lost her hair ribbon; her auburn tresses were scattered, hanging past her shoulders. Dirt and something like blood streaked her face. A bruise bloomed near her jawline.

"What in the shocks happened to you?" *Good moons,* had someone taken a cheese grater to his throat? "Water. Do you have water?"

She nodded and left, coming back a moment later

with a cup. When he couldn't sit up on his own, she helped him. Her hand was tender on his back. *What in the blasted suns happened?*

He didn't recall falling asleep in his room, but he was there now. In fact, he didn't remember much of anything. How had Hallie gotten so beaten up? Why did his side feel like someone had sucker-punched it? And his head?

"Where's Zeke?" he croaked once he finished the cup. He still sounded bad, but it didn't hurt as much. Looking over at his brother's empty bed, Kase took it as an excellent sign Zeke felt well enough to get out of bed. Worry about his brother's wellbeing had been eating at him for the past few days.

Hallie took the cup from him and sat back down in her chair, cradling the small piece of pottery in her hands.

"You don't remember?" She avoided his gaze.

With a grimace, he sank against the wall. He tried to think back, but his brain hurt. The throbbing pain reminded him of one of the times he'd gotten in a fight with Jove when he was younger. Kase couldn't recall what started it, but Jove had landed a solid punch to the side of Kase's face. Their mother had been so furious her ears had turned red. Zeke had been the one to tell on them, and he was the only one who didn't get a lecture afterward.

"My head's spinning, and it blasting hurts," Kase answered. "I don't understand. Why isn't he with you? Why are you all dirty? Is that *blood?*"

Hallie inspected her fingers gripping the cup. After a minute, her eyes, brimming with tears, found his. "Do you remember the Cerls attacking last night?"

"*What?* They attacked the city?" He clutched his

bedsheets in tight fists. "Stop messing around and tell me what happened!"

Hallie sniffed. "You don't remember anything at all? The fighting, the Gate, anything?"

"What in the blazes are you talking about?"

She bit her lip. "They got into the city, and you fought them. They wanted the Gate, and..." Her voice caught, and she glanced back at her lap. "And Zeke...and Zeke, oh stars, Kase..."

He scrunched his face, tearing through his brain and grimacing against the pain throbbing on the right side. At last, flashes of light flickered in his memory. Blue and gold. He grasped at that and held it tightly. Shapes and sounds blurred and fizzled. Gradually, he recalled bits and pieces, and the more he strained, the more came back to him. He felt the grip of the pistol in his hand, and he remembered...he remembered...

"He's dead." His voice broke as a tear slid from the corner of his eye to drip off his chin. The trail burned against his skin as another followed.

"Yes," Hallie whispered. "I...Kase, I..."

Kase closed his eyes as his memory replayed Zeke falling to his knee, his chest jerking, and a cold metal door shutting in Kase's face. He couldn't remember how he'd gotten here, or much of anything else, but his brother's last moments were a burning inferno in his mind.

Zeke, the brave soldier, the favorite son. Gone in an instant.

Anger bubbled in Kase's stomach. Why was he so useless when it mattered? He could land a nose-diving airship in the middle of a storm, but he couldn't stop a bullet from hitting his brother in the chest. *Why can't I ever do anything right?*

And they'd argued before joining the fight. He'd never gotten to apologize.

"Why is it always me?" The anguish in his own voice dug deeper into his chest as it cracked again. *"Why can't I stop it?"*

Hallie's fingers were soft on his hand as she gave it a weak squeeze. "I felt the same way once, and it's still hard. But I've had to learn how to keep on living."

"You don't know how I feel. No one does."

"Kase…"

He tore his hand out of hers and covered his eyes. "You don't. I couldn't stop Zeke from sacrificing himself. I couldn't—couldn't stop—"

The cup rattled against the floor, and the bed sagged as Hallie took a seat on the edge. Why wouldn't she leave him alone? Just let him wallow in his misery, for *moons-sake*.

"Zeke made his own decision," she whispered.

Kase tried to hide the tears he couldn't stop from flowing by wiping them furiously. They kept coming. "I haven't been able to save anyone. Anyone at all. Zeke, Ana…"

She shifted. "I know little about Ana, but—"

Kase's chest lurched. *"I blasting killed her.* I got into a fight with my sorry excuse for a father, and then…and then…the fire. I could've stopped her, but I—" Hallie sucked in a sharp breath, but that didn't stop him. "I was right there as she ran into the flames to save him…and I didn't stop her. I froze. I'm nothing but a coward."

The pain in his chest nearly crushed him. Why was it always his fault? He didn't save Ana. He didn't save Zeke. His breaths were scattered and made him ache all the more. Tears flowed freely from his eyes as his shoulders shook. He no longer bothered to hide them.

All the memories rained down on him at once. The haplessly-thrown cigarette after arguing with Harlan three years ago burned at the front of his mind. He remembered the blaze's orange glow as it ravaged the lower city, his arms streaked with ash. His father's condemnation of Ana for running off with the only boy she'd ever loved ringing in Kase's head while he watched his sister run into the building to save the boy, only to perish herself.

It was all Kase's fault. And now he'd lost Zeke, too. If only he had been quicker, smarter, stronger. If he'd only...

Hallie grabbed his arm. "Kase, look at me."

He stiffened under her touch. "Go away. You don't want to be near me. I can't—I can't—"

Her hand fell away as his sobs took control of his body once more. Why couldn't he save them?

"Kase," Hallie choked. "You saved *me.* Remember?"

His retort froze in his throat.

She continued, her words growing angry, desperate. "In the storm. From the dragon. When the *Eudora* fell from the tree. You fought off...you fought off...the Essence in the Gate chamber. For me. So I could escape. You sacrificed your chance for me." Tears spilled down her cheeks. *"You saved me."*

He didn't know what the last one was, but he assumed it had been during the fight. His head ached and throbbed still, but he watched her anyway, studying her closely.

She clasped both hands in her lap as she peeked at him through wet lashes. Blood and dirt smeared where she'd wiped her face. Her hair still had a mind of its own. Her honey-gold eyes didn't let go of the pain she felt, but there was something different. There was a determination, a desire to keep fighting, no matter the cost. In the beginning, this girl had infuriated him at every turn. She'd yelled at him, slapped him, pushed and prodded until he'd exploded, but slowly, without him realizing it, she'd become the woman who'd pulled him from the brink. In his heart, he knew her words were true, and while it would be a long time before he truly believed them, she was evidence he could.

Although his left side burned like fire, and his head pounded, he dragged his legs to the edge of the bed and stood. He stumbled, but Hallie caught his arm. "Kase, you shouldn't stand just yet."

He shook his head and grimaced. He didn't *quite* remember why his body was so banged up, but he was sure it would all come back to him soon. Swallowing the pain, he grabbed her hand.

Hallie's mouth fell open slightly. "What're you doing?"

He didn't say anything, just pulled her up and into his chest. He tucked her head under his chin, holding her tight. After a moment, she relaxed and slid her arms around his waist.

He gently kissed the top of her head. A whisper of a kiss. "Thank you, Hallie. For everything."

Her shoulders shook, and his own tears mixed with her quiet sobs. He didn't know how long they stayed that way.

He found he didn't mind.

CHAPTER 29

ALMOST HOME

Hallie

RECOVERING FROM THEIR WOUNDS TOOK a week. The physical ones, at least. Hallie's jaw still ached from time to time, but it wasn't broken. For a little while, she'd worried she wouldn't be able to eat the food the Yalvs provided during their stay. Apparently, they'd been holding out on them, but Hallie and Kase had finally gained a little more trust, which was a highly-esteemed quality to have in the Yalvs' eyes.

While the mysterious Vasa had healed Kase's most egregious wounds, he still tired easily, but on the fourth day after the attack, he'd griped and complained enough about not having anything to read that the Yalvs allowed him to leave his room.

As his condition was still of slight concern, the Yalvs

insisted they carry him in a litter down to the library, Hallie at his side. Kase hated it, but it was the only way Saldr and Healer Jera would let him leave the palace.

Reading helped take the edge off the grief. A little. Hers more than Kase's, but he was trying. Hallie hadn't found anything about what the Essence controlling Ben had said about collecting them all, nor did she find information about how the Gate actually functioned. She assumed that if the Lord Elder wouldn't tell her, then they probably wouldn't simply have the information she sought in a book readily available. Frustrating, but what could she do? She hoped Professor Christie was more forthcoming, seeing as he'd given her *The Gate of Time* to begin with.

The Yalvs used a different sort of Vasa on Zeke to preserve his body. Kase agreed he would rather take it back to Kyvena and conduct a proper ceremony there, and Hallie had been the one to negotiate the use of a wagon and horse to carry Zeke.

On the morning of their departure, Hallie, Kase, and their retinue stood ready in front of the Temple doors. Saldr had been chosen to accompany them through the Passage and to Kyvena itself. Hallie felt a little pleasure at being able to accomplish another one of their objectives. They'd completed them all, but it sure didn't feel like it. Strapped on the wagon beside Zeke's body was a small block of Zuprium, a gesture of good faith. Hallie had been assured it wouldn't knock out the electricity or anything once they'd returned to Jayde. Another mystery for her to explore.

"Lord Saldr, will you honor us?" The Lord Elder asked.

Nodding, Saldr took a slender dagger from his pocket and unsheathed it. He slit the tip of his index finger and pressed it to the door. When he pulled back, the blood glowed, and the door opened. Hallie nodded to the guards as she and the others passed into the tunnel beyond.

Saldr hadn't been the same since the death of his brother. Hallie didn't understand the implications of the sword, but Saldr hadn't shown any emotion after Hallie tearfully recounted the story to him with help from the Lord Elder.

She grabbed Kase's hand from beside her and squeezed it softly. He had refused to go near this place in the week since, and she understood. He still couldn't remember much of what happened that night, but he recalled flashes in detail, like Zeke's death and Ben being an Essence.

That conversation had been almost worse than the one about Zeke. Kase didn't speak to her for an entire day, only read silently in the library beside her. He didn't even eat the nameless fruit she'd snuck in for a snack.

He also hadn't said anything about the door she opened with her own blood, but she didn't dare bring it up. She needed to talk to her father first, and then she could figure out what to do with the information, which might be nothing. Besides, who knew if Kase even remembered?

Kase squeezed her hand and let it drop. He put his other on the wagon itself as it rocked a little on the uneven floor. During the week of recovery, the Lord Elder had sent people to clean up the gore from the battles within the Temple, but as they entered the first chamber, she had to quell nausea at the lingering bloodstains.

After taking the left corridor and entering a room

Saldr opened with his blood, Hallie found herself in a cavern much like the one with the Gate, only smaller. The solitary light came from the archway in the wall in front of her, but the images didn't flash by at the furious pace of the Gate.

"Is that Kyvena?" Kase's hand slipped from the wagon, and he stumbled forward. Saldr caught his shoulder.

"Careful, Master Shackley." The Yalv's pointed teeth flashed. "A Passage can be dangerous."

Hallie joined him. "Those are the airfields!" She stopped. "Wait, can the other side see us here?"

The Lord Elder shook his head. "It can only be opened by a Chronal on this side."

Hallie bit her lip. "How will Saldr let you know what the High Council decides?"

"That is not for you to worry about, child." The man's ageless eyes softened. "May the stars rise upon you."

Hallie bowed and completed the saying in perfect Yalven.

The points in his teeth showed in his smile. He turned to Saldr. "Go, my son. May the heavens guide you."

Saldr's sharp features and pale skin glowed in the light from the Passage. With a few words in a dialect Hallie didn't recognize, he put his hand through the image.

"Follow me."

He grabbed the horse's reins and tugged it toward the Passage. The animal didn't flinch when it entered the image.

Hallie turned. "You promised to get me home."

Kase's small smile warmed her heart as he took her

hand in his and led her to the archway. She squeezed it tightly as light enveloped them.

Almost home.

EPILOGUE

Jove

USING THE ASHTRAY ON HIS office desk, High Guardsman Jove Shackley snuffed out the cigarette. Heddie sat across from him, reading, rogue silver hairs falling into her narrowed eyes. The gruesome report detailed the crime scene and known facts of the murders of Stradat Richter and his entire household. She chewed on one end of her eyeglasses' frames as she read.

Every single person who had the misfortune of being at the Richter's family estate in upper Kyvena on the night of Tuesday the 17th of November, year 4500, was dead. Either shot to death with strange, frayed bullets, or slashed about the neck in a bloody smile. Morbidly, Jove wondered if Stradat Richter's red hair matched the color of his blood.

Still senseless killings.

No one had taken responsibility for it yet. The Watch had virtually nothing on the case, and Stradat Sarson wanted answers. *Isn't that the purpose of the Watch?* she'd demanded. *To find out if things like this are going to happen?*

Jove didn't blame her. How had the Watch failed so miserably? He covered his eyes with his hand as he said, "How did they manage this? Richter's guards are some of the best-trained anywhere."

Heddie set down the report on the desk. "Our informants in both Ruby and Sapphire have nothing. Our domestic contacts haven't come up with anything either."

Jove uncovered his eyes and threw his pencil. "How could we fail this terribly?"

"We're human," Heddie answered, idly dodging the writing utensil. "However, that doesn't make it acceptable."

Jove glanced around his office, trying to think. It wasn't much, just a few personal effects: a small portrait of Clara on his desk and a landscape painting of the mountains on the wall. The light from the morning sun peeked through the gray window curtains his wife had sewn.

"What do you think our next move should be?" Jove asked.

"We should alert the response teams to dig for more information. Then, we should—"

The door burst open, a messenger yelling, "High Guardsman! I apologize for intruding, but I've got a message—an urgent one—here."

"Thank you." Jove held out his hand. While this

particular messenger was always a tad too excitable, it must have been *truly* urgent for him to burst in without knocking. Jove needed to talk to him about that, but doing so would make him feel too much like Harlan. He scratched his stubbled jaw.

He dismissed the lad with a wave and turned the envelope over, finding his family seal: four swords in a diamond formation with a star in the middle.

From the Lord Kapitan. Fantastic.

He and Harlan hadn't spoken much since the murders. The Lord Kapitan was busy with his new duties, as he was the one to take over Stradat Richter's place in the interim until they cobbled together an official election. Jove waited until the messenger shut his door again, then slit open the seal. He unfolded the message.

"It's from the Stradat Lord Kapitan. He says . . . blast. Blast. Blast. *Blast*."

Heddie tilted her head. "What?"

"He's calling an emergency Council meeting. Says they've found the assassins."

Heddie shot out of her chair so fast it clattered to the floor. "How? Our informants haven't said a thing."

"I don't know, but he's doing it to undermine— *blasted* man."

"*Stars*, can you not think of another curse?" Heddie straightened the collar of her jacket. "We need to go. Now."

Jove grabbed his own coat from the back of his chair and slung it around his shoulders. The two Heads of the Watch sped out of their headquarters near the Jayde Center and made their way to the large structure. Once inside, they hurried up the stairs and down the hallway to the Council Room. Jove knocked his specific code, and the doors opened to reveal the others already waiting in their seats.

Old Stradat Loffler was awake for once, and Sarson's lips were thin. On the other hand, Harlan sat with his chest puffed out and mustache trimmed neatly. This was the day he'd been waiting for. Too bad Richter had to suffer for it.

"Stradats," Jove said with a small bow and salute. Heddie followed suit, then they took their seats.

Harlan stood up and spoke as soon as Jove pulled his chair in. "The kingdom of Cerulene has taken credit for the murders of Stradat Forrest Richter and his household."

Of course, they did. *Blast.* Jayde was going to war, whether Jove wanted it or not.

Over the course of the next hour, they still hadn't come to a cohesive decision of what to do. Jove wanted to gouge his eyes out with the dull pencil on the table in front of him; maybe a little extreme, but he'd do anything to get out of this meeting. Declaring *official* war was a process, an extensive one. Jayde also hadn't been in a major conflict on that scale since the Great War. Sure, skirmishes, border disputes, and minor rebellions had happened, but nothing that required the *process.* Maybe the High Council was just a little rusty in that regard; that could be the only reason for the mess he found himself in. While he knew he should have been listening, it was difficult to hear Harlan bragging— in his own way—that he'd been right to want to attack first the entire time.

According to Harlan, it was the rest of the High Council's fault Richter was dead.

"We call the City Governors together and take a vote. Send out the summons today, now," the Lord

Kapitan said, his frown deepening. "If you're all so stars-bent on following the process for declaring war, stop wasting our time. This act demands an answer, and we've already sat on our hands for days!"

Heddie tapped her own pencil on the parchment in front of her. Maybe she was also contemplating sticking it somewhere unpleasant. Her voice was stretched thin when she said, "We need to tell the public. The reporters are already starting to sniff around. It's a miracle no one's found out yet."

Sarson's eyes were red-rimmed as she snarled, "If the Watch had been working to their full potential, we would have had this information days ago, or maybe we'd have *stopped* the assassination to begin with!" A tear skittered over the deep scar in her cheek. A crack in her otherwise steel exterior.

If proper decorum would have allowed it, Jove would've started banging his head on the table in front of him. From eye gouging to head banging. At least the latter wouldn't be as bloody.

He knew the Watch had failed, but at this moment, there was no use arguing over that fact or casting blame. What was done was done. They could only prepare and make sure it didn't happen to anyone else.

"And I'll keep telling you until it finally resonates through your thick skull." Heddie waved her reading glasses in her hands. "It was an inside job. That's the only explanation. None of our field agents knew anything. Someone's turned traitor for that blasted scum of a Cerl king, and you know it."

"And that is still under the jurisdiction of the Watch. If you're so incompetent, we should consider replacing you." Harlan's tone was like the thin edge of a knife. "We need to strike Sol Adrid. Now."

"We're *all* incompetent, seeing as the only thing we're doing is sitting around shouting at one another." Jove stood up, both palms pressed against the table. Time to end this ridiculous sham. "If we need the full Governor's Council approval to declare war, we need to get moving."

"Young Shackley is correct," Loffler said, his eyes clear. He looked more alive than he had in the entirety of Jove's acquaintance with him. Maybe the thought of being offed by a Cerl assassin was the only thing that could wake him up. "He has a good head on his shoulders."

"Thank you, Stradat Loffler," Jove said with a nod. "I'll send out the messages, unless any of you have objections, which would be incredibly *stupid* of you."

Inside, Jove cringed at his word choice, but he was at the end of his tether.

"Go," Harlan said when no one spoke up to oppose. No emotion crossed the Lord Kapitan's face. Just like a stone wall.

Jove nodded and left the chamber, slamming the door behind him. The wireless telegraph office was just down the corridor from the Council Chamber. Jove wished he was forced to walk further. Alas, the operator, a pudgy, mustached man named Porter, jumped when Jove entered.

"High—High Guardsman, I wasn't sleeping. I promise, sir," he fumbled.

Jove pushed past him. "You're dismissed, Mr. Porter. I need to make a private transmission."

"Yes, yes, sir. Will you not be mentioning this to—to Stradat Sarson?"

Jove closed his eyes and took a deep breath. "I don't mean to be rude, Mr. Porter, but you have three seconds to leave this room."

"Of course, of course, Sir High Guardsman," Porter squeaked as he left the room, slamming the door behind him.

Finally. Jove snatched the notepad and pencil from the desk and wrote out his message. He'd burn it later, but it always helped him to write it out with the correct dots and dashes before he sent something. He'd have to send it six times to the cities in each major province, including the Governor's office there in Kyvena.

Governors report Kyvena STOP 23 Nov 4500 STOP Hovers coming STOP

That should be enough information without revealing anything sensitive, in case of interception. Jove walked to the Kyvena machine and prepared to send the message, but just then, one of the machines behind him began tapping.

Jove cursed, flipping the page. He shouldn't have sent Porter away.

He transcribed what he could, but he knew he missed the first bit as well as a few dots here and there. *Stars*, this job was hard. He really should've been nicer to Porter. Once the tapping stopped, Jove translated the message, his pencil tip breaking as he finished the last word.

"Crashing, burning stars," Jove gasped. He tore the sheet from the notebook and ran down the hallway. Passing Porter, he yelled, "Go back in there and interrupt me if you get anything else from Fort Achilles!"

Whether or not Porter acknowledged the order, Jove didn't know, but he skidded to a halt in front of the Council Room doors and tried to knock his passcode. It took him three tries to get it right.

The other members of the Council did not look amused. Harlan in particular. Jove held up the message. "Cerl troops have attacked Fort Achilles. The company stationed there is engaging, but Correa has sent at least a legion, and reinforcements are a half day's march away."

No one spoke. All eyes were on Jove, unblinking.

Then, it erupted.

"And this is why you should have listened when we told you to send more troops, Lord Kapitan!" Heddie growled.

Harlan's eyes were ablaze as his fist pounded the table. "Enlistment is down! And our soldiers are far better than anything Cerulene can fling at us."

Jove tried not to crush the message in his hand as he watched the three go back and forth, Sarson adding in her useless two coppers.

"The Passes are all snowed in for the winter. They can't go anywhere," the woman shouted. "Sacrificing a few for the good of the whole is our only option. Achilles is well equipped to take care of it."

Loffler got up from his chair and walked to Jove. He had a slight limp in his right leg. If Jove had heard correctly, he'd gotten it in one of the border skirmishes nearly fifty years ago, when the Yalvs were still on this side of the world. He put a hand on Jove's shoulder.

"I'll go help the young man in the Telegraph office figure out if they have more information." Even his voice sounded like it might give out any day now.

Jove closed his eyes but nodded. The old man probably only wanted a quiet place to take a nap. Why in the stars did he not just retire?

"Koppen, Shackley, why didn't we know about this attack beforehand?" Harlan demanded.

So, I'm just Shackley now?

"Weren't they just in Sol Adrid? How did Correa get an entire legion to the border so quickly? Tell me that." Sarson's face turned red in her frustration.

Jove tuned the rest of it out. He couldn't take it anymore. Foolish, idealistic Jove from three years ago had thought he could change the world. But at that moment, watching three of the most powerful people on Yalvara bicker like children, he didn't want to be a part of it any longer.

He strode calmly to the table and smoothed out the transmission on top of the papers he'd been reading earlier. Picking up his pencil, he stuck it in his pocket for a souvenir and promptly turned and walked out of the Council Room.

"Where do you think you're going?" Harlan barked.

Jove spun on his heel, hand on the knob. "No one can agree on anything because of your overinflated egos. Consider this my resignation as High Guardsman. Good day."

"Jove!"

He didn't turn this time. Instead, he slammed the door, cutting off Harlan's voice. No one followed Jove. No one stopped him as he exited the Jayde Center and emerged into the chilly November afternoon.

That might've been the dumbest decision I've ever made. He fingered the pencil in his pocket, and after a minute, flung it to the side of the road.

But Clara's making those fantastic buttered potatoes tonight. I'd much rather worry about that.

He'd talk to Heddie tomorrow and see about taking a desk job. Someone else could handle the rest. Because for the first time in years, Jove felt a weight lift off his shoulders he hadn't even known he'd been carrying.

CONTINUED IN BOOK 2

WANT MORE?

Read EXCLUSIVE bonus stories from Kase and Hallie's backstories when you sign up for my newsletter: *https://www.alliearnest.com/members*

Follow Me on Social Media

Instagram: *@alli_earnest_writes*

YouTube: *Alli Earnest*

ACKNOWLEDGMENTS

Where do I even begin?

I started this book back when I was still teaching middle school Language Arts, and now, I'm an author. CRAZY. *Cities* began as a rather motley crew rocketing through the stars trying to steal time with Kase and Hallie at the helm of this ship! Granted, Hallie's name was Rav, and many other crew members were cut in subsequent drafts, but I digress. Ahem, maybe I'll write some bonus content like such for all my adoring fans later? Haha, my husband might be the only one interested...and even then, that's a long shot. He's very much NOT a reader.

Moving on.

I guess I should first thank Jason. Without his encouragement, this book wouldn't be in your hands right now. Of course, he also did tell me I should stop editing this book into the ground and move on, but those are minor details. Thanks, husband. Love you! I'll move on to book 2 now, which should make you happy.

Next, I'll thank my firstborn, my little baby boy, who'll be nearly six months old by the time this book baby is published. STOP GROWING UP SO FAST. I'm grateful for your help getting this book to the finish line. Your coos and giggles were very encouraging while you watched me type furiously away.

I'm, of course, grateful to the rest of my family. Without them, I wouldn't be an author in the first place. Mom and Dad, you enabled my reading habit, and I'll be forever grateful for that. To my sisters, I love that we're all big readers, though in different genres. I still think that you, Colyn, should join Haven and I on our next *Lord of the Rings* extended edition marathon. To all my grandparents, aunts, uncles, cousins, in-laws, stepparents, stepsiblings...you all are incredibly special to me. This book wouldn't be here without your unwavering support and love! I'd also like to give a shoutout to my brother, Knox Owen, who has a character named after him in this book...

And now for the special shoutout to my fur babies, Shaggy and Misty, who never failed to interrupt my writing time because they wanted a treat.

OKAY. Now for all my writer peeps who made this book AWESOME.

I'll start by thanking my incredible editors. Cassidy Clarke, you are the BOMB when it comes to developmental edits. And line edits. Renee Dugan, my copy editor, thank you for polishing this manuscript so it could shine. You ROCK. And don't worry, I definitely know how to use apostrophes. I did before, but I REALLY know now.

To my critique partners, who each saw this book in different stages but made it better nonetheless. Becca, you read such an early draft, didn't run screaming, and helped refine my writing in SO many ways I didn't know I needed. Not all heroes wear capes. Blake, your love for my characters and world makes me so happy. I'm also sorry about Zeke. I really am. Brittany, though you got to see the draft closest to the finished product, your insight into the story was (and still is) invaluable. AND you read it while feeling incredibly sick being pregnant and all. Therefore, I expect the second book you read to baby will be mine. You can read him yours first, of course. Also, why do all my CPs have names that start with 'B'? I just noticed this...haha.

To my beta readers. I did three rounds, and two of you read my book TWICE at different stages because YOU are the real MVPs. No really. Thank you, Cam and Alina. Your feedback both times through was just fabulous. My other betas, THANK YOU: Victoria, Sue, Michael, Beth, J. Kap, Michelle, Sara, David, Katharine, Samantha, Kayleigh, and Dania.

Thank you to Haven, who read a very, VERY rough draft of this book and didn't think it was total and complete crap. You're my favorite sister named Haven. Now stop reading this and go work on your own book. Thanks.

To my proofreaders: Aunt LeAnn and Bonnie. THANK YOU for picking out all my errors I missed on that last pass through. You also finished my book in record time. Many, MANY thanks.

NOW, to my fabulous cover artist, Dea. Oh my stars. Seeing my characters come to life like that? A DREAM. You were wonderful to work with, and I'm so glad I stumbled upon your Cosmere fanart. Thank you SO much.

And thanks to Derek Murphy, who will probably never read this book, but I wanted to say that your formatting template saved me so much time, effort, and money.

And to you, reader. Without you, I wouldn't be writing this now. Thank you from the bottom of my heart for making my dream become a reality.

GLOSSARY

Ben Reiss [RYSS]: Watch agent, lead on the *Eudora Jayde* mission
Cerulene [SIR-oo-LEEN]: powerful kingdom on Yalvara, ruled by King Filip
Clara Shackley [CLAHR-uh]: wife of Jove
Ebba Fleming [EBB-uh FLEM-ing]: mechanic
Ellis Carrington: Hallie's friend and classmate
Engineer Corp: group of brilliant minds in Jayde tasked with developing new technology/recovering old technological secrets from First Earth
First Earth: third planet from the sun in the Milky Way solar system, destroyed over 1000 years prior to the story
Fiver: denomination of Jaydian money, equal to 5 pieces
General McKenzie: man who led the Life Ships, established Jayde on Yalvara
Great War: began as a conflict over resources, world-wide, ended with the disappearance of the Yalvs
Hallie Walker [HAA-lee; 'Hallie' rhymes with 'valley']: Yalven scholar at the University, hails from Stoneset
Harlan Shackley: the Lord Kapitan of Jayde
High Council: Jayde's governing body consisting of the Stradats, the Lord Kapitan, and the High Guardsmen
High Guardsman/woman: head of the Watch
Hover: general term for aircraft using hover technology
Hover Bike: motorcycle-like vehicle used by the Crews to train new pilots on hover controls, cheap
Hover Crews: sometimes called simply 'Crews', force of hover ships, an offshoot of the Jaydian military
Hunder [HUN-dur]: denomination of Jaydian money, equal

to 100 pieces

Jayde [JAYd]: nation ruled by an oligarchy, founded by refugees of First Earth

Jove Shackley [JOHV]: High Guardsman of the Watch, oldest Shackley brother

Kase Shackley [KAEss SHACK-lee]: Senior Pilot, youngest son of the Lord Kapitan

Kyvena [Kigh-VIN-uh]: capital of Jayde

Les Shackley [LESS]: mother of Kase, Jove, and Zeke

Life Ships: enormous vessels that carried remnants of humanity from First Earth to Yalvara

Lord Elder: leader of the Yalven nations

Lord Kapitan [KAP-ih-TIN]: high commander of the military

Myrrai [muh-RAE]: Yalven city, known as the realm of starlight

Owen Christie: Yalven professor at the University

Petra Lieber [Peh-TRAH Lee-BUR]: Hallie's friend and classmate

Silver Coast: small coastal nation, used to be a part of Jayde

Sol Adrid [SOL uh-DRID]: capital of Cerulene

Stoneset: small mountain village in the Narden Range, on the other side of the Narden Pass

Stradat [straa-DIT]: highest elected official, three sit on the High Council

Tev Rubika [TEV ROO-bih-KUH]: oldest non-Yalven nation, dealing with civil war aftermath

Watch: Jayde's intelligence and police force

Yalvar Fuel [YAAL-var]: caustic resource found beneath the surface Yalvara, used in engines, being fazed out by the introduction of electricity

Yalvara [YAAL-var-UH]: planet near the edge of the Milky Way

Yalvs [YAALvs]: people native to Yalvara

Zeke Shackley [ZEEK]: Lieutenant Colonel, medical specialist, middle Shackley brother

Zuprium [Zuh-PREE-um]: metal found on Yalvara that doesn't rust, is difficult to destroy, and when combined with electricity, creates hover capabilities

A B O U T   T H E   A U T H O R

ALLI EARNEST drinks way too much coffee and is obsessed with redwood candles, but growing up with two sisters, she's always been a tad overdramatic. It doesn't help that she enjoys books with dragons, wizards, and laser swords.

Graduating with a bachelor's degree in Middle Grades Education, Alli taught English Language Arts for five years and tried to convince thirteen-year-olds that Poe wasn't nearly as crazy as he sounded.

At present, Alli writes science-fiction and fantasy from an office filled with books and other collectibles. She's active on Instagram and YouTube, fangirling over her favorite books and documenting her author life. She lives in the southern US with her husband, son, and dogs.

www.alliearnest.com

Made in the USA
Las Vegas, NV
03 March 2024

86673260R00288